W9-BCD-024

BLUE HORIZONS

***Other Five Star Titles
by Irene Bennett Brown:***

Long Road Turning, Women of Paragon Springs, # 1
The Plainswoman

BLUE HORIZONS
Women of Paragon Springs Series #2

Irene Bennett Brown

SOUTH HUNTINGTON
PUBLIC LIBRARY
2 MELVILLE ROAD
HUNTINGTON STATION, N.Y. 11746

Five Star • Waterville, Maine

F
Brown

Copyright © 2001 by Irene Bennett Brown

All rights reserved.

This novel is a work of fiction. Names, characters, places, and incidents are either the product of the author's imagination, or, if real, used fictitiously.

Five Star First Edition Romance Series.

Published in 2001 in conjunction with Multimedia Product Development Inc.

Cover design by Shanna Chandler.

Set in 11 pt. Plantin by Myrna S. Raven.

Printed in the United States on permanent paper.

Library of Congress Cataloging-in-Publication Data

Brown, Irene Bennett.
    Blue horizons / by Irene Bennett Brown.
        p. cm.—(Women of Paragon Springs : bk 2)
    (Five Star first edition romance series)
        ISBN 0-7862-2815-6 (hc : alk. paper)
        1. Women pioneers—Fiction. 2. Kansas—Fiction.
    I. Title. II. Series.
    PS3552.R68559 B58 2001
    813'.54—dc21   2001040105

For
Serenity Ragone
Beloved granddaughter
who knows how to reach for
her own horizons.

Chapter One

Meg held her lantern high to cast aside the December gloom of evening and looked back over her shoulder with a deep sigh. Her good friends weren't about to let her out of their sight. Wouldn't let her go until she repeated her story to all three of them together—though earlier she'd reluctantly made the rounds to tell them individually of her past, facts that now had their rustic little community of Paragon Springs all a-fuss.

Shawls over their heads and shoulders, the women's booted feet picked their way single file in the snowy shadows toward her low-slung soddy that also housed the mercantile.

Aurelia was first with her long swift stride, her fine Kentucky breeding and respect for Meg were the only things preventing her from throwing a fit. Next came eighteen-year-old Lucy Ann Walsh, clutching her small daughter Rachel's hand. Lucy Ann's own past made her forgiving of almost anything in anyone else's life. Bringing up the rear was Emmaline Lee, half white, half Cheyenne, the oldest and best educated of the foursome.

Light from Meg's swinging lantern glittered off the frosted window glass of the mercantile. Below the windows the flower beds of summer—hollyhocks and matrimony vine—dead now, were snow-covered and ghostly behind a thigh-high, woven twig fence.

Meg limped to a halt, then opened the door. The store was owned by Meg but overseen by Aurelia. It was tidy, well stocked, and smelled deliciously of spices, pickles, dried fruit, and tobacco. With Meg in the lead, the women marched past shelves of canned meats and fruits, sacks of sugar and flour, and barrels of tools and hardware.

At the door to her private quarters, Meg invited, "Come in, ladies, and make yourselves at home." She put the lantern on the bureau and took off her cape.

Emmaline and Lucy Ann sat on the edge of her quilt-covered bed, Aurelia took the rocking chair. They waited, insistence that she leave out nothing in their eyes.

Meg leaned against her bureau for a moment's support. She'd kept the secret so long that revealing it now was like tearing stitches from a wound partially healed, but festering. She took a deep breath and pushed back a brown tendril of hair, her fingers grazing the scar at her temple. Pacing before them with her slight limp, she studied their faces through silver-gray eyes. She empathized with their puzzlement; she'd given them quite a shock this evening. "You do understand why I couldn't tell you about my past before?" No one commented, so she continued, "I'll be leaving for St. Louis as soon as the weather clears enough for travel, to try to get a divorce. I hope not to be gone long—"

"A divorce! You're a married woman, Meg Brennon, and you've never said a word about it!" Aurelia repeated disbelievingly for the umpteenth time that evening. "You've had a husband in St. Louis for going on the four years we've lived here together and you haven't breathed a whisper that he existed?" She looked cheated, as well as shocked.

Lucy Ann fingered Meg's quilt and shook her head. She spoke quietly, her blue eyes sincere when she looked up. "Don't scold, Aurelia. Sometimes a woman has to do what she has to do. Meg was in terrible danger from her husband. A word about him to anybody might've helped him find her. She couldn't go back to his beatings. He broke her hip, caused her to be—lame. Don't forget, after she got away, he

sent a bounty hunter after her. My little brother had to shoot
Frank Finch dead to keep him from killing Meg."

"We thought he was a claim jumper because Meg storied
and *said* he was," Aurelia answered. "I'm glad she finally told
the truth, the whole of it, to the law in Dodge City! And
anyhow, I'm not scolding, nothing of the sort." Pink-faced in
the lamplight and rocking fiercely, her winged, gold-brown
brows locked in a frown, she went on, "I do understand. But
we're Meg's friends. We're as close as family, nigh sisters.
She could've told us the truth, the same as we've told her
about ourselves. She's dear to us, we would've protected her,
no matter what."

Maybe this wasn't going to be so bad, Meg thought. She
smiled. "Thank you, Aurelia, but I believed not telling was
the right thing at the time. It'll bother me the rest of my life
that Lad, just a boy, had to kill Frank Finch to protect me. I
pray that nothing like that'll ever happen again. When all is
said and done, you have protected me even though you didn't
know my secret. You've helped me build a home, a whole
new life, out here in western Kansas. Paragon Springs
wouldn't have seen the light of day without help from all of
you." She hesitated. "There's one more thing—"

"You have children?" Aurelia sat forward, nearly upset-
ting the rocker. They all stared, waiting.

"No children, although one of the reasons I'm going back
to St. Louis to divorce Ted Malloy is that I'd like to meet
someone, get married, and have a family like the rest of you
have." As long as she was legally tied to Ted Malloy, she was
living a form of bondage and would remain in danger. If he
should find her, everything she'd worked hard to gain would
be his as her husband. That was law. He'd rule her with brutality again. She cleared her throat. "My real name is not Meg
Brennon. I had to give up using my true name, Cassiday Rose

9

Curran *Malloy,* to avoid being found."

There was a thick silence as they pondered that and then Emmaline asked, "What do you want us to call you from now on, dear?" Her brown, exotic features broke into a quiet smile of concern. "You've always been Meg to us."

Emmaline looked worn out and Meg regretted bringing this on her. On top of her duties as newspaper editor and schoolteacher, Emmaline was raising her two children alone and caring for her elderly father, who wasn't at all well. She had been up with him several nights in a row.

"*Cassiday* would seem like a stranger," Lucy Ann was saying, her blond head bobbing, "but we could call you that if you want, Meg, it's your true name."

Meg shook her head. "The young person I once was is a stranger to me, too. I'm used to being Meg and I'd like for you to keep calling me that."

They all looked relieved not to have to grapple with a strange name for someone they thought they knew very well. Hearing that she had a past they would never have guessed was enough.

"I'll worry about all of you when I'm away," she told them, beginning to pace again. Nervous fingers pushed back her hair. "Things seem quiet this winter, but you never know when Jack Ambler will stir things up again."

From the beginning, she'd been the women's leader and the one to encourage other settlers to homestead around their little settlement of Paragon Springs. With everyone's help and Aurelia's excellent cooking, she'd made their sod shanties, dugout, and corrals into a road ranch where travelers could spend the night, be fed good meals, and replenish their supplies from the mercantile store.

Jack Ambler, first to come to that area, owned the huge Rocking A cattle ranch in the Pawnee Valley eleven miles northeast of them. He'd done everything possible to harass them and others into not staying, believing the open range was his alone to use. He was violently against the range being cut up into small farms and towns. Last month, two of his hirelings, an ugly, vicious, weak-brained pair, had shot at Meg and killed her team of horses, hoping to frighten her and her friends into leaving the country for good.

That's when she realized that she had to let her own past out into the open, so that she could go to the law whenever she needed them. The horse killers, Hammett and Frey, were serving time in Dodge City. Jack had been away at the time they'd shot her team and supposedly had not given that specific order. But she knew, wherever he was now in December, that the problems from him wouldn't end until he accepted that she and the other homesteaders were there to stay, to build their homes and communities, and that he'd lost.

"All of you have your own chores, your places to keep up. I hate to ask you to take over my ranch chores, too. My work at the quarry and the freight-line—"

They shushed her into silence.

"You don't have to ask, Meg." Aurelia had calmed down. Her rocker creaked rhythmically. "Between us, we'll do what has to be done. Owen will help me in the mercantile and with getting out the mail, as always. My two boys, as well as Lad Voss and Emmaline's boy, Shafer, can help Ad Walsh in your place at the rock quarry and with any freighting that needs to be done, when they're not seeing to the cattle. Neighbors'll help, too, if we need a hand."

"You've done enough for us," Emmaline added, and they all nodded.

"Aren't you afraid?" Lucy Ann asked then, tentatively. "St. Louis is a big city, it has to be very different from Paragon Springs. Your husband—I guess maybe you don't want

11

us to call him that—this man, Malloy, is a terrible person who'd do most anything seems like . . ." her voice trailed off.

"I'm scared," Meg admitted. "More scared of Ted Malloy than of St. Louis, but this is something I have to do. I've put this off far too long already."

Later, the women rose to leave, much less agitated than when they'd arrived. Meg drew Emmaline aside. "Do you think your father will pull through this time? Is there something I can do?"

Emmaline's father, Whitcomb McCurty, had spent an adventurous youth on the plains before he became a mission schoolteacher and married Emmaline's mother, a Cheyenne. It was his final request of his daughter and grandchildren to bring him here to western Kansas to die. Emmaline's mother had died years before and the old man never got over missing her.

"He's very weak," Emmaline answered sadly. "He wants to go, but his body seems to hang on of its own accord. The twins are sitting with him tonight; Selinda is reading to him although he may not hear it."

"Let me know if there's anything I can do."

"I will. But you have worries enough of your own, Meg."

Paragon Springs was buried in drifts of snow for weeks and it was February before the weather cleared enough for Meg to get through to Dodge City and the train. The morning of her departure from the settlement, each of the three women arrived with something of their own to round out her wardrobe for the trip. Meg would have done the same for any of them, but still she was touched and for a minute couldn't speak. She held Aurelia's blue-striped grenadine dress against her. "This is your best dress, Aurelia," she protested, "I can't borrow it."

Aurelia took it from her, carefully folded it, and put it in Meg's satchel. "I can do without it fine for no longer than you'll be gone."

Emmaline's plum-colored wool shawl went in on top of Aurelia's dress. "I have others," Emmaline said, "and you may need it in bad weather."

Meg was protesting the shawl when Lucy Ann held out a piece of jewelry for her to take. She shook her head, backed away and held up her hands. "No, I really can't borrow your mother's brooch, Lucy Ann, though I thank you." The fine filigreed gold and red stone brooch was all Lucy Ann had from the time before her mother and other members of her family were killed by Sioux in Nebraska.

"It'll keep you safe, bring you luck, and make you even more beautiful, Meg." She took Meg's hand and placed the brooch in it, curling Meg's fingers over it. "Please honor me and wear it."

Lucy Ann's eyes were shadowed despite her smile as she remembered the attack. She'd been raped by the renegade Sioux; her three-year-old Rachel was the result. Her brother, Lad, had been partially scalped and though he'd survived, he'd been stunned into traumatic silence for months.

After Lucy Ann gave birth to her beautiful baby, Lad regained his voice. Later, Admire Walsh married Lucy Ann and made her, her child, and Lad his own family. Ad, a young dark-haired cowboy, had quit as a rider for Jack Ambler's Rocking A ranch and taken a claim two miles south of Paragon Springs where he'd begun farming.

"Th-thank you," Meg said huskily, giving in, "I can see none of you are going to listen to me." They all burst out laughing when each friend brought from hiding an extra item or two of unmentionables: embroidered flannel drawers, a chemise, a petticoat, woolen stockings. "I love you all so much," Meg said, hugging them each in turn.

Through the thin walls separating the store from Meg's quarters came the sudden sound of voices. Aurelia said, "Sounds like Owen has customers." Her voice softened saying his name. "I'll go see if he needs help. The rest of you stay and help Meg finish packing. Admire's already waiting out front to take her to Dodge."

They hurried, not wanting Admire to get too restless waiting in Meg's stone-loaded wagon behind her team of oxen. After Ad saw Meg onto the train, he'd deliver the stone to a Dodge City blacksmith who wanted to build a shop.

Lugging her satchels, dressed in a gray serge traveling suit with a black velvet bonnet tied under her chin, Meg led the others from her room into the store and the middle of a confrontation.

"But that's a mighty lot of shot you want to buy, Mrs. Morris," Owen was saying to a shapeless but formidable little woman in brown. Owen's hand rumpled his hair worriedly as he exchanged puzzled frowns with Aurelia who was next to him behind the counter.

"Two, three pounds of shot, I'm pure desperate and I need aplenty," Persia Morris insisted.

"Is anything wrong?" Meg asked, fearful that the Morris family, homesteaders from Tennessee, were arming themselves for serious trouble—maybe from varmints or claim jumpers, but also possibly from Jack Ambler. And just when she was leaving.

"It's the wind," Persia explained, motioning with her work-worn hands. She looked embarrassed. "Blows my skirts up and shows my naked ankles! I ain't no Jezebel. I'm sewing shot in all my hems to hold 'em down when the wind blows which is nigh all the time!"

A dead silence followed. Meg swallowed and said, "Oh."

Her heartbeat receded to normal. "What a fine idea, Mrs. Morris. Buy all the shot you need, we can always stock more. Owen, will you assist Mrs. Morris, please?"

Owen's eyes twinkled. He struggled not to laugh; relief had softened his handsome features. He thumped the counter with a knuckle. "Right away, Mrs. Morris." His shoulders heaved as he bent over the shot barrel in the far corner of the store and scooped shot into a canvas sack.

Owen had arrived from the East last fall and was a favorite in the community. Aurelia, who'd been sadly widowed years before, had taken an immediate shine to him and he to her; they often walked out together of an evening. They were a wonderful team in the store, but their relationship looked to go no further unless Aurelia could make up her mind about marrying him.

Maybe a small miracle would happen between the two while she was away, Meg thought. She headed for the door with Aurelia, Lucy Ann, and Emmaline following.

"Be right out," Owen called after them, "soon as I finish Mrs. Morris's order."

Outside, the children of the community played tag around Admire's wagon while they waited to say good-bye to Meg. She hugged each of them, starting with Aurelia's flock. Dark-haired Joshua, eleven, told her solemnly, "Be careful, Aunt Meg." David John, a gold-brown boy a year younger than Joshua, grinned shyly at her but didn't say anything. When Meg leaned down to Aurelia's active little four-year-old daughter, Zibby, the child kissed Meg's cheek with a loud smack, making all of them laugh. Aurelia's other daughter, Helen Grace, had died of croup a few years before and lay buried in the small graveyard above the community.

"Good-bye Shafer, good-bye Selinda," Meg said as she hugged Emmaline's handsome almost fourteen-year-old

15

twins. "Help your mother all you can, although she seems to be doing fine." The old Professor had died ten days ago. Meg felt very sad for the little family although much had eased for them.

"Don't get lost in the city, Aunt Meg," Shafer warned with a fleeting, devilish grin, "an' don't let them city folks hornswoggle ya."

"I'm hard to fool," Meg replied, reaching to ruffle his hair. "And you behave yourself!" Shafer tended to be a little wild, but he was a likable boy.

Selinda, her dark eyes shining in her lovely face, said softly as she played with the ribbons of her bonnet, "I know you'll be busy, Aunt Meg, but if a chance comes, would you visit an art museum in St. Louis? When you get back you can tell me about it."

"I'll most certainly try," Meg answered the budding artist, "but you're right, I'm going to be frightfully busy."

She looked down at Lucy Ann's little Rachel, who was tugging at her skirts and saying, "Me, too, Auntie Meg. I want to kiss you."

Laughing, Meg picked her up and hugged her. She stroked her pigtailed hair and returned Rachel's kiss before putting her down again. "Be a good girl."

Last she hugged Lad, Lucy Ann's young brother, a strapping boy the same age as the twins. He held her hand in his strong calloused one for a moment. "We'll miss you, Aunt Meg." Lad was going to amount to something. He loved books when he could get them and he was very smart. She would always feel indebted to him for saving her life when Frank Finch would've killed her.

Meg's eyes were smarting when she climbed up into the wagon with Admire. These were her people, and she couldn't wait to get her business done and return to them.

They rolled away in the heavy rumbling wagon, the oxen's hooves squishing softly in the mud of the snow-lined road. The Paragon Springs folk streamed after the wagon for a while, shouting good-bye, telling her to hurry back. She turned and waved, urged them to get inside out of the cold wind, and then she was on her way.

After a bit, Admire shoved his black felt hat back on his head and said, "Remind me when we get to Dodge, I got a little pocket gun I want you take with you, a Remington .46 caliber."

"I don't think I want to carry a gun, Ad."

"Can't tell when you might need it in a big city of strangers, Meg. And from what I hear tell, a gun could mean your life when you meet up with your husband."

She couldn't argue that point. "Thanks, Ad."

Several days later Meg stepped from the train in St. Louis's Union Station, overwhelmed from all she'd seen through her grimy coach window coming into the city. She hadn't remembered that the buildings were so tall and magnificent, the streets so bustling—thick with vehicles and people. She waited wearily on the depot platform for her bags, dizzied by the mass of humanity swirling around her. St. Louis was going to take some getting used to after all this time.

A chill wind carried the putrid odors of the stockyards and industries, and a fishy smell off the Mississippi. Steamboats on the river wailed mournfully.

Aching with weariness from the long trip, feeling hollow and edgy with panic at her surroundings and the task that faced her, she longed for the clean blue skies of Kansas, the open plains, and Paragon Springs. But there wa no going back until her mission was completed. For all she knew, Ted

Malloy could be dead and she a widow not needing a divorce, but she had to find out.

With her bags in hand, she caught a streetcar that would take her to Kerry Patch, the predominantly Irish neighborhood in north St. Louis where she was born and grew up. Where in one foolish moment she'd joined her life with a charming young rake, Teddy Malloy, a moment that she wished had never happened and that she must now undo.

The city grew shabbier as the horse-drawn streetcar rattled and clanged toward Kerry Patch. At its outskirts, she pulled the bell rope and got off to walk. The Patch had changed little; it was still a poor neighborhood of dirt streets, rubbish-strewn alleys, unpainted shacks and tenements. The streets were empty, most folks inside eating supper at this hour. The smell of fried potatoes floated on the crisp wintry air.

Her walk slowed and her heart thumped as she approached the shanty where she'd lived with her parents. It was freshly whitewashed, the coal-shed out back sported a new roof. Ragged clothing flapped in the chill wind from a line. Somewhere out of sight, youngsters laughed and shouted in a game of ante over.

She walked on, her thoughts on the past. Her father had never meant for them to live in the Patch for long. He'd dreamed of a big sheep farm, an estate in the country, and a life of ease for his highborn wife, Maria, from County Leitrim in the old country. A worker with stone and brick, he had been killed in a construction accident just six months before her mother died in childbirth. The new infant, the only sibling Meg might have had, died, too. Meg was alone at sixteen, and she made the biggest mistake of her life later that year. Chiefly from loneliness, she recognized now, she had married Ted.

She stumbled and came to a halt when she arrived at the ramshackle cottage she and Ted had shared during their brief marriage. She trembled as she took in the tumbled roof, cracked windows, and rubble-strewn yard. Ted's father had wanted to make a man of his son, he'd thought it would build his character if he forced him to start out with nothing in the Patch and work his way up.

The gorge rose in Meg's throat. She didn't want to remember, she desperately wanted to run, but her feet were glued to the dirt path.

The stew she'd fixed that last night they were together was boiling hot and burned Ted's mouth. He'd beaten her nearly to death in retaliation. He'd struck her for trifling matters before that, but each time she had hoped he would change, that he'd be again the charming boy she fell in love with.

That night was the worst, the end of it for her. Bleeding and bruised, her hip fractured from being slammed about, she'd crawled to Meara Dolan's for help. Meara, a spinster and a seamstress, had been a friend of her mother's. Meara hid her away from Ted as long as possible, getting a doctor, and nursing her to the point that she could slip away from St. Louis on her own. Recovered and still on the run, she'd saved her small earnings from several odd jobs, sold a nice piece of jewelry of her mother's and formed her own business selling millinery goods from town to town. Later, she met Lucy and Lad, and an old woman named Grandma Spicy, now deceased and buried on the hill at Paragon Springs. The four of them had joined uneasy forces to make their way west.

It still seemed a miracle that she'd escaped Ted's brutality. Now here she was, back at the scene of the worst time in her life. Suddenly, her feet came free. With her heart roaring in her ears, she raced toward the cross street ahead and Meara's house, nearly losing her satchels in the run.

Panting, she pounded hard on the door of the little blue cottage. A chip of old paint came off on her hand. She brushed it away and pounded again. "Meara! Meara, please, open up!"

A muffled woman's voice on the other side of the door asked, "Who you be?"

The voice didn't sound like Meara. Meg replied in a soft, desperate whisper, "It's Cassiday. Cassiday Curran." She refused to use Ted's surname. Meara would remember her best by her maiden name, anyway.

The door creaked open a crack showing a bit of an unfamiliar face. The eyes squinted suspiciously. "Who are 'ya? W'd'ya want?"

She decided to use her other name. "My name is Meg Brennon. Is Meara home?"

"Meara who? There ain't no *Meara* here."

"Meara Dolan. I lived with her once in this house." Her throat dried to dust from panic that she might not find her old friend.

The door opened another inch. Wrinkled hands with stained fingernails gripped the doorjamb. Blue eyes blinked repeatedly. "I been livin' in this house two and a half years, me an' my husband, Glenn. No Meara's been livin' here since I come. Ain't no Meara Dolan livin' in the Patch at all."

But I need her! Meg thought, her mind a-whirl and her knees gone weak. From the moment of her decision to come here, she'd hoped to stay with Meara. If need be, she meant to ask her to testify as a witness to Ted's cruelty.

Goosebumps traveled her flesh. She felt dread to her bones at her situation and wondered what to do now.

could get a word in, she asked, "Do you re-
a Dolan? I understand she doesn't live here
you know what happened to her, where she
?"

shed with the pot. A knife flashed in her small
chopped vegetables for a noontime soup. She
into a carrot, and told her, "Sure an' I re-
a Dolan. A nice one, she was, and nobody in
ood could sew as fine a seam as 'er. What hap-
'll tell ya! A German fella moved into the Patch
ve know, Meara up and marries 'im! We was all

married?" Meg was surprised. From things
d in the old days, she had expected to remain a
r life. After Meg had fled the Patch, there'd
d between them. They had been afraid to write
vould find out and trace Meg's location, de-
God that each was safe and happy. "I'm glad to
married. Do you think her husband's a good
happy?"

as in love as a pair of doves!"

ed. "Good. Do you know where they went to
ivorce went to a nasty trial, she was going to

ya that, but it's not in the Patch. They lived on
six months after they got married, then Meara's
ted to take 'er to meet 'is people. They never
ey stayed where 'is people was, I suppose. Like
vhen they leave the Patch, that's the last ya 'ear
you, for instance. I remember ya bein' called
n ya was 'ere years ago, just a girl. Now you're a
man an' say ya like to be called Meg, ain't that
emember Maria, your mama, and your papa,

Chapter Two

Meg had to find a place to stay; it would be dark before long. She calmed herself and took a deep breath. She had an idea. "Does Bridget Flemming still take in boarders?"

The head beyond the crack in the door bobbed in affirmation. "Two streets down and one over. Tell her Lillie Clary sent you. Bridget's a friend of mine."

"Thank you, Mrs. Clary, I'll tell her. I'm sorry I bothered you."

"Ain't no trouble." Her voice lowered, "A young woman alone in this neighborhood ain't never safe, so watch yourself."

"I will." She brought the collar of her cloak up tighter around her throat, picked up her bags, and stumbled on toward Bridget's. As she hurried along, she wondered at the fact that she hadn't asked Mrs. Clary about Ted Malloy, whether or not she knew him and if he still lived in the Patch. The truth was, as much as she wanted to be divorced, she dreaded facing him as much as she feared few situations in her life. Their old shanty had been abandoned. He might not live in the Patch at all.

She supposed it was possible that Ted's father, John Malloy, had found the key to making a man of Ted and had moved him up and out of the Patch—employed his son in one of his businesses. She doubted it, though, very much.

The two were so different. John J. Malloy, a stern, dignified, but tough man, had himself started out in Kerry Patch as a lowly masonry-worker. With hard work and diligence he had eventually established his own building supply manufactory, and then had gone on to construct many of St. Louis's fine office buildings.

Irish men of sum and substance, such as the elder Malloy, didn't stay in Kerry Patch. In fact, the Irish weren't as clannish as others often saw them. It was just that many of them were poverty-stricken, they could identify with one another, and they found safety in numbers. When they became educated and made money, they couldn't wait to leave.

That was understandable, Meg thought, looking around her in the evening twilight at the shabby cottages and dilapidated tenements up and down the rutted road.

Ted had hated hard work, hated doing without his father's money. He took out on her his resentment against his father, blaming her equally for his situation and because she had no money of her own, although relatives on her mother's side were wealthy folk in Ireland.

Meg turned the corner toward Bridget Flemming's into an even colder wind. At a sound behind her she whirled, afraid she was being followed. A yellow cat played in debris by the roadside. Her fear subsided.

She supposed she could look for Ted at his parents' mansion in the grand neighborhood several blocks west of the Patch. But John Malloy was a powerful man in days past and he would be, still. She could be as defenseless as a butterfly fluttering into a net if he didn't want her released from marriage to his son.

There had to be another way to find Ted and make him see reason. She hoped it wouldn't take long. She wished with all her heart that he'd be changed, that he would quickly and quietly consent to a divorce and be done with it, so she could go back home. But who could believe in a fantasy such as that?

She reached Mrs. Flemming's ramshackle cottage. Maybe

Red Pat. After they died, ya married that good-for-nothin' Malloy, an' then ya vanished." She stood there wiping her hands on her apron, her expression clouded and clearly waiting for Meg to explain where she'd been.

Until things were settled between her and Ted, and maybe not even then, it was best not to mention where she lived now. She was tired of lying, hiding facts, and keeping secrets, but she saw no other choice. "I've lived in different places and for a few years I traveled." Taking a deep breath, she changed the subject, "Does Ted Malloy still live here in the Patch?"

A voice called suddenly from the front of the house, "Hullooo, Bridget, you home, then?"

"That's Lillie Clary," Bridget told Meg. "She comes over ever' mornin' to have tea with me and a chat. She'll be curious about ya, for sartin." She cupped a hand around her tiny mouth, "Come on to the kitchen, Lillie. We been expectin' ya."

"Hello, Mrs. Clary." Meg smiled.

The floor shook slightly as Mrs. Clary, a short stout woman, came into the room. A brief smile in Meg's direction showed that Mrs. Clary had no teeth. Her blue eyes sparkled above her chubby cheeks.

"Did you get a good rest, Miss?" Mrs. Clary gummed the question as she removed her bonnet and plaid shawl, tossing them aside on a bench. She settled herself at the table and held her cup for Bridget to pour tea.

"I slept like the dead."

"Bridget runs a fine place, don't she?"

"Yes, she does." The boarding house was as shabby as everything else in the Patch, but spotless. The food was plain, but nourishing.

"Our friend Meg, 'ere, was askin' about Ted Malloy, Lillie. Did ya know this young lady was married to 'im, an'

25

still is? No," she answered herself, "ya likely don't know that, ya bein' a newcomer, almost, to the Patch."

"I never met this young lady before last night but I do know that Malloy!" Lillie made a sour face. "A good-for-nothin' he is, worthless and bad as they come. He likes nothin' better than to get my man drunk and take his money gamblin'. You're his wife? Didn't know he had one!"

Meg tried once more to find out if he lived in the neighborhood.

" 'E don't live nowhere for very long," Bridget replied, with a shake of her head. "Comes an' goes. 'E don't work at real work. Spends 'is time in the saloons when'e comes to the Patch. 'Is father, John J. Malloy, is an important man in St. Louis, and rich. But the way I hear it, 'e's ashamed of his son and don't give 'im a nickel."

"What about his mother? Does she feel the same about Ted?" Meg remembered Mrs. Malloy as a shadowy person, always in the background. But still she thought Mrs. Malloy would defend her own son and give him aid, even if it meant displeasing her husband.

Bridget answered, "John Malloy's wife died about two years ago. Died in 'er sleep one night. 'Er heart up and quit, I believe they said."

"Died of heartbreak over the arguments between her worthless son and her husband, is more like it," Lillie claimed. "Too bad Ted Malloy weren't more like his father. But here he come up in the family like a stinkweed in a patch of lilies. Worthless. When Ted Malloy's not abed with a woman, he's gamblin' at the races or makin' bets at the local prizefights." Lillie was angry. "He makes his money that way, an' from cheatin' good men like my Glenn."

Bridget looked at Meg over her spectacles with sad apology. "Don't know why ya ever would've wanted to marry

Chapter Two

Meg had to find a place to stay; it would be dark before long. She calmed herself and took a deep breath. She had an idea. "Does Bridget Flemming still take in boarders?"

The head beyond the crack in the door bobbed in affirmation. "Two streets down and one over. Tell her Lillie Clary sent you. Bridget's a friend of mine."

"Thank you, Mrs. Clary, I'll tell her. I'm sorry I bothered you."

"Ain't no trouble." Her voice lowered, "A young woman alone in this neighborhood ain't never safe, so watch yourself."

"I will." She brought the collar of her cloak up tighter around her throat, picked up her bags, and stumbled on toward Bridget's. As she hurried along, she wondered at the fact that she hadn't asked Mrs. Clary about Ted Malloy, whether or not she knew him and if he still lived in the Patch. The truth was, as much as she wanted to be divorced, she dreaded facing him as much as she feared few situations in her life. Their old shanty had been abandoned. He might not live in the Patch at all.

She supposed it was possible that Ted's father, John Malloy, had found the key to making a man of Ted and had moved him up and out of the Patch—employed his son in one of his businesses. She doubted it, though, very much.

The two were so different. John J. Malloy, a stern, dignified, but tough man, had himself started out in Kerry Patch as a lowly masonry-worker. With hard work and diligence he had eventually established his own building supply manufactory, and then had gone on to construct many of St. Louis's fine office buildings.

Irish men of sum and substance, such as the elder Malloy, didn't stay in Kerry Patch. In fact, the Irish weren't as clannish as others often saw them. It was just that many of them were poverty-stricken, they could identify with one another, and they found safety in numbers. When they became educated and made money, they couldn't wait to leave.

That was understandable, Meg thought, looking around her in the evening twilight at the shabby cottages and dilapidated tenements up and down the rutted road.

Ted had hated hard work, hated doing without his father's money. He took out on her his resentment against his father, blaming her equally for his situation and because she had no money of her own, although relatives on her mother's side were wealthy folk in Ireland.

Meg turned the corner toward Bridget Flemming's into an even colder wind. At a sound behind her she whirled, afraid she was being followed. A yellow cat played in debris by the roadside. Her fear subsided.

She supposed she could look for Ted at his parents' mansion in the grand neighborhood several blocks west of the Patch. But John Malloy was a powerful man in days past and he would be, still. She could be as defenseless as a butterfly fluttering into a net if he didn't want her released from marriage to his son.

There had to be another way to find Ted and make him see reason. She hoped it wouldn't take long. She wished with all her heart that he'd be changed, that he would quickly and quietly consent to a divorce and be done with it, so she could go back home. But who could believe in a fantasy such as that?

She reached Mrs. Flemming's ramshackle cottage. Maybe

Mrs. Flemming could tell her something. Bolstered with hope, she struggled up the path with her bags.

Next morning, weak sunshine seeped through the small window of Bridget Flemming's kitchen. Meg was Bridget's only boarder, and sat at a small corner table with a bowl of oatmeal and a cup of fragrant, steaming tea in front of her. Bridget, four feet tall, humpbacked and silver-haired, was a childless widow. She was awfully glad to have Meg stay, welcomed her few coins in payment.

"It rained in the night, did ya know, dear?" Bridget asked as she scrubbed the oatmeal pot in a pan of suds at another table nearby. She looked at Meg over the tops of wire-rimmed spectacles settled on her button nose. Her faded blue eyes matched the washed-out blue of her striped gingham dress. Over the dress she wore an apron made of bleached flour sack.

"I slept very soundly, I didn't hear the rain." The truth was, she had only a faint memory of being shown to her small room after she arrived. Her decision to immediately pepper Mrs. Flemming with questions had had to wait. Exhausted from the long journey and riven with fear and worry over the task facing her, she'd simply crawled between the covers on her small cot and fallen asleep. This morning she felt better, ready to find Ted and get their separation over with. In the meantime, there was comfort in Bridget's friendly chatter.

"Ya remember the Donnellys, Jim and Joannah?" Bridget didn't wait for an answer before going on, "Both dead. Jim got killed in a saloon brawl, Joannah died of consumption two months later. Their children scattered—moved on. Finn and Katie MacCormac don't live 'ere no more, either. They took their family back to our homeland, to County Clare. Others ya might know are gone from the Patch."

When Meg could get a word in, she asked, "Do you remember Meara Dolan? I understand she doesn't live here anymore. Do you know what happened to her, where she might've gone?"

Bridget finished with the pot. A knife flashed in her small hands as she chopped vegetables for a noontime soup. She hesitated, bit into a carrot, and told her, "Sure an' I remember Meara Dolan. A nice one, she was, and nobody in the neighborhood could sew as fine a seam as 'er. What happened to 'er? I'll tell ya! A German fella moved into the Patch an' first thing we know, Meara up and marries 'im! We was all glad to see it."

"She got married?" Meg was surprised. From things Meara had said in the old days, she had expected to remain a spinster all her life. After Meg had fled the Patch, there'd been little word between them. They had been afraid to write for fear Ted would find out and trace Meg's location, deciding to trust God that each was safe and happy. "I'm glad to hear Meara's married. Do you think her husband's a good man, was she happy?"

"They was as in love as a pair of doves!"

Meg laughed. "Good. Do you know where they went to live?" If her divorce went to a nasty trial, she was going to need Meara.

"Can't tell ya that, but it's not in the Patch. They lived on 'ere for about six months after they got married, then Meara's husband wanted to take 'er to meet 'is people. They never came back. They stayed where 'is people was, I suppose. Like a lot of folks when they leave the Patch, that's the last ya 'ear of 'em. Take you, for instance. I remember ya bein' called Cassiday when ya was 'ere years ago, just a girl. Now you're a grown-up woman an' say ya like to be called Meg, ain't that somethin'! I remember Maria, your mama, and your papa,

Red Pat. After they died, ya married that good-for-nothin' Malloy, an' then ya vanished." She stood there wiping her hands on her apron, her expression clouded and clearly waiting for Meg to explain where she'd been.

Until things were settled between her and Ted, and maybe not even then, it was best not to mention where she lived now. She was tired of lying, hiding facts, and keeping secrets, but she saw no other choice. "I've lived in different places and for a few years I traveled." Taking a deep breath, she changed the subject, "Does Ted Malloy still live here in the Patch?"

A voice called suddenly from the front of the house, "Hullooo, Bridget, you home, then?"

"That's Lillie Clary," Bridget told Meg. "She comes over ever' mornin' to have tea with me and a chat. She'll be curious about ya, for sartin." She cupped a hand around her tiny mouth, "Come on to the kitchen, Lillie. We been expectin' ya."

"Hello, Mrs. Clary." Meg smiled.

The floor shook slightly as Mrs. Clary, a short stout woman, came into the room. A brief smile in Meg's direction showed that Mrs. Clary had no teeth. Her blue eyes sparkled above her chubby cheeks.

"Did you get a good rest, Miss?" Mrs. Clary gummed the question as she removed her bonnet and plaid shawl, tossing them aside on a bench. She settled herself at the table and held her cup for Bridget to pour tea.

"I slept like the dead."

"Bridget runs a fine place, don't she?"

"Yes, she does." The boarding house was as shabby as everything else in the Patch, but spotless. The food was plain, but nourishing.

"Our friend Meg, 'ere, was askin' about Ted Malloy, Lillie. Did ya know this young lady was married to 'im, an' still is? No," she answered herself, "ya likely don't know that, ya bein' a newcomer, almost, to the Patch."

"I never met this young lady before last night but I do know that Malloy!" Lillie made a sour face. "A good-for-nothin' he is, worthless and bad as they come. He likes nothin' better than to get my man drunk and take his money gamblin'. You're his wife? Didn't know he had one!"

Meg tried once more to find out if he lived in the neighborhood.

" 'E don't live nowhere for very long," Bridget replied, with a shake of her head. "Comes an' goes. 'E don't work at real work. Spends 'is time in the saloons when'e comes to the Patch. 'Is father, John J. Malloy, is an important man in St. Louis, and rich. But the way I hear it, 'e's ashamed of his son and don't give 'im a nickel."

"What about his mother? Does she feel the same about Ted?" Meg remembered Mrs. Malloy as a shadowy person, always in the background. But still she thought Mrs. Malloy would defend her own son and give him aid, even if it meant displeasing her husband.

Bridget answered, "John Malloy's wife died about two years ago. Died in 'er sleep one night. 'Er heart up and quit, I believe they said."

"Died of heartbreak over the arguments between her worthless son and her husband, is more like it," Lillie claimed. "Too bad Ted Malloy weren't more like his father. But here he come up in the family like a stinkweed in a patch of lilies. Worthless. When Ted Malloy's not abed with a woman, he's gamblin' at the races or makin' bets at the local prizefights." Lillie was angry. "He makes his money that way, an' from cheatin' good men like my Glenn."

Bridget looked at Meg over her spectacles with sad apology. "Don't know why ya ever would've wanted to marry such as 'im. 'E takes one mistress after another to look after 'im. They give 'im bed and board, affection, likely, too, and spending money. It ain't long, though, 'til a woman with good sense gets wise to 'im. They find out 'is charm don't mean a thing. They get tired of 'is beatin' 'em, breakin' their bones sometimes, and they throw 'im out."

So in five years he hadn't changed at all, unless he was even worse. She could toss out the window any hope that he'd be a gentleman and give her what she wanted willingly.

Lillie said, "I heard he's been stayin' with that silly woman, Selma Flannagan, if she ain't tossed his carcass into the street by now. Before that it was Katie O'Toole, Gilda Feeny, Daisy MacDara. Katie was a widow that thought Ted would take care of her. She found out she was better off alone. Gilda and Daisy was wild girls that went on to be uptown prostitutes."

"What makes a man act like that, do ya suppose? What makes 'im beat on a defenseless woman?" Bridget wondered.

Meg, who wished she wasn't an authority on the subject, said quietly, "Beating a woman who is no match for him in physical strength makes a spineless man feel he's strong and manly. Or maybe he's angry at something else, and she's handy as a punching bag. If she's a woman with spirit and a mind of her own, a man like we're talking about sees that as a threat. He beats her to keep her in her place, subservient."

"That's what Ted did to ya, didn't 'e? I remember 'e beat ya so bad ya was in bed at Meara's for weeks before you disappeared." Bridget's little face was pinched with concern.

"Yes, that's what he did to me." Meg clasped her hands tightly before her. "A woman shouldn't have to put up with such abuse. I got away from him and built a new life, thankfully. Now I've come back to get a divorce from him."

For a few seconds the word *divorce* bothered the other two

women, then Bridget declared, "Well, a good thing, too!"

Meg took her cup and bowl to the pan of suds and washed them herself. "Seems like the local saloons are the places to look for him. Would you give me directions? I remember one. Maybe there are others after so many years?"

"You can't go to places like that!" Lillie exclaimed in horror, her fat cheeks quivering.

"You wouldn't be safe, lookin' for Ted Malloy yourself." Bridget wrung her hands in her apron and shook her head. "The worst places is where 'e'd be."

Meg looked at them, waiting, saying nothing. She had to look for Ted wherever she was most apt to find him. She didn't have a lot of time; the sooner she let him know of her intention to be divorced, the better. She wanted to face him and make him see that she meant business.

"Awright, then," Bridget gave a flip of her apron and backed down with a look of misgiving. They gave her directions to three area saloons. Although most men frequented the bars in the evening after work, Ted could be found there any time of day. Also, when Meg asked, they gave her the name and location of the tenement house where Ted's most recent female acquaintance, Selma Flannagan, was said to live.

It had indeed rained, Meg saw when she got outside, and she danced to miss the puddles of water in the rutted dirt path. After a walk of a few blocks, she reached the first saloon, a dismal shack called CLANCY'S.

Hoping not to bring too much attention to herself, Meg glanced inside through a dirty window. She could make out a couple of men seated at a table playing cards, drinks in front of them. The barkeep was a bald, buffalo-sized man who immediately noticed her outside. He frowned fiercely and pointed toward a sign in the window that said NO WOMEN

INSIDE. He motioned for her to move along. Meg pretended not to notice. She pressed her face closer to the glass, wanting to see into the deeper shadows of the establishment. She made out no one else in the room and neither man playing cards looked like Ted. The barkeep, glaring at her now, was striding toward the door. She chewed the inside of her cheek, shielding her eyes for one last careful look. Satisfied that Ted was not there, she hurried away. The barkeep had come out to the street; she could feel his eyes on her back. She didn't turn, didn't hurry, acted as though peering into saloon windows was an everyday habit with her. Still, she was relieved when that particular place was well behind her.

She could stay put at Bridget's and let Ted find her, she supposed. If gossip still spread as fast in Kerry Patch as it had in the old days, word of her return would be known by most within a matter of hours. She was sure if he knew she was there he would come looking for her. She hoped he would want to be legally free of her, as much as she wanted to be free of him. But he might want something else entirely. He might want her to pay dearly for leaving him in the first place, pay with her life, possibly. He might even, God forbid, want her to resume their marriage.

Until they were face to face, she couldn't know what his reaction to her return might be, but she must take him by surprise. She wanted the upper hand from the start.

Meg checked the other two saloons the women had told her about, but saw no sign of Ted. She walked on, not sure where to look next, but not ready to give up. A shabby, familiar-looking figure came toward her on the roadside path. "Mr. Sheahan?" He'd aged a lot in five years; in the past he worked hard as a street-cleaner for downtown St. Louis. "Mr. Sheahan?" This time he heard her and stopped.

Grizzled and stooped, he leaned on his cane, and his watery blue eyes studied her. She explained who she was and that she was looking for Ted Malloy. Mr. Sheahan didn't recognize her, but he did know about Ted Malloy. His voice was thin and quivery, "Yesterday I saw him with the no-goods at the dog races. Might be there today."

"Where's that, Mr. Sheahan?"

He turned and pointed with a wobbly finger. Shaky words dribbled from his mouth on saliva, "There's an empty lot on the alley back of Cass Avenue. They run dogs there."

After another long walk, Meg found the place. In answer to her wave, a pimply-faced boy left a noisy game of stickball in the lot to tell her that no races were being held that day.

The rickety stairs of the tenement opening onto the Fifteenth Street alley creaked as Meg slowly made her way to the second floor. Wallpaper peeled in dribs and drabs from the walls. The floor was dirty and cluttered with rubbish. The smell of urine, burned cabbage, and other unpleasant odors she couldn't identify, nearly took her breath away.

According to the bone-thin landlady Meg had spoken with downstairs, Selma Flannagan had the second room on the left.

Meg knocked on the door and waited. She couldn't hear anything from inside. She waited, then knocked again. The landlady squawked up at her from the foot of the stairs, "Selma might not be to home. Sometimes she goes visitin' her mother over to Biddle Street. If Selma was out all night an' is up there in bed you won't raise her, either."

Meg gave up after knocking several times with no response. It was possible Ted didn't stay there. Back downstairs, she asked the landlady.

"Sometimes he's here. Comes an' goes. I ain't seen him around lately, which suits me fine. All those two do is scrap, the screamin' and fightin' is enough to wake the dead. I've told Ted I don't want him here, but he just laughs. Maybe Selma's got fed up with him, got rid of him."

For hours, pushed by urgency, Meg crisscrossed that side of St. Louis, seeking places where she might locate Ted. He wasn't one of the men sitting on the benches in front of the barbershops she passed. He wasn't among the hangers-on throwing dice, dozing, or talking outside the livery stable, the blacksmith shop, or the fire station. When she saw someone who looked friendly and non-threatening, she asked about him, but got no helpful answers.

Then she passed an old abandoned livery barn where a prizefight was to take place that night, according to a poster on the door. The building was quiet, locked up tight. She studied the hand-drawn poster. The artist was very good; the two men looked so real she blushed when she saw how revealing their long tight drawers were. Both men were bare chested, their necks, shoulders, and arms bulged with muscle. They wore soft slippers. The younger fighter had thick curly hair and was more handsome than the older one. There'd be a fight that night, the poster said. She would come back later.

Ted's way of life made her think of a flea, hopping constantly with no stopping place for long. But at some point he had to land long enough that she could approach him and insist on his cooperation in a divorce.

She returned to the tenement rooms of Selma Flannagan and this time Selma, a thin young woman in a loose dragon-green wrapper, answered Meg's knock. Meg stated her case, noting sadly the purple bruise on Selma's cheek, her swollen upper lip, and the patch of missing hair in her dirty blond locks. Selma's gaping wrapper revealed another bruise on her left breast.

"I don't know where Ted is," the young woman told her,

anger in her brown eyes, "an' today, I don't care. He could've fallen into the Ol' Mississip' and drowned, and I wouldn't care. First the bastard beats me and tears up my clothes, then he steals my money. That was three—four days ago, I dunno, maybe last week—but I ain't seen him since."

"Do you know where he might be found?"

"Jesus, Mary, and Joseph, no! I told you!"

"Yes," Meg nodded. "Thank you." She turned to leave, then turned back. "You shouldn't have anything to do with Ted Malloy, Miss Flannagan. He's dangerous, as you likely know from the way he treats you."

"An' who are you to be givin' me advice?" With hands on her hips, Selma glared.

"His wife. He once nearly killed me, and would've if I hadn't gotten away."

Selma stared at her in a weighty silence that seemed to go on forever, then she pulled her green wrapper close around her and slammed the door.

Meg shrugged and headed down the stairs. After walking all day, her hip hurt fiercely. She headed back to Bridget's.

After supper and a brief rest, she prepared to leave again, dressed in her dark gray suit, smoke-gray cloak, and black bonnet. Several people that day had said she would mostly likely find Ted Malloy at the fights. It would only worry Bridget if Meg told her she was going to the prizefight, so she said only that she was going for a brief evening walk, that she might call on old neighbors. She saw by Bridget's soft blue eyes that she didn't believe her.

"Wait!" Bridget said, and scurried away. She came back to where Meg hesitated inside the front door. Bridget handed Meg a ten-inch hatpin, the top of which was an enameled red rose. "You put this in your bag, and if you need to use it, don't think twice, *jab!*"

Meg thanked her with a hug and put the hatpin in her bag.

By the light of the moon, an occasional street lamp, and lamplight spilling from shanty windows, she found her way along the streets to the site of the prizefight.

The livery barn was a different place at night. In front, horses were tied to rails, trees, bushes. There were countless rigs: crude wagons, fine black buggies, small hacks. She zigzagged a path through the vehicles, ignoring the men who watched her. She acted as if she were deaf when some of them called out to ask if she was alone and wanted their company inside.

She entered the packed, smoke-filled room and saw that it was centered by a big, canvas-covered stage enclosed with ropes. Two heavily muscled men, in long johns and shirtless, pranced in opposite corners of the ring; they weren't quite as fine looking as the poster had shown, but close. An excited hubbub indicated that the fight was about to start; people were pouring in the door. She found it hard to breathe because of cigar smoke and the foul odor of at least a hundred unwashed bodies. There were a few women in the room, though they were a different sort than you would find at the local market or in church on Sunday, Meg reflected wryly. She moved slowly through the crowd, her eyes searching. She shouldn't be here, but she couldn't leave. He could be here.

As discreetly as possible, she studied individual men in the crowd, their build and size, their faces. *No matter how long it takes* she was thinking, when sausage-like fingers reached out and grabbed her arm, nearly startling her out of her mind.

"Hey, beyootiful lady! Let's be friends, awright?" The man holding her powerless was corpulent; his vest, missing half its buttons, gaped across his wide front. His heavy-lidded eyes surveyed her suggestively, and a pink-lipped smile split his bloated face, showing stained teeth. He yanked her up tight against his huge belly.

"Stop it!" Meg struggled, pulled an arm free, and gave him a hard fist. She pushed away and moved on quickly ready to open her handbag and grab Bridget's hatpin. She heard his rumbling laugh behind her. She sighed shakily. As big as he was, he could have overpowered her if he chose, although she liked to think she could outrun him if the need arose.

The prizefight started with a deafening roar while she continued her urgent study of faces. She was reminded of wild dogs thirsting for blood but resisted covering her ears. She grimaced as the thud of fist against flesh and bone and the grunts of the fighters melded sickeningly with women's squeals of horrified delight and men's shouts for their favorite fighter, "Kill 'im, kill the bastard!" Around her, men watching the fight recoiled and moaned as though they took each blow that smashed the fighter's faces. Others danced on their toes and punched the air, shouting instructions that no one else paid attention to.

They were out of their minds, all of them, Meg thought. Twice she was nearly knocked off her feet by boisterous would-be fighters acting out in the audience what was happening in the ring. She pushed on, hatpin at the ready now, shaking off hands that tried to grab her, ignoring invitations that fired her cheeks.

She was not sure how much time passed. The more she searched for Ted, the more tired and frightened she became. She felt foolish for venturing there in the first place, but now that she had, she couldn't give up. She had to find him. He could be close. In her anxiety, faces blurred.

The uproar grew deafening as the fighters slugged it out. Then it was suddenly over as the heavier fighter went down with a quaking thud. There was a hush, then screamed pleas from the crowd for the ox to get up swinging. He lay still while the referee counted. Meg looked and saw the younger fighter wiping blood from his nose onto the back of his arm. The referee handed him a towel, then lifted the young man's arm and declared him the winner.

The referee shouted, "Right there, that pretty lady right there in gray. Bring her up here to award the prize to the winner and give him a big KISS!"

Until a sea of eyes turned on her, Meg hadn't realized she was the topic of the referee's speech. "Bring her on up here, now. C'mon little lady, this is your chance to kiss a champion!"

Hands caught her waist and she cried out, "No! No, please! Stop!"

Every pair of eyes in the room was on Meg as she fought the hands lifting her and carrying her through the cheering crowd toward the ring. She tried to use Bridget's hatpin, but felt it slip from her hand to be lost on the floor. A sob of fury caught in her throat.

Chapter Three

Meg was defenseless against the heavyset man who yanked her from the others. He slung her over his shoulder and carried her upside down with swinging strides, his rear just below her bobbing face. Laughter and cheers rang. Humiliation and fury strengthened her pounding fists as she struggled to free herself. She heard a sudden order from the direction of the ring, "Put her down! I'm tellin' ya now, let the lady go! Let her go on home now."

She saw from her blurred and bobbing side-glance that it was the younger fighter ordering her release. The rowdy crowd, a moving sea around her and her captor, roared refusal. "Take 'er to the ring!" they yelled in chorus, "take 'er up there where the champ can claim his kiss!" She fought off hands that pulled, patted, and grabbed at her, then she heard her skirt rip.

All at once the crowd parted and Meg was released so suddenly she fell to the floor, losing her handbag. In dismay she scrambled among booted feet and a forest of trousered legs until she found it. "C'mon, Miss." Her arm was clasped and she was helped to her feet, clutching her bag to her chest and gasping for breath. Her hair was torn from its pins, straggling in her face, her clothing askew and torn; she was too angry to speak.

"Go on about your own affairs, now," the fighter ordered the crowd. Some grumbled at being robbed of their fun and others chuckled in embarrassment at what they'd been doing, but they accepted his order and in twos and threes, turned away from her.

"Th-thank you," she said sharply, her fevered glance level with the fighter's sweat-shiny chest. She looked up into his face, ready to do battle if he wanted anything from her other than to let her go. But there was no ill intent and only kindness in his expression. "Thank you," she said again in relief and attempted to straighten her clothes and hair.

"Come with me." Meg's arm was again caught in his strong grasp. "You can wait while I get dressed and then I'll see you safely home."

"No." She swallowed dryly. "I appreciate your offer, but I can manage alone. Excuse me, please, I have to go now."

He stood very close, concern in his eyes, then he stepped back, shook his head, and shrugged. "If you're sure, miss."

"I am." She rushed away from him, pushing her way through the milling crowd only to find herself completely turned around with no knowledge of where the main door was located. In confusion she went one way and then another, her heart pounding as she looked frantically for an exit. She found the door at last. Tears of relief were close as she plunged outside into the cold gloom.

Much of the crowd was also spilling into the street, moving toward their rigs. Others inside could be heard loudly collecting their bets.

Meg picked up her skirts and ran along the dark street, chafing with regret that she'd been the focus of attention in that terrible place, even for that short period. If Ted was there, he'd surely seen her. Now she prayed that he hadn't been there, or if he was, that he hadn't recognized her. She looked over her shoulder. No one followed, yet.

Darkness smothered her as she ran; her pounding footsteps matched the frantic beat of her heart. Several times she looked over her shoulder to see if anyone followed. Perhaps she should have let the fighter walk her home. But she didn't know him any better than she knew any of the others. She had to take care of herself.

A half-hour later she opened Bridget's door and tiptoed inside, hoping she wouldn't wake her hostess. But Bridget was waiting and came from her room with a lamp. Aghast at Meg's disheveled hair and torn clothes, Bridget's sweet face flooded with sympathy as she put the lamp on a table and hurried forward. "Poor thing, poor thing," she clucked. "Are ya all right, then?"

"I'm all right." Shaking like a tree in a windstorm, Meg began to remove her outer garments. Hot tears flooded her cheeks. "I got into some trouble," she tried to explain, "but nothing serious. I'm really all right, just a bit upset."

Bridget's hug was warm and comforting. "There, there," she said, patting Meg's back. "We'll be cleanin' ya up and fixin' ya some nice warm milk. Sit in the chair there, darlin', and I'll be right back." She turned, "Did ya use your hatpin?"

"I'm awfully sorry, Bridget, but I lost the hatpin. I'll get you another."

"Don't matter." She scurried off.

Meg stumbled to the chair, unable to stand any longer with or without Bridget's order to sit. While Bridget fussed over her, she rambled, mostly in an attempt to clear her own mind, "I was thinking I might find Ted Malloy at the prize-fight tonight—" Bridget gasped and her hands froze in midair.

"Ya went there? Oh, ya shouldn'ta!"

"I suppose it was foolish to go there alone, but I'm desperate to find Ted. Some rowdies got hold of me and they were trying . . . trying to play a prank, before a . . . a young fellow came to my assistance. He made them leave me alone. I got away and came home; that's really all there is to it. I'm sorry if I worried you."

"Somethin' a whole lot worse coulda happened to ya tonight, Meg, don't ya know? I hope ya won't go doin' nothin' like this again!"

Meg shook her head. She was beginning to feel numb. "I hope I won't have to, but I must find Ted Malloy." She removed Bridget's hands from where they fussed at her hair. "I'm keeping you up. Let's turn in. It's been a long day."

Later, Meg lay in bed, sick with embarrassment and frightened at the thought of what might have happened if she hadn't gotten away from the crowd. There were some very rough men there tonight. She was lucky the young fighter had stood up for her and made the others stop. She tossed for some time, then purposefully turned her thoughts to home, to Paragon Springs. Her tears began to dry on her cheeks, her breathing eased, her mind slowly calmed. Anything, everything was worth it, to be able to return home again a free person. She yawned, turned on her side, and with her palm under her cheek, let sleep come.

The neighborhood of elegant homes where Ted's father lived was so quiet and tidy compared to Kerry Patch, that one would think it was an exhibit and no one lived there, Meg decided.

Elms, their naked branches outlined against the blue sky, lined the wide paved street. She looked up and down, remembering the trees as saplings. It was hard to believe how much they'd grown in the years she'd been away.

Her steps slowed as she approached the Malloy mansion, a massive, three-story structure set in wide, well-kept grounds and built of lavender-blue limestone capped with a red-tile, mansard roof. Arched windows, tall doors, and ornamental dormers made it seem like a rich, well-dressed, and self-satisfied matron, but she wouldn't let it intimidate her.

There was a time when she believed that she might live

here as Ted's wife. Then, after she got to truly know him, she'd wanted nothing so much as distance between them. She'd wanted never to see him or this house again. Now she had to face both.

Shaking off bad memories, she stood at the ornamental iron fence, noticing for the first time a warmly-bundled, middle-aged housemaid on her knees scrubbing the front steps with soap and water.

"Hello," Meg called, "may I come inside?" Without waiting for an answer, she opened the gate and planted herself firmly on Malloy ground.

"Hullo, yourself," the cleaning woman said, looking up. "Are you the new nurse?"

"Nurse? Hmm, no. I'm . . . a visitor."

"Well go on up, then, and ring the bell. Hannah will let you in. Mind that you wipe your feet and don't track this water inside."

"All right, thank you." She hesitated. "Is someone sick?"

The woman frowned in suspicion. "You ain't a close friend of Mr. Malloy or you wouldn't be askin' that. You'd know he's sick, dyin' as a matter of fact."

She stared at the woman, shaken by her comment, and let the news sink in. Ted's father had been such a strong, overbearing man when she knew him that it seemed he would live forever, like a mountain. "I didn't know, and I'm sorry. I've . . . been away from St. Louis for years. I'm . . . a relative." She reconsidered for a second. "When you speak of Mr. Malloy, you don't mean Ted Malloy, do you?"

The woman scoffed, "Course I don't!" She scrubbed harder, filling the air with the clean smell of her soap. "That scoundrel don't live here. I mean old John Malloy, he's the one sick."

"I see. Thank you." She sidled past and on up to the wide

front door, where she rang the bell.

Hannah, a tall, rawboned maid in black, also mistook her for the new nurse they were expecting and ushered her inside without question.

Meg explained, "I'm Ted Malloy's wife." Surprise filled the other woman's face. Meg rushed on, "I understand that Mr. Malloy isn't well, but it's very important that I talk with him, if it's possible for him to receive visitors." She stood on the cool marble floor and looked past Hannah up the curved mahogany stairway. She'd forgotten how beautiful the interior of the house was.

"Who did you say you are?"

It put a bad taste in her mouth to say it but she repeated, "Mrs. Ted Malloy. John Malloy's daughter-in-law."

Hannah frowned. "No one's ever mentioned a daughter-in-law. Mr. Malloy won't have nothing to do with his son, Ted. We have orders not to let him in."

"I have nothing to do with Ted. I'm legally married to him, but I haven't lived with him for years. Please, tell Mr. Malloy that Cassiday is here and that it is urgent that I talk with him."

Hannah look unconvinced, but she said, "I'll ask." She turned away, leaving Meg alone in the entry hall. She returned a short time later. "Whoever you are, Mr. Malloy says you aren't his daughter-in-law. She ran off years ago and is probably dead."

"But I am his daughter-in-law, very much alive!" She stepped forward, her gloved hands outstretched in a plea to be understood. "I was called Cassiday Rose Curran when I lived in Kerry Patch. Mr. Malloy will remember my parents, Red Pat and Maria Curran. Please tell him I beg to see him for just a few minutes."

Hannah frowned and stood steadfast. "He's not well, you

know. I don't like pestering him when he doesn't want to be bothered. He's sure he doesn't know you, he says you're an impostor."

Meg sighed and said apologetically, "I understand, but if I can have just a few minutes' audience with him, I'm sure he'll recognize me. I don't want to tire him or be a nuisance, but I must see him. I won't keep him but a few minutes."

"I'll ask again, but I doubt it will do a shred of good. Come with me."

Hannah led the way into a sitting room where Meg nervously took a seat on the edge of a pillowed chaise lounge. The room was as she remembered, only a little more worn. It was furnished in lovely light and dark woods of maple and walnut, with a thick floral carpet. The fashionably tall windows were draped with blue satin. In front of one window were glass shelves on which sat blooming geraniums, calla lilies, and ivy, a homey casual touch.

It was in this room that John Malloy had ordered her marriage to Ted, after discovering them kissing half-clothed in the honeysuckle arbor on the back grounds. Mr. Malloy had hoped that marriage would settle his wild son. He knew that Cassiday came from good stock and might come into money of her own from her mother's side. None of what he hoped had come to pass, and the marriage had been a disaster.

Meg licked her lips and waited. Her knees were beginning to feel weak; her stomach churned.

At a sound, she looked up. Hannah was pushing Mr. Malloy into the room in a wheeled chair padded with thick pillows.

"Mr. Malloy." Meg leaped to her feet. "Thank you for seeing me."

He looked the same, yet smaller and incredibly old. He was obviously weak and in pain, but his strong mind and will came through in his manner and his expression. He growled, "Who are you? I don't think you're that girl."

"Yes, I'm Meg. I mean I am Cassiday. I am Ted's wife."

"Come closer into the light so I can see you. You don't look like Cassiday Curran to me."

"It's been years, sir. I've changed." In her mind she pictured herself today compared to the last time he saw her. She was still slender, but had filled out in bosom and hips. She wore her dark hair pinned up, rather than in curls to her shoulders as she had when she was younger. Her personality and manner had changed most; life in western Kansas had given her backbone she didn't have when she lived in St. Louis. She went to stand in front of him. He leaned forward in his chair, glaring at her from under snowy brows. He studied her face for a long time, then her build and clothing, her hair. His head shook, partly from age and sickness, partly from doubt.

He sat back and snorted. "You're not her. You're not Cassiday. Hannah, take this person out of here."

"No, wait, please." Meg shook Hannah's hand from her arm. "I am Cassiday, sir. It's been a long time and I'm older. I've lived harshly and probably don't look the same because of it."

He was motioning for Hannah to wheel him away.

"Do you remember the color of Cassiday's eyes?" Meg asked quickly. Her eyes, dove gray and ringed with black, appeared silver.

He hesitated and thought about it. "They were grayish, silver, I suppose. Your eyes are dark blue."

She knelt in front of his chair. "Please look closer, Mr. Malloy. My eyes are silver. This scar on my temple," she brushed her hair back and traced the scar with her finger, "happened when Ted beat me. I'm lame because he beat me.

I had to leave him, because he beat me."

For a long time, Mr. Malloy looked at her and didn't speak. He seemed to sag in his chair as recognition dawned, although he continued to glower.

Hannah stood by with her hand over her mouth, fascination in her eyes.

Meg spoke quietly, imploring Mr. Malloy. "I wouldn't lie to you, sir. I'm Cassiday, although for a long time I've gone by another name. I call myself Meg. I had to do that, to keep away from Ted."

"I told him to let you go when you disappeared," John Malloy muttered, more to himself than to anyone else. "I told Ted he didn't deserve you."

"Then you do believe me? You recognize that I am Cassiday?"

"You could be her." He spoke with effort, force of will hauling him up straighter in his chair as he gripped its arms. His glance bored into her. "But that doesn't matter one bit to me. I know why you're here." His lips curled. "You've heard that I'm dying and you've come back to watch, like a vulture. As Ted's wife, you plan to claim my fortune when I die. But I've disowned Ted, I have no son with a wife. You've come here for nothing!"

Meg was so shocked that for several seconds she couldn't say a word. She felt sick that he would accuse her of such a thing, but maybe in his place she would believe as he did. "That's not what I'm here for, Mr. Malloy." She stood up. "I came to you for just one thing: I need to know where Ted is, because I intend to divorce him. I want to be free of him once and for all."

"How would I know where he is?" With shaking effort he turned his head to look up at her.

"I don't know, sir. I thought he might be here, or that you

could help me find him."

"I don't know why I should help you."

"It would be a kindness, Mr. Malloy, that's all. Ted and I should never have married. That was a terrible mistake, but you have the power to help make it right. You don't really owe me anything, but the rest of my life depends on this divorce. I believe I deserve my freedom, and with or without your help, I will have it."

"You're her, but you're different." There was grudging admiration in his tired voice. His hand shakily picked at the wool coverlet covering his knees.

Meg thought that was the end of it until he said, "Come back in two days at four o'clock in the afternoon. I'll have Ted found and brought here for a meeting." He looked up at Hannah and ordered tiredly, "Take me to my room." He had no further words for Meg. His head went back and he closed his eyes. He looked very weak and vulnerable in that moment, but Meg knew that he would never be either as long as he lived, and even after death his memory would be a force for his son and anyone who'd known him to reckon with.

"I appreciate this more than I can say, Mr. Malloy," she told him softly, but he didn't respond.

Hannah gave Meg a slim smile, nodded, and wheeled her employer away.

Minutes later, Meg hurried down the street feeling as elated, and at the same time as frightened, as she had ever been in her life. She had no doubt that Mr. Malloy would have Ted found and brought to the mansion at the appointed hour. A meeting was going to happen and the divorce could go forward, providing she could make Ted see reason. After so long, he would be a stranger, but the fear she felt toward him was very familiar. It had never gone away.

Chapter Four

The law office was small and cramped. Row upon row of shiny-backed books lined the walls; a brass lamp hung low over the attorney's desk. In the corner there was a bench for clients who must wait, and in front of that a couple of chairs flanked a spittoon. The very businesslike attorney, Hiram Smith, was younger than his beard and receding hairline had at first led Meg to believe. His smile was kindly. "Let me get you a chair, please."

"Thank you." Meg's arm brushed a dusty fern as she moved aside to allow him to place a chair for her in front of his desk. She sat down and tried to ignore the nervous fluttering in her stomach.

He bustled behind the desk and sat down, leaning forward with his hands clasped in front of him. "Now then," he said, "let's see what we can do for your troubled marriage."

A flag of alarm went up in Meg's mind. "I don't want to do anything for my marriage, Mr. Smith, I want to end it." She'd found the attorney by walking the streets beyond Kerry Patch, where she'd come across a cluster of small businesses on Seventh Street and noticed the sign in his small office window. In earlier conversation he'd been sympathetic. He practiced in the matrimonial field, he was well qualified according to his credentials, and the fee he'd quoted was within her means, although barely. She hoped she'd chosen wisely. There wasn't time, nor did she have the money, for a lengthy search for a lawyer. He simply had to be the right one for her cause.

He smiled and nodded. "Not all marriages are made in

46

heaven, I understand that. It's my job to hear you out, advise you of your rights and obligations, and point out to you the consequences of ending your marriage. I only advise, the final decision is yours."

She gave a ragged sigh of relief. She knew that getting a divorce was a huge decision and usually placed scandal—on the woman, especially—but she didn't want someone to try to convince her to stay married. "I wed my husband, Ted Malloy, in good faith," she told Smith, "but he changed almost immediately after we married. Possibly I was too young to see his true character before I married him. I did love him at first, but he was enraged by the smallest things and took out his anger on me. He was brutal to me on many occasions. On our last day together he beat me so severely that I had to leave him or risk dying at his hands."

Smith frowned, and she wondered if he thought that she exaggerated or had provoked Ted and it was her fault. "I have scars to prove what he did, Mr. Smith, and I am lame from that last beating. I realize now that ours was never a true marriage. He saw me as someone to wait on him, to submit to his bullying. For over four years I've lived in freedom from him, but now I want to make that freedom legal and permanent."

"I see," he said, although she was still not sure that he did. He seemed reluctant to proceed with her directions, unconvinced of what she was telling him. He leaned back in his chair, tented his fingers, and said solemnly, "You understand that I'll need to hear Mr. Malloy's side before we continue with proceedings. Did you request that he come here with you today? I like for a couple to be in agreement on a matter of this importance."

"I haven't yet been able to locate him, and even then I'm afraid he'll only lie."

He ignored her comment, one hand held up to still her

while he explained, "I must remind you that society and the courts are on the side of marriage and like to see a union remain intact. Divorce is a last resort. Both you and Mr. Malloy must appear in court and tell your stories before a judge." He tapped the desktop in a monotonous rhythm. "If what you say is true, you should succeed in obtaining a divorce."

"I must have a divorce, Mr. Smith, and I am telling the truth!"

"It's the court's business to determine who is at fault for failure of the marriage." Tap, tap, tap. "The court will also decide who is financially responsible for all persons involved after the marriage is dissolved." A frown settled between his eyes. "Are there children?" He dipped his pen in the ink bottle on his desk and squared a sheet of paper in front of him.

"There are no children. As for myself, I want nothing from Ted Malloy except my freedom."

He shrugged, his pen scratching as he wrote on the paper. "I will advise, and so will the court, in the matter of financial responsibility." He put the pen into its holder, his eyes squinting as he studied her. After several seconds he nodded, satisfied at his calculations whatever they were. He dipped his pen in the ink bottle again. "Can you give me an idea how to find the defendant, Mr. Malloy, so we may summon him? Please give me his full name, and its proper spelling."

"In a day or two I'll be better able to tell you where to find Ted. He evidently has no permanent address. The two of us are meeting at his father's house tomorrow afternoon to discuss the divorce. His name is Theodore Malloy," she spelled it for him, "but he is called Teddy, or Ted."

"I'd like to see you both here in my office at ten o'clock on Friday." Smith explained other matters of Missouri law. The circuit court had jurisdiction in all cases of divorce. The complaining party did not have to be a resident of Missouri to obtain a divorce if the offense and injury complained of was committed within the state while both parties resided within the state.

Ten minutes later she was saying good-bye. He reminded her of one more item that only served to increase her headache: "Divorce cases are given a low priority by the courts," he told her, "and it may be some time before your case is heard."

She nodded, although she privately hoped her case would be different. She wanted the divorce quickly so she could return to Paragon Springs. It bothered her to burden her friends there with her share of the work—running the road ranch and quarry, managing the freighting business. All of them had their own work to do without her adding to it. They were too considerate to complain, but she must get back there as soon as possible.

Meg's legs were like clabber as she once again approached the Malloy mansion, this time for her meeting with Ted. Hannah showed her into the sitting room where she'd met with his father days before, then excused herself. Meg noted absentmindedly that a lily bloom at the window had withered and fallen to the floor.

Ted hadn't yet arrived. She was wondering if he would come at all when the soft echo of bells chimed from the direction of the front entrance.

She took a deep breath.

When Ted walked into the room a minute later, Meg hid her shock. For all he'd done to her, he'd been undeniably handsome in his youth, always well dressed, full of charm. He was still handsome, she supposed, but he looked seedy and dissipated. His eyelids were puffy, his face crepe-skinned and jowly. His once youthful body had developed a paunch. His suit was well cut but thready and food stained; he looked like a peacock with tattered and faded feathers.

From across the room he stared disbelievingly at her through gooseberry-green eyes. "How are you . . . *Cassiday?*" He said it as though he wasn't sure it was she. After a moment his face wreathed in a smile. "I hardly recognize you! When I heard you were back I didn't believe it." He chuckled. "I'm not sure I believe it now. You've changed. You're more beautiful, for one thing." He started to where she stood with his hands outstretched. Her lifted chin and warning glance stopped him in midstride. He clasped his hands in front of him, still rakishly smiling.

In the past that smile could have marked either the onset of sweetness or an explosion of violence from him; she had never known what to expect. Now her stomach churned and she moved farther away from him.

The way he saw her was unmistakable, from his expression and his manner. She was a ticket to something he wanted badly, a ticket he hadn't expected but that had dropped out of the blue. He was overjoyed that she'd come. His long-missing wife had walked right back into his life with no effort on his part, and just in time. She was attractive, strong, and (except for her limp) in apparent good health. She might even be a woman of property from her appearance. Best of all she legally belonged to him. Nausea rose in Meg's throat at the thought of his touching her.

She was about to set him straight, but in that moment, Hannah wheeled in his father.

Ted's expression changed dramatically. He suddenly seemed serious, grateful, in slight awe. He rushed to his father's side. "How are you, Father?" He took the chair from Hannah and wheeled it into the light from the window; one big wheel crushed the lily blossom as he turned the chair to face the room. He knelt by his father and started to place his hand on the old man's knee, but was stopped by the look on his father's face.

If she hadn't known Ted so well, Meg might even have pitied him. Instead she felt nothing for him, only a rush to get on with the matter at hand. But she controlled her impatience.

Ted stood up, untouched by his father's rejection, still hopeful. He moved a pace away from his father's chair, mindlessly straightening his cuffs as his words spilled one over the other, "Thank you for inviting me here today, father. I'd have come sooner if you'd allowed it. I've worried about you, I wanted to see you."

"You've never had a thought except for your own pleasure and what you want." His father waved Ted's concern away. "I brought you here to face up to this young woman, to do right by her, if you've got the gumption and decency."

"I don't know what you mean?" Ted appeared to be surprised.

Meg addressed him for the first time. "I want a divorce. I came here to find you and get you to agree."

He looked hammer-struck, seeming to shrink in size, sagging deeper into his clothes. Then a look of anger and resistance flared in his eyes. He found a chair and sat down, crossing his legs. "I might *not* want a divorce, Cassiday. In all truth, I couldn't be happier to see you. It's as though the years have fallen away. We can be together again."

Together again to achieve his own aims! His audacity sparked her anger. Reasoning with him would be a waste of time but she tried, anyway. "Ted, ours was never a good marriage. You treated me badly, injured me. If I'd stayed and reported what you did to me, you'd have been sent to prison."

She knew better; the law often overlooked abuse of a wife, counting such things as a husband's right and responsibility. Ted knew it, too.

"We could get to know each other again, Cassiday. I lost my temper a few times and I'm sorry about that. I loved you; I never wanted you to leave."

He looked on the verge of begging, something he never would have done in the old days. He would have shouted at her, beat her, to get what he wanted. Tonight she was the answer to his prayers, savior of his future, if he handled matters cautiously.

If they came together again, resumed their marriage, it would surely please his father. Ted could even clean up his life for awhile, at least. Cassiday had to give him a second chance so he could convince his father to reinstate him in his will. Then it wouldn't be long until he'd inherit his money.

She saw it all, read his mind easily. It'd be a hard fight, but she wouldn't give in to what he wanted. She was not surprised, only furious, when he said, "I refuse a divorce, because that would be a big mistake. You might have been gone a long time, but you're still my wife. You have obligations, legal and wifely obligations, to me, Cassiday."

"I haven't been known as Cassiday in years, I am Meg!" she told him firmly. "No matter what the law says, I don't consider that I'm your true wife. I belong to myself now, Ted. I'm not your livestock to abuse as you choose."

"Now don't get upset," he ordered. His right hand fisted, repeatedly opened and closed; he wanted to strike her but struggled for calm.

"Don't get upset? You sent a bounty hunter after me, to bring me back!"

"Because I needed you, I wanted you. You're my wife. You had no right to abandon me," his voice rose, "or to abandon your duties as my wife. I had a right to send someone after you."

"You sent Frank Finch to bring me back dead, if need be. I'm sure you've wondered what happened when he didn't return to St. Louis with me in tow?"

His look of guilt was followed by curiosity, but only for a second, and he shrugged.

She went on, "Finch would have killed me with his own hands if someone else hadn't shot him first. The only reason you didn't come for me was that you knew a man like Finch would be a better tracker. A more clever killer, if that's what it took. In your good-for-nothing laziness, you wouldn't have to lift a finger or give up your low-life carousing here in St. Louis to come after me. I'm right and you know it. I have a lot I could tell the court!"

"Cassiday, please," he spoke softly, although his face was red, his eyes flashing, and he looked ready to explode. "I didn't send Finch to hurt you. You have it wrong. He was to be your escort to see you safely home again."

"Bullfeathers, Ted. Bullfeathers. That's a lie."

Both of them had forgotten that his father was in the room until he gave a weak cry. Meg looked in his direction. Mr. Malloy's face was ashen and he looked so ill she was afraid he might expire that moment. She felt pity for him, and guilt. He'd done her a favor in bringing Ted here tonight. "I'm sorry, sir, that we've upset you and tired you. I'll go now."

His shaking hand lifted an inch or two in acceptance of her apology and thanks. His voice was barely audible and he spoke slowly, "I did what I could." His eyes found Ted in disgust, then closed. "I tried." That he spoke not only of tonight, but referred to Ted in general was obvious to everyone in the room.

"Now, father," Ted began, but Hannah was already

53

wheeling Mr. Malloy from the room.

"I'll see myself out." Meg hurried from the room and down the hall to the front entrance, her spine tingling as she sensed Ted close behind her.

"Wait, Cassiday!" he shouted as he followed her down the steps from the house to the street.

"I'm called Meg, and I've said all I'm going to say to you tonight except this: My lawyer's name is Hiram Smith. His office is on Seventh Street. Be there at ten o'clock on Friday." Her heart thudded in fear of him. She measured the distance to the street corner where she would catch a streetcar. She hurried away, her pace swift. His footsteps pounded behind her.

He shouted angrily, "Cassiday, Meg whatever you call yourself, you stop where you are! I demand to know where you've been all these years! As your husband I have a right to know."

"Leave me alone, Ted," she called back over her shoulder, "I don't have to tell you any such thing."

His voice, ugly, carried up and down the street, "I suppose you have another man somewhere; is that it? Is that the real reason you're trying to pull off this nonsense about a divorce?"

He caught up to her, grabbed her shoulder, and whipped her around. "You will answer me, damn it! I'm your husband. You won't be seeing a lawyer, either."

"It's none of your business where I've been. I've already seen a lawyer and you'd better be there, too, on Friday. Let go of me, or I'm going to scream for the police."

He laughed. "What good would that do when I explain to them that you ran from our marriage, abandoned our marriage bed, and all I'm trying to do is get my disorderly wife to behave?"

An ocean of fear washed over her. "I have a knife in my pocket, Ted," she lied, "so let go of me this instant before I have to use it." She wished now that she'd carried Admire's pocket gun; from now on she would. She'd hate to use it; she never wanted to feel again as she had after Finch was shot to death on her account. But if Ted forced her, she'd kill him.

"I don't believe you." Ted yanked her hand from her pocket and saw that her fist was empty. He chuckled, pulled her against him and attempted to kiss her.

She moved her face and fought back, beating him about the head and face with her fists. He managed to duck some of her blows, but she landed more than a few.

In anger, he began to drag her toward some bushes at the side of the street. "No," she cried, trying to kick him, struggling furiously in his strong grip. "No!"

"You're still my wife," he panted, "and you'll do your duty."

"Help!" she screamed, "Help me!" The bushes tore at her as he shoved her down on the hard ground and threw himself on top of her. She gasped as the wind was knocked out of her, her head reeling. This couldn't be happening, it couldn't. *Dear God, don't let him do this.*

Chapter Five

Regaining her breath and strength, Meg twisted and struggled beneath Ted's weight. Unable to move him, she sunk her teeth into the hand covering her mouth, then jerked her face aside and screamed again, "Help me!" She pounded at his face, at his head. Fear that he might succeed in the act gave her uncommon strength. She beat at him. "Let me go, you monster, let me go!"

He breathed a heavy foulness that filled her nostrils and made her want to retch. Furious and frightened, she struggled to throw him off. He responded with a stinging slap across her face. She cried out and tried to hit him back. Then he caught her arm and held it against the ground in a hard grip. She sobbed, "You're breaking my arm," and tried to draw up a knee but he held her down with such force that she couldn't move.

"What's goin' on in there?" The bushes suddenly parted and a police officer peered in at them.

Ted was crouched over her with his knee holding her down painfully; his arm pinned her chest. He laughed as he fumbled with his trousers. "She's my wife, officer. Just getting what's mine. Leave us alone."

"I don't know this man!" Meg screamed, "he's trying to—trying to—oh, God, please get him away from me!"

"She's my wife," Ted insisted, pushing her back as she tried to raise her head.

"You ain't doin' this here, no how!" The officer, a big man, grabbed Ted and hauled him up like he was a parcel of garbage. "You oughta' be ashamed, treatin' her that way!"

Meg scrambled free, pulled her skirts down and got unsteadily to her feet. She was too stunned to cry. Her heart thudded in her ears.

"I know you!" the officer said suddenly, when he got a good look at Ted. "You're Malloy, Ted Malloy. Your father lives up the street." He snorted. "I've seen you hanging around with women in the saloons and at the horse races. Never saw you with a wife."

Keeping an eye on Ted and fearful that the officer might release him, Meg crept slowly away, her heart pounding, her skin covered in cold perspiration.

Ted stomped in fury and frustration and he shouted in the officer's face, "I'm telling you officer, that woman is my wife." He waved and pointed. "Stop her. That's my wife."

"And I'm Queen Victoria. You're lucky, Malloy, that I got here when I did or you'd be spending jail time." The officer waved at Meg with his stick, "Go home, miss, I'll keep this scum here for company."

"Thank you, Officer." She took off running. At the corner, she leaped aboard the streetcar before it stopped. All the way to Bridget's street, she gripped the brass pole of the car, her forehead pressed against it, trembling hard. She'd give her soul for the blue skies of Kansas again. Only a few more days, God willing, just a few more days. Ted Malloy would be lucky if she didn't kill him.

That same evening, he appeared at Bridget's door asking Bridget to allow him to see his wife and clutching a bouquet of hothouse violets. Meg had warned Bridget that he might come and what they could expect. However, she had foreseen violence, not stale charm and flowers.

The spry little woman told him through the narrow crack that she'd opened in the door, "If you mean Meg Brennon, who ain't your wife for long, she don't want to see ya. Git on now, git off my porch and be gone with ya!" She closed the door and then, motioning Meg to help, shoved a heavy chair against it.

He pounded on the door. "I want to see my wife! I have a right!"

The women stood in the middle of the small room, not moving, just worrying together in wordless communication.

On top of her fear, Meg found Ted's behavior galling. He'd come bearing flowers after the way he'd assaulted her today? She wished the officer had locked him up, but he must have decided that *no real* harm was done and there was no just cause. Or Ted had convinced him that she was his wife and he had a right to his disgusting behavior.

Meg was on the way to the kitchen for a drink of water for her dry throat, when she saw his face looming suddenly at Bridget's front window, off the porch. She trembled violently and started in that direction, but when she looked again his face had vanished. Chills raced along her spine as she hurriedly closed the curtains. "I'm so sorry, Bridget. I didn't mean to bring you this trouble."

"I know ya didn't mean to, and I don't fault ya," the little woman answered, hovering close. "If we don't have no truck with 'im, 'e'll get tired of waitin' out there and go away. I doubt if 'e can go long without tippin' a glass at the saloon."

They waited, both listening for the sound of his leaving, shaking their heads at one another when they heard nothing. Meg peeked out the window and saw him lazed back against the porch post, smoking a stogie. "He's still there!" she hissed. "He's going to camp on your porch until I give in."

"Well don't ya do it, dearie," Bridget hissed with an encouraging nod. "We can out-wait 'im if we try." She sat down in a chair in the corner and took up her needlework, humming softly an old Irish ballad about sweet Molly Malone, the fishmonger's daughter.

Meg took a chair next to her, but itched with impatience and anger at Ted. When she rose later to look outside, he was still there. Her skin crawled as she went back to her chair. Why didn't he go, why must he torment her this way when in the end he'd lose? She'd never give him what he wanted. She'd rather die than go back to him. Her destiny was not with him, it was back in Paragon Springs, where she meant to spend the rest of her days forgetting that he had ever existed.

He knocked again and again, while Meg chewed her lip in fury and Bridget sewed with tiny, angry jabs.

Enough was enough. Meg went to the door and yanked it open. "Leave us alone, Ted, or you're going to be very sorry. I'm warning you."

"I'm not leaving until I've talked to you." In a quick move he wedged his foot in the door and smiled at her. He held out the violets, and from his pocket withdrew a cheap-looking bottle of perfume with a drawing of a gardenia blossom on the label. His tone was silken with apology but sounded only empty and desperate to her, "These are for you. I'm sorry for this afternoon, I truly am. That won't happen again, not like that."

"No, it won't, absolutely." She shook her head and ignored the gifts that he held out. "Use your good sense, Ted, if you have any sense at all. I'm not interested in you. I'm not interested in keeping this marriage. I want you to go away right now. I'm not the foolish young girl I once was. You can't charm me with flowers and sweet words and you might as well not try. I'm a whole lot wiser now."

His eyes flashed as he said staunchly in the tone of a domineering husband, "You won't have anything to do with the lawyer." He shook his finger at her. "You will stop this nonsense once and for all. I'm glad you're back, that's all that needs be."

"I've told you, I've already talked with Hiram Smith and proceedings for our divorce have begun. Be there at his office on Friday. There's nothing you can do to stop this. I will divorce you."

"Not if I can help it," his voice and face turned ugly. "I know the courts favor marriage over divorce. When they find out that I don't want a divorce, that'll be the end of it. I'm head of the house; as my wife, you're nothing."

"That's nonsense!" she protested, but she knew there was truth in what he said, as far as society and the courts were concerned. She tried to shove the door closed at the same moment that he forced his shoulder through the small opening. She held it fast, pushing back.

He smiled at her, his rancor washing away. "Let me come in. I'll stay here with you and it'll be like the old days, I swear, Cassiday. I'll do everything to make you happy. Father likes you. He'll help us. He'll give us a fine house, maybe let us live with him until he passes on." His chin quivered, "Give me this chance, Cassiday."

"Never. You've got a lot of gall to even ask. You had all the chances you'll ever get when we were together. Now if you don't leave, I'm going to start screaming. Bridget has . . . some pretty burly neighbors," she invented, "Joe and Daniel . . . big as oxen. If I tell them you're bothering us they'll likely pound you to a pulp. Plus, the police will arrest you for disturbing the peace. This is Bridget's home and she deserves quiet, not all this commotion."

He looked at her for a long moment as though he'd like to spit in her face. He stuffed the perfume in his pocket and threw the flowers on the ground. "You'll always be my wife, Cassiday, if I say so, and I do. Wait and see!"

She shivered and watched to make sure he left. When he disappeared down the street, she closed the door and sagged against it. Her eyes rounded when she saw Bridget waiting behind her with a cleaver in her tiny hands. "Oh, Bridget, Lord help us if it ever comes to that! Put it away now, he's gone. I'm so, so sorry I've brought this on you."

"Not so sorry as that Malloy'll be if 'e ever touches ya again," Bridget vowed. She turned and stepped smartly to the kitchen, hanging her cleaver in its place next to the stove. " 'E better watch out, I say."

The next morning when Meg came out of the outhouse in Bridget's back yard, Ted was standing there. He needed a shave, there were bags under his eyes, and his suit was as wrinkled as if he'd slept there in the yard.

The hair rose on her neck. Couldn't she go even to the outhouse without being molested? She spoke harshly to cover her fear. "Don't you have anything better to do than to spy on me?" She smelled his strong body odor as she pushed by him; her feet fairly flew up the path toward the back door.

He raced after her and grabbed her arm. "If you'd listen to me, we'd have this over and done with. We're not getting a divorce, Cassiday! You tell that lawyer you've changed your mind."

She trembled with rage. "I haven't changed my mind, I couldn't possibly. Look what you've become, Ted. You're disgusting, not only to me, but to your own father. If you want to win his approval, do it on your own, without me."

His face hardened and he doubled his free hand into a fist, wanting to hurt her. His lip curled. "If I'm not up to Father's standards it's your fault! If you'd remained my dutiful wife as you swore to do in your vows, the troubles I've had wouldn't have happened. You're the bad luck that's brought me down, Cassiday. I'd be somewhere now, I'd be the boss of one of father's businesses if you'd stayed with me. Father's house, his fortune, would be mine." He changed that quickly, "Ours. We'd have everything."

Her arm was aching in his grip. "You took the path you're on long before we married, Ted. I would have liked to have changed it, but it was impossible."

"It's not too late, Cassiday! You can help me, I know you can. You've saved our future by coming back. I'll forgive you for what you've done, for what you're trying to do, but you must drop this silly idea of a divorce. That's all I'm asking for, don't you see?"

"I see a very repulsive man begging for the impossible. I'm tired of trying to talk sense to you. You're hurting my arm and in another second I'm going to scream." She whipped away and told him over her shoulder as she reached Bridget's back door, "Be at Hiram Smith's office Friday at ten!" She swept inside and with swift, fumbling fingers locked the door, leaning against it as waves of revulsion flooded her. Like it or not, she was going to carry Admire's gun and use it if she had to.

When she arrived at Hiram Smith's office Friday morning, Ted was there. He and Smith were smoking cigars companionably, chuckling over a story they had just shared. She watched them in disbelief. The air in the small room was blue with cigar smoke; she coughed and covered her nose. Smith became businesslike when he saw her face, but it was too late.

"What's going on?" she asked, although she had a good idea, already. Ted had made her lawyer his cohort.

Smith waved at the cigar smoke. "Sorry. Mr. Malloy was so kind—" He brought her a chair, which she refused. He told her, "Mr. Malloy has told me of his devotion to you, in spite of the fact that you abandoned him and left the marriage without good cause. He's asked that the divorce proceedings be dropped."

She stood rigid with anger. "And you believed what he told you?"

"He tells a very convincing story, Mrs. Malloy."

"He's a born liar."

Smith didn't seem to hear her. "I believe in the institution of marriage, Mrs. Malloy, very, very much," he said.

"And I believe in my life, very much. This man beat me to within an inch of my life, Mr. Smith. I had to run away or risk dying at his hands. He sent a bounty hunter to bring me back. A bounty hunter! Does that sound like a loving husband to you? A man who truly loved his wife would have come for her himself and gotten down on his knees. The bounty man was ready to bring my body back in a box if he had to, and collect his fee. Someone else killed him before he could do that. That's the only reason I stand here alive today."

"Mrs. Malloy," his tone tried to smooth her ruffled feathers, "all marriages have problems. We need to discuss this. Mr. Malloy has offered to take you back. He promises to do his utmost to repair your marriage."

"He wants to use me to get back into his father's good graces so he can inherit his fortune, that's what he wants." She shook her head. "Mr. Smith, you no longer represent me, you're fired! If you have a fee due you from my earlier visit, collect it from my husband, this *good* man sitting here." She looked at Ted in disgust. "And good luck." Shaking her head, she turned and stormed out of the office.

Without a recommendation from someone she trusted, Meg worried about how to hire another lawyer, a good one. Most residents of the Patch were too poor to employ a lawyer even if they badly needed one. Divorce was practically unheard of—intolerable marriages were simply endured or one party took off one day and disappeared.

For herself, from this point on she wanted her separation to be legal, definite, permanent. She wanted to go home to Paragon Springs with proof of her freedom in hand.

She decided to look where most legal actions took place— at the courthouse. Whomever she hired this time, he must take her cause to heart, not shape the case to his own beliefs.

She took the streetcar to the courthouse on Fourth and Broadway Streets. Inside the huge building, she pulled her wrap tighter around her, finding it as cold within as outside, or possibly her nerves were to blame. Her footsteps echoed on the floor of the cavernous main entry. She had no idea where to begin, but the place looked very official and— helpful. She began to feel hopeful.

A flock of women were polishing the floors and beautiful woodwork of the huge main hall. One of them a few feet from Meg looked up to comment, "You look mighty lost, miss. You got trouble I can help with?" The cleaning woman had a friendly face in spite of one eye that looked off to the side. She straightened and wiped her chapped hands on the long apron she wore over her faded striped dress, and asked again, "What ya lookin' for?"

Meg smiled in frustration, "I was just thinking I might need a compass to find my way in this place, it's so big. I don't know who or what I'm looking for, or where to begin."

"What is it ya need?" The woman kept polishing, although she watched Meg's face.

Meg hesitated, wondering how this person could help her other than to direct her to the ladies' water closet.

The woman read her expression and laughed, her chuckle surprisingly musical. "Maybe I can help you, maybe I can't." She brushed loosened tendrils of hair back from her face.

"You'd be surprised, I'm thinkin', at how much me and the other cleaning ladies know from spending fourteen hours a day in this place. We see plenty, we hear plenty. But I got work to do if you don't need me."

"Yes, yes, I do need you. Thank you, and I apologize." She disliked telling her personal problems to anyone if she didn't have to, not even to close friends and especially not to strangers. But she found herself pouring out that she needed a very good lawyer to help her get a divorce from a man she hated who might kill her if he got the chance.

"Divorce, huh? Your man beat ya, huh? You want to see Mr. Hamilton Gibbs, he takes cases like that. Everybody likes him. A woman in trouble can't do no better than to get Mr. Gibbs to help her."

"Mr. Gibbs? You're sure?"

"Like I said, fourteen hours a day in this place teaches you plenty. Sometimes I think *I* could be a lawyer." She laughed, a symphony of sound, then grew serious again, "Mr. Gibbs has a fine reputation. He's the man you need."

"Where might I find him?"

"He's in court right now, Room thirty-six." She motioned toward a door far down the hall. "They'll all be comin' out of there for their noon meal before long. Watch for him. He's a tall, beanpole-built fella, ugly as a fence post but as kind as they come. He's one of the few lawyers in this place that stops to say hello to us and ask after our families. Don't he, Gladys?" she asked a meek-looking cleaning woman close by.

Gladys nodded and spoke timidly, "He helped one of our friends, Elma Jordan, get rid of her man. Didn't charge a cent because he knew Elma didn't have it. He said he was payin' her back for her hard work here." She ducked her head and went back to polishing the floor.

The first cleaning woman asked Meg, "Now ain't that somethin'?"

"Indeed it is. He sounds fine. I'll wait down there." She nodded and moved away, smiling. "I thank you, very much."

She waited nervously for about a half hour. When the door opened and a group of mostly men filed out, she recognized Hamilton Gibbs right away. He was tall and lanky as the woman had described, and he had wide shoulders and thick, unruly brown hair. He was not handsome, but neither was he as bad looking as the cleaning lady had described. He moved over by the wall with another fellow and they stood talking. Meg waited until he moved off alone and then hurried after him. "Mr. Hamilton—" She realized that she had used his name wrong. "Mr. Gibbs, sir. Mr. Hamilton Gibbs, may I have a word with you?"

He turned, saw her, and walked toward her, giving her a nearsighted stare from behind his wire-rimmed spectacles. "Yes? I'm Gibbs."

"I need a lawyer, Mr. Gibbs."

"I see. Your name?"

"I have a couple of names, but I prefer to be called Meg Brennon, Miss Brennon, although I'm not really Miss, I'm Mrs." She caught her breath and made a face. "I sound like a babbling idiot, but I can explain—"

"Of course," he said. "My office is two blocks west, next to the Mercantile Library, but we can find a quiet spot here where we can talk. Come with me."

"This is your mealtime. Maybe I should come to your office another time?"

"No need for that." He lifted his leather case. "I have food in here. We can talk while I eat and maybe—" he looked shy and afraid of rejection, "—you'll share my lunch with me?"

She was flabbergasted at the unexpected offer from

someone she'd just met. "Oh, I couldn't do that. But if you don't mind, I'd like to talk to you about taking my case."

"Come on, then."

He led the way to a small alcove off the hall and motioned for her to take an overstuffed chair. He sat down across from her, clasped his hands in his lap, and waited.

Below his craggy brows and behind his glasses, Meg saw that his eyes were a very deep blue and held the most sincere expression that she'd ever seen on anyone, anywhere. She sighed softly, and sat forward. She had the strangest feeling, looking into his eyes, of coming home.

Chapter Six

Gibbs opened his large leather case and took out a paper-wrapped parcel. He smiled, and his deep voice held an appealing shyness, "Mrs. Lyle, who keeps the boardinghouse where I stay, makes the best grahambread, and cheese. Will you share it with me, please?"

Meg smiled. "You're kind, but I don't believe so. Thank you very much."

"I'll enjoy the food more if you'll join me," he insisted, "and Mrs. Lyle would be very pleased to hear that I shared her tasty makings with a lady." He watched her with a twisted grin and it appeared that he wasn't going to touch his own food unless she relented. In spite of his shy manner with her, he was persuasive.

"All right. Thank you."

Pleased, he broke off a portion of bread and cheese for her. Meg thought she would be too nervous to chew, but the food was as delicious as he claimed and she realized that she was starved.

"Pardon me for a minute," he said, putting his food aside on a small table nearby and rising, "I'll be right back." He returned a minute or two later with an extra cup, into which he portioned out for her some of his cocoa from a small cloth-wrapped jug. "It was nice and hot this morning," he said, "but of course it has cooled."

He listened while she talked between bites. She found him easy to converse with. He was a good listener; his bony, intelligent face held a sensitivity that appealed to a deep corner of her soul. She talked and talked. Occasionally he stopped her to ask a question. Many of her answers led him to frown and shake his head.

She was unaware of the passing time until he told her that his time was up and he was due back in court. She jumped to her feet. "I'm so sorry. I've likely told you more than you need, but I couldn't seem to stop babbling—"

"You didn't babble. I'm very interested in taking your case. Please come to my office so we can complete our discussion." He scribbled the address on a piece of paper and handed it to her. "I'm sure I can help you."

"Thank you." When he asked how she happened to seek his representation when there were many lawyers in the city to choose from, she told him that he'd been highly recommended by one of the courthouse cleaning ladies. "She was very nice, she has a laugh that's almost musical . . ." she didn't finish.

He chuckled. "That'd be Louise. With a little training, she could work as my clerk, she's very smart. They're all good women, hard workers. I'll be sure to thank Louise for recommending me."

They hadn't discussed his fee, but Meg wanted his service so badly that she was already thinking of ways to raise more money if she had to—she could sell part of her ranch, or one of the businesses, something. Whatever it would cost her, Hamilton Gibbs was the answer to her prayers, she was positive.

Meg had a four-day wait between meeting Mr. Gibbs at the courthouse and her appointment with him at his office. She took that time to do her laundry, chores for Bridget, and to write a letter home.

Dearest Aurelia,

I've been here little more than a week and it seems like a lifetime. Matters move much more slowly than I'd hoped.

I've found a lawyer whom I feel I can trust and who comes highly recommended... she smiled to herself, *so that may change.*

If Admire has a lot of orders for stone, please tell him to wait to fill them until I get home. There's no need for him to kill himself with hard work on my account. Tell Emmaline, please, that I'm thinking of her and the twins. Surely they will stay on with us at Paragon Springs even though her father's wish to die on the plains has been fulfilled? I hope things go well at the store. I suppose you are running low on supplies, and winter weather is making it difficult to replace them. I'll build the stock up again when I get home.

I worry that bad weather could trap me here, but I pray not. If there's trouble from Jack Ambler that can't be handled otherwise, contact the Dodge City Sheriff and get his help. I think of you all, and of home, all of the time.

Fondly, Meg.

Ted came by Bridget's house twice, on evenings when Meg was helping Bridget with a quilt she was making for a donation to her church. They locked the doors and pretended not to be home. Meg knew that the time might come when he'd break in, and that nothing would stop him. She wished the whole divorce matter were over and done with.

The day of her appointment with Gibbs, she put on Aurelia's blue-striped grenadine dress and, for luck, pinned Lucy Ann's brooch to the lace fichu collar. She brushed her hair to a sheen then caught it in a cascade of curls down the back of her head and tied on her black velvet bonnet. Wrapped in her cloak, she hurried to catch the streetcar thinking that it wouldn't hurt to be a few minutes early. Following the directions Gibbs had given her, she found his office next to the Mercantile Library. She saw other professional establishments, small brick buildings nearby for doctors, lawyers, dentists. The gold-etched sign on the glass window of his office said HAMILTON GIBBS, COUNSELOR AT LAW.

Meg knocked softly, hesitated when there was no answer and then went in. He wasn't at his desk and the door to a back room stood open. She looked around, noting that Gibbs's office was larger than Smith's and nicely furnished in wood and leather that was a warm burnished brown. Signs of success, she thought, that could be attributed to Gibbs's hard work, his compatibility with people, and his fine reputation. She was proud of herself for having found him and grateful to Louise.

"There you are!" he said as he came from the back room. "Hello!" His smile showed relief. "I could've kicked myself for letting you go home alone the other day, after what you'd told me about your husband. How are you? Are you all right?"

"I'm getting to be an expert at avoiding Ted Malloy, thanks to practice. I'm fine." She smiled. "You have a very nice office," she complimented, taking a comfortable chair. The room had a clean smell of books and leather and the pleasing fragrance of vanilla, from a large potted plant blooming with clusters of purple flowers in the corner. "What is the plant? It smells wonderful."

"Heliotrope. Mrs. Lyle gave it to me when I moved into my new office." He grinned that twisted smile she was getting to know and appreciate. "My first office was hardly bigger than a closet. I lived there and slept on a pad under my desk."

"You've come a distance in your profession then," she commented.

"I've been lucky, and I've worked hard. There's no shortage of work here in St. Louis; whether that's a good thing or bad depends on the viewer." He drew a file from his desk drawer and laid it beside his inkwell and pen holder. "I've given your case a lot of thought since we talked."

"We haven't discussed your fee . . ." she began worriedly.

He dismissed that with a shrug. "It won't be as painful as you might think. I will charge according to what you can pay."

"Thank you, but how can you?"

"I take a lot of cases," he answered, looking at her from under thick brows, "and those who benefit greatly from my services and can afford to pay well are charged accordingly. A case like yours means a lot to me. I take them whenever they appear."

"What do you mean?"

He explained, rubbing his jaw with his big hand, "I had a sister, Jenny, a timid soul who was married to an abusive man. She was not attractive, not especially clever. She felt indebted to her husband for marrying her at all, and she loved him. Nothing I could say or do would convince her to leave him for mistreating her."

"What happened?"

"She stayed with him until he killed her."

Meg gasped, and silence filled the room.

A glimmery shine showed in Gibbs's blue eyes. If they were tears he didn't seem embarrassed by them. He cuffed his mouth and coughed. "Taking cases like yours, doing my best for my clients, is the only way I have to vindicate Jenny, the only way I can live with the guilt that I could not prevent her death."

"What happened wasn't your fault."

He shook his head to dismiss the subject. "Maybe not. But let's talk about you. I think I have what I need but I'd like for you to tell me again so that I'm perfectly clear on everything."

She repeated for him the sordid tale of her marriage to Ted, ending with his behavior toward her now that she'd returned to St. Louis for a divorce. "He's fiercely against ending the marriage. I'm afraid of what he'll try, what he'll do, to stop me."

He nodded, his expression serious. After a moment he told her, "Our best chance for success is to be heard before Judge Whitney Williams. Whit Williams is very fair and honest. In the past he's shown sympathy toward women in cases like yours."

Meg sat more relaxed in her chair. A cloud that had hovered over her for a very long time began to slip away. Of course turning over problems to Mr. Gibbs was only a beginning.

"Judge Williams is a busy man," Gibbs continued, "and it may be some time before we can get our case into his court. Dockets are full for months at a time and divorce cases get low priority, unfortunately. In the end, we may not get the judge we want." At Meg's expression of distress, he said quickly, "I feel that it's only fair to give you a true picture of the problems facing us so we know what to expect."

"I understand. I don't suppose there's anything we can do to hurry matters?" She explained her responsibilities back in Paragon Springs and why she had to get back there.

"I wish I could promise you what you want. I'll try to get us a court date with Judge Williams. I believe that's the most important step we can make. I'll do my best to get a date sooner than normally happens. We mustn't count on that, however."

"How long do you think it might be before we get into court?"

He frowned with empathy. "This is the bad part. I'm truly sorry, but it could be months, possibly a year even, before our date in court is scheduled."

"Months? A year?" she whispered in dismay. "But I can't stay in St. Louis that long. I don't have the money, I'm needed at home at Paragon Springs . . ." her voice trailed off. She'd wanted so much to go home a free person by spring.

"I'm sorry," he said again. "If there's anything I can do to move our date closer, I'll do it."

She hid her disappointment as best she could. For years she'd taken care of herself, not counted on another soul. Now she had to turn her life, her destiny, over to others. To laws and rules, and courts and time schedules, none under her control. At least she could trust Hamilton Gibbs, she was sure of that. She looked up at him. It might take time, but with her destiny in his hands, she was convinced her wishes would eventually prevail.

He read her sorrowful face and said softly, "I believe it is best that you return home as soon as possible, in any event. As long as you remain in St. Louis, you are in certain danger from Malloy. He's legally your husband and as such he has legal rights. Because of his recent attack on you and his history of past abuse, we could get a lawful order to keep him away from you, and we will if you like, but I've rarely seen that piece of paper change anything."

"It wouldn't stop Ted." She sighed. "I'll go home."

"Whatever you do, don't let him know where that is," Gibbs warned sternly. "He's determined to have you back to win over his father. This time he's desperate enough to track you to the ends of the earth if he has the least clue to go on. I'd like to see you safely on the train and make sure he's not following."

Her heart gave a fluttering leap. His offer surely went beyond his usual professional services. She told him, "That won't be necessary. I'll keep away from him. He won't know

I'm gone until it happens. He's cruel, but he's not very smart."

He nodded. "Even though a lengthy wait is probable, please don't worry, we'll get your divorce. If you can't be here at the scheduled time, be assured that I can stand in for you in court the same as if you were there in person."

"I'll be here absolutely for my court date," she admonished, unable to consider anything else. "It would be hard for me to believe it happened if I'm not present to witness the proceedings with my own eyes and ears, and have my own say. Send me word of my court date by wire, and if there's time, I'll get here as fast as a train can travel."

He held her hand in both of his as she was leaving. "I'll do my very best for you. Have a safe journey home."

Meg was reminded again how safe it felt to place her life in those hands.

"I'll be leaving soon for my home," Meg told Bridget, back in Kerry Patch. "For your own safety and mine, I won't say exactly when I'm going, or where to, or how I'll travel. I'll just be gone." She held the little woman's hands. "I want you to know how much I appreciate your kindness and your hospitality. I won't ever forget."

Bridget hugged her with tears in her eyes. "Godspeed, Cassiday Rose, and be careful."

For an extra measure of care in case Ted should try to force from Bridget details of Meg's whereabouts, Meg then went to Bridget's neighbors to ask them to keep a close eye on her for a while. She arranged for Glenn Clary, Lillie's husband, to keep Ted busy at the saloon gambling and fortified with extra drinks on the night she planned for her departure. Meg didn't have to reveal her motives; Glenn Clary was just glad for the opportunity to get even with Ted for cheating him so often.

A cold moon lit the night as Meg slipped out the door at Bridget's. She hurried along the chilly streets, keeping to the shadows. Closer to the main part of the city, she caught a streetcar and rode the rest of the way to Union Station. She was sure Glenn Clary was keeping Ted occupied, but she kept watch anyway as she sat on a bench in the depot, ticket in hand, awaiting the departure time for the train headed west. She'd bought a small food basket at the depot, hoping the sausage sandwiches and apple would last the trip.

As soon as she'd arrived at the station, she had sent a wire to Paragon Springs folks telling them she was coming and asking that Admire or Owen pick her up at the Dodge City depot. She might have to wait in town a while for their arrival, depending on when word got to Paragon Springs. Each word cost dearly, or she would have let them know in advance that she didn't have her divorce yet. It was going to be hard to explain when she got home. A return trip to St. Louis wasn't going to be easy, either, on any of them.

At last she was on the train. The conductor tipped his billed hat to her and punched her ticket. She sat back in relief on the wooden seat covered in thin red plush. She was going home, not free yet from Ted, but she was going home.

Her fellow coach passengers included nattily-dressed gamblers and drummers, farmers and their wives, ragged urban dwellers, and several immigrant families in colorful European dress. There was much movement and chatter as everyone maneuvered to get comfortable on the hard seats for the long, jolting night ride. The small potbellied stove in the corner of the car gave little heat and people covered themselves with whatever was at hand.

Meg hoped the immigrants were headed for her own area of western Kansas where settlers were sorely needed. When she asked the conductor in a quiet whisper, he told her that the Russian immigrant party would not be going that far. Their destination was Newton, Kansas, north of Wichita.

In the time she'd been in western Kansas, Meg had seen many immigrant families come and go. Some found adapting to a new land too difficult—the hardships more than they could endure. Others, itchy-footed folk by nature, moved on. When they came and settled, Jack Ambler was furious; when they left, he was glad.

She hated to see folks give up. It took numbers of them working together to tame a land, to build good lives for all. That day was still in the offing for Paragon Springs and the surrounding region. For some, homesteading life held an unholy loneliness; for her it had always been, and would always be, a haven from the poverty and despair of the urban squalor she'd come from. Paragon Springs was a haven ripe for building into something special.

The train shook and rattled along. After a while, a cowboy got out his harmonica and played several soft tunes. The music brought calm, helped to settle the children into sleep. Down the aisle, a man began to snore loudly. A baby in the seat across from Meg whimpered until its mother patted it quiet.

Meg smiled. The young mother was one of the immigrants, and talked to her child in a foreign tongue. The baby, who was perhaps a little under a year old, eyed Meg from large blue eyes in a chubby face. He removed his thumb from his mouth and flashed her a smile, showing four perfect white teeth. Later, Meg set an example and pretended to sleep. When next she peeked, the little one had also closed his eyes, his rosy lips parted in soft breathing. The poor mother looked worn out and relieved that the child slept.

The night passed slowly for Meg. Each time she fell

asleep, the bone-jolting stop and start at a station would wake her, or the jolting would wake a child—the one across from her or another—who would then set everyone in the car astir with its crying. Twice she got up in the night to use the tiny water closet, and was nearly thrown off her feet by the jerky sway of the train as she traversed the aisle back to her seat.

Snowflakes swirled outside the train window all the next day as they rumbled and shook westward. There were great empty spaces in the bleak and wintry landscape, broken only by occasional woods, a farmhouse or cabin. At other stretches small towns were strung like drab brown beads on the necklace of tracks.

At one stop, Meg left the train to buy a cup of lukewarm coffee in the café attached to the depot. The depot platform was slippery with frost; the cold bit her face. She went back to her seat shivering. The coffee was wretched, but it washed down the sausage and bread she'd bought in St. Louis. When she saw that her red apple had caught the eye of the baby across from her, she offered it to him via his mother. The mother looked surprised but pleased, and finally accepted it with a smile and gesture. The baby gnawed the apple like a little rabbit.

When the immigrant mother saw that Meg shivered with the cold, she handed her an extra blanket.

The young mother had been having difficulty with her restless baby for hours. She'd gotten little sleep and was having a difficult time keeping her eyes open.

"I could hold him for you," Meg offered. The young woman tilted her head in puzzlement. Meg repeated her offer with facial expressions and gestures. The woman looked doubtful but wishful. Meg tapped her chest, "My name is Meg. Meg."

78

The woman touched her chest, "Elsa." She held her baby's hand and said, "Is Friedrich." Carefully, she held the child toward Meg as though still not sure she wanted to relinquish him to her.

The baby was happy to be moving anywhere. He sat in Meg's arms and looked up at her. He touched her brooch and bobbed his head. "Pretty," Meg told him. "Pretty." She played clapping games with him and he laughed in delight, wanting her to continue. The mother watched carefully, and then, in another few minutes, her head bobbed and she fell asleep.

Meg clapped hands with the baby until they were both weary of it. She let him play with her bonnet; he enjoyed putting it on and staring up at her for her reaction. She sang him a little song she remembered her mother singing to her ages ago. Although he couldn't have understood the words, he laughed each time she sang softly, "Pop! Goes the weasel!"

He went to sleep in her arms, his head against her breast. It felt wonderful, and Meg experienced an intense longing for a child of her own. She touched her lips to the wispy hair on top of his head. "You're wonderful, little Friedrich," she whispered.

She did so want to get married again and have a family before it was too late. Her mind wandered to Hamilton Gibbs and she wondered if he was married. She really hadn't thought about it before, but realized she'd assumed he was unmarried because he lived at a boarding house and the owner made his lunch. Which wasn't proof of anything, really. He could have a wife. The fact that he'd been so nice to her meant only that he was kind, a good man. She liked him, married or single, there was no disputing that.

Some time later, Elsa took little Friedrich back and changed his clothing. She gave him a chunk of bread from her

79

basket and the child ate ravenously.

Later everyone attempted to get comfortable for a second long night. Early the next morning, the young mother and her child and the rest of the immigrant party left the train at Newton. Meg stepped out onto the depot platform to tell them good-bye.

For the remainder of the journey she sat in a numb daze as the train rocked across the miles.

She came alive hours later when they approached Dodge City and the engineer blew the shrill whistle for their arrival. They chugged into the dusky, drab town—a huddle of brown buildings along the shining tracks. The sky was gray with cold, and the wind tossed curls of smoke from the chimneys. There was little activity on the streets, the weather confining most people inside.

Meg shook off her weariness and gathered her belongings. She followed others down the aisle and to the door. She stepped outside into the wind and cold, prepared to walk to the hotel and put up there until her people came. Then she heard her name called.

Admire and Lad walked around the corner of the depot and headed toward her on the platform. Ad's dark eyes snapped with friendly welcome and Lad wore a wide grin. His hair was carefully combed to hide the scar where he'd been partially scalped.

"How could you have time to know when I'd arrive? I thought I'd have to wait for you."

"We came to Dodge for supplies and found your wire," Admire explained. "We just got in yesterday so we waited over for you."

"Thank God for it!"

Meg took a long draught of sweet Kansas air, coughed

when the chill of it hit her lungs, then dropped her bags to the platform. She embraced them both with wordless joy. Her bad news that she had no divorce could wait.

Soon after Meg arrived home, she walked with Emmaline up to the graveyard. Emmaline wanted to show her the tombstone Aurelia had carved for the Old Professor's grave. Aurelia, at the time of her little Helen Grace's passing, had shown a special talent for carving a monument from the magnesia marble found up at The Rocks.

Meg knelt by the mound of turned earth and traced the elegant wording on the white stone, and the book and buffalo design. "Aurelia does beautiful work," she said softly, looking up at Emmaline. She stood up and put her arm around Emmaline's waist. They stood quietly for some time. A chill wind whipped around them. Not far away was the much older burying place of Aurelia's daughter, Helen Grace, and a few steps from that, Grandma Spicy's grave.

"You did the right thing, Emmaline, bringing your father here to western Kansas for his last days," Meg broke the silence.

"Yes," she answered, "I'm glad we came. At first I couldn't see how the children and I could give up our comfortable life in Lawrence and my teaching job there, but I couldn't deny the professor his last wish."

"I was afraid you might not be here when I returned. I worried that you might go back to Lawrence, now that your father has passed on. Do you plan to go back?" Meg hoped not. Emmaline was a valuable, contributing member of their small band—teaching their children, publishing their small newspaper, the *Echo*. The paper tied together the community and far-flung neighbors on their homesteads, who came in when they could for their paper, and other mail.

Emmaline considered, "I think not. We've been welcomed here the same as if we're family. It wasn't like that in Lawrence. Although I'd been born and raised there, educated there and both my father and my husband, Simeon, were white men and teachers, I was always an outsider because my mother was a Cheyenne." She looked at Meg, "You know that my parents met at the Shawnee Mission School where my father taught my mother?" She sighed and looked off into the distance. "My children were treated as 'breeds,' too, although they have only one-quarter Indian blood."

"I'm sorry, Emmaline. It's so unfair."

Emmaline shrugged away her sympathy, and smiled. "I like it here; I love teaching and putting out the *Echo*. I want to take part in this country's growth. It's going to be exciting, Meg."

Meg hugged her and sighed happily. "I'm so glad you've decided to stay. I was afraid you'd go back to Lawrence, since that was your original plan when you came out here."

"When Simeon went west to look for gold and never came back, I thought I'd remain where I was the rest of my days, that I'd raise our children alone there. But Shafer will be glad we're staying, he likes it out here much better than in Lawrence. Selinda is another matter. She's a bright girl and there's so much more she'll want to learn than I can teach her. I hope to find a way to give her all the education she craves."

"We'll find a way! Paragon Springs may be but a little above an earthen prairie dog village now, but someday it's going to be a *real* town with fine, tall school buildings—wait and see!"

Emmaline chuckled, "You are a dreamer, Meg. Luckily,

you're a real fighter for those dreams. I believe you." Arm in arm, they walked back down the hill, Meg wishing she had only to battle for those dreams, and that she didn't have to struggle so hard to be free of Ted Malloy.

Chapter Seven

It was a cold, windy evening. The community had gathered in Aurelia's cozy soddy to welcome Meg home. Even after supper, the house smelled deliciously of beefsteak and corn pudding.

Meg appreciated their kindness, especially Aurelia's in making the meal, but wished that she had good news, wished they were celebrating her freedom.

"I don't believe I can recall you failing at anything before, Meg," Aurelia said, as she and the other women cleared the kitchen.

Admire and Owen had disappeared to the stables to smoke, with orders to bring in more chips for the fire when they returned. The boys—Joshua, David, Shafer, and Lad—had gone with them, chattering about the muskrat and mink they'd caught in their traps along the Pawnee and speculating how much money they might make selling the skins, or the bounty they'd collect if they could trap a few coyotes and wolves.

The little girls, Rachel and Zibby, scooted their rag dolls in boxes across the kitchen floor, singing "Oh, Susanna" off-key and pretending they were going to Oregon.

Aurelia spoke not with malice but in a tone of wonder and honest respect. "I thought when you went to St. Louis you'd get a divorce right off as you planned." She went on with teasing affection, "Of course there's the tree claim you took, Meg. Can't quite call that a success. Those cottonwood seedlings you keep replanting aren't ever going to thrive in this country's blistering summers and bitter, cold winters. I mean, just listen to that wind howl out there! It's a wonder anything survives."

"I wouldn't have failed this time," Meg reminded her, "if the divorce didn't depend on legalities, unfair time schedules, and the courts." She put her hands on her hips and favored Aurelia with a thin smile. "And you never can tell about the trees. I'm not giving up on them yet. We need trees out here as much as anything I can think of, except more folks. We need homesteaders most of all." The greater the numbers taking up farms, helping one another and cultivating the land, the better life would be for all of them, not to mention what greater numbers of settlers would mean in victory against Jack Ambler.

"Would you cut the pumpkin pies, Meg?" Aurelia asked after a few minutes, setting aside their mild disagreement. "I'll put on coffee. Lucy Ann, in a bit would you go out and tell those foolish men and boys to come inside and not forget to bring chips for the stove? Brrrr," she shivered, "just listening to the wind gives me a chill."

Lucy Ann came to pat Meg's arm. She said encouragingly, "Time'll pass quickly and you'll hear from that nice lawyer. You'll go back to St. Louis and get the divorce and it'll be done with. Don't worry."

Meg sighed. "I've lived this long tied to that fool-demon Ted Malloy, I suppose I can survive a while longer. I'm glad he's far away in St. Louis and I'm here, though. But enough about St. Louis and my troubles." She finished cutting the pies, licked a bit of spicy pumpkin from her finger, and looked around at the others. "Any excitement here at home while I was away?"

"I saved the three weekly issues of the *Echo* you missed," Emmaline Lee told her. "Jack Ambler got married—"

The room went abruptly quiet. The other women watched Meg's face.

"He did *what?*" Not long after Meg and the others settled there, Jack had hinted at wanting to marry Meg, or—a prospect even more disgusting—to make her his mistress. He'd offered to set her up in Larned or Dodge City. He'd take care of *her,* he'd said; her friends could pack up and go back where they came from. It was one of his many efforts to break up the community, to nip settlement in the bud. But she was already married, unknown to him—to any of them at the time—and she thoroughly disliked Jack to boot.

"He married a young woman down in Texas," Emmaline answered. "Named Dinah Something-or-other. Someone he's known for years from buying cattle down there from her father. I saw the story in the *Dodge City Times* and I reprinted it in the *Echo.* I thought settlers in the valley ought to know where he is and what he's up to. They constantly have to watch their backs and guard their claims, when he's around."

Meg nodded. "I worried about that while I was in St. Louis. Did the Dodge paper say he planned to stay in Texas?" She was hopeful, but she doubted the folks at Paragon Springs and their neighbors would be so fortunate.

"No, it didn't say he'd stay in Texas, but it didn't say he'd return here, either. Maybe Jack isn't sure what he wants."

"If that miserable man stayed a thousand miles away from western Kansas the rest of his life, it'd make me happy!" Meg said.

All his dirty tricks to drive the homesteaders out were vivid in her mind. Early on he'd run his cattle over the women's dugout home, crushing it in. Thank goodness none of them were inside, but afterward they'd been forced to build their sod houses, repairing the old dugout for storage.

In another tack, Jack had had his men take up fraudulent claims in an effort to gobble up land for his own use; he'd threatened burnings and beatings to scare homesteaders into leaving. He'd even attempted to salt their water supply to make it unfit. There wasn't anything he wouldn't try, to drive them out.

"Owen's getting tired of staying in the spare dugout," Lucy Ann suddenly changed the subject as she tidily arranged cups on the table for coffee. "It's not really a home anymore, anyway, what with all the feed, seed, and garden crops stored in there." Her expression turned lively as she said, "He wants his own place. He's asked Aurelia to be Mrs. Symington."

"Aurelia!" The news wasn't totally unexpected, but Meg was filled with excitement. She took Aurelia's hands in hers. "I'm so happy for you! When's the wedding day? We'll all help!"

Aurelia blushed, but she removed her hands from Meg's and shook her head, "I told him I wasn't ready to get married again. Shush," she said, when Meg started to protest in disbelief. "My husband got himself killed by horse thieves and left me stranded in Kentucky with my little children, forcing me to come out here to Kansas to his brother, Harlan. Then Harlan took off," she waved her arms, "and abandoned me and my children to your care, Meg. Why would I want to get married and risk losing another husband? It's been hard, but I've learned to take care of my family on my own. I'm doing fine without a husband, thank you."

"But, Aurelia, don't you care for Owen? From all the signs, you've been sweet on one another from the day he came here." Owen hadn't known he'd be working with a group of women when he landed in Dodge last fall looking for a job, and a new life. But Meg had hired him to help run the store at Paragon Springs and help in the fields as needed. They'd all taken to him immediately, especially Aurelia.

"I think the world of Owen," Aurelia admitted, a softness crossing her face. "Spending time with him makes me happier than I've been in a long time. But I don't think there's any thing wrong with keeping him my . . . my . . . well, my special friend, and not my husband."

Meg's eyes rounded and she threw her hands in the air. "What if he gets tired of being just your friend, Aurelia, what then? Like he's tired of living in the old dugout? What if he up and leaves? If I were free to marry—" Meg began emphatically. She shook her head and didn't finish.

Aurelia looked startled and a little frightened. "You're not interested in Owen for yourself, are you, Meg?"

She caught Aurelia by the shoulders. "Romantically, no, although I think he's as good a man as most of us will ever see. What I am saying is that if I were free and cared for someone as much as you obviously care for Owen, and the fellow asked for my hand, I'd agree before he could catch his breath, while he's still on his knees, and he wouldn't have a chance to change his mind!"

"You think Owen might change his mind?"

"I don't know what Owen might do." Meg tried to quell her exasperation with Aurelia. "I do believe it's a mistake for you to fret yourself over something that likely won't ever happen, and spoil your chance for real happiness. If Owen were your husband, he'd never leave you. A chance for a special life is staring you in the face, Aurelia, and I think you ought to take it. That's what I think."

Aurelia didn't appear convinced. She'd suffered a lot of pain when she lost her husband and had been humiliated terribly when her brother-in-law sold his homestead and left Aurelia and her children for Meg to care for, as part of the property deal. Even so, Meg wanted to shake her so badly that she had to drop her hands and clutch them behind her back. Aurelia needed to realize that the pain would be equally great if Owen lit out because she wouldn't marry him. He could get tired of waiting and leave.

Meg was sure she wouldn't chance such a loss if she were free to love again. She remembered a time when Aurelia declared that it was unnatural for a woman not to have a husband. All the women at Paragon Springs ought to marry, she had claimed. But now that an opportunity was at hand for her, she shied away like she was about to be rattlesnake bit.

"It's my life," Aurelia said stiffly, "and I suppose I know how to manage it. I'm a grown woman."

Meg nodded, thinking that maybe she was as upset with her own situation as she was with Aurelia and was taking her personal disappointments out on her friend. "I'm sorry," she said.

Lucy Ann quickly put an end to the fuss. "I'm going to fetch the men and boys. It's time for our pie and coffee!"

Meg and Aurelia worked together the next day at the store on a list of stocks they needed to put in for the rest of winter and the coming spring. Meg noticed what a perfect team Owen and Aurelia were in the store; she watched and she envied them.

Although their tasks were interchangeable if necessity called for it, Aurelia was chiefly in charge of stocking, selling, and keeping track of foodstuffs, clothing, and household goods. Owen oversaw men's hats and boots, tobacco and whiskey, ammunition and guns, hardware and tools. In his time there, he'd become expert at explaining and demonstrating a newfangled tool or a machine's use, such as Gantling's horse-drawn drill for planting grain, and Emerson and Company's rotary and slide corn planter. They hadn't sold any of either yet, but men liked to come in and see them demonstrated and often bought other items.

Owen refused to let Aurelia do any of the heavy lifting in the store, or the sweeping up—he treated her like a queen.

Aurelia thanked him by making him special treats at meal-time, laundering and patching his clothes. She plainly enjoyed talking with him, she laughed at his jokes—she was thoroughly charmed by him—yet she wouldn't consent to being his life's partner.

It made little sense to Meg and she felt sorry for poor Owen, but as Aurelia pointedly stated, she was a grown woman and had a right to manage her own life however she saw fit. She didn't want to return to the way it was when her first husband was alive: her happiness dependent on a husband who might not be there a week, or a month, or a year from now. She was afraid.

Winter struck a last terrible blow after Meg's return from St. Louis and hard work kept her too busy to think of much else. It was a constant chore to keep the ice broken on the sinks, where the cattle drank, but her herd must have water. After breaking ice at the spring pond, she hauled water by the barrelful to the house for household use and baths. She herded her stock close to home, feeding them hay when snow covered the ground. When roads and weather permitted, she and Admire freighted for customers and her store. Sometimes she found herself carrying in fuel for the store's stove, although the youngsters usually took care of that chore. Twice she went to evening quilting parties at Aurelia's, then nearly fell asleep over her stitches from exhaustion.

At last she had an opportunity to read the papers Emmaline had saved for her. She read the story of Jack Ambler's marriage and couldn't help wondering what it might mean, if anything, to the future of Paragon Springs, and to her own personal future? Would marriage with Miss Dinah Lowell settle Jack down and rid him of some of his hate for settlers? Would he start over in Texas and not bother Paragon

Springs folks anymore? What a relief that would be! If he returned and picked up the fight again, what could she and the other settlers do to stand fast, to end the torment and bring the peace the settlement so desperately needed to ensure survival. She reminded herself guiltily that she was borrowing trouble that might not occur in the same way she'd warned Aurelia against. But it wasn't the same. Where Jack Ambler was concerned, all of them had better look ahead and be prepared.

Meg was surprised when an official-looking letter arrived from Mr. Gibbs not long after her return from St. Louis. She tore it open immediately, wondering how the weather might affect a return to St. Louis if she needed to go right away. She scanned the letter and saw only that Mr. Gibbs was worried about her. She smiled to herself as she read:

Dear Mrs. Malloy,

I write to you today to ask your kind reassurance that you reached your home safely. I have berated myself in no small measure that I allowed you to make your way unescorted to the train on the day you left St. Louis. I should have overridden your objections, your declaration that you could take care of yourself. If any misfortune befell you at the hands of your estranged husband, it would be entirely my fault, knowing your case as I do. I would lay blame to myself—where it would belong—for the rest of my days. I beg a letter from you as soon as possible, letting me know you are well. My conscience, and my concern, will then be eased somewhat.

Respectfully,

Hamilton Gibbs, Attorney At Law

Attorney Gibbs's worry over her was unnecessary, Meg

thought to herself as she sat down to write him a return letter, but it was nice of him to be concerned, even so. She ought to have written him the minute she got home, that her trip was uneventful and she was safe. She'd worried about Bridget, was she safe from Ted? She'd ask Gibbs to look into it and let her know.

Frigid weather continued and for days at a time the temperature hovered between twenty and thirty degrees below zero. Folks suffered from the cold all over western Kansas and it seemed that warm weather would never come.

The few customers who straggled into Meg's store to buy supplies brought heartbreaking stories from around the valley: Everything edible—potatoes, squashes, pumpkins—froze as hard as rocks. Bread had to be thawed by the fire before it could be sliced. In a terrible instance, a woman's feet were frostbitten while she went about her home chores inside the house and she lost three of her toes. Farm animals were being brought inside with families to keep them from freezing. In one instance the ears of an ox had frozen and broken off.

Meg was in the root cellar one day, adding additional covering to their store of vegetables and fruit, when she heard an odd sound above ground. Curious, stiff with cold, she made her way out of the cellar. A young man's form, nearly white with the blowing snow, stood hunched in the cold as he held the reins of a horse. A woman covered in frost and snow—and looking more dead than alive—was propped in the saddle, her shawl and skirts whipped by the wind.

"Lad, is that you?" Meg cried. "Lucy Ann?" she raced forward, catching the woman, who fell stiffly into her arms. It wasn't Lucy Ann. "Lad? Go inside, son, right away. You're half frozen."

He shook his head, "I'll help get her inside," his voice crackled. "She's in bad shape. I gotta go back; she said she had a child with her."

A child, lost in this weather? God forbid! Meg's heart constricted at the image his announcement brought, but she argued with him, "You can't go back, Lad Voss, you're going inside and thaw out. We'll get help to look for the little one. Right now we have to get the child's mother in by the stove or she's going to die."

Inside the mercantile, Aurelia hurried to help. They put the woman on Meg's bed, then Aurelia told Lad to go out front by the stove. "There's some hot soup on the stove; have Owen give you some. We'll take care of her," she told him.

"Tell Owen about the child," Meg said. "He'll know what to do."

The woman's muscles were stiff. Her skin looked strangely tallowy where it wasn't bluish red. Her breathing was shallow.

"Mary Hague," Aurelia said, "I believe that's this poor soul's name. She's come into the store a couple of times. Thin as a stick, always tired."

"Yes, she's Mrs. Hague," Meg replied, recognizing her. "I helped her and her husband file a claim. It's on past Lucy Ann and Admire's place, another five miles. I don't think much of her husband, I'm afraid he's a no-good."

They cautiously removed the woman's clothing, then placed her in a tub of barely warm water. "We've got to bring her temperature back to normal slowly," Aurelia said.

Meg nodded, "If we're not too late," she said grimly. The bath didn't seem to help much. They dried Mary Hague, dressed her in one of Meg's nightgowns, and put her into bed, covering her with several thick blankets. Meg got a cup of water from the pail in her small alcove kitchen and added a

touch of whiskey. She returned to her sleeping quarters and
could tell with one look at Aurelia standing by the bed that
the worst had happened.

Aurelia's eyes were shiny with tears. "She's gone, poor
soul, just like that. She sighed like a little baby and then she
. . . didn't breath anymore."

A heaviness settled in Meg's heart. Severe weather was always a terrible foe to be reckoned with out there. "Where was
her husband?" she wondered disconsolately. "What on earth
was she doing out in such weather, with a small child along?"

When they went out into the store they learned that Owen
had gone to summon Admire and others to form a search
party. After getting details from Lad, Owen convinced him to
stay put.

Now Lad, seated close to the stove with his half-frozen
feet in a pan of water, told Meg and Aurelia, teeth chattering,
"Lucy Ann and Ad s-sent me here for s-supplies. They said I
was to s-stay here if the weather was too bad for me to come
back home right away. I found the lady on the way in. She was
all mixed up, but talked s-some. She lives on past our place.
Her man is fond of drink and had gone to Dodge City and
didn't come back, she said. She'd run out of food, and cow
chips to burn, and she was headed here to Paragon Springs
for help. Sh-she got lost on the way."

"Her child?" Meg questioned softly, her hands clutched in
front of her.

Pain shadowed Lad's youthful face and a shine of tears
came to his eyes. He gulped, "It's hard to talk about. She says
she had her little three-year-old boy with her. She called him
Ollie." He closed his eyes for a second and bowed his head,
his voice trembling. "She lost him, went around in circles
looking for him, but she couldn't find him in the blowing
snow. I tried following her directions and I looked with her

94

for a long time, but I couldn't find him, either." His voice caught and he leaned forward, his elbows on his knees, his head in his hands.

Meg rubbed his shoulders. "You did the best you could, Lad."

"No. I gotta go back. I'm all right, now. Where's my boots, my coat?" He looked around. "I can catch up to Owen and Admire. I can help." He drew his feet from the water, pushed the pan aside, but grimaced from pain when he tried to stand.

Meg grabbed his shoulders and pushed him back into his chair. "You'll stay right here! You'll lose your feet and hands if not your life if you go out there again. If anything happened to you I wouldn't want to be the one to answer to your sister."

For three days the men searched as long as daylight lasted. On the third day, the snow had begun to melt and they found the child's frozen body near the far southwest line of Admire's claim. Ollie's rigid little face was caught in his two frozen hands, showing a painful, frightening death.

The image wouldn't leave Meg's mind and she felt some responsibility. She hadn't brought the child's family to that country, but she had helped them find land, had encouraged them to stay.

The story of what happened to Mary Hague and little Ollie reached Dodge City and spread throughout the valley.

Grover Hague, Mary's husband and Ollie's father, finally ended his drunken binge and arrived at Paragon Springs. He was a stubby fellow, swag-bellied, with dirty unkempt hair and frog-like features. He smelled bad and he needed a shave.

It was hard for Meg to speak kindly to him, but she said simply, "I'm terribly sorry about your wife and child, Mr. Hague. We kept their bodies here, knowing you'd want to bury them near your home when warmer weather comes."

"Damn this country for what it does to people," he cursed and sobbed. "Ain't fit for humans to live in, never shoulda come here. This country's what killed my wife, my little boy. Well, I ain't stayin', I tell you that. Not in this sorry country, I ain't."

Meg felt such distaste for his puling attitude, laying the blame anywhere but on himself, that she refrained from answering. *If you'd been home with them where you belonged,* she wanted to tell him, *this likely never would've happened. If you'd prepared properly for winter—put in enough fuel and provisions— your family would be alive now, they wouldn't have had to strike out from home in a storm . . .* She had plenty she would have liked to say, but because he'd lost so much, and could be honestly grieving inside, she held her tongue.

Unfortunately, a number of new settlers to that country agreed with his view. Literature about western Kansas claimed sunny weather, mild winters, and other fantasies that simply weren't true. Folks needed to learn to live with, and deal with, harsh weather, or they couldn't survive. How often Meg had heard the lament, "Ain't no use to buck Ma Nature," from some lazy soul abandoning his claim for a fool's paradise that didn't exist.

Meg would never forget the Hagues, especially after the brief funeral service held when the ground thawed. Though they were buried in the slowly growing graveyard above Paragon Springs with headstones carved by Aurelia, Mr. Hague was long gone, so no family were there to mourn them. However, Meg remained convinced that many such heartbreaking tragedies were preventable.

It was April before a soft warm south wind broke the icy grip on the land. With the change in the weather, Meg felt, as always, new hope, new determination.

Up at The Rocks, she returned with Admire to the back-breaking work of quarrying stone for sale. She scraped away the overlay of damp soil to expose the soft limestone. As she marked the stone for cutting, she said to Admire, "I remember thinking, when I traded my father's fiddle and some millinery goods to Aurelia's brother-in-law for this claim, that these rocky acres were particularly worthless."

"Well they sure ain't," he chuckled.

Far from being worthless, the quarry had yielded many wagonloads of stone and she was making a fairly decent living from the sales.

There were treasures in that country that weren't always evident right away. Several times Meg served up that argument to grumblers who chose the end of winter to come into the mercantile and stock up for a journey back to where they'd come from or to new opportunity and warmer climes in New Mexico or California.

She told them that if they would only stay long enough to learn the land and the climate and how to deal with it, things would improve. They answered her with the story of the dead child and its dead mother. None wanted that to happen to them. If the tragedy hadn't happened, some of those leaving would have gone anyway, of course. But it was disappointing that her intended encouragement was paid so little heed.

They lost more settlers than she would have thought possible that late winter and early spring. She was reminded of the grasshopper scourge in the summer of 1874 that caused so many folks to pull out. With dread, she knew how happy this most recent homesteader exodus would make Jack Ambler, who, word had it, was returning to the Rocking A and bringing his new wife.

One day Meg and Owen made a trip to Dodge to pick up

the mailbag for Paragon Springs and a large order for her store. After loading their shipment, they took her shaggy horses, Pete and Dan, to the livery, where they grained them and left them to rest while they walked in thin spring sunshine to a nearby café.

In her pocket, Meg carried a second letter from Hamilton Gibbs. While she and Owen were waiting for their hot meal to be brought, she held up the letter and asked, "Do you mind?"

"Not at all. I hope it's good news."

As she read the letter, the Dodge café and Owen faded; she could almost hear Mr. Gibbs's warm, deep voice:

Dear Mrs. Malloy,

I was very relieved to hear from you and know that you are safe and well. My mind is easier on your behalf, for now.

Bridget seems safe enough. She says she has her trusty cleaver handy if Malloy ever comes to bother her. Also, her neighbors keep a close eye on her.

I am doing everything in my power to get you as early a court date as possible. I've let it be known that you are in danger from your estranged husband and that it is most important for this matter to be taken care of quickly. Unfortunately, the courts move more slowly than molasses pours in winter.

We are having a serious railway strike in St. Louis and Missouri in general. I pray that the strike will be over when you need to make your return trip here, but be assured that if you cannot make the journey, I will take your place and speak well for you in court.

Thank you for your good wishes. I hope you won't feel that I'm stepping out of bounds to say that your pleasant letter was as welcome and peaceful as a lovely sunset, following the difficult day in court that I had just experienced. I was most pleased, and I return your good wishes.

With deep regard,

Hamilton Gibbs, Attorney at Law

She folded the letter and put it away, her eyes smarting. "Not good news?"

Meg shook her head. "Not very good, I don't have a date yet for my divorce trial." She sighed in disappointment. "I want so much to have it over with." But she told herself as she and Owen ate their meal that it was good of Mr. Gibbs to write and keep her informed. He had a very fine writing hand. In spite of no good news, she felt comforted by his letter.

As she sipped her coffee, Meg turned her attention to Owen and blithely asked, "Owen, what're your true feelings toward Aurelia?" Too late, she realized that she was being very personal.

He didn't seem bothered by her question and answered sincerely, "I love her very much; I think she's lovely and fine." A shadow of disappointment flickered for an instant in his face. "You probably know I proposed marriage and she turned me down?"

Meg nodded.

He told her, toying with his fork, "I do understand, and I'm willing to wait until she's ready. Aurelia has good reason to be afraid of caring about a fellow, then losing him and being left to fend for herself alone. It may not be for a while, but I believe as surely as the sun comes up in the morning that eventually the two of us will marry, quite happily."

"Good for you, Owen!" Meg smiled at him in admiration of his solid conviction, his goodness. She reached over to pat his hand. "You won't be sorry. Aurelia is a wonderful person, and more capable than she has any idea. The way she's taken over for me at the mercantile, you'd think it's something she's done all her life. And she's a fine postmistress. I don't think anyone else could keep everything so tidy and in its proper slot so it's easy to find. Folks like it when she takes time to chat when they come for the mail and supplies. She's an asset to the community we couldn't do without."

"If she agrees to marry me, I wouldn't take her away."

"Oh, goodness, no! I wasn't thinking anything like that. Paragon Springs needs both of you. I just hope for your sake she comes to her senses soon and says yes to being your wife."

He wore a tentative smile. "Can't argue with that." In a moment he asked her, "What about you, Meg? Do you plan to marry again when your divorce is final? How about this attorney of yours? I watched while you read your letter and I swear you turned even prettier than usual."

"That is foolishness, Owen. I did not!"

"You did, and you caressed his letter as though it were special, although you said it held no good news."

She laughed at him, embarrassed at his wild suppositions. "Owen Symington, you're imagining things! Merciful heaven, I have no special feelings for Mr. Gibbs. I admire him, I trust him, but I've only just met him. Our relationship is professional, nothing more. And anyhow, it'd make no difference if I did have personal feelings toward him—he's in St. Louis, and I'm here in western Kansas. Hardly a situation for romance."

His simple question had burst a dam; once she'd started talking about Gibbs, she didn't want to stop. "I'm not free to think of anyone in a romantic way, anyway, not yet. But one thing I'm convinced of about Mr. Gibbs, is that he's a good man. Like you, Owen. Maybe that's what you detect in my manner. The man I married turned out to be a terrible person. I admire a man who is honorable and decent. It seems almost a miracle when such a man comes into a woman's acquaintance."

His eyebrows rose in mock surprise and he chuckled, "Well, whatever your true feelings for this Gibbs, I'm flattered that you've included me in your category of good men."

She sipped her coffee and after a thoughtful moment said, "My father was such a man. I should've judged Ted Malloy by the standard of my papa. I didn't, probably because I was young and blind, and I've paid dearly."

"Are your parents living? I've never heard you say."

"No, they're gone, my father died first. In a way, you could say he gave his life for my mother."

"How so?"

"He was killed at work when a load of brick fell and smothered him. He worked very hard to give my mother everything he felt she deserved. Her family was gentry, back in Ireland. A person had only to see how my mother and father looked at one another to know how much in love they were."

She would feel she'd landed the miracle of the ages to have a marriage like that. For years she'd been on the run from a dreadful marriage, focusing her attention on escaping Ted and keeping herself alive. Now she wanted more.

"Good luck to us both," Owen broke into her thoughts softly.

"Amen," she said, and touched his arm.

Chapter Eight

A few weeks later Meg stood in the shadows of Dodge City's Santa Fe depot, her eyes narrowed as she observed newly arrived cattle cars being unloaded down the track. Drovers on horseback whistled and shouted as they circled the bellowing, long-horned cattle spilling from the cars. Using their ropes as whips, the riders herded the cattle out across the tracks and headed them north.

To one side of the melee and half-hidden by flying dust was Jack Ambler, in a dark suit and Stetson. So he was back, and with him, trouble. Two men Meg didn't recognize, Texas cowhands from their garb, flanked Jack. The fourth person in the party was a slender woman in a blue traveling suit and plumed hat. Was this Jack's new wife?

She's attractive, Meg conceded irritably, but if she had good sense, why would she marry Jack?

Meg rubbed her chin as she sized up the situation further. The two Texas cowboys with the couple were probably fresh riders Jack had hired. Admire claimed that some of the old-time riders for the Rocking A, peaceable men, had quit. They didn't like Jack's methods of dealing with settlers, and they didn't want to chance serving time like the jackals who'd killed Meg's horses.

Unfortunately, there were still plenty of Jack's hands who remained loyal. Longtime cowhands, they believed as strongly as he did that homesteading farmers didn't belong in that country. They felt that the settlers gave Jack no choice but to drive them out by any means possible.

Concern weighed heavily on Meg as she hurriedly finished

loading freight onto her wagon for the long trip home. From what she'd seen today, Jack wasn't cutting his cattle operation to make room for settlers, but just the opposite—he was increasing the size of his herd, meaning that he would need even more grazing land than before.

On a bright sunny morning a week later, Meg was out riding Pete counting her cattle and making sure the small herd was not wandering from their own range. Strayed, they could be rebranded with a running iron and taken into someone else's herd. She couldn't afford to lose even one.

"Shhh, what's that?" She halted Pete, reaching down to stroke his dappled gray neck. Most of her herd milled around her, grazing, but the distant, plaintive bawling of a cow in distress carried on the soft spring wind. "We'd better see," she told the horse softly.

The commotion seemed to come from the direction of the sinks, her two natural ponds. She reined Pete that way. Whatever the cow's problem, it wasn't thirst. They'd had good rains since spring thaw and now in May they still had showers off and on and the sinks were brim-full.

At her urging, Pete broke into a heavy, bone-jarring trot. A few minutes later Meg spotted a short-horned, liver-colored cow that was belly-deep in mud at the edge of the farthest sink. Meg's T Cross brand that she'd inherited from Aurelia's brother-in-law, Harlan Thorne, showed on the cow's hip. The unhappy critter moaned and bawled, saliva flying as it tossed its head.

"Now how'd you get yourself in a mess like that?" Meg railed as she dismounted. "What am I going to do with you?" With hands on her hips she walked over to determine how she might dislodge the cow from the muck. After another minute of contemplation, she got her coiled rope from her saddle, formed a loop, shook it out, and swung it over her head several times. She let the loop play out over the distressed cow and drop, missing the cow by two feet.

"The boys are much better at this than I am," she muttered, yanking the muddied rope back in snaking jerks to try again. On the fourth attempt the loop settled nicely over the cow's head and horns. Feeling satisfied with the throw, she climbed back onto Pete, wrapped the rope around her saddle horn and backed her mount, hauling back on the rope. "Hey, come on out of there!" The rope tightened and the bogged-down animal made a strangling bellow but didn't budge from the mud. Meg tried a few more times. Then with a frustrated sigh, she let the rope go slack. She dismounted and mopped her forehead on her arm as she stood puzzling over her predicament.

She didn't want to choke the darn critter to death, that would be more beef to eat than they needed right now. She wanted to keep the cow as long as possible for birthing calves.

The wind blew Meg's skirts about her ankles. She brushed her hair from her face and wondered if she should go home for help.

A strange woman's voice called out loudly, "You haul and I'll push from behind." Startled, Meg shaded her eyes and looked in the direction of the voice. The slender blonde she'd seen with Jack last week in town was riding around to her side of the pond on a sleek black horse. She was attractively dressed in a brown skirt, a white shirt-waist under her jacket, trim boots, and a handsome hat. Meg, holding old Pete's reins, felt dowdy in her worn and faded calico.

She gaped as the young woman dismounted, yanked off her boots, pulled the back hem of her long skirt up between her legs and tucked the hem into her waistband, and plunged into the mud and water to shove on the cow's behind.

"Why on earth would you—you're going to be all over mud, a mess!"

The young woman laughed as she soundly slapped the cow and shoved at it. "I've had to do this sort of thing aplenty in Texas. I'm not sugar that melts, any more than you are. Get back on your horse and haul!" she motioned, "I'm pushin' all I can."

Meg remounted quickly and hauled back with her rope; the other woman pounded and shoved at the cow's backside. The words she used on the cow sounded like Mexican cuss words. With a great sucking sound, the cow slowly emerged out of the mud onto dry ground. Mud and water dripped down its legs.

"Silly thing!" Meg said as she removed her rope from the muddy animal's head. "You could've gotten yourself out without all this trouble. You didn't really try." She turned to her helper. "Thanks, you saved me a cow!" She drew a breath and asked tentatively, "Are you Jack Ambler's new wife? We heard he got married."

"One and the same. Dinah Ambler, used to be Dinah Lowell, from west Texas, near Sweetwater." She held out her hand. They both laughed and grasped wet and muddy fingers.

"Meg Brennon."

A fine wrinkle creased Dinah's brow. "Ahh, as I thought, you're one of the Paragon Springs women. I've heard plenty about you. You seem to be the main thorn in my husband's side."

Meg was a little surprised at her forthright comment. "I suppose you could call me that," she said cautiously, "as he is in mine."

Dinah Ambler smiled and nodded.

Meg decided her friendly manner didn't necessarily mean

that Dinah didn't agree with her husband's belief that settlers were a scourge in those parts and had to be eliminated. Although it was possible that she was a woman with a different opinion, a mind of her own.

"I was on my way to meet you all," Dinah said, "when I heard the cow caterwaulin' and you talkin' to it." She shook out her skirt. "I'm a sight now, but if you and your friends don't mind?"

Meg hesitated for only a second. "Folks are more than welcome at Paragon Springs, and I owe you a cup of coffee and a change of dry clothes." Having Jack's wife as company would be odd, but it was only neighborly. She regretted having to chance Jack's wrath, though. Meg didn't doubt for a minute that he would be mortally against his wife socializing with the women at Paragon Springs. She wanted no trouble, but what would be, would be.

As Meg and Dinah rode in, Lucy Ann drove up in front of the mercantile with her little Rachel in the Walshes' buckboard. Sunshine spilled over the scene back-dropped by an azure sky.

"I needed thread," Lucy Ann said with a shy smile, "and some of the denim goods you got in the last order, Meg. Admire needs some new breeches."

Meg introduced Dinah, and Lucy Ann told her politely, "I'm glad I picked today to come. It's a pleasure to meet you."

Dinah smiled and then knelt in front of Rachel. "You're a very pretty child, every bit as beautiful as some little girls I know down in Texas." She brushed her hand clean on her skirt, then stroked Rachel's dark pigtail. "Would you like to ride my horse sometime?" she nodded over her shoulder at the black Morgan.

Rachel's face screwed up in a frown, her black eyes showed doubt.

Dinah laughed, "That's all right if you don't want to, you're still little."

"She's three," Lucy Ann said with a smile. She held out her hand for Rachel's to go inside, but Rachel took Dinah's hand instead and they marched toward the store. Lucy Ann looked at Meg with raised eyebrows.

Inside, Aurelia looked up from unpacking a crate of dress goods. Meg introduced the newcomer to her, and to her little girl, Zibby. At the moment, there were no customers other than Lucy Ann. Meg explained how Dinah's clothes came to be muddy.

"I have a skirt you can change into," Aurelia said. "We'll rinse yours out and hang it on our clothesline, which is the big elk rack you saw outside. Won't take any time to dry in the warm winds out there today." As she left the store to retrieve the skirt, she mouthed silently to Meg, "Jack Ambler's wife, *here?*"

Meg gave a slight nod, lifted her shoulders in a shrug, and went to serve coffee and a plate of bread-and-butter sandwiches.

If the Paragon Springs women were concerned that Dinah could bring trouble just by visiting them, Dinah herself seemed to have no such worry. She chatted happily, telling them of her difficulties settling in at the ranch, and other information. They listened, always glad for womanly news from outside. For a brief while, it didn't matter that she was wedded to their worst enemy.

"It's been ages since a woman has lived at the Rocking A," Dinah told them, "but you all likely know that Jack was married before, a long time ago. There's a lot of fixin' to do. I thought I'd buy piece goods here at your store to make curtains."

It was yet another surprise that Jack's fine wife would sew her own curtains. Jack could well afford to have curtains made, if Dinah wanted. The women finished their coffee and sandwiches and moved in a body to examine the yard goods Aurelia had been in the process of unpacking.

A great clamor filled the room as the women, excited as children, exclaimed over each bolt of fabric drawn from the crate. Little Rachel and Zibby sat by and stared at this strange behavior. Occasionally, one of the little girls would reach out to touch a bright-colored fabric, although they seemed more entertained by the carefree delight the adults were showing in mere cloth.

"I think I like the copper-toned madder prints," Dinah said, "but do I choose stripes, plaid, or checked? It's so hard to decide."

"That soft pink gingham reminds me of a dress you loaned me when we first met, remember?" Lucy Ann said to Meg. "We were on our way here to western Kansas."

"I remember."

"This," Dinah exclaimed, "is wonderful!" She held up a bolt of butterscotch-yellow print, then drew fabric from the roll and stroked it. She passed it to Aurelia. "Seven yards for a dress, please. It's perfect to have made into a day dress for spring and summer."

"It's all so pretty," Lucy Ann said, kneeling by the pile of riches. "Look there at the indigo blue with the yellow flowers on it, and that white with aqua sprigs—have you ever seen anything so pretty?"

Meg had a more difficult time than the other women in showing interest in the dress goods. Even though she felt sure Jack knew nothing of Dinah's visit there, she half-expected him to barge in and ruin their enjoyment.

While Aurelia measured and cut Dinah's chosen fabrics

and Meg and Lucy Ann gathered up the other bolts to shelve them, Dinah lifted Rachel and swung her until she squealed in delight, her skirts a bell around her small bare feet.

Zibby, a year older than Rachel, smiled shyly and held her hands out when Dinah put Rachel down to claim a dance with her. Around and around they bounced and jigged. In no time at all, both little girls had been totally charmed by the friendly newcomer.

Meg felt a trifle silly to think it, but wondered if Dinah had been sent there by Jack? Had she come to spy, to find out something about the women at Paragon Springs for him to use against them? He'd made life miserable for them almost daily for years. What did he want now?

After Dinah left, Meg told the others, "I could hardly throw her out; she was very good to help me get my cow out of the mud. Jack would have a fit, though, if she socialized with us. Maybe she won't be back."

"I liked her, and I hope she does come back," Aurelia said firmly.

Lucy Ann nodded agreement, although she looked a bit frightened.

Meg soon abandoned her feeble hope that marriage to Dinah might mellow Jack and soften his attitude toward settlers. Indications of just the opposite were everywhere that spring and early summer. Without a by-your-leave, he moved some of his new Rocking A cattle onto claims abandoned by homesteaders who'd gotten discouraged and vacated as winter ended.

He ignored established settlers' boundary lines and allowed his herds to roam onto homesteads where crops of corn, squash, and potatoes were springing from sun-warmed ground. The plantings, meant to flourish into crops that would sustain a homesteading family through a long hard year, were trampled, and ruined.

More than once, a harassed settler, already with more troubles than he could count from the weather, from a wife unhappy to be there in the first place, plus afraid he'd be unable to grow another crop in time to save his family from starvation, would quit his claim and move on—exactly what Jack wanted.

One early morning, Meg saddled Pete and rode toward the Rocking A, determined to speak her mind to Jack. She crossed onto his land, a great expanse that looked deceptively flat but which was actually corrugated with ridges and draws. Cattle grazed everywhere; some of those closest to her sported horns like giant rockers.

A hot wind gusted dust in front of her and for a second she was blinded. She rode on, her mind on what she was going to say to Jack, when a shot from off to her right broke the silence; at the same moment a wolf, practically flying, flashed past her across the prairie. She drew up, her heart pounding. In another second, Jack Ambler rode up out of a draw some distance to her right, a rifle in his left hand. He jerked his mount to a halt and shouted at her, "What the hell are you doin' here?"

She took a deep breath and loped toward him. As she rode up, she spotted the lifeless, bloodied form of a calf a short distance down the draw—the wolf's kill. She told Jack firmly, "I'm here to speak with you!"

He slouched in the saddle with the rifle resting across his lap. His wolfish face wore a faintly contemptuous smile, but, more from habit toward a woman than welcome, he touched his hat to her as she approached.

She wasted no time on niceties, it was hard enough to keep her own dislike of him reined in. "What on earth do you think you're doing, Jack?" she asked with straightforward calm. "You keep buying cattle when you don't have enough range to support them. Your herd is chasing all over the place ruining folks' crops." She paused, then gave up trying to keep anger at bay. "Of course you know that, because what you're doing is intentional!" She said angrily through her teeth, "It's got to stop. I'm warning you, Jack, keep your cattle off land owned by the homesteaders, unless you want the law brought in or settlers shooting your cows! I hope you understand what I'm saying."

His gold eyes narrowed and his lips tightened over his pointed, wolf-like teeth. "Nobody better shoot a single Rocking A cow or they'll wish they hadn't," he said. "This is all your stupid nester friends' fault, anyhow, so don't blame me. They think that plowin' a furrow around their claim makes it theirs. Is a cow supposed to know what the hell a plowed line means and not cross it? I haven't done anything wrong."

"Legally, those furrows are recognized the same as fences!"

"Tell that to a hungry or thirsty cow," he snapped. He pulled his hat down tighter, and anger colored his perspiring face. "As I keep tellin' you, Plow Lady, you homesteaders asked for it. You invaded cattle country, not the other way around, and you oughta remember that and stop puttin' the blame on me!" He clicked his tongue and kneed his horse into a fast walk westward. "There's a wolf out here that needs killin' for gettin' my calves an' I've wasted enough time talkin'. Get yourself off Rocking A land, Plow Lady. You're the trespasser!"

"You could hire more riders to tend your cattle, you could put up fences! You could obey herd laws!" Meg shouted after him as he rode off. He ignored her, his back stiff. She sat on

111

her own horse, trembling, a knot of anxiety in her stomach.

Meg never considered herself an avid letter writer, but she enjoyed writing to Hamilton Gibbs and hearing from him as summer wore on. For one thing, it was a pleasant diversion from the troubles at home. He wrote periodically to say that he was still trying to arrange a court date, to ask after her safety, and to warn her to keep watch for Ted who was turning St. Louis upside down trying to locate her.

She wasn't foolhardy, but she was sure that if Ted couldn't find her after this long, that she was relatively safe. She worried more about Bridget, but Gibbs assured her that although Ted had pestered Bridget for a while, he evidently was convinced that Bridget had no idea of Meg's whereabouts and he left her alone.

Feeling a bit of schemer for it, Meg began to include casual questions in her letters that had nothing to do with her case, that would bring a reply from him. She'd noted many changes when in St. Louis. Had he been to the new park she'd heard so much about while she was there?

He wrote back:

I take pen in hand tonight to answer your questions about Forest Park. I hadn't seen the place for myself, and your inquiry spurred me to do it. I spent the most pleasant Sunday I've known in recent memory. Forest Park is a very lovely place, with many flower gardens, bridle paths, and a lagoon for boating. I would recommend it highly to anyone. Perhaps when you return to St. Louis, you would like to spend an afternoon there? It wouldn't be safe for you to go alone, but I could accompany you if you wished.

She wrote to him in one of her letters about her young

friend at Paragon Springs, Selinda Lee, who was interested in art. He wrote back that her letter had prompted him to visit the Mercantile Library one lunch time and view their special exhibit that day of George Caleb Bingham's scenes of everyday life in Missouri. "I'm not a knowledgeable judge of art, but I enjoyed Bingham's paintings very much," he wrote, "they are wonderfully realistic. I particularly like his 'Jolly Boatman' and 'Daniel Boone Coming Through The Cumberland Gap.' I felt drawn into his scenes, a part of them."

He told her to encourage her young friend in art, because art, like flowers and music, fed the soul. Only now did he realize how much he missed such things, struggling as he did in the mines of law. He hoped her young friend might see such art for herself, someday.

Had Gibbs preferred to keep their association on a strictly business basis, he could have done so easily, but he seemed glad to correspond with her, on any subject. She suspected that he was a lonely man due to dedication to his work, and she was a new friend whose requests were a reason for him to sightsee and explore. Meg lauded herself for doing a good deed, writing to him, and for her the incidents he described were so different from her own rustic, worrisome life on the plains, that his letters were brief, happy vacations.

It would be a pleasure to see him again, when her court date was eventually set.

Dinah Ambler continued to drop in at Paragon Springs. Sometimes she came to buy ribbon or another trifle; mostly she came to visit.

The women relaxed around her, recognizing that she was lonely with Jack away out on the range or in Dodge City. They enjoyed Dinah. She talked openly about herself, at times answering questions she only saw in the other women's eyes, their manner, things they'd like to know but were too polite to ask.

They quilted as they visited. Owen had built Aurelia a quilt frame, and, never one to be idle, she kept it in the store so that she could quilt between caring for customers. Women customers often drew up an extra chair at the blue and white quilt with its Birds in Flight pattern, adding a few careful stitches while they caught up on gossip. Equally often, Aurelia removed stitches that weren't small and fine enough to her liking, but no one complained.

"I'm pure Texan, only child of a rancher," Dinah told Aurelia, Meg, Lucy Ann, and a distant neighbor, Bethany Hessler, who had gathered to quilt and chat that day. "My mother died a year and a half ago." A shine of tears came to Dinah's cornflower-blue eyes and she brushed them away. "We were very close and I miss her. My father didn't wait a year to remarry, after my mother died. His new wife," she made a face, "is younger than me. After she moved in, she couldn't wait for me to move out."

A murmur of sympathy went around the circle; with needles poised above the quilt, the women waited to hear more.

"Papa's new wife couldn't believe I hadn't yet found a husband, old as I was. That I still lived with my father, kept house for him, and worked with him on our ranch. I was definitely in her way."

"And Jack—?" Lucy whispered, looking anxious, curious. "How'd you two come together?"

Meg was glad she asked. It amazed her that anyone as nice as Dinah would be happy with somebody like Jack.

Dinah poked her needle into the cloth so she wouldn't lose it, then sat back with her hands in her lap. "For years Jack came to our ranch to buy breedin' stock from my father. Jack's known me since I was a young girl. He watched me grow up. I flirted with him, I suppose, as soon as I learned how to flutter my eyelashes and learned that that might get me warm grins and compliments. All along we enjoyed one another's company."

"You did?" Lucy Ann blurted the question, eyes wide with doubt, then ducked her head in embarrassment and began to sew.

Dinah didn't seem to notice as she continued, "I'm not sure, other than that, what the attraction was. I was very proper, and I reckon Jack's wild ways kinda fascinated me. I'm sure he didn't mean for our adult attraction to extend beyond flirting, but then, at first, neither did I. My father, though, wanted to see me married. He liked Jack, and believed I could do worse."

"How about some coffee?" Aurelia asked. "And Bethany's brought some of her delicious shortbread." She motioned at Dinah, "Go on with your story, Dinah, I don't want to miss it. I'll be quiet."

"There was my stepmother," Dinah went on with a wry laugh, "and likely others, too, who believed I was sinking into the oblivion of spinsterhood." She shrugged, and looked mischievous. "I admit I wore Jack down. I know I took him off guard and he likely didn't know what he was doing when he proposed marriage, but then it was done. Life with my young stepmother had gotten to be intolerable, and a new life with Jack in Kansas sounded like an exciting adventure, new horizons to conquer, all that."

She said quickly, after a moment of silence, "I love Jack, don't misunderstand me. But I can't say that I always understand him. He gives you all trouble, I know that. I've asked him to stop, but he's set in his ways, believes what he believes, and won't listen. Raisin' hell and raisin' cattle is all Jack's ever known."

115

"What does Jack think of your visiting here, befriending us?" Meg finally asked the question she'd wanted the answer to for weeks.

"He doesn't know, yet, and he wouldn't like it. I just tell him I'm out ridin'. But I knew I had to meet you all from the first moment I heard about you."

"Whyever so?" Lucy Ann asked, astonished, picking a floating blue thread out of the air, "when your husband hates us so?"

"After I'd heard him grouse and complain and lose his temper for the fiftieth time talking about you all, I thought to myself, doesn't that beat the moon? This little ol' group of women has a strong, hard man like Jack Ambler buffaloed 'til he doesn't know which side is up. Women such as that, I've got to meet! And," she added into their echoing laughter, her expression turning sober, "it gets awfully lonely on the Rocking A with no other women close, you know? It was lonely at home after my mother died. Jack'll have to understand. Do you all mind?"

They didn't mind, but that didn't mean they didn't worry about what might happen when Jack found out.

116

Chapter Nine

"That oughta be enough," Admire told Meg one day, thumping a squared white rock into place on the heaped wagonload.

"Plenty," she answered, catching her breath. She rolled her sleeves down and buttoned them. Her clothing was covered with snowy dust from the stone and she could feel grit in her mouth. She brushed at her bodice, her skirts. "If Sol Green wants more we'll see he gets it. I told him he could buy on credit. I'd rather do that than have him pull up stakes and leave the country. Jack's cattle grazed right through Sol's corn, bean, and melon crops last spring. He put in a second crop and prays to harvest this one. He has to do something to keep those animals out."

Solomon Green was a gaunt Missourian whose claim was several miles west and south of Paragon Springs. Of course his crops were not the only ones ruined by Rocking A cattle. Meg leaned back against the wagon. She wiped her forehead on her sleeve. She was tired, although today's load hadn't been as difficult as some. Larger slabs of stone required block and tackle to load, or she and Admire dug into the slope and backed their wagon in, then pushed the stone onto the wagonbed. Luckily for their tired backs today, Sol wanted the smaller bits and pieces of broken stone for building his fence.

"Sol will help me unload when I get to his place," Meg said. She stared into the wide expanse of empty plains under a robin's-egg-blue sky. "You can stay here, Admire, and after you've rested you can start marking and cutting another batch. A lot of folks have agreed to buy our stone as long as they can have it on credit. Don't kill yourself with overwork, though."

"I won't," he answered wiping sweat from his neck with his handkerchief. "Now you be careful yourself. Better keep watch for Jack, or some of his men who don't mind doin' his dirty work for 'im. Maybe he didn't give the order to kill your horses that time, but he still wants you outta this country in the worst way. If there's a trick just inside legal to get rid of every last settler in this valley, Jack'll do it. He'll do it illegal, if he figgers he can get away with it and not have to pay with his neck strung up."

"I know, Ad." She patted the gun strapped on her hip, "I carry this, but I wish I didn't have to." It would always haunt her that Lad was forced to kill the bounty man Ted had sent after her. Finch deserved it, but she hated bloodshed. She was a peaceful person for the most part and preferred peaceful answers to problems.

Bidding Admire good-bye, she climbed up onto the wagon and drove toward Solomon Green's. The oxen snuffled and blew as they plodded along; crickets chirred in the grass alongside the dusty trail. The sky was clear and blue from horizon to horizon.

It was a long, warm, and tiring trip after a morning loading stone. Meg was half-asleep when she spied three riders encircled by dust and approaching from the direction of Sol's claim.

"The devil himself," she muttered aloud as they drew close. Her mouth dried. A shiver traveled her spine. She didn't like the looks of Jack's companions any more than she liked Jack. Both Texans were lean as wild dogs, their hats tipped low over their eyes. One man was older than the other, wrinkled from the sun and gray in his beard; the younger Texan was clean shaven.

All three tipped their hats to her as they rode up. Meg's return smile was as grim and unfriendly as theirs.

"Howdy, Miss Brennon—or whatever your real name is," Jack mocked. "Talk is you've 'fessed to a shady past. I knew all along you weren't what you claimed, and were runnin' from the law."

"You speak nonsense, Jack." Meg brushed at her skirted lap, looking past his shoulder, then directly into his mocking gold eyes. "I came out to Kansas to get away from a mean husband, that's all, not from the law or a 'shady past' as you put it. None of which is your business, of course."

He shifted in the saddle, his voice hard. "I just wish your man'd come claim you, get you out of here."

"Don't hold your breath for that to happen because I'm divorcing him," she said quietly, hiding the fear his suggestion brought.

He nodded at her load of stone. "If you're takin' that to Sol Green you might as well keep it—he won't be needin' it."

She went rigid; her eyes flew from Jack to each of his grinning companions and back again. "What do you mean? What've you done to Sol?"

Jack eyed her steadily and he spoke slowly for emphasis, "He drew down on me and I had to stop him from killin' me. After a little discussion, he decided he wants to head back to Missouri."

Nothing in what he had said surprised her, but Meg was infuriated. "You're a mean, hard-hearted, unreasonable fool, Jack Ambler!" She lifted the reins and cracked them over her team's backs, shouting as the wagon jerked into motion, "Leave us folks alone, Jack, or you're going to find yourself rotting in jail with Hammett and Frey!" The chance of Jack's going permanently to jail was so impossible it was laughable, but she had to threaten at least.

119

He turned his horse and pounded up close to her lumbering wagon. She could smell his sweat, sense his grim attitude. "That, Plow Lady, doesn't have a chance in hell of happenin', and you know it!" He swiped his fingers along his hat brim in farewell, then turned back and rejoined his companions.

The wind carried their laughter, grating on her screaming nerves.

Meg drove on through the heat toward Sol's, worrying about what she'd find. Tension made the hair on her head hurt and grew worse when she finally arrived and her eyes took in Sol's place.

Beyond the small sod house, his entire corn field once again was destroyed. Green stalks were trampled into the dust and lay dying in the sun. A few clucking chickens scratched and pecked at the ripped leavings in his bean patch, and noisily relished his smashed melons. A thin milk cow grazed on the other side of the house. There was no sign of Sol or his wife Tilda, outside. Sympathy filled Meg, along with anger.

She got down from the wagon and went up to the house, calling out, "Sol? Mrs. Green?"

The hide door was pulled aside and Tilda Green, a wrinkled, dark little woman, told Meg to come in. "You come with the stone, I reckon," Tilda said. "C'mon in and rest yourself, Miss Brennon. Sol's stove up. Don't knows we'll be needin' the stone, now." She nodded at her husband who lay on a cot in the corner of the room.

Meg hesitated for her eyes to grow accustomed to the dim interior after the brightness outside. When she saw Sol more clearly, she drew a sharp breath. He looked as if the cattle had been driven over him, too. Both eyes were starting to swell shut. There were marks of a beating on his face; blood was caking on his mouth.

He told Meg haltingly through his battered lips, "Sorry . . . you brought the stone . . . all this way. We ain't gonna need it, after all. Jack Ambler ain't gonna let us stay, we got his orders to git off this land."

"But he can't do that, this claim is rightfully yours, you're proving up. Tell me what happened. We can go to the law, have him arrested—"

Meg took the Arbuckle box Tilda offered as a chair, and sat close to Sol's bed. "We've got to keep fighting Jack," she urged him and Tilda. "One of these days he'll know we've won, that we're here to stay, and he's got nothing left to do but back down or spend the rest of his days in jail."

"Won't do no good to fight 'im." Sol touched his tongue to his lip and winced. "Men like Jack's got all the power, the law on their side. I was talkin' to him and reached for my jack-knife to do some whittlin' while we talked. He claimed I was reachin' for a gun, and he did this to me. Said I was lucky he let me live, for what I was tryin' to do. He and his friends will swear before the law that his story's true. Wouldn't do me no good to try an' fight it, tell my side. Ain't no use to fight Jack Ambler."

I've been fighting him for years and he hasn't beaten me yet, Meg thought, but she was sick to death of the fighting. She turned to Sol's wife. "What do you think, Tilda?" The wiry little woman might have more backbone than her husband. She seemed less fearful.

Tilda, in faded peach calico and a long soiled apron, sat on a bench, her bare feet planted on the dirt floor. "I'm plumb tired of movin'. I'd like to stay here if there's a way to stop Jack Ambler from comin' at us. I'll go, though, if that's what Sol wants. It hurts me to see him beat bloody this way."

"It hurts me, too," Meg said, a knot starting to form in her throat, "but I hope you folks will stay. We can fight Jack, to-gether."

Sol was studying his wife's face. "I know you don't want to move no more, Tilda, I don't want to, neither. I reckon we can stay on a while yet, try it anyways. Our chickens an' cow will have to supply our vittles, it's too late to be plantin' crops again this season. I hope you're right, Miss Brennon, that Ambler gets stopped before somebody is kilt."

Meg nodded and said through tightened lips, "We'll stop him." When and how were answers she couldn't give as con-cretely as she'd like to. Holding on was the best she knew how to do, and so far it had worked for Paragon Springs folks.

Two days later, Meg went to check on the Greens. She saw sadly that they'd picked up and left, after all. A forlorn wind whipped around the barren sod shack. The horse and wagon, chickens and cow, were gone. The load of stone she'd brought them was in a pile right where she and Tilda had un-loaded it.

With a heavy sigh, Meg turned for home. She and Admire would come back in the wagon to load it. The stone hadn't been paid for and they might as well take it back for someone else who could use it. As she rode away, she saw three Rocking A cows grazing close to the soddy. Meg was so angry she could hardly see. She dismounted and threw stones at them, screaming until her throat hurt.

A few days after finding that the Greens had abandoned their homestead, a letter arrived for Meg from Hamilton Gibbs. He'd arranged a court date for her; she was to come to St. Louis right away. She read the letter with mixed feelings— excitement and gratitude that the day she'd long awaited had arrived, but dread that she must leave home when things were in such a fearful state.

"Keep watch for trouble from Jack," Meg cautioned her friends when she told them her news from Gibbs. All of them knew by now that Jack had "persuaded" the Greens to quit the country. They'd gathered at Aurelia's for supper and sat at her table discussing the matter. Meg took a sip of coffee. "Go to Sheriff Bassett if you have to, especially if you have something that can be proven against Jack, a watertight case. But whatever you do, don't try any vigilante-type justice, please. Back off if you must, I don't want anyone hurt."

"Let us worry about matters here," Owen told her, pushing his chair back from the table. "You have enough to concern yourself with in St. Louis."

Admire, elbows propped on the table and hands clasped, agreed. "Ain't nobody goin' to get hurt as long as Jack Ambler watches hisself."

"Owen is very levelheaded," Aurelia reminded Meg, "and Admire is, too."

Lucy Ann nodded. "They're good men, they can take care of things."

"I trust you all to do the right thing," Meg told them on a quick breath. "It's just that I trust Jack so little."

The minute Meg stepped off the train in Union Station, she spotted Hamilton Gibbs shouldering his way through the crowd toward her. Her heart gave a surprisingly joyful rush. She scanned the crowd for Ted Malloy, but there was no sign of him. She looked up at Mr. Gibbs as he came over to her. "Hello," she said softly.

He looked at her for a moment. "I'm so glad you're here, I was afraid you might not be able to come. You had a good trip?" he asked, as he took her elbow and guided her toward where the baggage was being unloaded. Heat waves shimmered over the city, and people moved more slowly than usual.

Meg took a handkerchief from her reticule and patted the perspiration from her face. She smiled. "It was tiring, but I'm glad to be here and get this done."

"I've found a room for you at the Sylvan hotel," he told her. "You'll be safer there than in Kerry Patch where Malloy will be watching for you. The hotel isn't far from my boardinghouse and Mrs. Lyle has invited you to take meals with us, if you like, while you're here."

"That'd be nice. And thank you for the hotel arrangement." She frowned, and added politely, "I apologize for putting you to so much trouble."

"It's my job," he said off-handedly.

Meg took this to mean that she wasn't necessarily a special case to him even after their exchange of several letters. Disappointment was so obvious in her soft "Oh" that anyone around them could have detected it and that included Gibbs. Realizing this, Meg hoped he wouldn't think she'd set her cap for him or anything like that. Embarrassed, her face flooded with color.

Behind his glasses there was surprise in his eyes. A quiet, pleased smile played at his mouth. "It was my privilege," he said.

Her bags came and he grabbed them and took her elbow in his other hand. "I have a rig waiting for us across the street."

Gibbs said as they drove toward the hotel, "I wish we could have had our appearance in court before Judge Williams. As I mentioned in my letter, any chance of that was still months off, so that's why I suggested we be heard before Judge Knox, now." His voice was nearly drowned out by the sounds of the city: the rattle of vehicles over brick pavement, a braying donkey hitched to a cart by the curb, the sound of steam whistles from riverboats. He continued, "Judge Knox is a good man, very intelligent, fair—"

"You're frowning, what's the matter with Judge Knox? He won't want to prevent my divorce, will he?" The thought shot worry through her.

Gibbs explained quietly, "Knox has a problem with strong drink, but when he's sober there isn't a better man to know."

Meg asked, dismayed, "He doesn't drink on court days, does he?"

"I'm sorry, but yes, he's been known to. Many judges, and attorneys, imbibe. A fact the public is unaware of, in all likelihood. I'm not privy to their private reasons, but I'd guess that for some men the responsibility—the life-continuing or life-ending decisions they have to make—comes easier with fortification from drink. We're going to hope that Judge Knox has a clear mind for us tomorrow."

Meg nodded. "As I told you in my wire, I didn't want to wait for Judge Williams, although you've made it plain he's the best choice. I can't tell you how much I want this divorce over with. The wait has been insufferably long as it is."

"I understand."

They drove in silence through the main part of town until they arrived at her hotel on a tree-lined avenue, a trip that seemed brief to Meg.

The Sylvan was a three-story, red brick building with a fancy arch decorating its otherwise plain facade. A uniformed attendant hurried out to hold their team while Gibbs helped Meg from the buggy. "May I come back for you in about an hour? That will be suppertime at Mrs. Lyle's."

She'd been afraid she wouldn't see him again until tomorrow. At the same time, she didn't want him to feel beholden, or to see her as a burden. But an evening with Gibbs after a long tedious trip held appeal. "Thank you very much. I'll be ready."

The dining room at Mrs. Lyle's was homey, attractive, and smelled deliciously of homemade bread and other good things. The walls were papered in a soft beige, green, and rose floral. There were potted ferns in front of the windows and a long table covered with a white cloth centered the room. Each corner had a private table. Several boarders were already seated when Meg and Hamilton entered. Two of them were women; the men appeared to be traveling drummers, clerks, or lawyers—like Hamilton.

Hamilton introduced Meg to Mrs. Lyle, a tidy, buxom lady with a warm, friendly smile.

"It's nice to meet you, Mrs. Malloy," Mrs. Lyle said. She led the way to one of the far corner tables. "Now I know you two need to talk, so you come sit over here. I think you'll like supper tonight. It's baked stuffed bass with egg sauce and potato balls, turnip greens, and piping hot biscuits with persimmon preserves."

"It sounds wonderful," Meg told her with a smile, but later, as much as she wanted to enjoy the meal, Meg discovered that she had little appetite.

"If you don't like fish," Gibbs told her quietly, "I know Mrs. Lyle would be happy to bring you something else." He started to rise from his chair but Meg motioned him to sit back down.

"Mrs. Lyle's an excellent cook and I love fish. My family ate a lot of fish—channel cat, trout, bass—when we lived here in Kerry Patch, so close to the river. I seem to have lost my appetite, that's all. I suppose I'm worried about tomorrow—what Ted might do or say, trying to ruin my chances for divorce. But let's talk about something else. Tell me about you, Mr. Gibbs. I've enjoyed your letters so much. Looking forward to them has become quite a habit with me."

He nodded, pleased. "If you'll call me Hamilton, I'll tell you whatever you'd like to know. A first-name basis might not be businesslike but I don't see a need for us to be businesslike every minute."

"No," she said, "I don't feel that's necessary, either. Now, tell me all about you."

"My health is hearty and sound," he said in an important, gruff voice, as he made a crazy face. "I have sharp hearing, let's say that goes well with a sharp mind?"

She laughed with him. "That's not what I meant. No teasing. Tell me where you grew up, what your family was like, where you were educated, things like that."

He was not homely at all when he teased, and when he smiled the change was so dramatic, his sideways grin so charming, that it nearly took her breath away. She sat waiting, her heart thumping in her breast.

"Mine isn't a terribly exciting story," he told her. "I was born on a farm near Clarion, Iowa. My father was the local magistrate—the justice of the peace—as well as being a farmer. My mother was a schoolteacher. My parents married late and were middle-aged when they had my sister Jenny and me. Both of my parents are dead now, as is Jenny. I believe I told you about her?"

Meg nodded soberly. "Yes."

"I still feel partly responsible that I couldn't change her miserable life, couldn't prevent her early death at her husband's hands. Such a tragedy." He shook his head.

"Did he pay for what he did? Go to jail?"

"No, he disappeared when I tried to see him punished. The local sheriff made a halfhearted attempt to track him down, then when he couldn't find him, he forgot the case and went on to other matters. Jenny's husband never had to pay, unless he repeated the same abuse on some other woman and she killed him. That's what he deserved." His voice had grown harsh with pain.

"I would've liked to have known Jenny and helped her," Meg said softly. She reached over and touched Hamilton's arm. "I'm really sorry."

"I refuse to let it happen to you!" He thumped the table with his knuckles and his usually kind eyes flashed with angry determination.

"It won't happen to me, Hamilton, I promise you that."

He took his hand from hers and shook his head. "We can't be sure. I worry what Malloy might try when no one's around to protect you. My biggest fear is that he'll harm you before we have a chance to make your divorce legal."

"You're doing all you can, and more." She hesitated. "Are you married, Mr. Gibbs?" He was so sympathetic to women, she was suddenly sure he must be betrothed, or married. Maybe she'd been forward in asking, but he didn't seem to mind.

"I'm not married, and there are no such plans in my life at the moment. I don't believe I'm the type to appeal to most women."

She barely contained her surprise. "What do you mean?" She wanted to protest his suggestion to the skies. She found him very appealing, could give him a whole litany of special qualities she saw in him.

"I've been a bookworm from the day I learned to read," he explained. "You can see for yourself that nature failed to notice me when good looks were handed out. I dress 'frumpy', Mrs. Lyle says, although she tries to make suggestions now and then." He pushed his spectacles back further on his nose and said, embarrassed but forthright, "I've always been shy around women because of the way I look, and also because

I've not had a lot of time for . . . courting. For years I've devoted myself to the study and practice of law."

"Where did you study?" She asked quickly, afraid he was about to end the conversation.

"I saw leaving Iowa as a great adventure, although I certainly didn't travel far," he told her in his deep pleasant voice. "I studied law here in St. Louis." A furrow creased his brow. "Maybe if I'd stayed closer to home in Iowa, I could've kept better track of Jenny—well, never mind, I've said enough about that." He cleared his throat and his smile returned. "At the same time I went to school to study law, I apprenticed with a practicing attorney. I swept out his office, cleaned his cuspidor, did other menial tasks. Didn't mind it much, though, because being with him gave me the opportunity to read every word in his law library. I became familiar with trial procedure, attended court, learned the knack of pleading cases and filling out legal papers. I met most of the leading lawyers in St. Louis, then eventually completed my studies and passed the bar. But—" he didn't finish.

"But what?"

"I'm proud of my practice, I take a lot of satisfaction in helping folks with their legal problems. But the work is often tedious, heartbreaking, frustrating. I've worked so hard for so long that I've not made a lot of close friends, certainly not many women friends. I wouldn't mind changing that. I'd welcome a less lonely life."

She thought that could happen sooner than he might guess. Now that he'd established his practice and built a fine reputation, he might find more time for leisure, for women friends. She was sure he would meet someone special.

Mrs. Lyle came to their table. "Didn't want to pester you folks, you seemed to be having such a nice talk, but would you be wanting dessert? I have some apple cobbler with pouring cream. I'll bring you some, if you like."

Meg spoke up, "I've had a lot on my mind and I'm afraid I didn't do justice to your fine fish dinner, Mrs. Lyle. I'm feeling better, now, and I'd love some of that cobbler."

"I'd like some, too, Mrs. Lyle," Hamilton said with a wide grin.

It had been a long day, the final leg of her trip from home, settling in her hotel room, and then supper with Hamilton. When they had finished their dessert she asked him to take her back to her room. "I'd like to turn in early," she told him. "I want a good night's rest before I walk into that courtroom tomorrow."

They arranged to meet at the courthouse for their ten o'clock hearing. Hamilton needed to be there early, but he would send a driver to escort her.

Meg had difficulty sleeping that night, from worrying about what might happen in the courtroom. Ted was not to be trusted. He was slick, cruel, and determined to control her as long as it might help him in any way.

She arrived at the courtroom twenty minutes early. She'd thought Hamilton might be waiting for her, but there was no sign of him or of Ted. Worry settled like a cold hand around her heart. Everything felt *wrong,* as though she had come on the wrong day or was in the wrong city. She found a chair outside the courtroom where Hamilton had said their hearing would be held.

"Meg?"

Hamilton poked his head around the door and motioned her to come. "It's time." He whispered as he took her arm and led her into the courtroom, "Are you all right?"

She nodded. Words wouldn't come to her dry throat at the moment.

"Have you seen Malloy?" he asked.

"No," she said huskily, "I haven't."

"He'd better come!"

They sat down at the counsel table and waited. The court clerk, a pimply young man in a dark suit, and the only other person in the room, sat patiently at a small table below the judge's vacant bench. The room was austere and so quiet that the slightest sound—the movement of an arm, or someone clearing his throat—echoed. Ten minutes passed, then fifteen, then surely twenty, Meg surmised. Hamilton looked at some papers in front of him. Now and then he turned to smile encouragement at her. Meg managed a shaky smile in return.

Where was the judge? Where was Ted?

After a while, Hamilton removed his watch from his vest pocket and looked at it. His brows rose and he looked angry. "The judge is a half-hour late," he said quietly, "and damned if I know where Malloy is. Pardon my language."

She shrugged that his words didn't bother her at all in comparison to everything else. Finally, the door off to the right opened and a man in a judge's black gown entered from his chambers. A small, gray-haired man, he held his head high, his steps determined but uneven as he moved toward the bench.

Meg's heart sank. Dismay came in a flood.

The judge missed the step up to his platform the first time he tried. He lifted his foot again, way out of reason, and almost fell forward on his face, gripping the bench just in time to pull himself up and into his chair.

"Damn!" Hamilton muttered under his breath. He reached over and caught Meg's hand and squeezed.

The judge sat stiffly upright and looked out at them. "Hamilton Gibbs, nice to see you. Shall we get started?" He tapped his gavel and it spun out of his hand, clattering onto the floor.

Tears filled Meg's eyes. If the man didn't hold her life, her entire future, in his hands, she might have chuckled in gentle sympathy. As it was, she was furious, devastated.

Beside her, Hamilton got to his feet. "Your honor," he said to the judge, "the defendant isn't here. And sir, I don't believe you're feeling well. I recommend that we postpone this hearing."

The judge reared back and tried to focus his eyes on Hamilton, then Meg. He nodded and wiped his mouth with the back of his hand. "Trial postponed!" he ordered.

Hamilton nodded at the clerk, who jumped to his feet and helped the judge from the bench and back to his chambers.

A thick, painful silence followed.

"This is not how it was supposed to be!" Meg cried around the anger and pain in her throat. Tears of disappointment and fury stung her eyes.

Hamilton Gibbs looked sorrowful and sick. "This is my fault," he said, "I shouldn't have gone ahead; I knew this might happen with Knox. I should've recommended that we wait for Judge Williams."

She shook her head, looking at him through a film of tears. "It's not your fault any more than it's mine. I insisted we go ahead in Judge Knox's court. I just didn't dream that he'd be sopping drunk, and that Ted or his lawyer wouldn't even bother to come at all!" She dashed a hand at her tears. "Life can be so unfair at times!"

She struggled against throwing herself into Gibbs's arms for comfort, but a second later, forgot propriety and flung herself against him. His arms tightened around her and the thud of his heart sounded against her ear. Her pain began to ease with his words, spoken close and sympathetically, "I wouldn't have done this to you, Meg, for anything. I'm so sorry."

She was in his arms for only a moment but it was enough to give her back her strength. She moved away, smiled at him, and nodded.

He gathered up his papers, and holding her hand, he led her from the empty courtroom.

Chapter Ten

They drove through the busy streets in hot, late summer sunshine back to her hotel. Hamilton continued to apologize, "I'm so sorry, Meg, I know how much you counted on having this over with. You left your home, traveled so far, and for nothing. This is all my fault."

"No, it isn't. We both did what we thought was best." She touched his arm. "Let's put what happened behind us, forget it, and go ahead from here. I have no choice but to wait for another day in court. In the meantime, I must return to Paragon Springs. Let's wait for Judge Williams, no matter how long it takes. Judge Knox may be an able official when sober, but I don't want to take another chance with him."

"Don't blame you for that. And I'll make sure Malloy is in court next time if I have to bring him in in shackles." He studied her for a long moment and his kindly eyes sparkled. "You're remarkable and quite lovely, Meg, if a homely fellow like me may tell you that."

"Of course I don't mind. A woman likes to hear such things, even when they aren't entirely true." She pulled off her gloves and showed her calloused brown hands, and they chuckled together. His own features, she thought, held a quiet dignity and intelligence that added up to so much more than typical good looks.

"You know," his expression grew more solemn, "I think it might be best if I accompany you back to your home."

Her eyes rounded in surprise. "All the way to Paragon Springs? Hamilton, that's ridiculous." She used his given

134

name so easily that it surprised them both and there was a fraction of silence.

His expression turned grave. "I'm worried about you. Malloy could be anywhere; he could be watching us this moment, just waiting for me to leave you. I'd feel better if I could see you safely back to Kansas. Yes, all the way there," he finished emphatically.

She shook her head. "In the first place, I wouldn't dream of taking you away from your work for that long. We both know you're busy, that I'm not your sole client. In the second place, I've been in dangerous situations many times before and managed to get out of them. I've taken care of myself for ages. It isn't necessary for you to do that, Hamilton."

In the end, he agreed to let her return home unescorted, but he didn't like it.

In the cool dawn next day, he was seeing her off at the train. He told her, "You're admirably independent, Meg, but the day may come when you'll have to depend on someone else to look out for you."

"I understand, and when that day comes, I might even like it," she answered with a mischievous laugh.

"Good-bye, then, until we get another chance to go to court." He held her hand a moment while noise and confusion swirled around them, the huge locomotive belched steam and smoke, and the sun turned the sky to the east rose-red.

"Yes, good-bye until our chance comes again." Travelers were thronging toward the passenger cars and Meg was bumped and nearly knocked off her feet. "Oops!" She laughed ruefully as she regained her balance with Hamilton's aid. It was time for her to board, and yet she felt deep reluctance to leave his company.

In those waning seconds she recognized that her feelings

were beyond anything to do with their professional relationship, or casual friendship. She was falling in love with him!

Suddenly dismayed by the prospect, she reminded herself as she headed for the steps to her train car that it would be very foolish to mistake his kindness toward her as anything more than that. And didn't she have enough already in her life to concern herself with?

She boarded her car, and took a quick look back at him. If she didn't take care, she'd be experiencing a whole new sort of heartbreak.

The cold months of winter dragged by. Infrequent trips were made to Dodge City to pick up the mailbag for Paragon Springs and vicinity. There were letters for Meg from Hamilton, but a new court date for them had not been set and there were days she felt that she might never be divorced.

Spring arrived with a sweet newness that as always gave a glad lift to her spirits. Wildflowers dotted the plains; the sky was so blue and the sun so bright, her eyes watered the day she drove her wagon to make a delivery of live young turkeys to Rudy Bosch, a new homesteader from Bavaria who had located up near the Hesslers' claim. On the way she met Will Hessler, out searching on horseback for a lost cow due to calve. She told Will of her mission and he informed her that she wouldn't find Bosch at his homestead.

"But where's he gone to, when did Mr. Bosch leave?" Meg asked above the noise the turkeys were making behind her in the wagon. Even without the facts, a sad premonition filled her.

"Bosch's been gone a week or two. Don't know where to," Will told her. He lifted his hat and ran a hand through his blond hair; his mouth tightened. "But my money says Jack Ambler convinced Bosch he had no right to his claim."

"But he did have a right! I helped Mr. Bosch locate that claim. What do you mean about Jack?"

"I know that Jack visited him couple of times because Bosch told me. He said Jack was sayin' that only an American citizen can claim land under the homestead law and Bosch is Dutchy, a foreigner. Bosch understood that if a man declared his intention to become a citizen, that was good enough to allow him to file on land. Jack argued that was just talk, and not so. I told Bosch he was right, that he could claim his land on intention to become a citizen, the same as other foreigners to these parts have. But Jack wore him down. He told Bosch that he wasn't a cattleman, anyhow, that he'd be better off to get a factory job in Topeka. Western Kansas wasn't a healthy place for him."

"What a dirty trick! Rudy Bosch had applied for citizenship, I'm positive. He would've been a fine addition to the valley. He was a hard worker, decent." Meg raised her voice to be heard over the squawking turkeys. "Look at the improvements he made on his claim in such a short time: a well dug, ten acres under cultivation. He planned to raise poultry if he could keep the coyotes and wolves away. He was going to provide the rest of us with chicks and eggs. I wonder, if he learns the truth, will he be back?"

"Don't think so," Will said, his blue eyes earnest. "He got tired of Jack browbeating him. Weather troubles an' all are enough to put up with out here, without another man's constant pestering that a body isn't wanted. Bosch just couldn't take it anymore, he was a gentle-hearted man. He signed over his claim to one of Jack's men who'll turn around and deed the land to Jack."

Meg was furious. After telling Will good-bye, she continued on to Bosch's claim to see for herself if what he said was true, that Rudy was truly gone. No one was about, but

Rocking A cattle flecked the land as far as she could see. She peeked inside the soddy and saw a half-empty bottle of whiskey and a pack of cards on the table; a skillet on the cookstove had remnants of gravy congealed around the rim. On the floor by the cot was a gunnysack that no doubt held the Rocking A hand's private possessions.

All Rudy Bosch's hard work had gone for nought.

Jack Ambler had gotten away with this outrageous lie behind her back. Who knew what else he was up to whenever she had to be away, or was holed up at home due to bad weather? She wanted so much to put an end to his skulduggery. At some point he had to be convinced that he couldn't possess the whole valley, that others had a right to be there as much as he did.

With the crates of gabbling young turkeys bouncing in the wagonbed behind her, Meg turned her wagon northeast. She passed other abandoned claims on the way to the Rocking A ranch. Jack's cattle grazed around the caved-in wells, the tumbled-down sod shacks. Garden patches were fast reverting to sod.

Jack picked on newcomers, mostly, finding those entrenched after years of toil harder to drive away. But if he found a way, he'd uproot all of the farmers.

Meg was steaming with anger by the time she parked her wagon in front of Ambler's rambling ranch house. A breeze sang through the cottonwood trees that sheltered the main buildings; a horse down in the corral blew and whinnied and Pete whinnied back.

Dinah opened the door to her knock. Surprise, then delight, filled her face. "Meg, do come in! What a pleasure to see you!"

"I'm afraid I haven't come on a friendly call. Is Jack home? I must talk to him." She couldn't hide her exasperation, her fury. And she liked Dinah, had nothing against her.

"He's not home," Dinah said, frowning. "Come sit down. I'll fetch us some lemonade and you can tell me what's wrong."

A few minutes later Meg explained about Rudy Bosch, how Jack had lied about Bosch's citizenship to get rid of him. She told Dinah about Sol Green, how he'd been beaten up on a pretext and frightened so badly that he and his wife Tilda had given up on their claim and left. "I don't know what to do, Dinah, but Jack can't keep this up. He's ruining the lives of good people who don't deserve it."

"No," Dinah shook her head, "he can't continue to hurt folks this way. I'm sorry for those folks, Meg. And I'm ashamed of Jack, truly. I don't know if he will listen to me, but I'll try talking to him again. I doubt I'll have much luck, because I know Jack is convinced he's in the right, and that immigrants to this land he calls his are in the wrong."

"I hope he'll listen to you," Meg said. "I don't want to do anything that will hurt you, or Jack, even, but I will look out for my friends. They have a right to move here, a right to stay."

Dinah walked her outside a while later. "What's that funny noise?" she craned for a better look at the crates in Meg's wagon.

"Young turkeys that Mr. Bosch ordered, that I was unable to deliver. I guess I'll give them to Lucy Ann Walsh. If she can keep the coyotes and wolves out of their pen, she'll love raising them."

As the women hugged good-bye, Dinah said again, "I'm so sorry about this, Meg."

"It's got to stop, it's just got to," Meg said grimly. She climbed into her wagon and took up the reins. For miles she drove in deep reflection.

Almost from the moment of her arrival in those parts, she'd acted as an unofficial land agent, showing home seekers where they might find the best free land in the valley. She'd given them information on how to file for their claims at the land office in Larned. She'd never charged a fee, believing that her efforts to aid land-hungry strangers were a service to them all, as every new inhabitant increased the value of the country and brought neighbors. With settlement there would eventually be schools, churches, and convenient businesses.

But hardship, bad weather, and Jack's skulduggery sent more homesteaders packing out than settling in for the long term. Holding settlers to that part of the country was like trying to keep water in a leaky pot.

She looked around her at the miles of wide empty spaces, untouched, unused except for scattered Rocking A cattle grazing on the wild buffalo grass, the gramma grass. It was land enough for all, if Ambler would just be fair.

In a while, a few miles above her own property, Meg came to the claim of a homesteader she'd helped locate, the claim now abandoned like so many others. D. B. Glover, a reedy, stoop-shouldered Civil War veteran with a constant bad cough, had been willing to battle hot winds, droughts, grasshoppers, coyotes, and blizzards, if in five years he could own his own quarter-section. He planned to ask a distant cousin back in Indiana to come west and be his wife. But Glover hadn't counted on a fight with Jack Ambler.

One night, some of Jack's men had smoked Glover out of his soddy by creeping up and pouring sulphur and gun powder down the chimney onto the coals in Glover's cookstove. There was heavy smoke, then a terrible explosion that sent dirt, pots and pans, and other belongings flying about in Glover's house. One of Jack's men, lariat in hand, was waiting when Glover burst through the door. Glover had a choice, to be strung by a rope from the ridgepole of his damaged house, or to take off down the road and not come back. He chose to leave.

Jack had taken over with no legal right to the land, believing power and possession were enough to hold it. She flicked the reins over Pete's back and clicked her tongue to hurry him home.

She wanted to be ready by first light tomorrow for a trip to the land office at Larned. She'd have to be gone for days, but she thought the government folks in Larned ought to know what Jack was doing. She was sure Jack wouldn't want a lawsuit against him. If he released his illegal claims, honest settlers could then have them.

Meg tied her rig at the hitching rail in front of the Larned land office and went in. There were several men and a woman waiting in line; another woman came in to stand behind Meg. She was as tall as a man and towered over Meg, who smiled at her briefly and then turned back to business.

Meg was relieved to see that the agent behind the desk was the one who'd taken care of her papers when she got legal title to her share of Paragon Springs. She liked Stowe McCormack. A man of slight build, wise-looking behind his spectacles, he was very efficient, and he treated everybody fairly, not just a few.

When it came her turn, Meg offered her hand, "Mr. McCormack, I realize you see hundreds of people passing through this office, but perhaps you remember me—Meg Brennon. I took property in trade, north of Dodge City and south of the Pawnee River."

He studied her for several seconds, then he smiled. Whether truthful or not, he said, "Yes, yes, I remember you. What can I do for you today, Miss Brennon?"

She explained her interest in bringing development to the country around Paragon Springs, how for some time she'd aided immigrants in locating claims.

"I know, I know! Folks mention you when they come in to file on the land you've shown them. You're providing a very important service, Miss Brennon."

So he did know who she was. Grateful, she still hesitated, then told him, "Perhaps I am helping these people, Mr. McCormack, but not without difficulty, and some tragedy, I'm afraid." His brow puckered while she told him, without mentioning Jack by name, "Settlers in my area are being forced dishonestly and violently off their rightful claims." She described what had happened to Sol Green, to the Bavarian Rudy Bosch, and to D. B. Glover, who'd fought in the Civil War and had only wanted to be a simple farmer.

The more she talked, the deeper McCormack's frown grew. He pushed his spectacles back tighter on his nose. "That's very serious. Have these gentlemen requested help from the law?"

She shook her head.

"Well, have them come to see me. We'll take care of this."

"They were afraid to go to the law, and I can't send them here. I don't know where they've gone; they've left the country."

"I see."

"Could you send a government employee to investigate the graft and claim-jumping taking place in my area, so that it doesn't continue? Settlers there don't feel secure in going to the law to complain; they're convinced they wouldn't win. The strong stay and resist being pushed, the weak flee. I'm afraid there are more of the latter." She hesitated, thoughtful, and took a deep breath. "We've considered organizing a homesteaders' league as has been done in other areas. But we're afraid that might turn into vigilante violence, all-out war, and the last thing we want is bloodshed."

"Of course. We don't want shootings or loss of life over claim disputes. We're the law, and we can straighten this out. We're shorthanded and very busy, but I'm going to see that a government spotter is sent to your area to investigate."

Meg sighed in relief and again gave him her hand. "I appreciate that very much. There are some good people in my country; I'd like them to have the peaceful lives they deserve, and not be under constant threat of being chased away."

The tall, expensively dressed woman behind her touched her arm. Her smile was warm and friendly. "I overheard what you told the agent. I'd like to have a claim out your way. The name is Miss Levant, Kate Levant."

Meg took her hand. "Meg Brennon." She hesitated. "You must've heard we're having trouble there? It wouldn't be easy—"

"If I can have my own place, I'll do what it takes to hang on to it. I heard you, and I'm prepared."

The woman did look as though she could handle anything that came along. "Fine, Miss Levant. Come look me up when you get there." She gave her directions to the hamlet of Paragon Springs. "We're not a town, just a store and post office. But we intend to grow."

The woman smiled and nodded. "You'll see me there." Then Meg helped Kate Levant file on Sol and Tilda Green's abandoned claim.

A week and a half later, Kate Levant rode into Dodge City and bought her own rig, an extra saddle horse, furniture and other household goods, and a milk cow. She seemed to have enough money. Meg warned her to stay armed in case of trouble from Jack, who would consider the claim his. Kate said that would be no trouble and Meg didn't doubt her.

The Fourth of July came and went, celebrated by Paragon Springs folks and their neighbors with a picnic on the banks of the Pawnee. Meg's corn and melon patches were thriving. She spent long days scything wild gramma to make hay and tumbled into bed each night dead tired, but satisfied that her stock would be fed come winter, regardless of weather tantrums. She lived for letters from Hamilton, and the mailbag's arrival from Dodge City was always an exciting event because he wrote often.

She was in her room reading Hamilton's latest letter—he didn't yet have a second court date for them—when Aurelia knocked, telling her from the other side of the door that Jack Ambler waited outside to see her.

"Jack?" Meg stood up quickly from her rocking chair. It rocked, empty, while she took a deep breath and pulled herself together. She'd been expecting this.

Aurelia poked her head in the door. "He's mad as a wet hen!" she hissed. "So be careful."

"I will." Meg took her time putting the letter away, and then went out to meet Jack. Wind stirred dust in the store yard, locusts zinged in the cottonwood tree. She invited him to get down from his horse, the prancy sorrel he usually rode, and come inside for coffee, but he refused. "Whatever you say," she said calmly, and waited.

"You turned me in, didn't you?" he stormed, the veins on his forehead standing out as though they would burst. "You went to the government and told them to investigate me!"

"I might've mentioned to someone that some graft was going on around here, but Jack, I swear I didn't mention that you were involved." She gave him a tight smile. "Not to protect you, mind, I just thought with a little hint those men'd find out for themselves what you're up to. Maybe your own illegal doings found you out, do you suppose?"

"Damn you! They've thrown me—my cattle and my men—off land that ought to be mine. Fools had the damn nerve to threaten lawsuit if I don't keep my cattle from the range I need. I'm not having my grazin' lands cut down to the size of a little old cow pasture. I've got to have grass for my herds."

"You can't have this whole valley, Jack. It isn't yours, no matter what you think you need it for. Other settlers have a right to their own pieces of land."

"This is not farm country, it's cattle country. Small farmers can't make it here, and they wouldn't try if you'd stop encouragin' em! You've been the one all along that keeps bringing grangers in. They stay a miserable season or two, only to fail."

"Many of those folks didn't fail, they got pushed out by you."

"They shouldn't have come in the first place."

"They have a right to make a life here if they can, Jack, and I have a right to help them if I choose. I see it as my bounden duty."

"I'm goin' to see you in hell before I let you ruin my range, Meg Brennon."

A shiver raced along her spine, but she spoke calmly, still wishing to reason with him. "Merciful heaven, Jack, why can't you see that we could all live here together just fine if you'd stop making trouble? Your wife understands that, why can't you?"

Mentioning Dinah was like lighting a match to a powder keg but it was too late. Meg couldn't retract the remark.

He gritted, "Dinah has nothin' to do with this. She doesn't understand what I'm tryin' to do, but she will in time if you leave her alone. I don't want her comin' here to Paragon Springs, and I don't want you comin' to my place to see her again, either!"

Meg started to tell him that his wife had a right to go where she pleased and see whom she pleased and so did Meg, but he was whipping his horse about and filling her face with dust before she could get out another word. His threat to see her in hell before he'd give up the range stuck in her mind like a cactus thorn.

After another week of worrying about what Jack might do, Meg returned to Larned and secured Stowe McCormack's aid in making her a real representative of his land office. She'd continue doing what she'd always done, keeping track of available claims and helping land-seekers to file on them, but now she'd be official. That gave her the power to advertise land, and her services. She lost no time in sending Hamilton Gibbs an advertisement to place for her in the St. Louis papers.

Jack wasn't going to like it, but if she got enough folks to settle, together they'd have more power against his bullying.

Hamilton did as she asked but wrote back expressing his concern. He had nothing but admiration for her, he wrote, but what she was doing was dangerous. Men became violent over land. Claim jumpers, he understood, would try to seize control for the price of a bullet.

She wrote back that she'd be fine, and silently prayed that it would turn out to be true.

Chapter Eleven

Meg was at her desk in the back corner of the mercantile checking her ledgers and feeling guilty that she wasn't out with her own cradle helping to scythe wheat. The Paragon Springs families' small patches of wheat, oats, and rye this summer combined to make forty or fifty acres. Until they could afford machinery, they harvested grain by methods used since the beginning of time: scythe and flail, then winnowing in the wind to separate the chaff from the grain.

Owen, Admire, and Lad were cutting in the terrible heat today; perhaps she could get out and help them tomorrow. In the meantime there were her business records to bring to date. Plus, just yesterday she'd picked up two wires in Dodge City in response to her ad in the *St. Louis Dispatch* for land opportunity and she wanted to answer them. She also owed Hamilton a letter. It had gotten to be a habit to write to one another the simple events of their lives, whether or not there was real news.

As she scanned the figures and notes in front of her, she was distracted by Aurelia noisily rearranging goods in the store section and dusting with a vengeance. Aurelia had looked dour all morning. Meg was afraid Aurelia was going to upset the pickle barrel if she didn't decide its final location soon.

A handful of customers had shopped briefly; their decision not to dawdle might be due to Aurelia's bad mood.

When Meg couldn't stand the tension in the room another minute she laid her pen aside and asked, "For pity's sake, Aurelia, what's the matter?"

For a moment Aurelia didn't answer; then, dusting a shelf of canned goods furiously, she told Meg, "Owen asked me again last night to marry him."

Meg smiled tentatively, knowing how Aurelia felt. "But that's good news."

"Not really, I had to tell him no again. It bothers me to upset him over and over."

Then stop! Meg sighed and took a moment before asking, "Did he give you an ultimatum?" She half hoped so; she was sure that if Aurelia were tested, she'd give in to Owen and they'd finally get married and be very happy.

"No, he doesn't try to force me. I just wish he'd stop asking. It's hurts us both to go through it, over and over. I don't know why he can't leave things as they are."

"Maybe because he wants to be your husband, Aurelia! My goodness, if you're not going to marry him, why don't you just let the poor man go. Cut him loose."

"Go? Cut him loose?" Aurelia froze, deeply shocked. "I don't want him to . . . go."

"Why not, because you love him?"

"Y-yes," she admitted, "I care for him very much. I couldn't bear it if he—wasn't around at all."

"You love him, he loves you. Why can't you go ahead and get married? Live like a normal married couple? You'd be a lot happier, both of you, and all this fussing could stop." Meg scribbled like mad as she added a list of figures. She made a mistake, scribbled it out, dipped her pen and tried again. She massaged her forehead, trying to think.

Aurelia came over to her desk, dustcloth limp in her hand. "I'm afraid, Meg. I'm more scared of marrying again than you have any idea. If Owen and I were . . . *attached* and he left me, or d-died the way my first husband, John, did, I don't know what I'd do. I'm just not going to take the chance of that."

Meg pointed her pen at Aurelia. "All right, suit yourself, dear. But mark my words, as long as you keep Owen at arm's length, you're making a mistake, a big one."

"Well, it's my business," Aurelia replied stiffly.

"Yes, it is. But all morning you've looked like you drank spoiled milk and a friend worries about you."

Aurelia's expression softened and she looked back at Meg, a trace of guilt in her eyes. "I know you worry about me, Meg, and I know you care. I'd like to take your advice, but I can't bring myself to make this big step."

"Owen would be a wonderful father to your children."

Aurelia's expression brightened. "He already treats them like they're his sons, his daughter. Why—" Aurelia started to tell of an incident, then stopped. "I suppose I am foolish not to marry him. I debate the matter in my head. Sometimes it makes sense, but I doubt very much that I'll ever, *ever* change my mind."

Meg was about to tell her to stop debating and look in her heart, but at that moment, Aurelia saw something outside, through the window. She rushed to the door of the store and yanked it open. "You boys, you stop that right now!"

"What is it?" Meg joined her at the open door. Shafer Lee and Aurelia's boys, Joshua and David John, had ridden in from their herding chores to take their noon dinner and get a drink of water. She was hoping that a couple of them could give a hand in the wheat this afternoon.

In the yard, the trio, their homespun clothes dirty and sweaty, danced back from a rattlesnake that Shafer, recently turned fifteen, teased with a stick. The snake coiled, lifted its head, and hissed, tongue flashing. Shafer stuck his booted foot at it and laughed. Joshua and David John, not quite as old and daring as Shafer, looked worriedly at their mother and backed away.

"Confound those boys!" Meg muttered and went to get Owen's Spencer rifle, kept above a shelf in the store. She marched outside.

"Shafer Lee, you're going to get bit one of these days!" Meg scolded, carrying the loaded rifle out into the yard. She ordered the boys, "Stand back." She lifted the carbine, aimed, and fired. The snake's head went spinning into the dust, the body writhed a second longer and was still. "Sorry to spoil your fun," Meg glared at Shafer, "but I'd like to keep you alive." She pointed the carbine at the snake. "Now get that thing out of here."

Shafer was still snickering as he picked up the dead snake and headed behind the store with it. Joshua and David John followed, looking back over their shoulders at Meg and Aurelia.

Meg shook her head. None of them were quite sure when Shafer had begun to show his daredevil streak. When he'd come there with his mother and his twin Selinda, and his grandfather, he was just one of the boys, not much different from the others. The first sign of trouble had come when he didn't want to do his full share of chores unless it was dangerous work: facing down a mad cow, or riding an ornery horse. Anything tame was a bore. The other boys constantly harped that Shafer loafed and got into tom-foolery, making their own load greater, which unfortunately was the truth.

Beside Meg, Aurelia spoke up. "Emmaline spoils the boy, that's the problem."

"I know. She tries to get him to behave, but he just doesn't listen, and she doesn't want to push him too hard. She worries that it's his nature to be a little different."

"Because of his Indian blood? Pooh, that's just an excuse; he's only a quarter Cheyenne, after all. He needs a strop to his backside, that would set him straight."

"Like you beat your boys, Aurelia?" Meg asked, hesitating on the entry doorstone before going inside.

"I don't beat them because I don't need to!" Aurelia plucked a hollyhock blossom from the flower bed by the doorway and brought it inside.

"And Emmaline doesn't want to beat Shafer, either," Meg turned to tell her. "She's doing the best she can with him. I feel sorry for her, alone with two children to raise. Luckily, Selinda is well behaved and doesn't give her trouble."

Aurelia mused, "Emmaline's husband went to Montana to search for gold, didn't he, and then just vanished? She's probably fears losing Shafer like that." She looked more understanding and shook her head sympathetically. She poured a dipper of water into an empty tomato can, added the hollyhock blossom, and placed it on the counter.

"I'd guess losing her husband that way is at least part of the reason Emmaline treats Shafer as she does," Meg agreed, hesitating before returning to her desk. "I'm sure she'd give her right arm if her man had never gone, if he was with her now. A boy like Shafer needs a father's hand."

"Lord knows what it's all going to come to," Aurelia said. "Persia's here," she changed the subject, nodding toward the window and outside where a wagon driven by the short, stout woman in a sunbonnet was pulling in. "She must be here for her and her neighbors' mail, and maybe for flour or sugar; she's bought enough shot to outfit an army."

Two days later, Emmaline came to Meg's quarters at the mercantile to speak with her about Shafer. "He's furious with me," she said. There was a shine of tears in her eyes. "He may never speak to me again."

"What's wrong, what's happened?" Meg motioned for Emmaline to take the rocking chair, and she sat on the edge of her bed. Whatever the trouble with Shafer, it couldn't be totally unexpected, she thought, massaging her forehead as she waited for Emmaline to explain.

Emmaline rocked for a moment, "Shafer, without my knowledge, has made friends with some of Jack Ambler's riders from the Rocking A."

"Oh." Meg wasn't sure why she wasn't more surprised. "That's not very good," she said quietly, "although some of Jack's men aren't bad fellows."

"Shafer's asked my permission to let him go with them to Colorado on a wild horse hunt. He's too young to ride with those rowdies; I told him no."

"You did the right thing, Emmaline."

"He hates me for it, though." Emmaline cleared her throat and blotted her eyes on the handkerchief she kept tucked in her sleeve. "I'd like for him to be more like Aurelia's boys, and like Lad Voss who studies hard and works hard, but Shafer just isn't like that. He doesn't enjoy reading the way I do, or painting and drawing, the way Selinda does. He hates chores. All he wants to do is ride steers and race horses. I honestly don't know what's going to become of him."

"He's still a boy, he may be altogether different when he's a grown man."

Emmaline shook her head. "I don't think so. I'm afraid Shafer will always be the way he is, and I might have to let him be what he wants. I just don't want anything bad to happen to him. Those riders from the Rocking A are going to be gone weeks. Shafer would be neglecting his work here. I had to put my foot down."

"He'll get over being angry," Meg said consolingly, going over to grasp Emmaline's shoulder. She leaned down to hug her. "Everything will be all right."

In truth, she wasn't sure at all about her prediction. Shafer was different from the other children. All of them liked adventure, fun, excitement, but Shafer thrived on it; it seemed to be his life.

Because his mother wouldn't let him go to Colorado with Ambler's men, Shafer sulked and simmered darkly for a day, then returned to his same laughing, devil-may-care self. Owen caught him carrying around a live rattlesnake in a lard can. Shafer was wanting to throw it to one of the other boys to see if he could catch the can and not get bitten. Owen took it away and let him know in no uncertain terms what would happen if he pulled such a stunt again.

The commotion had brought the women outside just as Shafer was about to throw the can to Joshua. They had watched the incident in shocked horror. As Owen took care of the matter, Meg gave Aurelia a look that said: *See how it would be if you had Owen to manage things?*

Aurelia's return look said: *I already have him; he's here and he took care of it.*

It would be easier to make plum preserves outdoors and all at once, Meg and her friends had decided, after days of picking the fruit that grew wild by the river. Over an open fire in the yard by the mercantile, the plums cooked in a large iron kettle, sending out a wonderful smell. A work table had been brought outside and clean crocks, already washed in a tub of suds, waited to be filled with the preserves. Melted beeswax would be used to seal the crocks filled with congealing fruit.

Shafer Lee had sneaked out during the night two days before, leaving his bed untouched, and all the women worried with Emmaline.

"He'll be back," Meg said to ease Emmaline's mind. She waved a dishtowel, shooing flies away from the sweet-smelling jam. "Owen will do his best to find him and bring him back. If Owen misses him, and Shafer follows the horse hunters all the way to Colorado, he'll be safer with them than by himself." She added encouragingly, "And he's learning a trade, kind of, breaking the horses and bringing them home."

"I don't know," Emmaline said sadly, taking her turn stirring the concoction in the large iron kettle. She held her skirts back from the fire; perspiration dripped down the sides of her smooth face. "I don't know why Shafer worries me so. I ordered him to stay home, and he defied me. I pray he won't get hurt. I'm so sorry, Aurelia, that Owen had to go looking for him—I know you need Owen here." Owen now spent the days helping to thresh, doing the heavier work at the store at night.

Aurelia, chipping beeswax into a kettle, didn't comment.

It was late afternoon and the last of the preserves were being poured when Lucy Ann, helping to clean up the day's mess, spotted the spiral of dust coming from the south. "Look there. Somebody's coming on horseback," she called to the others.

"Riding hard, from Dodge," Meg looked up to comment. She frowned.

The women stopped and shaded their eyes, and watched the rider come. "Whoever he is, he's got bad news, or he just rides his horse to death for the fun of it," Meg said thinly. Her skirts whipped in the hot wind, and she held them down. She wiped perspiration from her brow.

"Is it Shafer?" Emmaline asked hopefully. A moment later, "It's him, it's Shafer! What on earth . . . ?"

He arrived in a cloud of dust, skidding his horse to a stop and flying out of the saddle to the ground in front of his mother. He threw his arms around her neck before she could say a word.

She hugged him hard, then pulled his arms free and frowned at him. "You were in Dodge City? You left and didn't tell me? We thought you were on your way to Colorado, the other direction. I've been worried sick about you."

He shook his head. His eyes were shining and he was short of breath. "Went to get you a present, Ma, to make up for giving you trouble about Colorado." He shoved a small object into an astonished Emmaline's hands. She gasped as she looked at the beautiful black shell hair ornament studded with garnets.

"Where did you get it? How did you pay for it, Shafer? You didn't . . . ?"

He shook his head. "I didn't steal it, if that's what you're thinkin'. I bet one of the gents in the Alhambra saloon that I could beat him in a horse race. He took the bet. I outrode him on his nag by a half mile," he boasted. "Used the winnings to buy you that pretty." He was enormously proud.

Emmaline's face softened. Her voice was tender although she tried to scold, "You were in a saloon? You gambled? Shafer, what am I going to do with you? You're only a boy, you ought not to be mixing with grown men in a place like Dodge. You have responsibilities here. You rode off without a word, worrying me nearly out of my mind."

"Ah, Ma, I'm sorry. I only wanted to get you something." He kissed her cheek and grinned. He wasn't intimidated in the least by the circle of women around him, workworn hands on their hips and fire in their eyes.

"And then," Emmaline said, "you ride in here like the world's ended. You ought not to run your horse that way."

His black eyes gleamed. "But I got news, and I couldn't wait to tell you all! Listen, now, there's goin' to be a hangin' in Dodge."

"What are you talking about?" Meg moved closer. "Who's

155

going to hang? What happened?"

He looked at her. "Remember those two men, Elam—what's his name—Frey, and Little Hammett? They shot and killed your team that time you was coming home from Dodge with freight an' they shot up your freight, too?"

"Of course I do, I'll never forget. They're serving time in Dodge City."

"They're goin' to hang!"

"Shafer," Emmaline said firmly, "I want you to calm down and tell us what this is all about. Come inside for some cold buttermilk."

Aurelia directed Joshua and David John to do a kindness and take Shafer's horse, rub it down after they got the saddle off, and see that it had water and grain. She halted their protests with a look. "Now!" she ordered. "Whatever Shafer's got to say," she muttered under her breath, "it's likely not fit for your ears." She might as well have said *good* boys' ears.

The women trooped into Emmaline's soddy after Shafer and took seats in the crowded dwelling while Emmaline went to the spring for buttermilk kept in a jug under the cold water. In one corner of her home was the printing press, plus shelves of paper and other material for publishing her newspaper. Pushed against the far wall were the desks and benches used during school time. The rest of the room was the Lees' living quarters.

Emmaline returned and got out an assortment of cups and glasses. "Now what's this all about?" she asked as she poured buttermilk and passed it around.

Shafer had caught his breath but still looked excited. He stood inside the door, lightly pounding a fist into his other palm. "Hammett and Frey killed a man a few days ago. Beat the daylights out of 'im."

"How could they? They were in jail," Meg said, leaning

forward on the bench where she sat beside Aurelia. "I don't understand." She accepted the cup of buttermilk from Emmaline.

"Killed him in jail!" Shafer said, his voice rising high and nervous. "The man'd been put in the same cell with 'em. This third gent was servin' time for woundin' somebody in a fracas over a claim up north near Dry Lake and the sand hills."

Beside Meg, Aurelia gasped but didn't comment.

Meg nodded, glad the claim jumping incident had taken place out of her region.

Frowning, Emmaline motioned for Shafer to go on and be quick about it.

Shafer gulped his buttermilk, leaving a creamy moustache around his dark mouth, and said, "The three of 'em were holding a cockroach race on the floor of their cell and got into a big argument about which man's bug won. Hammett and Frey beat the third man to death. Talk around Dodge is that Hammett and Frey were sure Jack Ambler wouldn't let them hang for killing another jailbird. They expected him to find a way to get them out of jail so they could go back to work for him . . ." He lifted his glass and took a long drink.

"Those two between them don't have a brain bigger than a pea," Meg muttered. "At least I'm glad something's being done about claim jumpers, that the law is looking into the situation. Jack surely didn't try to get those two out of jail?"

Shafer shook his head. He looked very tired, suddenly, and was losing interest in his story. "He didn't do anything. Not a thing. Sheriff was sayin' it wouldn't have made any difference. Hammett and Frey aren't fit to live, he said. They're going to hang day after tomorrow. Can we go watch?" he asked his mother.

She looked sick and discouraged, and also with concern for him. She set her buttermilk aside untouched, going over to grasp his shoulders and say sternly, "We will not. We're all going to stay here at home and tend to our chores as always. I'll tie you to your bedpost if I have to, Shafer Lee. But you're staying home where I can keep an eye on you. Do you know that Owen is out there somewhere searching for you?" She waved her arm toward the west, eyes flashing angrily. "You've caused him to leave on a wild goose chase for days, when he had more than enough work to do here because you shirk your share. You've caused us all to worry."

"Your present, Ma," he replied, "I just wanted to get you a present."

"And I appreciate that, but not how you went off without saying a word to me, making it hard for all of us here. You're being punished, Shafer. You're going to work harder than you've ever worked before raking wheat straw from all the family patches. I want that straw raked into perfect wind-rows, then you can help gather it into shocks. After that's done you'll help fork it into the wagons and bring it from the fields. There will be precious little resting time, and no time for your tomfoolery. You won't set foot off this place again until I say you can. Do you understand?"

He nodded, although from his disinterested expression Meg worried that Emmaline's message had simply traveled in one ear and out the other.

"Is there anything to eat?" Shafer asked. "I'm hungry."

At that moment, Joshua and David John slipped in the door, looking disappointed as they realized they'd missed the main conversation.

"It's about time for supper, anyway," Meg said. "We should all eat as soon as we get the jam divided and stored."

"And Shafer, you're not leaving my sight!" His mother shook her finger at him. She was really angry.

"I'm awful tired, Ma."

"You're going to help carry our crocks of preserves." She hauled him to his feet by his shirt front and shook him. "Now wash your hands and get on over to the store yard with the rest of us."

Meg and Aurelia exchanged glances as they went out. Emmaline might have to tie Shafer to his bedpost to keep him from riding off to Dodge to see the hanging. The boy had a taste for excitement that was beyond worrisome; it was frightening.

Chapter Twelve

Surface calm settled over Paragon Springs during the next weeks, although it was a period of hard work for everyone.

Owen marshaled the boys to the fields each day, sending some out to watch cattle and keep them close to home, others to forking wheat straw into piles and then into a wagon for delivery to that patch's owner. He worked Shafer long and hard, until he was covered with dust and too weary to get into mischief. For the most part, Owen's methods were working. Emmaline worried less and was beginning to hope that under Owen's strong, fatherly hand, Shafer might yet change.

None of the residents went to the hanging of Frey and Hammett, although the incident was vividly and gruesomely described by customers who came to the store; Little Hammett kicked some longer than Elam Frey, they said.

"I'm just glad it's over," Meg told the Hesslers with a shudder. They'd come to the store for supplies and to pick up their mail, including the latest issue of the *Echo*. "Those two deserved their punishment."

"That they did," Will replied. He thunked a bag of beans onto the counter, then one of flour. "Add those to our tally." He rubbed his jaw thoughtfully and said, as though he couldn't quite believe it, "There's folks who think the hanging will damper down Jack's all-fired push against settlers, maybe end it all together."

"We hope so, anyway," Bethany added. She placed two spools of thread and a packet of needles on the counter with their other purchases.

"Well, it ought to serve as a warning, but who knows about Jack, ever?" Meg asked.

Aurelia, tallying the Hesslers' purchases, spoke up in an embarrassed tone, "I'm not one to spread gossip, mind, but folks coming into the store here say they've seen Jack around Dodge City in the company of a beautiful dance-hall singer."

Will hesitated, then nodded. "I wasn't going to say anything, but I saw him with her myself, a couple of times. Admire's seen them together, too. The *Dodge City Times* wrote it up when she came to town. Her name's Marly Miner and she's a beauty, no doubt about that, and she sings good."

"Will Hessler, her singing and beauty is not what's important here!" Bethany scolded, her normally calm blue eyes flashing and her ample bosom rising. "Think of poor Dinah, how embarrassing. Jack has no business treating her like that, his own wife, as fine a person as ever lived."

"Like Meg said," Aurelia added mildly, "who can ever tell about Jack? He's an all-around scalawag and only a fool would expect anything decent from him. A lot of men are like Jack. They think dallying with women not their wives is their right, part of their nature, and so nothing's wrong with it."

"I don't know if you're speaking about anyone specifically, Aurelia, but Owen would never be like that," Meg said reproachfully.

Aurelia looked guilty. "No," she said, "I know he'd not be that way."

Will shook his head, "Nobody else I know's like Jack. Since the government men tied his hands from using lands that don't belong to him, he's been spending more time than ever in Dodge, drinking and carousing away from home and his wife. That'd never be Owen's way."

"No," Aurelia agreed again, a flush filling her face, "that

wouldn't be Owen's way. Owen's a good man, the best there is."

Meg looked at Aurelia for a moment, shook her head, then went back to the subject at hand. "Since I'm behind the land grab investigation, you might say I'm the cause of Jack's drowning his rage in drink, but I don't see it as my fault."

"Heavens to Betsy, no, Meg," Bethany said, "you've got nothing to do with the kind of man Jack is."

"No," Meg sighed, "I suppose not. But I feel sorry for Dinah."

Grasshoppers flew up from the grass as Meg walked to the knoll above the store one late afternoon, thinking to be alone and to catch a breeze there while reading Hamilton's latest letter.

She was deep in his words, almost feeling as though she were with him in St. Louis, when the snort of a horse made her look up. Dinah Ambler rode toward her. Dinah's usual bright manner was missing; she rode as though a burden weighed on her shoulders, and no wonder. Recently she had told Meg in tearful confidence that Jack didn't see dallying with Marly Miner as being unfaithful because Marly was a whore and acts with a whore came natural to a man; it didn't mean he didn't love his wife. Even though he knew that Dinah was aware of his misbehavior with the other woman (he made no secret of it) and although he was seldom home himself, he still forbade Dinah to have anything to do with her only friends, the women at Paragon Springs. This was an order she disobeyed often.

"What else am I supposed to do?" Dinah said once. "After my work is done at the ranch, there's no one to talk to after I tell Walker Platt, our cook, what to fix for supper." She and Jack argued fiercely about it, whenever he did come home from his drinking binges.

There was deep sympathy behind Meg's smile and wave of greeting as Dinah rode up. Jack was monstrously unfair, as well as unfaithful. He ought to see that his new young wife was lonely for company; that it wasn't easy for her to adjust to life in Kansas after leaving the familiarity of Texas. She needed Jack, and she needed friends. She didn't think Jack lifted a hand physically to Dinah, but having been subjected to abuse herself, she realized that wasn't something a woman could count on never happening from certain men when they were angered.

"Hello there!" Meg put on a brighter smile as Dinah drew her black Morgan to a halt and dismounted with a creaking of the saddle.

Dinah left the Morgan ground-reined and dropped to sit beside Meg. "Aurelia said I'd find you up here." She looked at the letter fluttering in Meg's fingers. "Am I intrudin'? Is that a letter from your lawyer? Do you have a court date for your divorce?"

Meg smiled. "Yes, it's from Hamilton. You're not intruding. I don't yet have a court date. He just wrote to tell me of some goings-on in St. Louis. He's handling a somewhat amusing case: a lady wants to sue the city for an outrageous sum of money because she believes her dog fell into a drainage sewer. She's sure the dog swam out into the Mississippi River and drowned or was stolen by a boatman, because her pet hasn't been seen anywhere."

Dinah chuckled for a moment and a comfortable silence followed. "Aurelia says there's quite a correspondence going on between you and Mr. Hamilton, Meg. She believes your exchanges may even be love letters." Her eyes flashed playfully and her hand flew up to cover her mouth. "Oops, maybe I said too much."

"His name is Mr. Gibbs; his given name is Hamilton. And Aurelia has no business gossiping about my letters."

"Aurelia will be upset with me for revealin' a private conversation. But you know that Aurelia means no harm, she's your good friend."

Meg nodded, feeling scolded a bit. "Of course, you're right. Aurelia is family to me, I love her dearly and I'm being too prickly." She held the letter in her lap against the wind. "I do believe, though, that Aurelia should tend her own romantic affairs with more care. Look what she's doing to poor Owen, holding him off near to forever when they're both so in love they can't see straight."

"That'll change. Aurelia'll give in and marry Owen before much longer. True love usually wins out, whatever the situation, or at least I've always believed that. Now, dear Meg, pardon me for pryin', but how about you, are you in love with Mr. Gibbs?"

Meg studied the far horizon, her face growing warm as she seriously considered the question. "I'm not sure. I thought I was in love once, and made a horrible mistake because of it. I like Hamilton, I enjoy his letters immensely; they're a wonderful distraction from all the worrisome goings-on around here. I believe I can say that we've become good friends. Letter-writing friends."

Dinah caught her hand. "Your face softens and somethin' new comes to your eyes when you talk about him. I think you're in love."

"I'll take your opinion into consideration," Meg replied, and they both laughed. She sobered, then asked softly, "And you and Jack, Dinah, are things any better for you?"

Dinah looked sad, distraught. "I wish I could say yes, but no. Jack's moody and hard to get along with these days. He's a man who thinks big, plans big. The idea that he may have to scale back his operations when he'd rather expand eats at him. Homesteads are makin' ribbons of the wide range he's always used."

"But all this country isn't his," Meg reminded gently, "and he never should have taken for granted that it was."

"I know. That doesn't change the fact that he sees every acre as part of his personal dream. He can't let go of the dream. I don't see that he needs so much—so many miles of range, so many thousands of heads of cattle. I think he could manage fine with much less. My father has had to cut back his operations down in Texas, and although he didn't like it at first, he's accepted it. Some of the farmers he once saw as intruders and enemies are now his good friends."

"I'd like to see that happen here."

"I know. I would, too." Dinah's frown deepened as she brushed back a blond tendril of hair that blew in her face. "I don't like what he's done to people around here, nor what he's doin' when he rides off to Dodge. If somethin' doesn't change—" she paused and swallowed "—I fear our marriage may not survive. He's about to explode, and I don't want to live this way."

She wiped at tears welling in her eyes and then went on, "I've warned him about his philanderin'. I've no intention of puttin' up with it, no matter how he lived his life when he was a bachelor. He's married now." She looked at Meg, her expression desperate. "I think if I could just have a child, if we started a family, Jack would like that and he might give up his wild ways. As a family man he might be more tolerant of his neighbors."

Meg's eyebrows rose in question.

"Could there be a baby on the way? Not yet," Dinah answered with a small smile, the tears sparkling in her eyes, "but I keep hopin'."

Meg tucked her letter into her apron pocket, then reached out and drew Dinah into the circle of her arm. "I know how you feel. I'd love to have children of my own someday. We can both keep hoping for the best."

That night just before bed, Meg read Hamilton's letter again. He'd ended the letter by complimenting her on her description in her last letter of Paragon Springs and the surrounding country. "I felt I sat beside you on a buggy ride around your country, you write of it so well," he wrote. "May I say that your letters have come to hold a very high place in my regard? They bring me such pleasure as well as news." He now signed his letters, "Your devoted friend."

Hamilton was a good person. A fine, honorable, and interesting man. She was more used to dealing with scoundrels like Ted and Jack. It was that difference between Hamilton and the others that impressed her so strongly. It wasn't necessarily that she was in love with him, despite Dinah's calculation. (And sometimes her own reckoning.)

The heat was terrible as summer wore on. Meg and Ad did not cut stone—it was easier to cut in the early spring and wet winter months—but they made a trip to Dodge City to fill orders with stone they'd stockpiled, and also loaded and delivered some to settlers near Paragon Springs. The cattle were kept herded close to the sinks. Garden crops were harvested early to keep the scorching sun from cooking them on stalk and vine, and were stored in the cool root cellar. At the end of a day, Meg's room in the cool sod house was most welcome, as were the pitchers of lemonade Aurelia provided.

During one particularly hot spell, Owen offered to make a freight and supplies trip to Dodge City and Meg agreed. She used the time at home to catch up on reading her newspapers, clearing her desk, and writing letters, when she wasn't out in the field.

She was in her corner office at the mercantile, the collar of her dress loosened for a tad of relief from the heat, when Owen returned with the mailbag, and Aurelia called out, "A letter from your lawyer, Meg."

"Be right there." Meg's hand shook as she set aside her ledgers and pen. Her legs wobbled as she stood up. She didn't know how she knew, but this was *the* letter—Hamilton's message that they'd been scheduled for a day in court after their long wait. "I'll take it back to my room to read," she told Aurelia as she accepted the letter.

Aurelia nodded and continued sorting mail and placing it in the partitioned box that was fastened to the sod wall of the mercantile.

Meg sat on her bed, holding her breath, and tore open the envelope. She took out the letter and read. After only a few words, tears of relief formed behind her eyes, and she had to blink them away to finish. Her heart pounded wildly in her breast.

She hurried into the store where Aurelia had finished with the mail and was returning to put a few stitches in her Birds in Flight quilt.

"Wait a second." Meg stopped Aurelia halfway and threw her arms around her; the letter crumpled between them.

"What is it?" Aurelia asked in surprise, wearing a half-smile.

"It's set," Meg told her, the wonder and relief she was feeling reflected in her choking voice. "Oh, sweet heaven, I have a court date. I'm going to be free. I thought it would never happen!"

Aurelia caught her in a hard hug and then drew back, smiling. "I'm so happy for you, Meg, dear! Tell me everything! What does the letter say? I had no idea when I gave it to you that it was the important one."

Meg drew a deep breath. "Hamilton says that we have a hearing date before Judge Williams—he's the one we wanted—scheduled for September 25th! Oh, my goodness, that's so soon." She clapped a hand to her forehead, then retrieved the letter that had fallen to the floor. She pressed the letter against her lips. "Thank you, Hamilton, thank you so much."

She let Aurelia read the letter for herself while she paced, finger to her cheek, mumbling aloud each busy thought that came. "I'll need to leave sometime around the second week of September to get to St. Louis by my court date." She wailed softly, picking up her pace, "So little time and so much to do. This is supposed to be my shining hour! Oh, well, it can't be helped," she decided, "but I wish I'd had a new dress made and had bought new gloves and a new hat, too. Nonsense, it's just too late to even think of it." Her pace slowed and she laughed softly, "My plain old things will have to do, but I really don't care, if I can just be finally *free.*"

After the letter came setting her court date and with the reassuring message that her case would be heard before fair and honorable Judge Williams, Meg existed in a state of calm joy. The work, heat, and dust didn't bother her, nor did the ever-present wind. The common and foolish acts of those about her were touching and funny and correctable; her friends were only human, after all.

In those days before she was to leave, she possessed unlimited energy, working like a demon as she took care of her ordinary tasks and preparations for the trip. Very soon she would be a free woman. In the recesses of her heart she was reminded that a return to St. Louis also meant another opportunity to see Hamilton Gibbs in person. As much as she loved to read his letters, she welcomed his very real company more. Time flew and it was time to leave.

In the golden expanse before Meg, driving alone in her wagon drawn by Pete, Dodge City was an uneven lump of dull brown against the blue horizon. Her heart filled with satisfaction to be completing the first leg of her final trip to St. Louis.

She drove on, whistling a remembered bird song as Dodge took on more defined shapes of clustered, low-slung buildings. She thought she could hear a strange sound riding the blowing wind. She urged Pete faster with a click of her tongue and a snap of the reins, her mind raised in curiosity.

With her head cocked, she listened to the clanging bells grow loud and furious as she neared the edge of town. Fire bells? Her eyes frantically searched for smoke, but other than thin spirals of smoke from chimneys, there wasn't a sign of fire. Her heartbeat slowed in dread. Something was terribly wrong and the fire bells were a warning, a call to action due to a calamity.

She wished now that Admire, Owen, or Lad had come with her, they could help with whatever the trouble was. She had to catch that train to St. Louis. The plan they'd made at the last minute was that she'd drive into town alone, leaving Pete and her wagon at the livery. Either Admire or Lad would drive her rig back home when they came to Dodge City in a week for the mail and supplies.

As she drove into Dodge City, she saw a dozen or so blue-uniformed soldiers from Fort Dodge, the military post located five miles west of town. The post was established in 1865, the primary task keeping a watchful eye on the Indian Territory to the south and patrolling the frontier around Dodge City. There had been scant Indian trouble in recent years and only a small command of soldiers lived at the post. At the moment they were talking animatedly with folks who clustered on street corners and in front of saloons and stores. Cowboys, soldiers, and regular folk were swiftly saddling their horses or readying wagons. Others dashed from the stores with sacks of supplies as though they were crazed, shouting commands and questions back and forth.

Her mind protested that none of this concerned her. She didn't want to know what was happening. Maybe there'd been trouble at one of the saloons, maybe Jack was involved, but whatever it was, it was out of her hands. She drove slowly on toward the Santa Fe depot. If anything stopped her now from her hearing in St. Louis, she didn't know what she'd do. This was her one chance and she had waited so long.

Then she saw the Hesslers in the wild commotion. She halted her wagon in the middle of the street. "Will, Bethany!" she called above the noise. The couple turned from where they were speedily loading their wagon in front of Charles Rath & Company's General Store. Meg shouted to them, "What's happened? What's wrong?"

Will raced into the street, dodging in and out of wild traffic. Bethany followed on his heels, her skirts flying. Will grabbed the side of Meg's wagon. "It's Injuns!" he told her, "headed this way from the territory."

Meg couldn't have been more shocked, and her eyes rounded. "Indians? But they're all on reservations. We've been safe from Indians for ages. They're civilized now; there's nothing to fear. Is there?"

"There's plenty to be afraid of!" Will retorted with a slap to the side of her wagon, spooking Pete for a second. "Word just come that Dull Knife's people, hundreds of warriors, women, and children, have run off from the Fort Reno reservation down south. Dull Knife and Little Wolf is leadin' 'em.

Local authorities got word days ago, but figured they was just some poor starved souls wantin' to get back to their homes in Montana and the Dakotas. Sympathy's done run out, now. The Indians killed a coupla ranchers, dumped their bodies in a wagon, and stole their horses. In Comanche County they killed some cowboys sittin' innocent around their campfire. Acted friendly to the cowboys, then jumped 'em and cut their throats. It's awful, I'm tellin' ya."

Meg said through a dry, tight throat, feeling suddenly numb all over, "I didn't think we had anything to fear, I thought the Indian peril was over. It's been ten years since anything like this happened in western Kansas."

"That's part of the trouble, folks let their guard down. Otherwise those friendly actin' Cheyenne would never've got by with slittin' those white men's throats ear to ear—sorry ladies. Took everything those men had. The red devils are plunderin' an' killin' their way direct to Ford County. Dodge City law, includin' Wyatt Earp, is gettin' up a posse of soldiers and cowboys to stop 'em. Everybody else is supposed to arm themselves and take cover."

An icy chill chased Meg's numbness away. She felt dizzy with horror; it was hard to think.

Bethany, pale and nervous, was eyeing Meg's satchel on the wagon seat beside her. "Were you on the way to St. Louis?"

"My train is due to leave in about an hour and a half." She reached up to touch her hair, her scalp was tight from tension and pained like the devil.

"Best be on that train," Will told her emphatically, "if the railroad folks haven't changed their plans and mean for it to go out on time. You'll be safer headed east than anywhere in this country. Those red devils are rangin' all over as they travel north, authorities are sayin'. You go on, we'll look out for your folks at Paragon Springs. We were headed that way, anyhow. We plan to warn everybody on the way to our place. Our children are home alone, we want to get there as soon as we can, make sure they're safe and we're all ready for those red devils when they show."

Bethany reached up to clasp Meg's hand and squeeze. "You go on now, dear. If that train's leavin', you be on it. You've waited years for this time, don't worry about nothin' else. We'll see to your friends."

Meg looked toward the Santa Fe depot where the iron horse and its train of cars sat waiting on the tracks. Trainmen were filling the steam locomotive's tender car with coal and water, preparing for departure. She looked back north toward Paragon Springs and her decision was clear despite tears that clotted her throat. "I can't go, they need me at home. They've heard nothing there about Indians escaping from Fort Reno and won't be expecting trouble. I have to go home."

Chapter Thirteen

News flew along Dodge City streets as the Hesslers and Meg prepared to leave town. Mayor J. H. Kelly had telegraphed the governor to send arms: "The country is filled with Indians." There were only nineteen men at Fort Dodge; few townsfolk were acquainted with Indian fighting and a direct attack on the town was feared.

On the southbound Santa Fe tracks a locomotive and passenger car were being readied to take the soldiers, town merchants, and as many cowboys as possible, west and south to try to turn 300 Indians—warriors, women, and children—back to their reservation.

Settlers across western Kansas must be on guard for their lives. The savages were desperate to escape confinement on the reservation, and anyone between them and their home would surely suffer.

Meg left Pete and her wagon at the livery after convincing the stable owner that she must borrow the fastest riding horse available. In less than an hour after her arrival in town, she was riding out again on a blaze-faced sorrel with an eager gait. For a while she traveled with the Hesslers, then with a hasty good-bye to her, Will and Bethany left the main trail and headed their wagon northwest toward their farm. On the way there, they would warn other settlers, and anyone else they saw.

Meg continued on toward Paragon Springs, pacing her mount for the long trip under a hot, hazy sky. Heat waves shimmered over the trail ahead, looking a lot like Indians in dance, and her skin crawled at the sight. Rabbits bounded out of her path. The zinging and chirring of insects in the otherwise deathly quiet made her edgy. Every dip in the rolling plains held an enemy ready to rise up and snatch her off her horse.

She rode on, in mental argument with herself that the Cheyenne from Fort Reno couldn't have come that far yet, and she was in no real danger unless her mount threw her and she broke her neck. From time to time she slowed the animal to a restful walk, but it was next to impossible to hold the horse or herself back. After a mile or so at that pace they would be off and running again.

It was evening when she rode into Ma Jewett's place. Settlers often put up there overnight on the long trip to Dodge. Meg had stayed overnight with her on the way in. Ma Jewett had a well-kept sod house, outbuildings, and several acres in crops. A cow and three horses grazed east of the soddy. Meg dismounted and led her horse the last few paces into the yard.

Ma came out of the house, talking cheerily and with hardly a breath as always, "Meg Brennon! What're you doin' back this way so soon? Well, it don't matter. I've got gingerbread and dried-apple sauce and a pot of beans planned for supper. Made bread today, ten loaves, and churned butter. You come on and rest yourself—"

She stopped when she saw Meg's face. "What's wrong, dear? You missed the train? Train didn't go out today? Somebody hold up the train an' they ain't goin' out 'til tomorrow? Well, you just spend the night here with me and go on back there in the mornin' an' take yourself to St. Louis."

"I won't be going tomorrow and likely not any other time soon, Ma." She clasped both of Ma Jewett's hands in hers. "There's been some trouble, Indian trouble." Ma gasped, and Meg rushed to finish, "Cheyenne have escaped from Fort

174

Reno down in the territory. They're headed this way. They've already killed some people, ranchers and cowboys and travelers on the road."

Ma Jewett looked around them, grabbed Meg, and began to pull her toward the house.

Meg drew away, shaking her head. "I won't be staying the night this time, I have to reach Paragon Springs and warn them there. I'd like to leave this livery horse here, I'll be paying for him dead if I ride him any harder. I'd like to borrow a fresh horse from you, if you don't mind. You come with me and stay at Paragon Springs. There'll be safety in numbers at my place. I'll be asking other folks to join us, too, after I stop at their farms and warn them what's happening."

"Course you can have a fresh horse, an' I'll fix you some grub to eat on the way, if you're determined to go on. You can ride Santa Fe Sam, that golden palomino out there." Ma Jewett pointed with simple pride, "Man who sold me that beautiful creature claimed that gelding is a direct descendant of horses owned by Queen Isabella of Spain."

"Ma, we have to hurry—" Meg coaxed as she pulled the saddle from the sorrel.

"Ain't no *we*, I ain't goin'."

Meg turned, looking at Ma Jewett in sharp surprise. The woman was tough, rough as a cob, but still—"You have to come with me."

The map of wrinkles in Ma's sun-browned face deepened with a stubborn scowl. "I'm stayin' right here on my own place. Somebody has to guard it from the red savages."

"Ma, please. It won't be safe here."

Ma snorted, "Won't be safe for them Indians if they come! I'll stay in my rocking chair an' wait for 'em, keep my loaded shotgun beside me. They'll be sorry souls if they try to bother me."

175

"I don't like leaving you here alone."

"It ain't for you to decide or to blame yourself that I'm stayin'. It's my own choice. Listen to me, I've fought ever'thin'. Near starvation, drought, blizzards, mean horses and meaner humans and rattlesnakes, in order to claim this place and hang on to it. If I have to shoot me some Indians, I'll do that. But I ain't leavin' an' givin' 'em a chance to tear up my house and take ever'thin' I got. Now, come on, let's get you fixed for the rest of your ride home."

Time was passing and further argument wouldn't do a particle of good. Ma Jewett whistled up the palomino. While Meg saddled the horse, Ma hustled to the house to bundle some meat and bread for Meg's supper on the way.

Meg rode on into the night. For a while it was very dark and she kept to the trail mostly by instinct. Then a bright silver moon rose and it was nearly light as day. She had no trouble keeping to the trail. Once, she thought she heard a sound behind her and was being followed by a wolf or some other creature. But when she turned to look there was no sign of movement or shining eyes behind her. Another time, a coyote howled mournfully from the top of a distant rise.

It seemed an eternity had passed since she had packed for the trip to St. Louis in such high spirits. But she couldn't think about that. More important, now, was to warn the folks at home to be ready for the Indian raid.

Much later, deep into the night, the late summer moon showed her the way off the main trail to Lucy Ann and Admire's place. Meg dismounted woodenly, her hip and all of her bones stiff and sore from riding so long. She stumbled up to the Walshes' soddy and pounded on the door.

After a moment or two, Lucy Ann, in her nightgown and half asleep, cautiously opened the door. When she saw Meg in the light from the lamp, she looked shocked. "Meg! What on earth are you doing here in the middle of the night? You're supposed to be on your way to St. Louis." She drew Meg inside and bolted the door. "What's happened?"

Meg was explaining about the Indian escape and killings as Admire, pulling trousers over his long johns, joined them. Lucy Ann, listening, turned rigid and the color drained from her face.

Meg had to repeat the story twice before Admire would believe her.

He growled, finally, "Damn redskins, why don't they stay where they belong. I'm gettin' some clothes on."

"I thought all that was done," Lucy Ann said, despair in her voice, "I thought we didn't have to worry about Indians anymore."

"We all thought that," Meg replied, accepting the cup of water Lucy Ann handed her and taking a long drink. "These aren't renegade Sioux, Lucy, like those that attacked you and Lad in Nebraska. These are tattered, starving Cheyenne trying to get home before they all die off from a life they hate on the reservation. They've killed some men on the way, but I've been thinking that even if they get through Dodge City without being stopped, they'll likely travel west and north of here. They'll miss us in these parts altogether."

"You can't tell anything about Indians," Lucy Ann said flatly. Her eyes were glassy with shock, remembering.

"I know, and they'll likely kill again if anybody tries to stop them on their way north, or tries to prevent them from stealing food, cattle, or horses. We do all have to be on guard. I want you and little Rachel to come with me to Paragon Springs. Admire, too, if he'll come, and Lad."

"It's going to terrorize Lad all over again, hearin' this," Lucy Ann whispered. "We both been just about to get over what happened to us, as much as we ever will. I thought nothin' like the killing of my family, and what those Sioux did to me and to Lad—well, I never thought that'd happen again in a lifetime. Admire," she said in a voice strident with worry as he came back into the room, "I want you to come to Meg's with me and the youngsters. I'll feel better with you there."

"I ought to stay and mind the place." His grimace turned to a look of soft affection as he studied her. "All right, if that's what you want, I'll come. But don't you worry, Lucy Ann, ain't nothin' or nobody goin' to hurt you as long as I'm around."

The children were wakened. Lad was brought into the main room and told what had happened. Shocked, his hand went up to the scar that remained from being partially scalped. Neighbors had rescued Lad and Lucy Ann just as the renegade Sioux were about to kill them and add them to the bloodbath on the Nebraska farm of their folks. Lad's scalp had been sewn back on and had healed.

"We got to hustle," Admire said. Everyone hurried and in a very short time they were on their way through the darkness to Paragon Springs—the Walsh family in their wagon, Meg riding alongside on Santa Fe Sam.

They arrived at Paragon Springs in the hours just before dawn. The inhabitants of the tiny village were awakened one by one and told of the imminent danger.

Meg was exhausted from the fear she carried, and from being on the road more than twenty-four hours without a chance to close her eyes. A steady pain knifed through her hip. It was hard to speak but she managed to tell Aurelia and Owen what was taking place and advise them: "We have to keep an eye on the children at all times. We'll gather all weapons and see that they're loaded, and see that extra ammunition is handy. Take it from the store if necessary. Other folks besides Admire and Lucy and the children are on the way to stay with us through this peril. In numbers we'll be stronger against attack. We need to check our food supply in case the siege is long and we have to ration what we have. We'll herd the cattle and horses in closer so we can keep an eye on them."

"Meg, we know what to do," Owen said, gently touching her arm. "Go to bed, woman, and let us worry about this. You've done enough by not getting on that train and staying to warn us, making the ride back."

"Yes," Aurelia agreed. She stood stricken, both hands clasped to her cheeks. "I'm so sorry, Meg, that you didn't get to go to St. Louis. We can be thankful, though, that you're safe and you got back home alive."

She nodded. "Soldiers from Fort Dodge have ordered that we remain on guard and together here until we get word that the danger's past. Even with a miracle, I wouldn't be able to get to the hearing on time, so I mustn't think of it. Hamilton will stand in for me." Swaying on her feet, she mumbled, "I have every faith in him. He'll be there for me." Owen handed Meg off to Aurelia, who took her to her room and sat her on the bed. She brushed Aurelia's helping hands away. "I have to help, I can't sleep, I'm not even sleepy."

Aurelia ignored her, knelt to remove Meg's boots, and then slipped her dress up over her head. Meg tried to resist as Aurelia pushed her back and pulled a blanket over her, but the blanket was so soft and comforting and she was so weary. "Thank you for being so kind, Aurelia," she said sleepily, "I'll only lie here for a minute or two."

The rattle of wagon wheels, neighing of horses, and mixed human voices woke Meg several hours later. She was shocked that it was broad daylight, that outside her window the sun was almost noon high. The yard outside churned with ar-

riving wagons, each loaded with family and valued possessions. Owen and Lad were directing the herding of stock—it
would be something trying to get that straightened out again!
Nearly everyone had driven their animals with them and now
they were all a-mix.

Meg quickly washed, dressed, combed her hair, and hurried to Aurelia's house. Aided by several women from the
valley—including the newcomer, tall Kate Levant—Aurelia
was in the midst of preparing a noon meal for fifty people.
Meg said hello to everyone and then pitched in and helped
peel potatoes to go with the spicy Norwegian meatballs in
gravy that Bethany was fixing. If not for the voices subdued
by fear and faces clouded with worry, it might have been a so-
cial gathering.

She learned in a whispered aside from Aurelia that most of
the women had contributed to the meal from the foodstuffs
they'd brought with them. The Potter family was an excep-
tion. Miserly Joe Potter had insisted on keeping their food
supply stored in their wagon and set his older sons to
guarding it, both from the marauding Indians, and from the
other settlers. The act had embarrassed Bella, his wife, but
she hadn't countered his order.

Meg wasn't surprised; Joe could make a coin cry he
squeezed it so tight. Bella, like most women, let him rule as
head of the house.

After lunch, while the women were cleaning up, Bella
Potter introduced Meg and the others to her widowed sister-
in-law Eliza Coats. Mrs. Coats was a fortyish, fox-faced red-
head dressed six times finer than most of them could afford.
"Eliza's here for a visit and to look over land. She may file
near us."

"Not if Indians are a problem!" Eliza sniffed. "I won't stay
here to be dirtied and scalped by redskins. I've already in-

formed my brother, Joe, to let me know at the first sight of savages. Those brutes would love to have my hair." Her fingers fondly traced her temple and back. "When it's not in a bun, it reaches to the back of my knees."

"Do tell," Aurelia said drily, handing Eliza a dishrag. "Would you wipe the table over there, please?"

Eliza frowned, but she took the wet cloth and did as she was bid.

For the next few days, life in the little village followed a pattern. Men took turns standing guard; someone was on watch around the clock to warn should Indians come. Other men, and several of the boys, watched over the stock and provided the kitchens with fuel. The women cooked, cleaned, did needlework, and kept their eyes on the playing children, visiting in quiet, careful voices.

"Is that woman an Indian?" Meg heard someone ask in a suspicious hiss on the third afternoon of their forced confinement. The women were in the store, some of them working on Aurelia's quilt while others sat about doing their own needlework or reading Meg's periodicals. Meg followed Eliza Coats's glance of disgust and discovered that she meant Emmaline. Eliza had acted odd around Emmaline from the beginning, staying clear of her as if she were diseased, so Meg wasn't surprised at the rude question now.

Emmaline's friends frowned with shock at Eliza's lack of manners. Meg got to her feet slowly, resisting the urge to jab the woman with her sewing needle.

"Mrs. Coats, you're new, and you probably aren't aware that Emmaline is one of our most valued citizens here at Paragon Springs. She conducts school for our children. She's the editor of the newspaper in your hand." Meg was furious. Emmaline was far better educated, better mannered, more considerate and thoughtful than Eliza Coats. She was one of the finest and most likable women Meg had ever known.

"I see," Eliza said, "my mistake." She sent Emmaline a cold smile, then laid the paper aside primly, as though it had dirtied her hand.

Meg could have smacked her, and later apologized to Emmaline.

Emmaline laughed and shrugged. "Such actions don't really bother me. It isn't the first time this sort of thing has happened. I look Indian, except for my clothes. How are other women to know I've lived the same as they, all my life, in a white world, and know next to nothing of Indian ways? For all they know, I have a knife hidden in my skirts ready to plunge into their hearts, or hack off their red hair. If I'm too friendly, that also frightens them. Before this is over, maybe Mrs. Coats will come to know me better by observing. The silly woman had no idea that I teach the children and publish the newspaper she was reading."

"You're very generous to feel as you do, Emmaline. God willing, Mrs. Coats won't take land here, and I hope she doesn't because I can't stand her!" Meg said.

Emmaline, more than having concern for herself, worried about Shafer. The boy strutted around, parading his few drops of Indian blood. He held his neck so rigid, it might have been holding up a headdress of eagle feathers. The children laughed at him, and when Aurelia told him he looked ridiculous and was hardly Indian any more than she was, he stopped acting haughty and sulked instead.

"I'll have to keep an eye on him, regardless," Emmaline confided to Meg, her own amusement thin. "If the Indians do come, he may get the foolish notion to ride off with them. He's a silly boy. His own Cheyenne ancestors would've scared him to death, but he doesn't realize that."

On the twenty-fifth of September, the evening of the day set for her divorce hearing, Meg was on her way to the root cellar for cornmeal and bacon to have ready for the next morning's breakfast. It was a peaceful evening. Shadows shrouded the village; supper had long been over, and children were being put to bed. The stock was quiet and lying down. Men were having a smoke, seated on the ground and on a handful of chairs, out in front of the mercantile. There was the distant yap of coyotes, the metallic zinging of locusts in the cottonwood tree.

As she approached the old dugout root cellar, sudden movement at its entrance caught Meg's eye. At first she thought it would be Owen, who slept there. Her eyes rounded and her heart stilled as two Indians emerged from the cave, their arms filled with bags of beans, slabs of bacon, corn. So far they hadn't seen her as they skulked away. How had they gotten past the guards? Why hadn't anyone seen them? How long had they been hiding in the root cellar?

They saw her then, a few feet away, and froze.

They were dressed in reservation garb: dirty and ragged denim trousers and faded calico shirts. Each wore his black hair parted in the middle and free to his shoulders. They were impossibly thin and starved looking. Meg uttered a small cry when Selinda Lee stepped out of the cellar behind them.

"Selinda!" Meg was shocked.

"Meg." The girl looked frightened, but in control. "They were hungry, they wanted food. They didn't bother any of Owen's things; he wasn't there." Selinda let out a sudden shriek as one of the Indians whipped about and grabbed her. His coppery arms held her against him, prisoner and hostage.

Lad came striding around the corner of the blacksmith shed, startling them all. His gun was leveled on the Indians. "Let her go!" he yelled. "You won't touch her!"

Admire and Owen came running, guns in hand. "Step aside, Selinda," Owen said softly, "move over to Meg." He motioned for the Indian to let the girl go.

"I'll kill the devils," Admire said, raising his gun on them. He took a bead on the forehead of the Indian who held Selinda.

The Indian muttered something, but he released Selinda and she moved away.

"Don't shoot!" Meg ordered, when it looked like Admire was still going to fire. "That's not necessary."

"What're you talkin' about?" Admire snapped, "We got to kill them."

"No. These two aren't going anywhere, we've got them and we'll hold them for the law. I don't want blood spilled on Paragon Springs land. They'll be treated to civil justice, hung like anybody else if they're found guilty."

"You're six kinds of a fool, Meg!" Admire stormed, "thinkin' thataway. These is savages, and they don't deserve savin' atall. The rest of their tribe is likely out there now, watchin', just waitin' for a chance to kill us all."

"I don't think so." Meg wasn't sure, but she said, "I think they're a couple of half-starved stragglers separated from the main group. Selinda, were they going to take you with them?" Meg put her arm around the shivering girl. "Because I'd be the first to want them shot, to stop them."

Selinda shook her head. "I don't know if they were, or not. They made motions that they wanted food, they wanted my help in getting it."

"You shouldn't have been out here alone!" Meg scolded.

"I . . . I wasn't by myself, at . . . at first." Selinda's glance darted toward Lad, then her eyes lowered. "Lad and I slipped out to . . . talk. We thought it would be safe, that nothing was going to happen. After Lad saw me back to my house, he went to help stand watch. I came out again to . . . relieve myself . . . and the Indians spotted me."

"Well, thank goodness, you're safe now. Owen, Admire, tie the Indians to the cottonwood by my house, and tie them tight. In the morning, we'll take them to Dodge. Lad, put your gun down." From the look of him, she was afraid he was going to fire any minute, if Admire didn't. She understood their feelings, how badly they'd like to have vengeance against past atrocities, but she said quietly, "You don't want any more blood on your hands, Lad."

"They could've taken Selinda," he argued.

"Yes, and I would've wanted them stopped, killed if need be. But it's not right to execute them, ourselves." Admire was opening his mouth to argue some more and she rushed to prevent his interruption, "Of course we could put these Cheyenne to death, here and now, but that wouldn't even the score with those Sioux warriors that attacked your family, Lad. These two had nothing to do with that. You know it, too, Admire. We'll let the law take care of them."

"You're wrong, Meg," Admire argued. "You don't know enough about these things, bein' a woman. You ought to be more like Lucy Ann, she knows how to keep her place."

Meg couldn't answer right away, then she told him, "Your Lucy Ann is one of the sweetest people I know. Maybe I should be more like her, but I'm not. I am who I am and I say we let the law deal with these Indians and not take it into our own hands."

"But they're savages!" Admire argued. "They're not human!"

"I'm not going to argue any further, Ad!"

"Here, son," Will Hessler separated himself from the group that had gathered in the dusky evening behind Meg and Admire during their standoff over the Indians. He walked up to Lad, "Give that to me." Will took Lad's gun and held it on the Indians. "Ad, don't fire. Let's talk this over. I'm for allowin' the law to take care of them, like Meg says."

"I would've had to kill them," Lad said adamantly, "if they'd hurt Selinda." Starting in October, the two young people planned to attend the high school academy at Larned, boarding with separate families for the school year. Lucy Ann, Admire, and Emmaline, as much as they would miss the youngsters, were thrilled that the opportunity was there for Lad and Selinda, but who knew when they could resume their plans?

The Indians, still holding the food, looked like statues.

"Tie them," Meg said. "And it won't hurt to give them a little something to eat."

Admire was furious with the decision, but the majority voted with Meg to take the Indians captive and turn them over to the law.

Meg tossed restlessly after turning in and she wasn't fully asleep when she heard two shots in the middle of the night. She threw her wrapper on over her nightgown and raced outside.

A group of men were gathering where the Indians had been tied. Joe Potter stepped from the group in the shadowy dark, his explanation stingy and quick, "The savages cut their ropes with a piece of stone. They were gettin' away, tryin' to steal my white mare. Ad and me shot 'em down."

The Indians lay in two dead heaps several yards from the tree and the cut ropes. Strewn around were the bacon, the bag of beans, and the corn that Meg had returned to the cellar last night. Potter's white mare grazed without halter or rope a few feet beyond.

"Did it really happen as Joe says?" Meg faced Admire and demanded to know.

"Yeah, what he said is what happened. They was in the midst of a thievin' escape. They ain't the ones hurt Lucy Ann, but they won't hurt no other women, now, either!"

Meg knew that was the last word she'd get from him on the subject. She wanted to believe that he and Potter told the truth, and she sighed, "All right, Ad."

There were no further incidents in that part of the valley involving the escaped Cheyenne. Word spread that danger had passed, although there was no specific news for a while of the army's success in their plans to stop the Cheyenne. Life at Paragon Springs resumed its normal pace and the settlers who'd been staying there returned home. The Walshes and Emmaline made preparations to take Lad and Selinda to the academy at Larned as planned.

Eventually they were to learn that Dull Knife and his people had slipped around Dodge City undetected and continued their trek north, wreaking havoc across the state. If the count was correct, forty-three settlers had been killed by the Cheyenne; twenty-five women and girls had been raped. Property damage and thievery were still being tallied.

Most of those atrocities took place in northwest Kansas in the area of Sappa Creek, where three years before an army command under Austin Henely needlessly slaughtered an entire encampment of Indians. Because of that it was said that Dull Knife's raid was in retaliation. Others said the rapings and killings were due to Indians being savages, not human.

The Northern Cheyenne under Dull Knife didn't reach their homeland, but were captured and taken to Fort Robinson, Nebraska. Sixty-four warriors were killed in an escape attempt. The survivors were later sent to trial. Little Wolf and his people, who had earlier separated from Dull

187

Knife's band, were taken captive in Montana.

The entire situation made Meg sad, for everyone. She was just relieved it was over and hoped that nothing like it would ever happen again.

Chapter Fourteen

As Meg had hoped and expected, there were two wires from Hamilton waiting for her in Dodge when she and Admire went to pick up their order of supplies and her horse and wagon, returning the livery stable horse she'd retrieved from Ma Jewett on the way.

She stood in the dim, airless depot, her heart thumping as she read the first telegram: "Very concerned. Positive no accident you missed court date. What's happened?" Even in a few words his worry was sharp and her heart warmed in gratitude. She read the second, "Must know you're all right. Can't rest until I know. Send word if you need me there."

She folded the telegrams and put them into her reticule. She wired Hamilton immediately and explained the Cheyenne raid, letting him know she was all right. In the bag of mail for Paragon Springs and surrounding vicinity she found a letter from him, dated later than the telegrams. She found a bench against the depot wall under a cobwebby window and sat down to read it.

It was not good news. He detailed in thoughtful, regretful words events that happened in court in her absence. Meg's throat filled as she read the letter twice more, wishing that she had misread it. Her hand holding the letter lowered; she looked around her and saw nothing. Ted had lied and the judge had postponed her case. Rage stifled her and it was some minutes before she felt in control again. She didn't fault Hamilton, he'd tried; and as he said, the matter wasn't done. They still had a chance. But oh, merciful heaven, it was taking so long!

★ ★ ★ ★ ★

At the mercantile on her return to Paragon Springs, she waited until Aurelia and Owen waited on a group of weary travelers, then explained to them and to Emmaline who'd come to buy coffee: "My attorney, Mr. Gibbs, stood in for me as he said he would. Ted Malloy was in court this time because Hamilton," she cleared her throat, "my lawyer—made sure of it. But Ted told terrible lies, claiming that I—I am a l-loose woman. He claimed that from the beginning of our marriage it was hard to keep m-me at home and out of other men's . . . beds. When the judge asked why he'd want to remain married to such an unsavory woman, he said that he loved me, he sympathized with my misguided ways and believed with attention and loving care I would settle down, cured."

"What hogwash!" Aurelia was shocked, a white line tightened around her lips. "My heart aches for you Meg, dear. If the judge only met you for a few minutes he'd know better, he'd know you're not that kind of person."

Meg continued numbly, "Judge Williams decided to put off the case until I can be there. He was suspicious that anyone so wronged as Hamilton said I was, wasn't there to defend myself in person."

"You couldn't help it!" Aurelia cried, her face filling with color. "Don't they know back there that the Cheyenne were making trouble and no one could move about without risking their lives?"

Owen shook his head. He went to restraighten a shelf of canned oysters to hide his disbelief and anger on Meg's behalf. Emmaline stood silently, her hand covering her mouth.

"They do know, now," Meg told them through a dry throat. "Hamilton said that it wasn't until after the hearing that there was news in the St. Louis papers about the Cheyenne's escape from Fort Reno through western Kansas. He was sure that's what kept me away, he just didn't know if I was alive or dead. I sent him a wire that I was fine."

"You have to go back again?" Emmaline broke her silence to comment. "Things seem so clear to me, it shouldn't be so difficult for a woman to get a divorce when she needs it."

"Yes, I have to go back and God willing, it'll be the last time. Not only does the judge ask that I be there in person to tell my story, he also wants to hear from witnesses to Ted's abuse against me." She sighed, worry crawling like worms through her mind, "All of that happened so long ago, it's my word against Ted's—unless we can locate my friend, Meara, who took me in after the last beating. We also hope to locate the doctor who treated me for my broken hip and other wounds Ted gave me."

"Do you know where these folks are—the doctor and your friend?" Owen turned back to ask worriedly. "And what happens if you can't find them?"

"The doctor was very old when he treated me; he may not be alive. Meara no longer lives where she did, I tried to find her when I was there." She took a deep breath, "I won't leave a stone unturned until I find them, or learn what happened to them. The judge says if they can be located and are ready to testify on my behalf, he'll move my case up. I won't have to wait so long next time for a day in court. Hamilton is sure that with witnesses to tell what really happened, I'll win my case."

That same evening, Meg rode over to Lucy Ann and Admire's homestead. As they sat at the Walshes' table sipping coffee, she explained that she had to be gone for some time and would have to depend on Admire to do her work while she was away. "I want to make you a full partner in the quarry and freight business," she told him.

"You don't have to do that Meg," he admonished her.

"You know I'll help you out however I can. Always have."

"Yes, you have, and that's why you've earned this, Ad. I won't take no for an answer. You're my full partner from now on, having a partner's say and earning a partner's equal share, not just a worker's pay and we'll sign an agreement to that."

Lucy Ann looked happy and very proud of him, but Ad put up an argument for a few minutes more before he at last conceded. "All right. But I woulda done the work just the same, without."

"I know you would've, Ad, but this makes me feel better about leaving, and better about the future. Who knows, I might marry one day, be a wife and mother, and not have so much time for the businesses."

Lucy Ann's eyes twinkled merrily. "You might find a husband in St. Louis, as much as you have to go there."

"A St. Louie man?" Admire scoffed. "A city dandy? Now that's about the foolishest thing you ever said, Lucy Ann, and most times you're a sensible woman! She's sorry for it, Meg." The silence that followed was suspicious. He looked at Meg, then at Lucy Ann, and back again at Meg. His eyes narrowed and his nose twitched. "You durn women," he said, swatting at the air and scooting his chair back from the table, "always seem to know somethin' nobody else knows."

The conversation had brought heat to Meg's face and she had the silliest urge to giggle. Instead, she avoided direct eye contact with either of them and calmly studied an embroidered sampler on the wall with Rachel's full name and birthdate wreathed with pretty flowers. She cleared her throat and made her voice stern, "There's a lot of surmising and gossiping going on around this community, for sure! I'm going to St. Louis for a divorce, not to look for another husband. Mercy, I've not gotten rid of the first one, yet!"

Admire nodded, "There's plenty of good Kansas men

when you do. Lucy Ann, honey, get us some more coffee, please."

"Back to business," Meg said firmly, but smiling. "You'll find the ledger I keep for the quarry business in my office at the mercantile, Admire. There's a list of orders to be filled, one order for Spearville, two for Dodge. You'll find invoices showing who still owes money. Collect from them if you can."

Next morning she rode northwest to the Hesslers'.

Will spotted her from the open door of his barn and waved; Bethany came out into the yard to greet her when she looked out the window of the soddy and saw her arrival. The Hesslers' sod ranch house was larger and grander than most in the area; Bethany welcomed Meg into their nicely-furnished parlor and Will soon joined them. Meg accepted a slice of Bethany's apple cake, and a thick white china mug of milk. She explained as they ate that she'd like Will to oversee her land-agent duties until she returned from St. Louis, if he would. "I've been a bit foolish, taking on so much, but they were things that had to be done. Can you help me out, Will? I know you have your crops to see to, but if there's somebody wanting a piece of land, maybe you can show them what's available and what claims are already taken. As you know, sometimes a claim looks vacant, but really isn't, the owner is just away maybe for the season. The map the land office at Larned provided me with is at the mercantile. Aurelia can show you where it is, and the other land office papers, too."

Will sat forward on his chair, hands clasped between his thin knees, and nodded. "Bethany and the young ones are a good help here on the farm, of course I can do this for you, be glad to."

"Good. Most landseekers stop in Paragon Springs to ask about land in these parts. I'll leave word with Aurelia and

Owen to send folks on to you, that you'll be able to help them locate claims. Bethany, this cake is delicious!"

Back at her mercantile late that day, Meg had a meeting with Owen. "I'm going to relinquish my tree claim," she told him. "I've tried very hard but I can't get enough seedlings to survive to make a decent stand and that's part of the rules for proving up. I know you've wanted out of the dugout, and to have a place of your own. I'd like to see you file on my tree claim, and homestead it. I'm telling you first that it's up for grabs, because I'd hate for it to become Jack's property."

Owen was delighted. "If your mind's made up and that's what you want to do, you bet I'll file on it! I've been looking over different claims but didn't dream I'd get a piece of land this close to the community—" he smiled, "—this close to Aurelia."

"I thought this would please you. I'll write a letter for you to deliver to the land office in Larned, saying I'm relinquishing. You can file while you're there, and as soon as you get back, start cutting sod for your new home. If you can keep the few trees still alive that I do have on the claim, they'll make you some nice shade."

As always, Hamilton met Meg at the train station. Although she stood sedately in the autumn sunshine, waiting for him to speak, she was so happy to see him that she felt she might spin off into the air, flying. He was tall and good-looking in his own special way—a mix of boyishness and dignity—and so dear.

"How are you, Meg? I've been worried to death about you."

"I'm here, and I'm fine," she said softly. "It's very good to see you."

He picked up her bag and his arm went protectively across the back of her waist as he took her to his waiting rig. As he helped her in, his look alone told her how important she was to him, and not just as a client. Her joy in the moment overrode her serious concerns, and she gladly let cares slip away for a while.

"Something's happened since I last wrote to you," he told her as they drove clip-clopping toward her hotel. He spoke seriously, and yet she sensed that his words weren't connected to how he was looking at her. There was gladness in his eyes and an emotion close to hunger.

She let herself enjoy the magnetic connection between them, then reluctantly turned her mind to his comment. As she looked at him she could feel in her bones that what he had to tell her dealt with Ted. "Is it Ted?" she asked on a sigh.

He nodded, his look was solemn. "His father, John J. Malloy, passed away two weeks ago. His funeral was impressive and sad. Much of St. Louis turned out for it; businesses closed. Hundreds of weeping folk followed the hearse carrying his casket to the cemetery. He helped a lot of people in his time, and they mourn him."

It was a few seconds before she could speak and then she said, "I'm sorry to hear that he's gone. He was a hard man, in his way, but a much better human being, even so, than his son." Further thought of Ted sent a shiver traveling her spine. "I wonder how Ted's taking his father's passing?"

"Not well, you can bet. How he feels emotionally is anyone's guess. Financially, he gets nothing." Hamilton clicked his tongue at the horse; it tossed its head and picked up the pace. "His father left much of his fortune to the magnificent St. Lawrence O'Toole church, the spiritual center and pride of Kerry Patch as you probably know. The church was built in 1855 and needs some refurbishing. He left money for the building of a high school in the Patch, and to other charities, as he threatened Ted he would do."

Meg replied quietly, worry in her voice, "Ted's going to blame me because I wouldn't stay and help him win over his father before he died, while there was still time to change his will. Ted wanted his father's money desperately."

"None of this is your fault, Meg." Hamilton's hand covered hers. "But it's undeniably a huge loss for Ted, and he'll want to blame someone for it other than himself. From all I've learned about him, he never could take responsibility."

"If he and I remained married, what's mine—my land, store, freighting business, and stone quarry—would be his. He'd at least have that. I think he has guessed that I have some property; he's going to fight this divorce more than ever, now that he's lost what his father had." She let her fingers curl around Hamilton's, taking comfort in his touch.

"I'm afraid so. That's why we have to find your witnesses and convince them to testify for you. We're going to build a very strong case, so that losing isn't even a possibility."

She nodded, unable to voice the deep concern she felt.

That concern carried into the next morning. Hamilton had to be in court for a property settlement case, one that was immensely important to the parties involved. The trial would probably take hours. He thought he'd be free by late afternoon and he and Meg would go then to Kerry Patch and seek information about her witnesses.

By the time she finished an early breakfast, Meg acknowledged that she couldn't wait. She could do this by herself and there was no need to use up Hamilton's valuable time. Someone in the Patch would surely be able to tell her where Doctor Kane lived, and if she asked enough folks, someone might know where Meara had gone.

She set off for Kerry Patch with high hopes and a prayer that Hamilton wouldn't be angry with her later, when he found out she'd gone ahead without him.

Ever concious that Ted might spot her, and taking care—her head and most of her face covered by a shawl—she spoke with the few people she found on the street and even knocked on doors with questions, without success.

Bridget spotted her passing on her way and waved her inside, first to scold her for putting herself in danger, then to fix her lunch. Over tea and potato cakes, Bridget had an idea: "There's a German grocer other side of the Patch, I buy from 'im when I want sausages or pork knuckles for my noodle soup. Don't know why I didn't think of 'im before. 'E might've known the gentleman Meara married, or at least have some idee where they went."

Meg reached over to hug her. "Thank you, Bridget, so much."

"I ought to send for that lawyer fella to come get ya, is what I ought to do," Bridget answered with a self-incriminating frown. "Ya take care, now, Cassiday Rose. I'll be askin' the saints to watch over ya."

After leaving Bridget's, keeping to alleyways and with her head and face covered, Meg lost no time finding Ludwig's Grocery Store. The small, intimate establishment was very clean and smelled deliciously of fresh-baked bread. Mr. Ludwig was a stout, friendly man, anxious to help Meg if he could. "Meara Dolan? Yuh, I think I do remember her. She married Helmut Gottlieb. I talked to Helmut a few times. He liked my rye bread and sausages."

"Do you know where Mr. Gottlieb was from, where the couple might've moved after they married?"

He shook his grizzled head. "Nuh, don't know that." His

face scrunched as he tried to grasp something mentally out of reach. "Now—wait a minute. I'm remembering him mentioning one time that he hailed from Hermann."

"Hermann, Missouri?"

He nodded. "That's an almost pure German settlement, you know. If he was from there, he likely took his new wife back there with him. It'd be a good place to look for them, anyhow."

Meg grasped his hand and shook it. "I'm in your debt, Mr. Ludwig, you've been very helpful." She studied the pastries in the glass case and then told him, "I'll have an apricot turnover, please." She dug into her reticule and paid him, smiling as she left.

Her next stop was the train depot to buy a ticket for an early-morning trip to Hermann. Then she went looking for the home of the old doctor who treated her after Ted beat her so badly.

According to Bridget, Dr. Kane and his wife had moved a couple of times, each time to a smaller, more humble dwelling as he grew too old to practice medicine.

Mrs. Kane answered Meg's knock. Meg told her who she was, and that she would like to speak with Dr. Kane. Mrs. Kane, silver-haired, petite, and wraithlike, invited her in with a quivery smile. She reminded Meg of a fragile white butterfly as she tottered in the lead toward the doctor's bedroom.

Meg looked at the figure dwarfed by his coverings on the bed and tried not to show her shock. Dr. Kane was hardly more than a rack of bones outlined under the coverlet. He was as gray as death, his eyes were hollow, his cheeks sunken. The tiny spartan room had a stringent, medicinal smell. "Dr. Kane," she said, taking his withered hand in hers. "I hope you don't mind talking with me for just a bit?" She explained who she was and why she was there.

His wife interjected in a soft, bird-like voice, "Doctor wanted to go to Mr. Malloy's funeral, they'd been friends for years. But of course, he wasn't able. He hasn't been able to be out of bed for a long time. He's very weak."

"Hummph!" Dr. Kane declared in a quivery thin voice, "John Malloy can't . . . come to my funeral either, now he's dead." He added in a shallow drawn-out whisper, "Doesn't matter, our long years of friendship were what counted, anyway."

Meg asked him if he remembered the night he had been summoned to Meara Dolan's house to treat Meg.

"I remember all of it." He lifted a bony shaking hand as if to touch her face. "That beast, John's son, nearly killed you. You were all over bruises and contusions. I treated them with tincture of arnica. You were bleeding badly from a cut on your temple; that blow alone was enough to kill you. Your hip was fractured, I had to set that. You were the worst case of a beating I ever saw."

The doctor waved for his wife to help him with a drink of water and then he continued slowly, "I ought to've taken a whip to Teddy for hurting you that way, Cassiday Rose. Sorry, now, that I didn't. John tried hard for years to make something of Ted, but he couldn't turn him. I guess a rotten apple is a rotten apple; you're not going to make a fresh one out of it."

"Doctor Kane," Meg asked, "could you give a written accounting of my injuries, a signed affidavit that I could present at my trial?"

He nodded, and motioned for his wife to get paper, pen, and ink. "Go to the folks' next door," he said feebly, "ask them to witness what I say to write."

Mrs. Kane returned in a few minutes, accompanied by two stooped, snowy-haired neighbors, a man and his wife. They stood by as Mrs. Kane took down her husband's description of Meg's injuries, and what caused them. The doctor signed his own name and the elderly witnesses added their signatures.

Meg had barely enough time to get back to her hotel before Hamilton's arrival. She was eager to tell him of the success she'd had on her morning quest. Maybe for the rest of the day they could forget their court problems and enjoy themselves. It would stretch propriety, for she was still a legally married woman and he was her representative, but maybe they could do something leisurely, just for enjoyment, for a change.

She was waiting in the lobby, refreshed, her hair combed, and dressed in her best dress when Hamilton arrived. She explained what she'd learned about Meara's probable whereabouts, and that she had a signed letter from the doctor detailing the results of Ted's beating.

He was amazed, wearing a wry smile. "I should have known you would proceed on your own. Lord, but you're a strong-minded, independent woman!"

"You don't mind?"

"I don't mind that you're strong and independent; I wish my own sister had been. On the other hand, it wasn't wise for you to venture into Kerry Patch alone. I'm sure you realize that if Malloy had crossed your path, it could have been dangerous. Because you're still his wife, he could have forced you into obedience, to do whatever he demanded. You took a big chance."

"I know," Meg answered, chastised. Some of her excitement at her morning's accomplishments dwindled. He probably wouldn't agree, but she asked, anyway, "Would you care to spend the afternoon with me, maybe seeing Forest Park? Set aside for awhile the worries over my divorce?" She added, her voice more subdued, "If you feel it wouldn't be proper, though, I'll understand."

He grinned at her, catching her hands. "Hang propriety, we're friends and I'd love to spend the afternoon with you, wherever you'd like. Let's ask Mrs. Lyle to fix us a picnic."

It was beautiful in the park in October. The leaves were turning to red and gold in bright sunshine, the temperature was just warm enough. They boated on the new lagoon, strolled through gardens of fall flowers, and later spread their blanket and ate their picnic. It was the best time Meg had had in ages. She couldn't ever remember talking so much in her life, or feeling so comfortable with the person she was with. She hated for the day to end, and returning to the hotel, Hamilton said the same.

It was late when they got back to her hotel room. Hamilton told her good-bye at her door, warning her to take care and make sure she was not being followed when she went to catch the train to Hermann in the morning. When he was gone, she undressed languidly, bathed, and slipped on her nightgown. She was humming to herself, turning back the covers, when a knock sounded at her door. She smiled thinking Hamilton had come to warn her one more time to take care. She opened the door, and cried out as Ted pushed his way into her room.

He grasped her hard around the waist with one arm and pushed her back against the wall, slamming the breath from her. With his other hand, he traced a finger under the low bodice of her nightgown across the rise of her breasts. He smiled, showing stained teeth. He kissed his finger. "Wife, you're so sweet, and I've waited so long."

She struggled against him but he held her hard against the wall with his body, her chest pained from having the breath knocked out of her. She struggled to speak, at last managed to cry out, "Let me go, Ted, before I scream and bring everybody in the hotel."

"Scream if you want, I'm your husband and I can explain that we're playing a little game."

Of course he would do that. Her mind raced in panic. All at once, what he was saying registered and she was appalled.

"Did you enjoy frolickin' with that lawyer, wife?" he asked. "That wasn't nice, walkin' out with another man, bein' unfaithful. Shame on you, what will the judge think, when I tell him?"

He'd followed her, was somewhere in the background when she was at Forest Park with Hamilton!

"We did nothing wrong." Her heart was thundering in her ears, she struggled to free herself from his grasp but he only gripped her tighter until it hurt. She caught her breath on a sob. "Let me go, please."

"The way he looks at you and the way you look at him, that's wrong! You're my wife. But we don't have to go to court, nosirree. All you have to do is take me back, let me be your husband. You're all I have now, Cassiday. We don't have to stay in St. Louis. We can go to Oregon, someplace like that, and make a new start. You'd like that, wouldn't you?"

"Never!" She twisted in his grasp but his hold tightened like a vise again.

He breathed into her face. "If we go to court, I'll have to tell what I saw; I might make it spicier. The judge won't agree to a divorce, if I want to forgive you. You decide, wife. We can sell what you got, wherever it is that you live, and leave for Oregon next week. *Or* I tell what I know in court, and we go, anyway."

"You're a liar and a weasel," she gritted through her teeth, "and I'll never, ever again do anything you want, Theodore Malloy!"

Before she knew what was happening, he released her enough to draw his hand back and give her a hard stinging slap across her face. "You'll do what I say, you damn goose!" Her head spun, her ears rang, she stumbled and almost fell. In a daze, she saw his hand draw back to hit her again. Then someone else was in the room, shoving Ted aside, and grabbing her. *Hamilton.*

She turned in his arms and clung to him, felt his muscled strength, smelled the clean smell of him, heard his wrath as he held her tight, "My God, man, how can you hit a woman that way? You scum of the earth, I ought to kill you!" She looked up then and saw Hamilton's eyes shooting fire and a muscle twitching in his jaw.

Ted stood spread-legged with his unshaven chin jutting, and bluffed, "She's still my wife, I can do as I please."

Held in the circle of Hamilton's arm, Meg could hear the whistle of his breath through his teeth, feel the thunder of his heart. Then his breathing slowed, each breath pulled from deep within as he calmed himself.

"She's been legally advised not to let you near her."

"Advised by you so she can be your personal whore, you're sayin'? Well, that won't hold water, she's married to me and she'll stay married to me."

"You damn fool, use some sense. If you have any decency, any feeling for Meg at all, leave her alone, let her go." Hamilton's expression was murderous, although by contrast his voice was calm and his manner professional. "It would be no trouble to involve the law to see that you stay away from her until this matter is decided in court."

Meg saw that Hamilton held to his professional manner by the thinnest thread. An explosion on his part could get him into trouble within his profession and would add deeper problems to her case. She put her hand on his chest. "It's all right," she said softly, "it's all right." She had to stop this, now.

Chapter Fifteen

"You're to leave these premises right now," Hamilton ordered Ted. "Stay away from Meg. We'll settle this in court and nowhere else. Do you understand me?"

Ted shrugged and his lip curled. "I understand you're sweet on her and she's got calf eyes for you. You'll never get her, though, I'll see to that. She's my wife and she'll stay my wife. If you're as smart as you think you are, big toad attorney, you'll keep your hands off her. I can tell the judge a few things I saw today."

"Get out!" Hamilton growled. "And keep away from Meg!"

Ted laughed, but he faded into the shadows of the hallway. They heard him laugh again, louder, when he reached the top of the stairway. Then the soft thud of his footsteps descending the stairs.

"Sweet heaven," Meg cried, covering her face with her hands, "how could I have ever thought I cared for such a person! He's horrible. He's nearly ruined my life before, and he's still going to, I know it." She reached for Hamilton, but he held her away from him and then took her hand in his.

"Malloy is right about one thing, dearest Meg," he said huskily. "You're very important to me personally, I've come to care for you deeply." When Meg looked up at him and started to reply, he shook his head. "Don't say anything. I shouldn't be saying any of this to you as it is. I'm your lawyer, you're my client; our relationship must be nothing more until this is over. If I were to endanger your chances for a divorce I couldn't live with myself. You have problems enough, Meg, without my affection for you adding to them."

She understood, but it was an effort not to put her arms around him and feel his closeness that she so needed. She moved further away so as not to weaken. "Thank you for what you did tonight. You showed admirable strength and control."

"I never wanted to kill a man so much in my life, and I probably should have."

"No, we'll handle this the right way. You were grand." Then she asked, "Why did you come back?"

He heaved a deep sigh, "To begin with, I'm glad I did and caught Malloy in time." He tucked his hands in his vest pockets as if to keep from touching her, and replied, "I've been uneasy about you travelling to Hermann alone tomorrow. Do you remember Posey Chadderdon, who boards at Mrs. Lyle's? I've asked her to accompany you and she's agreed."

It would be hard not to remember Posey Chadderdon. She was a flaxen-haired Amazon, full-bosomed and muscular. She could break Ted like a stick without half trying, if it came to that. If having a traveling companion was the only way Hamilton would be agreeable to Meg's trip, that was fine with her. "Thank you, Hamilton, I'm happy to have Posey accompany me."

"She'll be here in the morning, waiting in the lobby. But even with her along, please take care." He shook his shaggy head as if nothing were the way he liked it. He pushed back a boyish forelock that fell into his eyes. "I'll see you when you get back. If you need anything before you go or while you're there, please send word and I'll take care of it."

She watched him go. In spite of the dirty shadow Ted had brought to the night, her heart was singing. Hamilton was in love with her, a fact that she couldn't look at too closely, yet. He was right that they mustn't reveal their true feelings, their romantic feelings, toward one another.

Posey Chadderdon, her brown hat askew, her full-bosomed muscular figure swathed in brown wool, was waiting in the lobby beside a potted palm when Meg walked downstairs early the next morning.

They exchanged greetings. Posey chuckled uneasily, her tone scandalized and her eyes mistrustful, "You're the first woman with a divorce I've ever met, Meg. Well, I guess you're not divorced yet, but you plan to be."

"I definitely plan to be, and I appreciate your help." She hesitated, sizing up the woman's manner. "Would you rather not do this, Posey?"

"Oh, no, I'm going with you. I like Mr. Gibbs, and he's paying me." Her forehead wrinkled in a frown. "I suppose he knows what he's doing, helping you get divorced from your husband, but I just haven't ever known another woman to do it, that's all."

"Sometimes a divorce is the best thing to do," Meg told her with a smile. "Without a doubt, it is in my case."

Posey still looked unconvinced but Meg didn't have time to discuss the matter further. She was anxious to reach Hermann and find Meara. If Hamilton felt it was necessary for doubtful Posey to accompany her, then she would make the best of it.

They set off for Union Station, both of them keeping an eye out for Ted, in case he should be watching her hotel, intent on causing trouble. There was no sign of him. Perhaps he'd decided he could have all he wanted by going to court. He could be right about that if she were unable to locate Meara in Hermann, Meg thought with trepidation.

They were three and a half hours on the train, arriving at

Hermann, a small immaculate village situated on the south bank of the Missouri River, about noon. It was a warm, beautiful fall day. Meg was delighted with the town's old-world flavor. The mostly red-brick houses with white trim and green cornices were built flush with the sidewalks. Autumn flowers in red, gold, and bronze bloomed in neat side-yard gardens. At the wharf, fragrant pine lumber was being loaded onto a waiting steamboat. Narrow brick-paved streets rose sharply from the waterfront and ran up the hillsides into a blue fall haze.

"Should we have something to eat before we look for your friend?" Posey asked.

Meg didn't want to, but when she thought about it she realized she was hungry. They turned into a small establishment with the sign, *Gasthaus.*

The café was cozy, with low-beamed ceilings and round dark oak tables. A heavenly smell made Meg's stomach growl. Just when she thought she couldn't stand her hunger a second longer, their food was served: sauerbraten and a side dish of fried potatoes for her, sausage and noodles for Posey. Slabs of pumpernickel bread spread thick with fresh butter accompanied the meal, and for dessert there were sweet dark cookies and tea.

Later, Meg thanked the owner profusely for the fine meal, then asked if he might know Meara and Helmut Gottlieb.

He gave her a quick bright smile and nodded. "Ach, yeah, I do. A fine couple. Mr. Gottlieb is an important man in Hermann, well respected, and everybody knows and loves Meara."

They were here then! Meg's relief was boundless. "Can you tell us how to find them?"

He led them toward the front window and pointed, "Street right outside is Market, cross it and take next four blocks to Gellert. Follow Gellert to the top of the bluff, as far as you can go. You find Gottlieb home and winery up there. You'll see their name on their gate."

As they climbed the hill, Meg explained to Posey that Meara had been a simple seamstress, a spinster, when she'd known her in the past. "I'm thrilled that she's married well. She's a wonderful person, and she saved my life."

Posey was short of breath before they reached the top of the hill. She stopped on the path and caught Meg's arm, holding on for support. Meg, used to the rigors of life in western Kansas, hardly noticed the climb even with her limp but stopped to give Posey a rest.

They went on and in another few minutes came to the Gottlieb estate. "So this is it," Meg said. Her eyes rounded as she took in Meara's home—it was a palace, almost! The three-story, red-brick, black-trimmed house was centered regally with other stone buildings on a knoll. Behind the house, undulating vineyards faded into the distance. A stone fence surrounded the property; a sundial design and the name DER GOTTLIEB SONNENUHR WEINERY were worked into the wrought-iron gate. The name meant "The Gottlieb Sundial Winery," according to the man who owned the café.

It was all very beautiful! Meg slowly opened the gate. She led the way up the path to the front door, afraid, now that she was here, that Meara might not be at home.

Meg rang the bell and waited, rang again. Suddenly the door opened and Meara stood there, tall and handsome in a cranberry red dress, her eyes kind and inquiring.

A sudden spurt of tears blurred Meg's vision. Although Meara looked older, with silver strands in her hair, Meg would have recognized her anywhere. "Meara, do you remember me?" she uttered the words with an effort, emotion running through her in tides.

"Is it you, Cassiday Rose?" Meara asked in astonishment. "Lord save us, it is!" Tears flew to her eyes, but her smile was wide as she pulled Meg into a close hug. Then she stood her away, looking at her up and down. "You're beautiful—a woman now, not the young girl you was. You got away from 'im, that devil Teddy, didn't you? Oh, I'm so glad!" She pulled her into a tight hug again.

There was so much to tell, and after Meg had introduced Posey Chadderdon and they were seated in Meara's lovely parlor, she let a lot of it spill out. "I'm not called Cassiday, anymore," she explained first off. "I had to change my name in order to escape from Ted."

Meara nodded. "I thought you might've. I never stopped praying you were alive and well, even if I didn't know where you were and couldn't write to you."

"I moved around a lot, besides changing my name. I was afraid to write to you, for fear Ted would be watching, somehow, for letters from me, and that he'd learn how to find me. I can't tell you how happy I am to hear you've married. Folks I've talked to tell me you're very happy."

"Oh, that I am. My Helmut is one of the best men ever lived. We're very happy. Tell me more about yourself, Cassiday Rose."

Meg told about her life at Paragon Springs, then she explained her mission. "I want to divorce Ted for good, but I need your help, Meara. The judge would like to hear from witnesses as to how he treated me, the beatings, the cruelty. If you remember, Dr. Kane tended my wounds after you brought him to your house where you'd put me to bed. The doctor is very old and not well, but he wrote a letter affirming what happened. I'll give it to the judge. I suppose you could write a letter, too, but I was hoping you'd testify for me in person."

"Sure an' I will! That scoundrel liked to have killed you. Cuts and bruises like I never saw before. You were crawlin', then draggin' yourself to get to me with your hip broken."

Posey, sitting by and listening, looked horrified, and for the first time showed honest sympathy toward Meg.

"A divorce isn't hardly enough, though," Meara said later, as she brought dark rich coffee and apple torte for each of them. "That beast Malloy ought to be strung up. I had a terrible time, him tryin' to get out of me where you'd gone, Cassiday Rose, when you started gettin' better. I thought a few times he was goin' to attack *me*. I had to keep myself armed with a poker. I let him know I'd take nothin' off him, but it was maybe the scariest time of my life, even so!"

"I'm sorry," Meg said.

"Wasn't your fault. You were a young girl, didn't know what you were gettin' into, marryin' him. None of us did. You were alone, 'cept for me. You were grievin' the loss of your parents, you were such a sad little thing. I thought he'd make you happy, thought the two of you'd be a good match, him bein' from the important Malloy family an' all. Had no idea he was the snake he turned out to be, or I'd a stopped you from marryin' him."

"You saved my life, and I'll always be in your debt."

"Pshaw, only did what any decent person would've. I was just sorry I kind of pushed you into Teddy's arms in the first place. I shouldn't have done that, it was a big mistake."

"It would help if you could come to St. Louis right away. The judge has said he'll move my trial up sooner, if I can provide witnesses to what happened. Could you come?"

Meara stood up, as if to head for the door and leave that minute. "Sure an' I will. It's the busiest time at the winery for Helmut, so I won't ask him to accompany me. I'll catch the train back with you this evening, to St. Louis. I'll visit his brother Karl, and his wife Virginia, while I'm in St. Louis. My Helmut won't worry about me if I stay with his family."

"You're sure it won't be any trouble?" Meg asked.

"Not at all."

Posey frowned as she asked Meara, "Just like that, your husband will let you go away on a trip, he won't make you stay home?"

Meara chuckled. "We have hired help if we need it in the house. Helmut wants me to be happy, most of all. He lets me do what I want, as long as it's safe. He says the luckiest day of his life was when he married me." She said it with a wide teasing smile and a flip of her hand, "And it's true. My luckiest day was when I married him. We get along just fine." She was silent for a moment, studying Meg with misty eyes. "And for my sweet little Cassiday Rose, I'd do anything. Anything at all, to make up for what happened to her."

"Too many men beat their wives, like Meg's husband did," Posey offered, "but all of them aren't like that."

Meg, thinking of men like Owen Symington, and Will Hessler, and even Admire Walsh—and particularly Hamilton, said, "No, all men aren't like Ted."

"An' thank God for it!" Meara added. "An' thank God I got one of the good ones."

Later, the four of them, Meg and Posey Chadderdon, Meara and Helmut, walked down to meet the early evening train. Meara's husband, a large, robust, jovial man, was so in love with Meara that it showed in his every gesture and expression as he saw her off.

Meg found him delightful and adored him for loving her friend.

It was late when the train pulled into St. Louis, and there were few people about at the train station. A thorough examination of their surroundings by Meg and Meara showed no sign of Ted.

Meara gave Meg her brother-in-law's address so she could call on her as soon as she was needed. Meg gave her the name of her hotel.

Meara looked at the address and hugged Meg. "You two can ride with me that far." She led the way to a waiting hack where both the driver and the horse looked asleep in the street's lamplight.

At Meg's hotel fifteen minutes later, Posey saw Meg to her room. She insisted on looking under the bed for Ted and behind her clothes hanging in the wardrobe—in every possible hiding spot—until she was satisfied.

"Lock your door, Meg," she said as she was leaving, "and shove that table up against it, too, just to be safe." She looked at her for a long moment. "I think I might have misjudged you at first, believing that you were a flighty woman wanting a divorce so you can chase after other men. I know now that isn't so. You're right to get free, whatever it takes. Before today, I thought that if a man beats his wife she had no choice but to let him do it. That, or grab something and beat him first, shoot him, or run away."

"Running away doesn't solve the problem, I tried that. And I've never had a taste for violence, for spilling blood. A legal divorce is the best answer in situations like mine, I believe. It had better be."

Posey nodded. "You're lucky to have Mr. Gibbs working on it for you. Couldn't do any better than Mr. Gibbs."

"That's true enough." Meg smiled. "Thank you again, Posey." She took her hand and held it in both of hers. "You were good company, and I'm just thankful Ted didn't show up anywhere on the way."

"I would have cracked his skull if he had, and been happy

to do it, now that I've heard more about him. Good night, Meg."

"Good night."

Next day, Meg sat in the hotel dining room having a mid-morning cup of coffee and pondering her situation, only half mindful of the clatter in the kitchen not far from her table. She'd found her witnesses, but was there anything else she could do to cement her case? She couldn't keep returning to St. Louis. This time, her divorce had to happen.

There was one more person in Kerry Patch she hadn't spoken with because she'd believed it wouldn't do her any good. Now she was wondering if it might help to speak with Phoebe Finch, widow of the bounty hunter who tried to kill her.

At the time Meg went to Dodge to confess to the killing of Finch in defense of her life, Lad had already spoken to Sheriff Bassett and had told him the truth of what happened—that he was the one who had fired the gun. Rather than press charges on a case clearly defensible, Frank's widow, Phoebe, had told the sheriff to drop the matter and let her husband's body lie in peace where they'd buried him. That had been the end of the matter, legally.

Meg's heart beat a little faster, thinking it over. Was there a chance Phoebe Finch knew about her husband's work and could help her, and would she be willing? Could she make clear for the judge that to collect the bounty Frank must either bring Meg back or show proof that he'd killed her for resisting?

She must talk to Phoebe. But Hamilton was right to insist that she couldn't risk another visit to Kerry Patch. Yet the Patch was where Mrs. Finch lived. For a second she considered sending Posey on her behalf, then decided that she must do the job herself. If only she could disguise herself really well . . .

For several minutes, over the rim of her cup as she sipped coffee, Meg had been watching a scene in the kitchen through the half-open door, listening to the conversation there while her mind was busy with her problems. She was on her feet, smiling wide, rushing for the kitchen where the main actor in the kitchen scene, a scrubby boy, had been selling fish from a basket to the Chef. Now he was headed for the door to the alley.

Meg zipped through the kitchen and caught him just outside. "Do you have any fish left?"

He nodded, "Some small-mouth bass an' some blue gill." He lifted the basket lid to show her.

Meg nearly swooned from the smell, but she told him, "I'd like to buy them, and the basket." She counted out several coins from her reticule. "I'd like to buy your hat and coat, as well."

A look of greed filled the boy's face. "Not for that, you can't buy my clothes, too. Just the fish and basket."

She added a half dozen more coins. "Will this be enough?"

He answered by setting the smelly fish basket at her feet. He peeled out of his coat, took off his hat, and handed them to her.

"Thanks, Miss," he showed scummy teeth in a grin, "but I don't think you got much of a bargain." With that he went running hard up the alley.

"I think I might've," she said softly, smiling at his retreating back. "We'll see anyway."

A while later, she slipped out of the hotel the back way, dressed in her plainest skirt, the boy's dirty ragged coat, and carrying the fish basket. She had tucked most of her hair out of sight under his filthy hat; she'd smeared her face with coal dust from the shed in back of the hotel.

The fish basket was heavy and Meg was glad to sell her fish and lighten her load on the way to Kerry Patch. When Bridget answered her tap at the door, she started to tell Meg that she didn't want any fish, but Meg interrupted, "It's me, Meg . . . Cassiday Rose." An astonished Bridget ushered her inside.

Meg explained to Bridget and Mrs. Clary, who was visiting, the reason for her disguise. They remembered Frank Finch and his widow, Phoebe. She was Mrs. Phoebe Dunlap, now. They gave her directions to Phoebe's house and an accompanying heavy dose of caution to be careful of Ted should she see him.

"Phew!" Mrs. Clary exclaimed when Meg picked up her basket again and walked toward the door.

Meg smiled over her shoulder, pulling the hat's brim down low over her face. "Sorry for the smell. I'll be glad to get rid of it, myself."

It was more difficult to convince Phoebe Dunlap, a plump, cherub-faced woman with graying blond hair, of her identity. Standing on Mrs. Dunlap's porch—Phoebe didn't want her inside the way she smelled—Meg told her whole story, which in the end left no doubt.

Shamefaced, apologetic, Phoebe readily told her, "Yes, Frank would've killed you if that was the only way he could get his pay from Malloy. Those were the orders he got, though I tried to get him not to do it. Ted had taken a lot of money from his father to pay Frank with. It was more money than Frank usually earned doing that kind of work and Frank wanted the money in the worst way. Wouldn't listen to me, beat me before he left. Ted gave him half to go after you and he would get the other half when he brought you back alive, or proof you were dead."

"You didn't go to the police and let them know what Ted

215

and your husband planned?" A wagon was coming noisily along the road, but Meg, waiting for Phoebe Dunlap's reply, paid little heed.

"I was afraid, you have to understand. You and me both could've ended up dead."

There was a tremor in Meg's voice. "Would you tell that in court before a judge and help me get a divorce?"

Phoebe wore a deep, thoughtful frown. She picked up her calico cat and stroked it for quite a while. Meg had almost given up when Phoebe spoke, "I wouldn't mind making up for what Frank did back then. It shames me, and I can't see as it would hurt me, anymore. I've got a good life now, with Mr. Dunlap. I'll come if you'll let me know when to be there."

"Mrs. Dunlap, I can't thank you enough!" Meg reached for her hand, but Phoebe looked at Meg's fish-slimy fingers and drew back.

"That's all right," Phoebe said, "I know you thank me. I'm sorry you had to go through so much grief because of Frank. And I hope you get free of that Ted Malloy so you can go on with a good life, like it's been my privilege to do."

Meg turned to leave, and found a wagon and driver stopped at the end of the walk. After a flurry of alarm, she saw that it was Bridget's neighbor, Mr. Harrah, a bashful, elfin-like man of middle age. In a thin voice he told her that Bridget had sent him to drive Meg back to the hotel in safety.

"Bless you, and bless Bridget," Meg told him thankfully as he helped her up into the wagon. He wasn't happy with how she smelled, she could tell.

On the other side of town, she had Mr. Harrah take the alley behind her hotel and drop her at the back door. She scuttled inside. She left the fish basket, coat, and hat, with the chef. "When the fish delivery boy comes again, give him his things, please. And would you tell him that I made a good bargain, after all, and thanks!"

Upstairs, she had the hotel maid fill her tub to the brim with hot water. She got in the tub, lathered herself all over with lavender soap, and then soaked for nearly an hour.

When Hamilton came to see her that evening, they both had news. He said that Judge Williams had an opening in court in two days, if Meg could have her witnesses there by then. A case previously scheduled for that time was found to need more investigation and had been put off.

"My witnesses are lined up and ready," she told him proudly. She explained about finding Frank Finch's widow, now remarried, and that she would testify on Meg's behalf. He wasn't happy that she had taken the risk of returning alone to Kerry Patch, but she could see he could hardly argue with her success. They agreed that he would notify her witnesses of the time and day to be in court. Ted would also be notified.

Hamilton's eyes didn't leave Meg's face as they were saying good night. She sensed that he wanted to hold her and kiss her—as much as she longed for him to do so. But the rules of his profession and his honor held sway and the moment slipped away, leaving a knot of disappointment in her chest.

He said quietly, "It's almost over, Meg. I'll send a driver for you tomorrow, to bring you to the courthouse."

Next day, the hearing was amazingly short. Like some weddings, Meara said later, it was over in the blink of an eye.

Judge Williams, short, balding, but handsome, was as Hamilton described him: a thoughtful, kindly man with a solid air of authority. Meg told her story, answering the judge's questions thoroughly and with care. The judge read the doctor's letter, listened to Meara's involvement in Meg's early life, her judgment of Meg's character, and what she had witnessed of Ted's brutality. It was Phoebe's testimony, however, that finally clinched the matter.

"My husband didn't have much conscience, Your Honor," she told the judge, "and he would do anything for money. Kill Cassiday Rose if that's how he'd get paid. And she never did nothing to him or Ted Malloy to deserve it."

Malloy's attorney, Hiram Smith, jumped to his feet to protest but Judge Williams waved for him to sit back down. "It's not that I don't believe you, Mrs. Dunlap, but what you're telling me is hearsay, your version of what took place. I'm afraid it's not admissible as fact."

Smith relaxed and smoothed his thinning hair. Next to him, Ted smiled cunningly.

The judge was regretful, "I could move on this case much more quickly if I had proof of your husband's agreement with Ted Malloy to do Mrs. Malloy harm."

"But, I have proof, Your Honor."

A stirring in the room sounded like bees taking flight. Meg stared at Phoebe who hadn't mentioned proof to her.

"Proof?" the judge asked. He clasped his hands in front of him and waited with a kindly smile.

"Yes, Your Honor. Frank trusted the word of some men but not Ted Malloy's. He made him write their agreement on paper. I only found it after I remarried and was throwing out some trash that was Frank's. It's right here—" she scratched about in her handbag. "Not sure why I kept it. Frank was dead. I figured Cassiday—wherever she was—was safe by then." She brought out a small piece of paper that rustled loudly in the quiet room. "Here it is. It says—"

The judge stopped her. "I'll read it for myself." He nodded for the bailiff to bring the paper to him. With a deepening frown, Judge Williams read the note, then he asked the bailiff to show it to Ted. "Is that your handwriting?" he demanded.

Ted examined it and his expression turned sick. "Yes, it is my hand, but she—"

The judge silenced him with a glare. "Mr. Malloy, your note says: 'Bring my wife back so I can make the bitch pay. If she resists do what you have to do but I'll need proof she's dead or you won't get another dime.' You wrote that?"

Ted was ashen. His glance darted about in panic seeking support. His lawyer was staring at him aghast. He offered no aid. Ted blustered, "Yes, I wrote it. I was angry. Wouldn't you be?" He looked at the judge, then at Hiram Smith. "Cassiday dishonored me by running off. I'm her husband! I didn't really mean that, to kill her, not like that. I wanted her back."

Judge Williams's voice was gritty with disgust. "To honor and cherish her, I suppose? Your agreement with Frank Finch indicates the opposite."

Ted leaped to his feet, fear had etched deep lines in his face. Smith tried to restrain him, but he shook him off. He jabbed a finger wildly in Meg's direction, and his eyes glared resentment. "This is all this woman's fault. She abandoned me, abandoned her duties as my wife." His voice turned thin and pleading, "She alienated me from my father and destroyed my life, Your Honor. She's an unfaithful woman. She's been dallying now with that lawyer right there, Hamilton Gibbs!"

"Sit down!" Judge Williams shouted. "You're a pathological liar, Mr. Malloy, and a wife-beater of the first order. I am awarding the plaintiff, Mrs. Malloy, the divorce she requests. If she will bring charges against you, I'll also have you thrown in jail for attempted murder. Mrs. Malloy?"

Meg thought for a minute, then whispered her directions

to Hamilton. He stood and addressed the judge: "Your Honor, my client, Mrs. Malloy, wants only to divorce the defendant and to have assurance that he'll never come near her again."

"Mrs. Malloy," the judge addressed her, "is that your desire? Would you speak, please?"

She nodded and stood up beside Hamilton. Her knees felt weak but she made her voice strong, "What happened is partly my fault. I used poor judgment in marrying Theodore Malloy in the first place. A life has already been taken for the attempt on mine. But I will leave it to your discretion, Your Honor, if you believe Ted should serve time."

"I do believe he should," the judge rumbled, "the defendant needs a year in jail to reflect on his actions. He needs to think about how he wants to spend the rest of his life, if he wants to stay out of court and out of jail."

Ted had shriveled in his chair, a beaten man. An officer of the court came and led him, dazed with shock and stumbling, from the room.

Meg turned and thanked Hamilton, then she went to Phoebe Dunlap and clasped her hand. "You saved me today, and I thank you very much."

"It was the least I could do, dear. After you left my house, I remembered the paper and thought it might help." Mrs. Dunlap smiled and with her gloved finger reached up and wiped away a tear that had appeared under Meg's eye.

Meg next threw her arms around Meara and cried into her shoulder. She pulled herself together after a few seconds and looked for the judge, to thank him, but he had left the room.

"You'll thank him for me, won't you, please?" she asked Hamilton.

"He knows how much you appreciate being awarded your freedom, but I'll convey your thanks, just the same."

"It's over," she whispered, disbelieving, "it's all over at last. I'm free."

"Yes," he agreed, "it's done." There was a shadow behind his smile and they both knew that, beyond filling out and filing some papers, Meg would have no further need of him. Her case was settled. She was free to return to her life at Paragon Springs and he would be taking on other law cases there in St. Louis.

"Hamilton—?" she said, her throat feeling raw.

He looked as stricken as she felt. "Tonight, let's have supper together."

She nodded. "Tonight." She stared at him, finding it impossible to believe that it would be the last time they'd be together. But how else could it be? Her life, her future, lay in western Kansas, and his was here in St. Louis.

Chapter Sixteen

At dinner that evening, Meg told Hamilton, "Your letters have been a joy to me and I'm going to miss them. Unless—" she didn't want to push but hoped he felt as she did "—unless you'd like for us to keep writing?"

In a few hours she would be gone for good and already she felt lonely. With her divorce assured, she and Hamilton no longer needed one another for professional reasons.

Their lives were so different and were led so terribly far apart, yet it pained her to think that their friendship was over. It was impossible to believe that she'd never see him again, would never again experience his warm wit and kindness, feel the sunshine of his smile. She toyed with her food, her appetite fading.

Hamilton's voice was huskier than normal. "Your letters have meant a great deal to me, too. Let's do continue to write." He gave her the smile she'd come to cherish and his eyes sparkled. "If you were to stop telling me of the goings-on at Paragon Springs, it'd be like having a fascinating book snatched away before I'd finished with it. I find your people out there very interesting. If I can advise by wire or through the mail on any matter, just let me know."

She swallowed against the thickening in her throat and took a sip of coffee, then told him ruefully, acknowledging his offer, "I have to admit it's a constant struggle on the plains. We battle the elements for survival; at times the simplest needs—food, water, and fuel—are hard to come by. As if that weren't trouble enough, there's considerable lawlessness, including a rancher who hates homesteaders and is determined to ruin us and run us out . . ." Her voice trailed off, then she went on forcefully, "Still, I'm convinced that with hard work and perseverance we can build good, peaceful lives out there."

"You'll do it." He studied her face for several seconds. "Unless an easier life in St. Louis might appeal to you?"

For a second she searched his face to see if there was special meaning in his comment, then she decided he was only making conversation. She'd be foolish to let her fancy run away with her. She felt sad but told him sincerely, "I belong at Paragon Springs. It's the only place I'll ever feel at home. St. Louis is very nice but only to visit, or for business reasons."

"If you come to St. Louis for anything, you'll contact me?"

"Of course." Actually, there was nothing for her in St. Louis but his friendship. She drew a deep breath. "I don't suppose you'll ever have a need to come out my way?"

"The wild west?" He grinned, but there was a desperate look of loss behind it. "You never know."

She nodded, unable to respond.

Their parting the next morning passed in a confused blur. Meg could feel the pull of home, where work—and friends that were more like family—awaited her. Except for Hamilton, there was nothing in St. Louis for her that could match the sunsets over the broad plains, the heart-stirring trill of the gray junco at this time of year. She ached for home, but the pain of leaving Hamilton's company was as intense, as harsh as if her limbs were being wrenched off one by one.

Hamilton looked as miserable as she was feeling.

Later, at the bottom of the train steps, he caught her in his arms. For one delicious moment, he held her tight against his chest—and then she was stumbling onto the train. She hurried for a seat, found him through the window, and didn't take her eyes from him until the train was moving and he had vanished from view.

At Paragon Springs, November brought the chill of coming winter. Meg sat at her small office space in the mercantile going over business records, while wind and ice tapped at the small window. She closed the book with a weary sigh. The notations and figures in the ledger were meaningless. All she could think of was Hamilton.

She'd received several letters from him in her first weeks back. Warm, friendly letters relating general goings-on in St. Louis, plus funny tales from Mrs. Lyle's boarding house and fascinating stories about his work. But for two weeks now, there'd been nothing. It felt more like months.

She was afraid that his friendship was fading. He'd had time to realize that it was fruitless to keep up a correspondence with no hope of a happy ending if he'd ever had anything more serious in mind for them.

She forced her hurt and sadness aside, put the ledger into its cubbyhole, and went to her room for her coat, scarf, and boots. Will and Bethany Hessler were butchering three hogs today, and everyone for miles had been invited to help out in exchange for a portion of the meat, and then to enjoy supper and a dance.

She wholeheartedly welcomed this diversion and the busy day of butchering. Because her friends looked for her to be endlessly cheerful and happy now that she'd won her divorce, she'd have to put on her best face and keep her chin up. She wanted no one's pity, although she missed Hamilton with every breath she took.

She went outside into the cold November wind to join the wagons of folks ready to leave for the Hesslers' and said a little prayer to be successful in her cheerful performance.

The men had killed the hogs in the early morning hours. Down by Will Hessler's barn, they hung the carcasses upside down from pole racks and cut the throats to let them bleed, the blood saved in pails for making blood pudding. Youngsters, noses red from the cold, played tag at the gory scene, laughing, chattering, all of them used to such necessity after a few years on the plains.

Aurelia called a halt when Shafer began to play with the intestines as though they were a lasso. The intestines were needed for use as sausage casings. "Bring more chips," she ordered. "We have to keep hot fires going here all day. Joshua, you and David John help. Zibby, you and Rachel play inside the house; out here is no place for little girls."

Vats of water were heated and the hog carcasses dipped into them. Then the women, using whatever sharp tools they could lay hand to, scraped the bristles from the hides. While the men quartered the carcasses, the women went inside to cut up the meat into hams, chops, and roasts. Scrap meat would be ground for making sausage. Fat trimmings would be rendered into lard for use in frying and baking; some would be used for making candles and soap.

Lad and Shafer, knees bent under their loads of heavy hindquarters and shoulder sections, brought meat inside for cutting up, letting in cold blasts of air as they came and allowing the warmth of the house to escape.

At one table, with knives flashing, Aurelia and Bethany trimmed fat off the hindquarters and rib sections. Lucy Ann and Emmaline then cut the fat into tiny pieces and dropped them into a large kettle placed on the stove.

Later, Meg was cutting a large loin into chops and roasts. Aurelia, caught up for the moment from washing intestines, came to help. They worked companionably, the women other than Meg chattering about what they were each making in secret for the children's Christmas. Meg, with no children of her own, felt left out of the conversation; however, she'd make or buy small gifts for all the youngsters. She loved each and every one of them as if they were her real nieces and nephews.

Meg hadn't realized that she had cut her hand until she saw the blood. "Would someone pass me a wet cloth, please?" she held her cut hand in the palm of the other while the blood dripped. "I'm sorry, Bethany, I'll clean your floor in a minute."

"I can't imagine what's going to become of you, Meg," Aurelia spoke with a worried frown as she took Meg's hand and mopped at the blood.

"I don't know what you mean."

"You know as well as the rest of us do that you haven't been yourself since you came back from St. Louis. Your mind wanders."

So her friends had noticed in spite of her pretense. She defended herself, "Nothing is different and I'm not changed. I'm doing all my work, as usual. I'm here today, just like all of you." She smiled, and licked her lips to stop their trembling.

Aurelia leaned close to examine the cut. She clucked her tongue. "It's going to have to be watched so you don't get infection, but I think it will heal without stitches." She looked Meg in the eye. "You know good and well what the trouble is. You've got your mind on that lawyer, Gibbs, and have had since you got home. You're in a daze half the time. The other day you left for Dodge City without the mail folks up here wanted sent on east from the Dodge City depot. Remember when you put a cup of salt instead of sugar in the gingerbread you were making?"

"Oh, for heaven's sake, the knife just slipped, and those other things were accidents like anyone has. I'm doing the best I can."

The other women ceased work to listen; they looked sympathetic, but Aurelia would give her no quarter. "You're going to have to forget him, Meg, or go after him, one or the other. If not, you're going to hurt someone seriously in an accident, most likely yourself, or you're going to work yourself to death pretending everything is the same as it ever was."

Meg pulled her hand away, bundled it in the cloth and held it. "Hamilton has been a good friend, as well as excellent professional help. And, well, I admit he's not easy to forget. But going after him, as you put it, isn't possible in the least. I can't leave Paragon Springs, and Hamilton has his work in St. Louis. We weren't meant to be together." Her misery turned into anger at Aurelia. "You and Owen are right here in the same spot living very similar lives," she pointed out. "You could get married tomorrow, and you're a fool not to, Aurelia Thorne! I know what I'd do if I were in your shoes."

For a second, Aurelia's lips thinned and a frown creased her brow. She said, "Well, you're not in my shoes, and you only think you know what you'd do if you were." She undid the cloth on Meg's hand and wiped it with a cloth dipped in turpentine that Bethany had brought.

"That hurts like Old Ned!" Meg protested.

Aurelia ignored her and went right on, "You left the man you married, because you had to, and it was your choice to be by yourself from then on. I loved my husband heart and soul. We had a good life until he went and got himself killed over stolen horses. He didn't need to go. He left me alone with four children to raise."

"That wasn't intentional, Aurelia! You know good and well that your husband would've preferred to live a long life with you and your youngsters. The chance of anything like that happening to Owen is probably a million to one, and you know he'd never ride off and leave you the way your brother-in-law did. You don't have anything to lose by saying yes to Owen, and you have a wonderful life to gain."

Aurelia scowled and mumbled under her breath, "I want to."

Meg's head shot up, unsure of what she'd heard, and she wore a puzzled half-smile. "What did you say?"

"She said she wants to," Emmaline, stirring the fat over at the stove, answered. Both Bethany and Lucy Ann nodded.

Aurelia's hands fluttered helplessly in the air. "I'd like to say yes to Owen when he proposes, but it isn't that simple. It's like, well, I feel like I'd be giving permission for something bad to happen. But if I don't answer him, things will be fine." She looked stricken, and at the same time embarrassed and guilty. She repeated an old adage without much conviction, " 'Kissing wears out, cooking doesn't.' I don't need romance at my age. Some things are better left as they are."

Meg caught Aurelia's hand in her uninjured one. "Not this, Aurelia, I swear to heaven, not this. Owen has his own homestead now, he's building a fine sod house, proof that he means to be around a long time. But it's your life, and I'm having trouble enough with my own."

The women had returned to work, but Lucy Ann offered over her shoulder as she strained liquid fat into a clean pail, "If things with you and the lawyer can't work out, Meg, maybe you'll meet someone else and fall in love with him. You're free to do whatever you want. There's some nice men here in the valley; maybe one day soon one of them will look awfully good to you."

She had an inclination to disagree but to save baring her private soul she answered, "Possibly." She made a joke,

"That wily Tog Elsberry in Dodge would be a good catch, don't you all think?"

Lucy Ann snickered, then covered her mouth. "Him?"

"Elsberry?" Aurelia scoffed, "with his dirty yellow moustaches that droop to his chest?" She pulled a long mocking face.

Meg replied drily, "He has lots of money from trading in buffalo bones and cattle—a lot of it made from my hard labors. I could get it back, be rich."

All of them laughed, then a brief silence followed.

"Charley Villard, that young bachelor rancher down by Spearville, was asking about you, was anyone courting you," Lucy Ann said. "He asked Admire. Charley's outside with the men, Ad invited him."

"It's all right that Ad invites his friends, but I really don't need anyone looking for a husband for me." Meg thought about Charley, a bony cowboy with ears so big they folded under his big hat. She mentally shook her head. Charley was a good man, but he was not for her. With each passing day she was more convinced that she'd met the only man she'd ever truly love. She was equally positive nothing could come of it. She'd go on in life, probably a single woman to the last, if she couldn't have Hamilton. And of course that was out of the question.

Everyone was worn to a frazzle from work by the end of the long day, but came back to life, Meg noted, after a delicious supper of boiled potatoes, fried pork and gravy, dried apple pies, and gallons of coffee to drink.

Later, the table was cleared and the dishes were washed. In a brief parade of carriers, the furniture was moved outside to clear the house for dancing. Three musicians including a fiddler, a fellow who played spoons, and a third who played the mouth harp, were tuning up.

Two or three hours of dancing followed; party dances that involved everybody and consisted of a lot of kicking, whooping, and swinging. Meg forgot her lame hip and the dull ache in her bandaged hand, and danced her cares away. Midway through the dancing, lanky Charley Villard, his eyes bleary and hardly able to stand on his feet, tried to convince her to go outside with him. She told him, out of breath and smiling, that she thought she wouldn't—he'd had a bit too much tanglefoot. Behind her smile was the aching wish to know what it would be like to dance all evening with Hamilton, to slip outside and be kissed by him.

It was a day toward mid-December and Meg had been out since first light feeding her cattle in the ice and snow. By the time the last bundle of hay was thrown, she was numb clear through; the snow had turned to sleet that bit her cheeks like needles. She went on to her next chore, fixing the corner of her shed where the roof and wall had caved in under the weight of snow. As the day wore on, she wanted nothing so much as to soak in a hot bath, and then to crawl into bed and sleep away her exhaustion.

As soon as she got to the house, her outside work done, she grabbed a couple of buckets and returned to the spring. She'd build a fire and heat up as much water as she could carry. She hoped the ice was melted on the spring-pond; she didn't think she had the strength to break ice.

She was leaning over the pond, prepared to stoop and dip her bucket, when her foot slipped on icy stone. She tried to catch her balance, twisting back to keep from falling headfirst into the pond. She crashed down, striking her head and cracking her ribs against stone, knocking her breath away. Dark slid over her like a dropped curtain.

Meg woke to a cold drizzle slanting into her face and her open mouth. She ran her tongue around the inside of her mouth. Slowly she sat up, only to be overwhelmed with a dizzying sickness as pain knifed her ribs. She reached up and felt a knot rising on her head, the answer to the pain there. She was so cold she was sure she could never thaw, she tried to stand, and couldn't, she fell back hard. As she sat there, her tongue between her teeth in an effort to endure the pain in her ribs and head, a sob of anger and despair at her helplessness caught in her throat.

She had no idea how long she'd lain unconscious in the sleet and rain, but her clothes were soaked and she was ice cold to the bone. Still, it couldn't have been so long that she'd been missed yet; no one had come to find her. Maybe it'd been only a few minutes.

Moving slowly, carefully, she struggled to her knees and then to her feet and stood weaving. Taking tiny steps that jabbed pain into her skull and ribs with every movement, she made her way to the mercantile. She couldn't reach the door, cried out and slid down to sit on the icy ground.

The door opened to show Aurelia's shocked face. "I thought I heard someone out here." She knelt by Meg on the frozen ground, exclaiming. "Meg! My goodness! What's happened?" Meg put up her hand to ward her off.

"I've bruised my ribs, or broken them," she gasped. "I slipped and fell, at the springs. Hit my head . . . my side . . . on the rocks. Help me up, but . . . please take care. I hurt so . . . bad."

Aurelia called out for Owen. He came, exclaiming, "Oh, my God, what is it?" when he saw Meg. As Aurelia explained, Meg was close to passing out again.

"Let me," Owen told Aurelia, and with care he scooped Meg off the hard, sleet-covered ground. Aurelia raced ahead into the store, waving Owen on toward Meg's room.

Shuddering from chill, her teeth clenched against pain and nausea, Meg allowed Aurelia to take over. She first removed Meg's chilled wet clothing, then washed her with warm water and bound her ribs. Meg held onto consciousness as Aurelia dressed her in a nightgown and inspected a cut on her head. "This lump up here is as big as a goose egg," Aurelia mumbled, "but it doesn't worry me as much as the chill you took, and your cracked ribs."

A few minutes after that Aurelia brought a little brown bottle of laudanum and talked Meg into taking a half-teaspoonful. "For the pain, and to help you sleep. This might not've happened, Meg, if you hadn't been driving yourself so hard. You need rest, a lot of it."

"The chores—"

"Hush about that!"

Meg couldn't control the shaking. She mumbled her thanks later as Aurelia tucked her into bed and drew the soft warm quilts to her chin. The last thing she remembered was Aurelia putting warm stones wrapped in towels at her feet under the covers, then bringing a chair close to her bed, sitting down and taking her hand and holding it.

She loved Aurelia. She was someone you could always count on.

Next morning, Meg woke with a rasping cough that tore her apart with each expectoration. Aurelia would allow her up only to relieve herself on the porcelain chamber pot kept under her bed. Then she helped Meg back into bed, washed her hands and face, and brought her a dish of hot gruel for breakfast.

By evening, Meg's cough had worsened and she had developed a raging fever. Nothing would stay in her stomach.

Aurelia tried beef tea, a little whiskey in milk, and for her cough, boiled onion syrup.

Sometimes in the days that followed, Lucy Ann spelled Aurelia and sat with Meg, or Emmaline or Bethany sat with her. They brought her treats of soft puddings and tea, bathed her feverish flesh, told her stories of the children's antics to keep her alert and with them.

Meg was only half conscious of their comings and goings and their murmurings over her bed. She hated the cough that built slowly inside and then tore her in two when it couldn't be held back. Her head wracked with pain that made being awake nearly unbearable. She was glad for the paregoric that Aurelia administered, that allowed her periods of relief.

After the sixth day, she began to feel better. Aurelia was happy about her improvement, but would let her out of bed for only short periods. "The cracked rib and the chill you took have given you pleurisy. You might feel better, but you're a long way from being on your feet again. We're going to keep you in bed, with hot stones at your feet to keep you warm and make you sweat. If the pain in your side gets worse, we'll apply a wet mustard plaster. A good dose of salts won't hurt you, either."

A few days before Christmas, Meg was still feeling weak and wobbly and subject to long periods of coughing that pained, but she told Aurelia, catching her hand when she came one noon with a bowl of soup, "I want to watch the children get ready for Christmas. Maybe I can help them with the decorations. Please let me out of this room."

Aurelia grudgingly okayed her request, "Only for a few minutes at a time, mind."

Owen had found a shrub down by the river that would serve as their Christmas tree, but he grumbled that it should be an evergreen like the Christmas trees he'd seen in Ohio.

The tree was placed inside the front window of the store, on the opposite side from the potbellied stove.

Bound to her chair by a heavy quilt, Meg sat by the stove, greeting customers who came to the store and neighbors who came to visit. She helped string popcorn and braid small straw wreath-ornaments, which were then tied with bits of bright ribbon. She could only be up for short periods of time, quickly losing the strength to even sit up, but she relished the moments out of bed and felt herself rebuilding her strength with each day. Her friends brought her carefully prepared dishes of egg custard, cream of pumpkin soup, hot beef broth with onion. She ate even when she didn't feel up to it. She was determined to be back on her feet before the time Aurelia predicted.

Her nights were broken by periods of sharp coughing that left her weakened and weary; she'd be glad for that to change so she could get more sleep.

She was in her room the day before Christmas, just stirring awake from a nap, when Aurelia came in wearing a mile-wide smile. Her eyes were luminous with wonder.

"What is it?" Meg asked, struggling to sit up against her pillows.

"It's him!" Aurelia clasped her hands at her breast. "He's come. Your Mr. Gibbs, he's come for a Christmas visit."

"You're joking! He can't be here."

Aurelia pointed. "Well, he is, he's out there in the store, big as life."

"Oh, Aurelia," Meg cried, throwing back the covers, "help me dress. Oh, my hair. I look a mess." She put her legs over the side of the bed and felt dizzy.

"Slow down, Missy, be careful. I'll help you. There's no hurry. Mr. Gibbs is out there visiting with Owen. Your friend had a hard time getting here in the rig he rented in Dodge, snow was drifted over the trail something terrible, he says. His train almost didn't make it. The weather what it is, he may not get back to Dodge and his train for a while. He's going to stay with Owen at his place. Slow down, Meg."

Meg took over dressing herself with trembling fingers. She couldn't lift her arms in the air long enough to brush and coil her hair so she let Aurelia do that. Then, with Aurelia's arm to steady her, she walked out into the store.

Rangy and tall, his thick brown hair mussed, he was standing by the stove warming his long-fingered hands. His clothes were rumpled brown as usual. When he smiled, his prominent cheekbones rose and his blue eyes sparkled. He said her name in his deep warm voice. It wasn't only her weakness that made her unsteady, her knees like water; it was seeing him, being in the same room with him.

He was staring at her, and she nodded. "I look awful. I'm sorry."

"I was thinking that even in sickness, you're beautiful."

Aurelia dabbed at her eyes with her apron, marched over and placed the closed sign in the window, and motioned for Owen to follow her. "We'll leave you two alone," she said. "We'll be back later to bring you both supper."

Hamilton led her to a chair. He brought the quilt Aurelia had directed was for Meg. He covered her lap, knelt and tucked it around Meg's knees. "I decided to give myself a Christmas present and come to see you."

"You are my gift," she said simply, "and I believe this is my happiest Christmas ever."

He stayed for five days. Meg's cough returned with a vengeance, and he warned her it was because she tried to talk so much. He convinced her they didn't have to talk all the time, he was happy to sit with her, watch the happenings in the store, and observe the folks coming and going. He loved the children, and one day Meg sat at the window and watched him play in the snow with them.

When she had to lie down, she insisted on having the door to her room left ajar. It was a comfort to hear the soft rumble of his voice when he talked with Owen and Aurelia and others out in the store. She smiled when she heard him discussing cattle and stone prices with Admire. Admire had fewer questions about Hamilton's profession.

She wanted to be able to talk to him herself, but every time she tried she went into fits of coughing.

The day he had to leave, she apologized. "What a Christmas for you. I picked a terrible time to be sick; I wish I could've been better company."

"I'm sorry that you didn't feel well, but I had a wonderful time." Once more he knelt by her chair, his kindly face not far from hers, his hand on her arm.

"You'll come again, then?" She hardly dared to hope. Her eyes searched his face, then she reached up to touch his face, wanting to know how his skin felt. It was smooth, with a bit of bristle, as she suspected.

"I'll come back as soon as I can." He covered her hand with his own, then brought her palm to his lips and kissed it. "There's something I want to discuss with you, when you're stronger."

"I promise to be well and not to cough one time. I'll show you Paragon Springs, the whole valley, next time." She covered her mouth as she went into a spasm of coughing, giving him a hopeless shrug.

For the rest of that winter, Meg took the best possible care of herself, resting as much as her work would allow. Hamilton's letters nourished her, along with the large meals she ate and the milk she drank several times a day.

She thought he might write of whatever he wanted to discuss with her, but all winter his letters came and he mentioned nothing out of the ordinary. Maybe he'd forgotten, or it never had been anything of importance, or he'd changed his mind.

In April, true to his promise, Hamilton traveled again to Paragon Springs.

Chapter Seventeen

From first light that April Sunday, Meg knew it would be a special day. Daily life was hard and lonely for nearly everyone in the valley; the past winter had been severe. Any cause for celebration was eagerly welcomed, so it was no surprise when folks came in numbers from every direction to the picnic she'd arranged in Hamilton's honor.

At the homesteads, fields were plowed and some crops in, new calves and colts had been delivered, soddies and dugouts had been aired and cleaned. It was a good time for a celebration.

Weather was sweet in April, and especially inviting on the banks of the Pawnee River where the picnic was to take place. The smell of wildflowers and newly planted fields gave rise to spirits. Folks arrived by wagon, by horseback, and on foot. The sound of friendly voices carried on the light wind as men unsaddled their mounts or unhitched their teams to let the horses graze, and women spread their blankets and quilts on the ground in clusters. Laughing children scampered everywhere.

"Let me help you with that," Hamilton said, coming around to take Meg's picnic basket as she lifted it from the wagon. The brush of his hand against hers sent a pleasurable shock through her. Judging from the warm smile he gave her, he'd felt it, too.

Hamilton stood out from the local men in his city clothes, but it was chiefly his relaxed, self-assured manner that set him apart. He might be shy with women in some circumstances, but with people in general he was very much at ease.

He was more manly and attractive than the other men, in a way Meg couldn't quite define.

The comparison between him and the locals brought her back to earth with a jolt: there was a difference between the two of them, as well. She was a seasoned westerner, he an accomplished lawyer from St. Louis, a tenderfoot in spite of his manner. She had best remember that they were as different as night from day. She'd be a fool to consider anything serious between them. Having him here as her guest, enjoying a casual flirtation, was stirring troubled waters enough.

"It's only fried chicken and a few other treats, but thank you." She smiled at him and pushed to the back of her mind the thought that this joy in his nearness couldn't last. In a few short days, Hamilton would return to St. Louis and she'd remain here. She couldn't think of it for more than a second before an ache formed inside her.

They unloaded her things and tethered the horses to graze. Meg put down an old quilt, then a prettier one on top of it, a little apart from the other picnic spots. Hamilton nodded toward where a group of men gathered, some squatting on their heels, others leaning against a wagon, to talk. Owen and Admire were among them. "If you don't need me for anything else, I reckon I'll join the men," he told her.

"Don't let them teach you any bad habits," she joked, eyeing the bottle that was being passed among them surreptitiously.

"Won't," he answered with a grin. "I have my own faults."

With her heart in her throat she watched him amble away. Every minute she spent with Hamilton she cared for him more, and it was such a mistake. She turned suddenly when Emmaline spoke at her shoulder, "I like your Mr. Gibbs. He seems to be a nice mix of kindness, good humor, and intelligence."

She'd described him perfectly, Meg thought, but at the moment she could only nod, her throat too full for words.

Lucy Ann joined them. "I'm glad Admire is having a good time today." She looked to where he was talking animatedly, using his hands, and sending the rest of the men into gales of laughter. She went on, "He misses the company of other men, working the farm and at the quarry how he does. It isn't like when he rode for the Rocking A, for Mr. Ambler. He was with a group of men all the time, then, and he liked that."

"But he loves you more than he misses that old job," Meg said, catching Lucy Ann's shoulder. "Ad did the right thing giving up cowboying and becoming a farmer so the two of you could have a life together."

"I suppose," Lucy Ann admitted with a wistful smile. "I just wish he liked farmin' better'n he does."

The talk turned to Jack and Dinah Ambler, who were invited but weren't coming. "Dinah wanted to come," Aurelia said, "but when she was in the store the other day she said Jack had invited his friends to the ranch for a weekend party. Jack is cooking a beef. She wanted to make sure they didn't run out of food and she bought quite a lot at the mercantile."

"What a party that will be," Emmaline said drily, "if the guests are Jack's friends."

"Dodge City's most unscrupulous businessmen will be there," Aurelia guessed, "and no doubt a large number of saloon bums and a few ranchers from outside the valley."

"Dinah is doing what she can to keep Jack happy," Meg defended. "And when he's not making trouble for us, I like it."

"I feel sorry for Dinah," Lucy said, "she's not responsible for the way Jack treats homesteading folk and—" The sound of a child's scream stopped her. "It's Rachel," she said and broke into run toward where the children had been playing.

David John, Aurelia's younger son, reached Rachel first. He picked her up and brought her in his arms toward the hurrying women.

"She fell and skinned her chin," the twelve-year-old said. "We were playin' tag an' we kind of run over her. Don't think she's hurt bad, though."

"Here, Rachel, let me see," Lucy Ann said, kneeling in front of Rachel as David John set the five-year-old on the ground. There were dirt and flecks of blood on Rachel's chin. Her face was awash in tears. "There, there," Lucy Ann said, wiping Rachel's face with the hem of her apron. "You'll be fine. Don't cry, now."

David John squatted next to Rachel. "We're sorry. But you can still play. Climb on my shoulders, Rachel, you can ride piggyback."

Rachel smiled, and with her mother's help climbed up on the boy's shoulders.

"David John is such a good boy," Meg said, watching him return to the game with Rachel on his shoulders.

"He loves Rachel," Aurelia said, "always has, since she was a baby."

Lucy Ann nodded agreement. "I've noticed that myself."

Emmaline said, "I think the children are hungry. Isn't it time we started setting the food out?"

One of the men by the wagons overheard and a deep male voice bellowed, "Shore is!"

"Oh, Sam," his wife, Maddie, scolded, "be patient." She told the other women with pride she couldn't disguise, "Sam can't get enough of my fried prairie chicken, or my carrot pie. If I'm not careful, the children won't get a bite of either."

Meg smiled by way of reply and went to ready her own food and utensils, remembering Hamilton's lunch that they shared together at the courthouse when they first met, and their picnic later at Forest Park. She hoped he'd enjoy today as much.

"They like you," Meg told Hamilton later, as they sat on her quilt, eating from filled plates in their laps.

He looked at her questioningly and she repeated, "My friends like you."

"I like them. They remind me of the folks back in Clarion, Iowa: straightforward, hardworking, honest. Except for that redheaded fellow, they're a good bunch of people. He's a little pushy and greedy, I think."

"Show me who you mean," Meg said, "although I'm sure you're talking about Joe Potter."

Hamilton nodded in the direction of Joe who sat with his family, his arm resting on their picnic basket as though to keep anyone from taking more than their share. "Mr. Potter asked me for legal advice."

"He did? Asked for free advice, I'll warrant. He has more money than any of us, but he's very tightfisted."

"He says he had freight shot up that time those hoodlums attacked your freight wagon and killed your horses. He wanted to know if he should sue *you* to recover the price of the goods, or if he should sue the company who sent them for not providing safe shipment."

"That rascal! I gave him a good cow to make up for his loss. What did you tell him?"

"I told him to sue the men who did the damage, the ones who riddled the load with bullets. They're responsible for his loss."

"But they were hanged, they're dead."

"I know. You told me about it in one of your letters."

Meg looked at him askance, trying not to laugh. "What did Potter say?"

Hamilton shrugged. "I don't think he liked my advice. I

think he'd rather sue you, and take your road ranch. I didn't tell him in so many words, but I let him know that anything like that happening would be over my dead body."

As she looked into his eyes, wanting to tell him how much she appreciated his thinking—every last thing about him—a shout went from blanket to blanket that when everyone had had enough to eat, there would be horse races over in the open grassy area west of the picnic grounds.

"Thank you, Hamilton."

"For what?"

"Everything."

He shrugged off her thanks, although he looked glad for it. He changed the subject. "Do you think they'll let me ride in the race?"

"Would you? Do you know how to ride?" On her knees, she began putting their things away. He helped, kneeling beside her.

He spoke close to her shoulder, "Back in Iowa when I was twelve or so, I fell for and was spurned by a little girl on a neighboring farm. I decided I'd run away and be a cowboy but needed practice first. I got into a lot of trouble with my father for running our farm horses so hard. Yeah, I want to race today."

"You're sure?" She sat back on her heels. Her hands crept up to her cheeks, trying not to laugh. He seemed such a city fellow.

His brow furrowed into a mock frown. "Do you doubt me? I do know how to ride." He took her hands and drew her to her feet.

She told him, "I don't want you to get hurt." *As though you belong to me when you surely don't,* she thought to herself.

"Won't get hurt." He scowled and shook his head at her in a mock scold.

She realized then that he wanted to show off for her, and he was going to do it come what may. She warmed inside. "Be careful, and good luck. I should warn you, though, nobody beats Shafer Lee in a horse race."

"Emmaline's son?"

"Yes. He loves horses better than anything in the world and he rides like the wind. Don't let it hurt your feelings if he wins," she teased.

"It just may be," he said solemnly, "that young Shafer has met his match."

She laughed and solemnly agreed. She followed slowly as he headed toward the area of open prairie where the run would take place. Will Hessler loaned Hamilton a mount, a tall, yellowish-dun. Ad looked dubious as he studied Hamilton, and mentioned in an aside to Meg, "If he just hangs on and don't fall off, he might make it to the finish line."

Owen shouted out the rules. "We'll start the race right here at this line." He nodded to where Aurelia's sons were marking a long groove in the grassy earth with sticks. "Finish line will be down there just at the top of the rise. We figure that's about a half-mile run. First to cross the finish line wins. We'll race two at a time. Winner of the first race will race the winner of the second race, and so on 'til we can name a top rider, or all our horses are worn out—whichever comes first."

Hamilton looked at Meg and tapped his chest. She laughed and waved a hand at him.

Shafer Lee, on an iron-gray cow pony that belonged to Admire—one Admire had caught wild as a mustang and broken—looked about to burst with eagerness for the race to begin. He volunteered to make the first run.

"I'll race against him." Hamilton held up his hand.

The crowd burst into laughter, then saw that Hamilton meant it. The chuckling continued for several minutes. Men poked one another in the ribs, some drawing coins from their pockets trying to place bets. Since everyone wanted to bet one way, no bets were taken.

Hamilton lined up on his claybank dun at the starting line, alongside Shafer on his feisty gray. Hamilton tipped his hat to Shafer, and grinned. "Good luck, son, you're going to need it."

Shafer nearly choked. "You've already lost, mister, might as well get down off that bangtail an' save yourself lookin' like a fool."

Hamilton leaned over and confided to Shafer, in a whisper loud enough for most to hear, "Too late for that, folks have already made up their minds that I look foolish. But they don't know for sure what they haven't seen yet."

Owen fired his pistol into the air and Shafer and Hamilton went flying past the yelling crowd on a streaming blur of yellow and gray horseflesh. The air filled with the thunder of hooves; flying dust made it hard to see. Meg breathed surprise, seconds later, when she made out Hamilton's dun nose to nose and stride to stride with the gray. Then, almost to the end, Shafer's little cow pony gathered his feet under him and flew ahead, the winner.

Meg ran to meet Hamilton as he came riding slowly back, tall and at ease in the saddle.

"Not too bad for a tenderfoot city man, huh?" Hamilton gloated in fun as he looked down at her and winked.

"Not bad at all! You're full of surprises, Mr. Gibbs."

He dismounted. Tucking Meg's arm in his, he led the dun back to Will.

A few men moved in to congratulate Hamilton even though he'd lost. "For a city feller, that warn't too bad a ride," Charley Villard, his hat pulled low and his ears folded down, told him with a big grin.

"Maybe you're in the wrong place, Gibbs, back there in St. Louis," Owen said, grinning, "you ride like a westerner."

Meg darted a look at Hamilton's face, wanting his response. He didn't reply to Owen in words, just shrugged off the good-natured compliment—which was all it was.

The races continued well into the afternoon, Shafer winning over all other riders, to no one's surprise.

Visiting went on a while longer. The last of the cold biscuits, beans, and pie was consumed, and then, with the gathering dusk, teams were hitched and wagons loaded, horses were saddled, and children were called in from their games for the return home and to waiting chores.

As Meg rode home beside Hamilton, who was driving her wagon, she was reminded again that only a short while remained of his visit. How could she survive without him near?

Next morning, Meg was up at dawn as usual, but found Hamilton already out with Owen cutting sod for the granary he planned to build on his new claim. Their cultivated fields were growing and a larger building was needed to store their grain. He would provide the building site and oversee it. Owen claimed in good humor that he'd spent so long sleeping in the old dugout, oats were beginning to grow out of his ears. He was eternally grateful to have a real home at last, a place to build on.

Meg helped Aurelia prepare breakfast and enjoyed watching Hamilton eat with a hearty appetite; delighted in his exchange of conversation with Aurelia's children as though they were his equals.

She assured Hamilton he needn't accompany her on her round of chores, but was glad when he insisted. When she went out to cultivate her spring oats and corn, he was there with a hoe, hacking weeds like a seasoned farmer although after an hour or so, his palms sported blisters. When they went in at noon, Aurelia layered lard on them.

Meg was a few paces ahead of Hamilton when they went back outside to finish their hoeing following the noon meal. She shrieked and broke into a run, skirts in hand. "No! Stop! Get out of there!" In the patch they'd weeded, three ugly wild cows with horns like rockers were munching and trampling the tiny green sprigs of corn.

"Meg, be careful!" Hamilton shouted behind her but she paid no heed.

In the patch, Meg flapped her apron in the face of the nearest animal. It started to turn, then tipped its head and lunged in an attempt to hook her; Meg danced away, stumbled, and nearly fell. The cow's eyes were wild as it tossed its head and bellowed.

Meg screamed at it, "Go! Get out of here!"

Hamilton whipped her aside just as the cow prepared for a second charge. Meg fell to the ground as Hamilton faced the animal, slapping it in the face with his hat and yelling. It bellowed again, throwing saliva, and showing the whites of its eyes. Hamilton ran at it, waving his hat and shouting.

The cow hesitated, then abruptly turned and loped from the patch, the other two trailing after.

Meg stumbled to her feet. Hamilton dropped his hat and caught her back against him, his arms across her chest. He mumbled against her ear, "Thank God you're all right."

They stood panting, watching the Rocking A cattle trotting off in the direction of Ambler's ranch. "I'll get my horse and run them the rest of the way, onto their own range," Meg said.

Hamilton leaned down to pick up his hat and said in cold anger, "There ought to be a law against a man letting his cows roam and destroy his neighbors' hard work. One of those beasts could easily kill a woman or child, or a man."

"There are laws," Meg told him, drawing deep breaths, "but that doesn't mean Jack Ambler follows them. He sets his own and as far as he's concerned every inch of this country is his by rights. Law officials in Dodge City feel they have worse lawlessness for their time and attention than homesteaders' picayune problems."

"That's not right, not the way to carry out the law."

"No, it isn't. But the law also shies from our troubles with ranchers because they don't relish being pounded to a pulp, their faces pushed into the prairie by a cattleman. That's a high price to pay for trying to enforce what they see as a trifling matter—a few wandering cows."

"This situation could lead to bloodshed if something isn't done."

"I'm afraid of that, but I'm hoping Jack backs down and obeys the law before it happens."

At the quarry that evening, Hamilton rolled up his sleeves and helped Meg load the stone she and Ad had cut the week before. "It's for the town of Spearville a little over a half-day's drive from here," she told him, brushing her skirts and catching her breath. "It'll be a nice ride, if you want to come along tomorrow when I deliver?" She was conscious of time speeding away from them, how soon he'd have to return to St. Louis.

He wiped the perspiration from his brow on his sleeve and grinned. "You bet I want to go."

At noon the next day, they stopped the wagon by the South Fork of the Pawnee River and found a shady spot to eat lunch. Meg spread the quilt and put out the food from her basket: brown bread spread with butter, cold slices of meat, watermelon pickles, and lemonade in a burlap-wrapped jug.

"It's nice to be by ourselves," Hamilton said, filling his plate and then pouring cups of lemonade for them. "I'm sorry it's so crowded at Paragon Springs, but that's how it's been since the beginning."

"Crowded, busy, and noisy," he agreed. He tipped his head, his expression thoughtful. "But then comes nightfall and folks go home, each family closing their door to the outside world. That's a nice combination, a wonderful life, it seems to me."

"Yes." She nodded agreement, glad he saw her life as she did. Unspoken feelings had sizzled between them from the first moment of his visit. Now that they were alone, sensuality hummed between them like electricity. "Hamilton?" As if he read her mind, he drew her into his arms and kissed her, a heady feeling, the touch of his mouth on hers drawing a soft happy gasp.

He said huskily, holding her close as he looked down at her, "I am so in love with you, Meg, I can't see straight. I'm not worthy of you, but with all my soul I hope you love me, too."

"I do, but Hamilton, please, don't say anymore." His face was so solemn, so filled with love. Yet where could it lead? There was no way for them to be together in one place. She knew she must stop this intimate moment, but it was hard to think, hard to be sensible as he kissed her again, longer this time.

When they caught their breath he asked, "Will you marry me, my precious Meg, will you be my wife?" He held her away, studied her face.

Her throat went dry; she wanted to answer but couldn't. She felt dizzied by his touch, his kisses.

His mouth roved lightly along her throat, behind her ear, down to the swell of her breasts as he slowly unbuttoned her bodice. Piece by piece, he removed her clothing, brushing it aside on their quilt.

The sun was hot on her bare skin. She couldn't, didn't want to stop him. Her breath was coming fast. All thought and reason fled her mind except for a single notion and it flickered like stardust behind her closed eyelids: their love was doomed, but they could still have this moment to remember. She helped him take off his shirt.

The sun gilded his cheekbones, his mouth, his shoulders and chest. "You're beautiful," she told him in a whisper of wonder as he moved over her.

His own voice was husky with feeling, "You're the beautiful one, your skin is like silk."

She responded, loving him wholly, adoring his touch, the feel of his hands caressing her over and over. His breath was sweet as his lips found hers, taking her to forever; she gasped as his mouth trailed down her naked body, later murmured in delight as together their love reached a supreme, glorious explosion.

Afterward, they lay back, catching their breath. "I'm sorry if I rushed you," Hamilton said, "but I've wanted you since the moment I first saw you. I love you so much, Meg. Are you all right?"

"I'm fine," she said softly. "More than fine. I've never felt so wonderful, so complete, in my life." She hesitated, "Am I being too daring, telling you that?"

"If you are, I love your daring, along with all the other wonderful qualities you have."

"Then?" She motioned for him not to dress just yet and reached for him. He drew her to him again, his eyes shining dark with delight and passion.

Meg sat close to Hamilton on the wagon seat the rest of

their drive, shoulder to shoulder, thigh to thigh. When he wanted to talk about the wedding, though, and where they might live, she moved, putting space between them. She had to tell him the truth: that she couldn't marry him.

"Why not?" Hamilton asked raggedly, his face engraved with shock as he looked down at her.

"Because I love you too much to marry you."

"That makes no sense."

"Listen, please, Hamilton." She touched his arm. "You've put every bit of your life into the study of law, into building your practice in St. Louis. You're very successful there, the work you love is there, you're well on the way to becoming one of St. Louis's most valued and important citizens."

"That remains to be seen, but regardless, you could be there with me, Meg. I'm in a position at last to give the woman I love a nice home, a comfortable life. You'd not want for anything, darling, if there were any way I could provide it."

"I know that, Hamilton." She laid the back of her hand against his jaw. "And I love you for wanting to take care of me. But I—I like where I am. I've only begun a dream I'm trying to build. Here at Paragon Springs I'm my truest self. I can't quit my dream and walk away now, don't you see? This place, these people here, count on me. I can't abandon them in the same way you can't abandon the folks who need your legal advice in St. Louis. We're from two different worlds, Hamilton. There's nothing we can do to change that. I can't ask you to change your life so drastically by coming here to stay, and I can't move there."

"If I were to leave St. Louis, it would be my choice."

"But if you weren't happy afterward, I'd always blame myself."

He nodded, but looked as though the world had ended. "I

could never see you unhappy, either, Meg, so I understand what you're saying as far it goes. Can we think about this further? Give ourselves some time? I can't give you up just like that, and never see you again. Not after today, not with all you mean to me."

It was hard to answer and tears welled in her eyes. "I don't know that thinking it over more will change anything. I love you with all my heart and soul. I could never love anyone else the way I love you, but I can't see how we can be together. There is no tomorrow for us." She began to cry and turned toward him. "Please hold me for now, just hold me."

He halted the team, kissed her tears, and drew her tight against him, but both of them felt the chasm that was their different lives.

Chapter Eighteen

Meg felt a restless unhappiness in the weeks following Hamilton's spring visit. She went about her work, physically involved as always, but with her mind burdened by confusion, sadness, and guilt. She was more and more convinced that she'd made a terrible mistake. She loved Hamilton and knew that she'd hurt him badly by refusing his marriage proposal.

Laboring in the fields, on the road making deliveries or picking up freight, and often in bed at night, memories of him, his good humor, his kindness, their lovemaking—were more vivid, more real than life going on around her. With each image she was reminded all over again how strong and tender, how passionate, how wonderful he truly was and how much she wanted him.

When she missed her menses that should have occurred a week or so after his departure, she attributed it to hard work or nervous strain. When in May she missed a second monthly, she was sure that she was with child. It took a bit for the realization to sink in.

She waited to feel unhappy about it, or scared, but instead she felt blessed. Feelings of joy overtook her and ruled all else. She was going to have a child, Hamilton's child. Overnight it was as though she'd become someone new and different. Her aspirations and convictions took on a different light. Whatever she did from now on—plans, dreams, work— she would mold to include this little one.

Most importantly, she wouldn't even consider bringing up her child away from its father. The baby's parents loved one another; they belonged together body and soul. They must decide where they would live, together. She recognized now that even if there hadn't been a child, for her and Hamilton to live their separate ways was all along a foolish, impossible idea.

In Paragon Spring's difficult environment, their offspring would grow up strong, self-sufficient, and wise. They could be leaders in that region as it developed. But it still wasn't fair to ask Hamilton to leave St. Louis and his work there. Nor would the city be so terrible a place to rear their children. There would be advantages: fine schools, cultural events. Doctors and hospitals would be close. She brushed aside pain at the thought of leaving Paragon Springs; she couldn't be selfish. Hamilton would prefer for her to move to St. Louis; for him and their child she would go and try never to look back or have regrets.

Hadn't she been preaching to Aurelia for ages the importance of love and uniting your life with the person you cared about? It was time she took her own advice.

For now she'd keep to herself the fact that she was leaving. She had property to be sold into the right hands. She wouldn't allow what she'd worked long and hard for default to Jack Ambler. Without a doubt, he'd give his soul to have even an inkling of what she planned, but he wouldn't know until everything was arranged.

The morning following her decision, in the privacy of her room, she began a letter to Hamilton. "I was wrong," she wrote. "I've changed my mind about staying in Paragon Springs. I wish more than anything to be your wife, I want to come and live with you in St. Louis." She rolled the ink pen between her fingers, her face flushing as her mind sought the most delicate words to let him know that she was with child.

An insistent tapping at her door interrupted and she sat up straight.

Aurelia's voice was urgent, "Meg? May I come in? I need to talk to you."

"Of course." She put the pen into its stand and rose to her feet. "Is something wrong?"

"I don't like to bother you, Meg," Aurelia said, her face creased with worry, "but Zibby is sick. I'm not sure what's wrong, but she lost her dinner last night and today she says her throat is sore—"

"Does she have a fever?" Meg was remembering, as she knew Aurelia was, their first winter there when Aurelia's other daughter, little Helen Grace, became very ill with croup and died.

Aurelia's hands twisted in her apron. She stopped for a moment to brush back the hair that had fallen into her eyes. "She feels a bit feverish. I don't want her to get worse. If you could mind the store and post office for awhile, I'd like to stay with Zibby."

"Oh, of course, Aurelia! Let me worry about the store and you just see that Zibby gets better. If there's anything else I can do, don't hesitate to ask. Do you think we should send to Dodge for a doctor?"

"I don't believe she's that sick, I just want to keep an eye on her."

"If you change your mind, let me know." She'd have to send one of the boys to Dodge. Owen had taken a wagon to the north branch of the Pawnee River to pick up wood along its banks—cottonwood and hackberry limbs blown down by a fierce wind they'd had a few days before. He might be gone two or three days; he wanted to bring home as much wood as possible—it was a scarce commodity in their country.

Zibby was nauseated and feverish for three days but got no worse, to everyone's relief. Meg tended the store and Aurelia's other chores. After the fourth day with Zibby,

Aurelia came into the store beaming.

"Zibby's going to be fine!" she chortled, "you can't believe what it was that was wrong with her, Meg!"

"Well tell me, because I want to know."

"Zibby's turned six years old! She was cutting teeth and not having a very easy time of it. She has beautiful new jaw teeth on both sides of her mouth."

Meg reached for a chair. "Oh, Aurelia, I'm so glad it wasn't anything else. I've been so worried because of . . ." She didn't finish.

"Me, too," Aurelia said softly. "I was afraid she was getting as sick as Helen Grace and I might . . . lose her. I'm so relieved I could sing, but instead I'll just get back to work. Owen is outside, he came home by way of Dodge City and he's brought the mail."

Later that day, Meg's heart leaped to see that she had a letter from Hamilton. Because she'd been busy at the mercantile as well as with her own chores, the recent letter she'd started to him lay unfinished in her bureau drawer. Meg took his letter to her room to read.

Dearest Meg,

I miss you more than words can describe. I've considered our situation very carefully and I've concluded that the worst thing we can do is to live our lives apart. I've never been so miserable in my life. I would never wish you misery of any sort, but my fondest wish is that you miss me in the same way, that your feelings for me are identical to mine for you. I cannot live without you.

I have considered the many good reasons you gave so conscientiously that I carry on my profession in St. Louis. But those very sensible and good reasons, even if multiplied a thousand times over, are no match for my one reason for moving to Kansas: you, my darling Meg.

And so I ask myself: what is a successful city law practice to the arms of an affectionate wife? Nothing, a paltry nothing. I love you; you must consent to marry me. I want to spend the rest of my life with you at Paragon Springs.

"Oh, Hamilton!" Meg whispered. Her eyes filled with tears and she couldn't see. After a moment she continued reading, his voice coming through clearly:

Before you protest once again, let me say that I sincerely feel there is a growing opportunity for a lawyer like me in your region. The brawls and tragic deaths, disputes over land and debts, are considerable; work in plenty for a good lawyer. In time, there will be civil proceedings as towns are built. I want to be a part of your life there, if you'll allow me.

Please, my love, say that you feel as I do, that the gravest mistake either of us could ever make is to remain apart another unnecessary moment.

I remain yours, forever and always.
Hamilton

Meg wiped her eyes with her apron hem. She touched his letter to her lips, than carefully folded it and returned it to its envelope. He knew—he knew how much it meant to her to live her life at Paragon Springs, to have her part in helping it grow. He knew, and he was coming to join her.

A woman couldn't ask for more in a man than that he understand her. If he understood her and she understood him in kind, then every other wonderful fact fell into place. The man she loved understood her very well. She got out the letter she'd begun to him, and tucked it into the envelope with his. That's where the letters would remain, to someday be discovered and read by this child she carried, or possibly by a grand-child or great-grandchild.

She was so fortunate to have met and fallen in love with Hamilton Gibbs, and he with her. She would accept his proposal by wire the next trip to Dodge City. When she saw him face to face, she'd tell him about their coming child.

"You're going to marry Mr. Gibbs, and he's coming here to live?" Aurelia's face was a mix of surprise and delight. It was evening and she was at home, folding a basket of clean laundry she'd just brought inside.

Meg had seen Aurelia taking dry clothes from the elk rack that served as a clothesline and had gone to talk. "Yes, to both your questions," she told Aurelia. It was impossible to keep the exultation from her voice. "Hamilton believes there's plenty of work for him as a lawyer here in western Kansas. He wants to move here, be with us."

"I'm so happy for you, Meg, truly I am!" As Aurelia chewed the matter in her mind, an expression of envy clouded her face. She looked forlorn. Tipping the laundry off her lap into the basket, she stood, and paced. "You're going to get married," she drew out slowly, "while I—" She didn't finish, but her sad look before she turned away said, *while I go on living half a life.*

Meg understood. When Aurelia turned back, tears in her eyes, Meg took her hand. "Let's make it a double ceremony, Aurelia, dear; you and Owen, Hamilton and I. Don't you think it's time for all of us to get on with our lives as we should?" She was tempted to tell Aurelia her secret, then decided that this very intimate news should be kept private until she and the father were lawfully wed. She said, "Owen would be a wonderful father to your children and a good husband for you, and you love him very much. What do you say?"

The worry lines in Aurelia's face were deep and there was doubt in her eyes, but a wistfulness was there in her face, too. She pressed her fingers to her mouth in thought. She let her hand flutter in the air. "Oh, my goodness, I don't know but that it might be all right," she answered. "It might be easier for me if I were to get married with you, my very best friend, beside me. Owen will be so thrilled, if I can just make myself go through with it. I've not been kind to him, holding him off for so long. I know he's hoped, now that he has his own place, that I'd marry him. He's asked me to take up the claim beyond his, saying it'd give us a whole 320 acres if we did someday get married."

"Then it's yes?" Meg could hardly control her excitement.

"Yes, I believe it is, if you don't mind sharing your ceremony, your special day, Meg."

Meg wanted to shake her but she laughed delightedly. Aurelia was at last giving in to the idea of marriage to Owen! "Wasn't I the one who suggested we get married at the same time?" She hugged Aurelia and kissed her cheek. "We've lots to do, dear, but first you'll want to tell Owen—he's not here, now, is he?" She remembered that Owen had gone to the Hesslers on an errand.

"He should get back late tonight."

"He's going to be a happy man."

"Oh my, yes, he is, and I'm happy, too! I'm obliged to you, Meg, for suggesting this, for giving me a push toward what I ought to have done on my own ages ago."

Plans moved forward very quickly after that, and Meg found herself in a constant state of dizzying joy. Her wire accepting Hamilton's proposal and his offer to join her at Paragon Springs seemed hardly to have left before he replied. He wrote, "I'm thrilled beyond measure that you're going to be my wife."

He explained that he'd already begun the necessary steps for closing his office. There would be cases he'd have to see through, others he was turning over to attorney friends. He might have to travel back and forth several times until his office was entirely closed, but in any event he'd be at Paragon Springs "with bells on!" for their July wedding.

Aurelia had suggested that they have a fall wedding, in September or October, when it would be cooler. Meg, knowing she'd look like a pumpkin by then, convinced her otherwise. She reasoned that if they waited that long, Aurelia might lose her nerve and back out again. The wedding should happen as soon as possible.

Owen, from the moment Aurelia told him she'd finally made up her mind and they could be married, turned into a habitual whistler. It gave a lift to their days to hear him whistling as he went about his work. He had personally appointed himself in charge of sending word to the circuit riding preacher to be at Paragon Springs to perform a double wedding on the twentieth of July.

In the meantime, Aurelia journeyed to Larned with Owen and filed on the claim next to his, expanding their holdings. While there, Owen insisted she pick out a wagonload of new furniture for the house they'd share, and any other household goods their store didn't carry. On their return, Aurelia told Meg, "Owen and I are going to be bona fide landowners and settlers as you've always wanted us to be, Meg."

"I always knew you would," Meg laughed, hugging her dear friend. "Maybe Hamilton and I can move into your old soddy, once you move out. The back of the store is pretty small for two people." *Three,* she was thinking, but she didn't say so aloud.

It was impossible to keep their friends out of their plans,

nor did Meg and Aurelia really want to—they needed help. Emmaline ran an announcement of the double engagement and upcoming double wedding in the next issue of the *Echo*. Word of mouth would do the rest. In western Kansas if one heard of a gathering, be it for a wedding, a dance, or any other celebration, that was considered an invitation.

Dinah was on hand to help order the fabrics for the brides' dresses: a cool lawn in dark lavender, to be trimmed with satin ribbon, for Meg, navy faille with a lace bertha collar for Aurelia.

They weren't first-time brides in their teens, so they wouldn't wear veils. A small, hat-like decorative headpiece would be proper though, Dinah insisted, and she'd make them. Meg's would be of lilac crepe de chine with a touch of lace and a small black velvet bow. Aurelia's would be similar, of salmon grosgrain and navy velvet.

"We'll want to get lots of wear from our wedding dresses," Aurelia advised, "so they should be suitable for other occasions."

Meg agreed, telling Dinah, who would make the dresses as well as the headpieces, "Please add some tucks in my dress at the waist." She looked at the women staring at her and told them, "I won't be slender all of my life! I may have a child—several children." She blushed, feeling as though her condition were written on her forehead.

Meg watched, amazed, as the population of Paragon Springs grew until it resembled a good-sized village by the time the wedding was two days away.

Bethany Hessler explained what Meg already had guessed: "Folks want to help, and they don't want to miss the excitement. There's few enough pleasurable times in this country. A wedding just naturally draws folks like flies to molasses."

Meg had made numerous friends all over the region

through her businesses. Aurelia and Owen knew lots of folks from work in the mercantile. Every hour brought more guests in their buggies, wagons, on horseback, and on foot. Some set up tents for sleeping; others would sleep in their wagons or on the ground under the stars for the duration of the celebration.

Those living close enough drove home at night to do chores, taking help with them to get done faster. Others, coming a longer distance, had arranged for someone to look after their stock. Those with only a lone milk cow, or a pig or two, brought their animals with them.

Two pits were dug several yards from the mercantile and fires were built in them. Two steers were butchered and the carcasses placed over the pits of hot coals. The meat would be cooked slowly until it was juicy and tender. In no time at all, the air was fragrant from the roasting meat.

Aurelia's soddy, as well as Emmaline's and Lucy Ann Walsh's two miles distant, was also fragrant as the women busily prepared additional dishes for the wedding feast: roast turkey, fried chicken, beans cooked with sorghum and onion, vinegary corn relish, several kinds of bread and rolls, pumpkin pies, raisin pies, custard pies, and Bethany's famous butter cookies.

The day before the wedding, Aurelia shooed everyone from her kitchen so she could stir up the twin wedding cakes.

At the same time, Meg helped to arrange tables and benches in the yard. More shade would be nice, but all they had was a struggling cottonwood tree or two and shade from the soddies. She was bringing an Arbuckle coffee box to be used as an extra seat under the tree by the mercantile when she heard the sounds of a buggy arriving. She looked up to see that it was Hamilton and ran to meet him.

His feet had no more than touched the ground before she threw herself into his arms. He kissed her long and hard, holding her so tightly that she could hardly breathe.

"Be careful of the baby," she gasped, before she knew what she was saying.

She felt him stiffen in her arms. He held her away and looked at her, puzzled. "What did you say?"

She realized then that she couldn't have held the news any longer; anyway, she'd been dying to tell him. Behind them, others were coming to welcome Hamilton, so she whispered swiftly in his ear, "We're going to have a little one sometime early in the new year." She met his eyes. "I suppose I should feel shame, or at least be embarrassed for conceiving our child before our marriage—but all I feel is sublimely happy, Hamilton!"

"Oh, my love, you mean—I get *two* of you? Sweetheart, are you all right?"

Their friends were in earshot now, so she told him loudly, giggling a bit, her face flushed and gray eyes dancing, "Busy, yes! But most everything is ready. The musicians have come—a fiddler, a guitar player, and two fellows who play mouth harps. Now that you're here, we're just waiting for the preacher to arrive."

It was hard to release him, but she let him be dragged off with the men who were tending the beef—why it took so many men for one job, she didn't know, but that's where they all gathered.

She went to join the group of women decorating the bower of willows near the spring, where the actual ceremony would take place, just as Lucy Ann's wedding had several years before. Wild grapevine was being draped on the bower and tied with bows. Pink bush morning glories, purple mullein, lavender prairie gentians, white yarrow and milkweed, waited in pails of water for forming into bouquets.

By evening, the circuit rider hadn't yet arrived. Aurelia

and Meg were surveying the preparations in the yard when Aurelia asked, worry sharpening her tone, "Where is he? Everyone's here but him, and he's the most important." She brushed a fly away from her face. "Heavens, but it's hot!" She held the bodice of her dress away from her skin and fanned with the other hand. "We ought to have waited for cooler weather—" she began, then looked at Meg. "I'm sorry, now's fine, I'm just nervous."

"The preacher will be here, maybe late, but he'll be here. Perhaps he got called to someone's deathbed for last rites, or he's officiating at another wedding. Any sort of thing might delay him."

"I know. But now that I've decided to get married, I'd just like to get on with the wedding so I don't have to worry about it."

"Isn't everything pretty?" Meg changed the subject. "Did you ever think our dusty road ranch could be made to look so fine?"

Aurelia stood with her hands on her hips, her head tilted and eyes squinting as she took in the yard and farther away the bower. She shook her head. "I see it lots better than this, in my mind. Someday, there'll be a church sitting . . . maybe right over there," she pointed and took a few steps in that direction. "Then weddings can be inside and proper, with pretty flowers and organ music. For other occasions, dancing and such, there'd be a town square over there." Her eyes went dreamy as if she could actually see it, and she swayed a little as though she could hear the music. "There'll be real stores, and a real school several stories high for all the children."

"A real school, for older students as well as the small ones," Meg repeated with a nod. In the fall, Selinda Lee and Lad Voss would return to the high school academy for young men and women in Larned. Nobody liked it that they had to go so far away from home and familiar surroundings, but education was important and both young people were serious students.

Meg took Aurelia's arm as they strolled toward the soddy. "I'm glad you have the same dream I have, Aurelia, to turn Paragon Springs into a real town eventually. I know you'll help to make it happen."

"That I will," Aurelia answered firmly. "If I'm going to live the rest of my life here as I expect to, there'll be a town in this very spot or show me the reason why! I couldn't abide living so poorly the rest of my life, I want finer things for me and mine than we've got now."

Meg hugged Aurelia's shoulders. "Thank you for staying all this time. I couldn't have done half of this without you. You're a dear, good friend."

Later that evening, Hamilton took Meg on a walk to the spring. "I brought you a wedding gift," he told her when they reached the tumble of white stones and could hear and smell the water. He took a package from inside his vest, and opened it for her to see. The light from the moon glittered off a matching necklace, earrings, and bracelet of amethyst and pearls.

Meg's breath caught; it was some time before she could speak. "Oh, Hamilton, dearest," she said in a minute, "they're splendid! I've never owned anything so beautiful." She threw her arms around him and held him tight, careful not to drop the small case that held her jewelry. "Thank you so much, my wonderful husband-to-be." She stood on her tiptoes and kissed him.

He drew her against him and kissed her several times, each kiss deeper and longer. After a while he raised his head and asked in a husky voice, "Will you wear the jewelry tomorrow—or," he chuckled, "whenever the preacher arrives to conduct the ceremony? I had it especially made for your wedding day."

"Of course I'll wear the jewelry! I'll treasure it all of my days. I have something for you, too, a wedding shirt, but I can't even say I made it myself—both Lucy Ann and Dinah gave me a hand with it."

"I'll love it, as I love you and our little one." He kissed her again, his lips tender and sweet and tasting of the peach brandy he'd drunk with the men earlier in a toast to his coming marriage, his farewell to bachelorhood.

"Listen," she told him, "they're starting the music." Since the arrival of the first guests, there had been music each night after supper. "Will you come dance the quadrille with me?" she asked. "I'm kind of a hop-toad with my bad leg, but I don't think I do too badly."

"Honored," he answered, and leaned to kiss her. His hand smothered hers as he led her back toward the dancing.

The preacher finally appeared on the twenty-third. The Reverend Horatio Meriwether Hampstead was small for his name, reminding Meg of a little gray prairie dog: slight, quick, and squeaky. He'd been called to console a sad, lonely woman over near Kinsley who'd been considering suicide, he told them. The mission involved some miles of travel and that's why he was late. He explained, while they listened sympathetically, "The woman's husband often went away for weeks at a time leaving her alone. She had no near neighbors to keep her company. A transient discovered her wandering the prairie, tearing at her hair, weeping inconsolably for her old home and family and her piano, back East. The wind blowing every day upset her nerves. There wasn't a single beautiful thing for the eye to see, she kept saying. Of course, her mind was slipping."

The reverend had made arrangements to send her back to the home she came from, the only answer in her case.

Due to the good reverend's days-late arrival at Paragon Springs, much of the beef and beans and cakes had already been devoured. The musicians and dancers were nearly worn out from nightly celebrating. But he was here now and the children's faces were hastily washed. Their mussed clothes didn't matter at this point. Men and women guests changed once again into their best clothes for the ceremony.

Meg and Aurelia, who each day from the twentieth had groomed their hair, bathing and perfuming themselves especially for their wedding, did so once again. This time they went the final step of donning their wedding dresses and allowing Dinah, who had ridden in that day to see if they had had word from the minister, to settle their wedding caps into place.

As weddings went, nearly everything that could go wrong, did so. The heat was insufferable, the air was thick with flies drawn by the beef pits. The guests were tired and needed to get home. Aurelia was pale and looked as though she might bolt any moment if not for Owen's grip on her arm. Cattle from out on the range had drawn close and their bellowing from thirst or troubling flies drowned out the words of the bland-faced reverend as he opened the ceremony in his squeaky voice. The racket from the cattle made it impossible to hear Bethany Hessler as she sang the song, "Faithful and True."

Meg didn't care. She was getting married and she was going to have a child—life was just fine.

It didn't even bother her that Jack Ambler had appeared and sat on his horse at the far reaches of the crowd, scowling.

Chapter Nineteen

In spite of her intention to not let Jack's presence ruffle her, Meg was very aware of him. He sat unmoving on his horse at the edge of the yard filled with their wedding guests. His hat was pulled low and she couldn't see his face, but it didn't take much to guess at his expression. He meant trouble.

It took an effort to focus her mind on the preacher's piping voice, his eloquent phrases: how each couple should lead their married life and how to rear their children in God's way as well as other Christian injunctions. Then came the proclamation, "I now pronounce you Mr. and Mrs. Hamilton Gibbs!"

Hamilton pulled her close and tenderly kissed her, whispering, "My darling, my wife."

"I love you so much," she whispered back.

The preacher then squeaked thinly, "And I pronounce you two, Mr. and Mrs. Owen Symington!"

Cheers filled the steamy afternoon and everyone in the yard surged forward to offer congratulations.

Meg was repeatedly kissed on the cheek and Hamilton slapped on the back; Owen and Aurelia, who appeared dazed but happy, were receiving the same treatment. A moment or two later, past Lucy Ann's shoulder, Meg saw Dinah with Jack beyond the crowd. Dinah was smiling up at him imploringly. From atop his restless sorrel Jack motioned vigorously with his hands and snapped angry words back at her.

If Jack thought for one second he could mar her wedding day or humiliate his poor wife on Paragon Springs property, he could think again! Meg grabbed Hamilton's hand and led him with her.

As they approached Dinah and Jack, Dinah was pleading, "Please behave yourself, Jack, and act like a civil human being. These are our neighbors. Come be with me for the rest of the party."

"Hell, no. You're coming home, now. You're not having further truck with these dirt-eating nesters. Go get your horse."

It took fortitude, but Meg gave Jack a friendly, amenable smile. "Jack, I'd like you to meet my husband, Hamilton Gibbs. Won't you get down and celebrate with us? There's food, and I know Dinah wants to be here for the dancing."

"She's comin' home with me," Jack insisted. His golden eyes couldn't focus for more than a second's time, and his face was flushed from too much whiskey. There were bruises on his cheek and chin and his clothes were soiled as though he'd been in a tussle with somebody. Fighting was a common pastime with him these days, according to word coming from Dodge City, and embarrassed confidences Dinah shared with the women at Paragon Springs.

"I want to stay," Dinah said, "for a little while. Please, Jack." She reached up to take his hand but he jerked it away, letting it rest on the saddle horn.

"Dinah's been a wonderful help to Aurelia and me, getting ready for today," Meg told Jack. "Let her stay for the party. Please, the both of you, do stay."

Jack looked at Meg with pure dislike. "I heard you were gettin' hitched." He sneered at Hamilton, "So this is him, the city-slicker lawyer who fell for the lady with no name and a checkered past. You look like a smart fella, smart enough to see this isn't farmin' country. I reckon you'll be takin' her to live back East—isn't that where you're from, Gibbs?" He swayed slightly before righting himself in the saddle.

"I'm from St. Louis," Hamilton answered, civil and

270

smiling, "but Meg and I won't be living there. I'm moving my law practice to this country. I may set up an office in Dodge City, but I also want to be a partner to Meg in her business affairs here at Paragon Springs. This is our home now."

At the pronouncement, a slow rage built in Jack's face. "Then you're as big a fool as she is!" he growled.

Hamilton's mouth tightened but he let the remark pass by. "We'd like you to join the party, Ambler. Your wife wants to stay. Out of respect for her wishes . . ."

Dinah moved closer to place her hand on Jack's leg, saying firmly, "I'll go home with you, Jack, but not until you've had some coffee and something to eat with our neighbors and danced a dance or two with me. First, congratulate these folks on their marriage. Anyone would do that, no matter their differences!"

He looked at her, his expression stony and stubborn. "You don't belong here." His lip curled, "These aren't your kind." He motioned with a jerk of his head, "You belong at the Rocking A."

"I belong where it pleases me to be. These are my friends, Jack. They've made me welcome in this godforsaken country, they've been good to me."

"So what the hell does that matter? They're damned nester vermin!"

"Shame on you, Jack!" Dinah exclaimed, her patience running thin. "They're good people with as much right to be here as we have."

"They got no rights at all. This is my range." He went on with a sweep of his arm, "If it's the last thing I do, every one of these bastards will be off my range, their milk cows and chickens with 'em." He slid off the sorrel and stood spread-legged, unsteady but ready to fight.

Admire had joined them and he spat into the dust. "You

don't want to try nothin' here, Jack. You're not so drunk you can't see that you're outnumbered. If you can't behave decent, then go on home and sleep it off."

"A hunderd ne-s-s-sters can't stop me," Jack slurred, lunging to take a swing at Admire and missing. He turned on Hamilton. "How about you, tenderfoot, think you can take me?"

"C'mon, Jack." One of Jack's more peaceful-minded riders and a friend of Admire's had come forward to take Jack's arm. "You don't want to do this. Let's get on home now, before somebody gets hurt or killed. These folks didn't ask for no trouble, this is a weddin'."

Two other Rocking A riders joined the first to take hold of Jack but he jerked away.

"Killin' 'em is 'zactly what I wanna do. I wanna kill ever' last nes-s-ster in this valley. You should help do that, if you're loyal to me. Are ya or ain't ya?"

Dinah flushed with anger and there was embarrassment in her voice when she spoke, "All right, that's enough, we'll go home! I'm sorry, Meg, Hamilton. I apologize to all of you for my husband. He doesn't know what he's saying; he's had far too much to drink." She told their riders, "Put him back on his horse and I'll take him home." She turned again to the settlers, watching, "I'm going to make him behave. I promise."

Hamilton, standing beside Meg with his arm around her waist and watching the Ambler entourage depart, commented, "Now I see what you've been up against. The drunken fool! I can imagine what he's like when he's sober. It's a miracle you've lasted against him this long. What a fight you've surely had." He sighed, "Mr. Ambler had better pay closer attention to the law from now on and cut out the harassment."

"I always hope for that," Meg said with a heavy sigh. "Unfortunately, Jack isn't without friends, powerful friends in Dodge City. It's hard to make a law stick with him and I'm afraid he won't ever let us homesteaders alone."

"Yes, he will," Hamilton said flatly. "Jack Ambler's day is coming, and I think he knows it."

Before Hamilton returned to St. Louis, he and Meg helped Owen and Aurelia move Aurelia's personal possessions into Owen's sod house on their expanded ranch. The foursome then moved Meg's belongings into the sod house Aurelia had vacated. The tiny back rooms in the mercantile could now be used for storage.

Meg directed where she wanted her things, telling Hamilton while they worked, "This is the first soddy that Aurelia, Lucy Ann, Grandma Spicy, and I built. We'd been living together in a dugout, four women and five children, if you can imagine—the same dugout we use now as a root cellar. Jack Ambler ran his cattle over the dugout, caving it in. Luckily, no one was inside. We picked that time to build two sod houses and fix the old dugout for storage. I'll always have a fondness for this place, but someday I'd like a real house built of stone, in the town we hope to have here eventually."

Somehow, she'd gotten too busy to proceed with the plans for a town. Getting her divorce had taken so much of her time and energy, and there was always the ongoing battle with Jack. She was a long way from giving up hope for the town, though. She agreed with Aurelia that it had to happen, for the betterment of all of them. For her children's future, it had to be.

A month later, Meg was just climbing out of bed in the morning when she felt a squiggle of movement deep in her abdomen, like a minnow swimming in a creek. She laughed out loud in wonder and caressed her stomach. When they met later in the morning to make baby clothes, she told her friends about the baby's movements.

"I'm feeling so broody, just like a hen making a nest. I love fixing up our house. You all saw the handsome cradle Hamilton brought with him from his last trip to St. Louis?" They laughed at her, because of course they had, but trooped together to see it once again because she liked showing it off so much.

Although Hamilton was away a lot those first months of their marriage settling his affairs in St. Louis, and then making himself known in Dodge City and taking a variety of cases scattered about that country, Meg was happy. Hamilton urged her to rest for her sake and the baby's, to let him do any worrying, and to hire out the harder work when he couldn't be home. She attempted to do what he wanted, and concentrated on the pleasures of making a home for them and their coming child.

She tried not to let her emotions fester and worry what Jack might be up to. Then, that fall at roundup time, Jack claimed that his tally was short. He swore that settlers had stolen his cattle and had "fed them to their flocks of little bastards," as the cows couldn't be found.

Settlers denied the accusation, then some of their own stock disappeared. To the last person, they believed that Jack had rounded up their cattle and sold it off with his own, that he'd arranged for his to be "stolen" so he could steal from them. Nothing could be proved to settle the matter either way and tensions remained high. As had happened more than once before, some settlers, weary of the conflict, pulled up stakes and left the valley. Meg tried to convince them to stay, but for them enough was enough.

Adding further salt to the wounds of the women at Paragon Springs was Shafer's growing admiration for Jack and his cowboys. At first, and in opposition to his mother's wishes, Shafer slipped off in secret to ride with Jack during roundup. Later, he boasted openly that he was one of "Jack's riders."

Meg, waddling about her chores in advanced pregnancy, grieved over the loss of the people she'd hoped to have as neighbors far into the future, and she worried for Shafer.

"I don't know why," Emmaline worried as the women sat sewing together one day, "my boy takes such a liking to a man who's always been so strongly against us being here."

"It's the danger, the excitement that appeals to Shafer, maybe," Meg suggested. "It's been trouble from the first from Jack; sometimes it feels like we're sitting on a powder keg waiting for it to explode. It's no wonder some people break under the strain. And if anyone is looking for the company of danger and trouble, he wouldn't need to look any further than Jack."

Aurelia got up to stand by Meg's chair, placing her hand on Meg's shoulder. "Now don't get to worrying, Meg, it's not good for the baby. None of us are leaving, and Dinah is doing her best to hobble Jack against making trouble. Let's put this out of our heads—for today anyhow—and have some coffee and my raised doughnuts."

"All right." Meg smiled and reached up to pat Aurelia's hand. "But worrying about what Jack might do has gotten to be a habit with me, one I doubt I'll ever get over until this feud is settled between us, once and for all."

If she'd had her way, Meg wouldn't have elected to make the birth of her baby a community event that wintry day in early January. Once begun, however, she was powerless to do anything but concentrate on delivering her child.

She entered the store out of a lightly falling snow and complained irritably to Aurelia, who was sweeping the floor, "My back hurts something fierce. It's ached like the devil this entire day, starting in the middle of the night. Guess I overdid it yesterday cleaning house. I need some sugar; I want to fix something nice for Hamilton. I think I'll make ginger cookies."

"Oh, you foolish girl," Aurelia exclaimed, taking a good look at Meg. She set aside the broom and grabbed her shoulders. "It's your time! I'm taking you home and you're going straight to bed." Aurelia turned to Owen, who'd been sorting some small tools in bins in the corner of the store. "Tell Emmaline it's Meg's time, then ride for Lucy Ann. Send word to Bethany Hessler, too, she'll want to be here."

"No, no need—" Meg tried to protest that the baby wasn't due quite yet, and if it was coming she didn't want a crowd around. In the same second she was slammed with a searing pain that nearly knocked her off her feet. "Oh, my goodness!" she gasped, grabbing the counter where tins of oysters were piled. "The baby is coming!"

"Like I said," Aurelia retorted matter-of-factly. "Let's get you home." She put her arm around her and hurried for the door.

With pain seizing her every few steps, Meg was glad it was only a short walk to her own soddy. She led the way inside and to the bedroom. She felt that if she could just lie down, the pain would ease.

"You have everything ready?" Aurelia asked as she helped Meg out of her dress.

Meg shuddered with pain and pointed to the chest where the birthing things were stored. "Over there. You'll find the birthing cloth, thread, scissors, and the baby's clothes and blanket." She panted from the waves of pain coming one on top of the other.

"This baby's coming fast," Aurelia exclaimed with her eyes on Meg. She hurriedly spread a thick white pad of cloth on the bed. "Crawl in here now, under the covers for the moment. You can keep your chemise on, but anything else will just be in the way. Lie easy if you can, while I boil some water."

Meg tried to "lie easy," but her pains were intense. She bit her lip to keep from crying out, and tasted blood. She was glad when Aurelia returned.

"Where's Hamilton today?" Aurelia asked.

Meg waited for the worst of a searing pain to ease, then gasped, "Out settling a property dispute. Some trouble northwest of here. I—I wish he was here."

"No, you don't. What's happening here would only worry him. Men like making babies, but watching them arrive scares them silly. I know. My first husband, John, fainted across my bed when Joshua came. You're lucky Hamilton isn't here. He'd only get in the way."

Meg had no chance to think about it, then. Pain seized her body and threatened to tear her in two; a vast flood of liquid burst from between her legs. "Am . . . am I dying?" she gasped, trying to rise, wondering if the liquid was blood. "Is the baby going to be all right?"

Aurelia laughed gently. "That's just the birth waters you felt, everything is right on course."

Meg gasped and strained. "I—I have to push."

"You go ahead then, honey, and push." Aurelia held her hand and Meg gripped it hard and pushed. Her whole body felt as though it was gripped in a vise. Afterward, the urge to push faded for a bit and she lay back, panting for strength.

She was in a daze of pain, and only half aware that Emmaline had arrived. Lucy Ann and Bethany came next. "We were on our way here, anyhow," Lucy Ann explained, "to see you, Meg. Isn't that something? We picked the very day that your baby decided to be born! Owen met us on the road on our way here, and said you were in labor."

"I'll go brown some flour in the oven," Bethany offered, brushing her hands on her apron. "My mother says parched flour is best to put on the baby's navel after the cord is cut."

Meg ignored the others as a gigantic urge to push possessed her. She pushed again and again and again, gasping for breath, praying for strength to bring her baby. Perspiration burst out all over her body. When sweat drained into her eyes, Lucy Ann wiped it away. Meg thought she was going to split when she pushed again.

Aurelia, strain showing on her own face, lifted the blanket. A smile of joy wreathed her face. "I can see the head, Meg, a little thatch of brown hair. You push again, keep pushing."

Meg strained and pushed and felt an immediate release.

"Almost out! Again, push again!" she heard Aurelia command through the fog of pain, and she did.

She was gasping for breath when Aurelia, chortling with glee, lifted the wet infant up and gave its tiny bottom a gentle swat. A shivery cry filled the air and Meg laughed weakly at the beautiful sound.

"A girl, Meg," Aurelia chuckled, "you have a fine, big baby girl."

Aurelia tied and cut the baby's cord, then wiped the infant all over with olive oil. She sprinkled browned flour on the navel, and then pinned on a belly-band. Lucy Ann diapered and dressed the infant, wrapping it in a blanket, and then gave her back to Aurelia. "Give yourself a little rest before you try to nurse," Aurelia said, stroking Meg's cheek and tucking the baby under her arm.

"All right," Meg said through a dry throat, relaxing. Later, she gasped as she felt the need to push again. "There's another one!" She pushed and something slithered out between her legs.

"That's the afterbirth," Bethany said. "I'll get it here into this bucket and take it outside." She came to kiss Meg's cheek. "You just have one beautiful baby daughter, Meg. Not twins this time."

"She is beautiful, isn't she?" Meg held her young one closer, then lay tired but euphoric as her friends worked over her, changing the bedding beneath her, washing her, and putting her in a clean gown. She was glad now that they were all there for the arrival of her child, but wished that Hamilton had been there, too.

When he came home three days later, she was up, sitting in a rocker, feeling as healthy as a horse and nursing her new baby. Meg let him have a good look at their child—her tiny hands and feet and bare legs—then bundled her up and passed her to him.

The infant might have been made of eggshell, Hamilton held her so carefully. "My God, Meg, she's so beautiful." He brushed his lips across the baby's face. "She looks like you. I was afraid she'd look like me, but thank God, she doesn't, she's as pretty as her mother."

"She's a little prune," Meg said with a soft laugh, rocking, "but that's all right, she looks beautiful to me, too."

"Have you thought of a name?" He kissed their child again.

"Don't laugh, but yes, I have. I'd like to name her Vesta, for the goddess of fire on the hearths of home in Roman mythology."

"Excuse me?"

"I learned about the goddess Vesta from Lad, our community bookworm. Fire was hard to come by in Rome, you see, and therefore desperately important to the people, Lad says.

Our little Vesta burst out of me like fire, truth to tell. She'll be warm and happy all of her life, we'll see to that. And is anything more important to us than her?"

He chuckled, and gave a nod. "Nothing is more important! Vesta it is." He was thoughtful for a moment then favored Meg with his twisted grin that never failed to reach her soul and delight her. He asked, almost childlike, the bundled infant tiny in his big hands, "May we name her Annabel, too, for my mother?"

"Of course. Vesta Annabel Gibbs is a strong, beautiful name."

"A strong beautiful girl to match her mother."

Meg stood then, encircling her husband and child in her arms, and laid her head on Hamilton's shoulder. She drank in his clean outdoorsy smell and the milk-sweet smell of their baby. She loved them both so much; they had given her a wonderful new life. Nothing must ever harm that precious life, especially not the likes of Jack Ambler, who would not like it that their small band at Paragon Springs was still growing.

Chapter Twenty

For many months, Meg focused her attention pleasurably on her new roles: wife and helpmate to Hamilton and mother to Vesta. Because in the past she'd been needed for outside work, she'd left cooking and some household chores chiefly to others. Now she enjoyed them as if they were brand new inventions. She sewed curtains and made pillows and learned to make sour cream biscuits that melted in the mouth.

Although she didn't entirely disregard the trials and tribulations of the community and the ongoing fuss with Jack Ambler, those matters took on lesser importance than her loved ones' immediate welfare and comfort.

Then one day she was hoeing weeds from her patch of half-grown corn, while nearby sixteen-month-old Vesta played by climbing in and out of an Arbuckle coffee box. At a sudden strange snort Meg's head jerked up in alarm.

A Texas longhorn carrying the Rocking A brand, horns swinging, was munching corn plants at the end of the row.

In the last year, Rocking A cows had gotten to be thick on the range. Nobody could keep them out of their crops or from trampling their dugouts or threatening their children. Many were afraid to complain. Others, who did, were ignored.

Meg fluttered her apron at the cow, and ran at it with her hoe. "Shoo, get out of here you confounded beast! Go home where you belong." She turned her hoe around and whacked the creature's backside with its handle. "Go!" When it had loped off into the distance, she grabbed Vesta and headed for the mercantile. She went in, letting the door slam behind her.

Aurelia looked up from where she sorted mail into the

proper pigeonholes. "What on earth? You look fit to be tied, Meg."

"I am! Where's that catalogue, Aurelia, the one that barbed wire salesman, Jones—or whatever his name was—left here last week?" She put Vesta on the floor to play with her rag doll, and took the catalogue Aurelia handed over.

Aurelia waited, studying Meg's red face and flashing eyes but saying nothing.

Meg waved the catalogue and sputtered angrily, "I didn't want to do this, but Jack Ambler has left me no choice. I'm going to stock barbed wire in my store, enough barbed wire to fence every farm in the region! Enough to fence the whole of western Kansas."

"He's not going to like it." Aurelia's hand crept to her breastbone, a worried frown creased her brow.

"That's just too bad."

She'd fenced her kitchen garden with stone, and she'd used stone to form her corrals. She sold stone to other homesteaders for identical use. But it took far too much stone, and time, to build a fence to contain range cattle. For settlers living a lot farther west there was neither stone to quarry nor trees to cut for fencing. Yet they had to have something to keep wild cattle out—mostly those ranging off Rocking A land—and their own stock in.

Holding Vesta in her arms, Meg was at the Dodge City depot when her shipment arrived. Roll after roll of stickery blue wire was being loaded into her wagon.

Half the town had arrived as word spread, and they gathered to watch the new invention being unloaded. "So that's what it looks like," a young store clerk in brown plaid said. "I heard of it, but never seen it till now."

"Me, neither," a butcher with blood on his apron responded.

"Take a good look," Meg said stoutly to the crowd, "because what you see is the salvation of the homesteader against the rancher who thinks the whole sea of grass out here belongs to him."

A new voice exploded suddenly behind her, "What the hell is that?"

Meg whirled from watching the loading to see Jack striding furiously toward her wagon followed on the run by the men who'd run to bring him from the saloon.

Standing back behind the edge of a wagon where he thought she couldn't see him, was young Shafer Lee, his hat pulled low to hide most of his face.

"It's barbed wire, Jack, invented up in Illinois but being used very successfully down in Texas. I'm sure you know about it. I'm offering it for sale from my store, if you're interested."

"Don't be an idiot!" Jack waved his hat in his fist. Wind riffled his hair, making it stand on end. "You know barbed wire will tear up my stock. Range cattle and horses are used to going anywhere there's grass."

"I'm sorry. The truth is, I don't much like it, myself, and I hope all our critters become accustomed to it before long. This stuff's become necessary because you won't keep your cattle off other folks' land and out of their crops. You forced this, Jack, and it's been a long time coming!"

"You're going be sorry as hell for the day you brought this here, Meg Brennon!"

Vesta cringed at hearing Jack's harsh voice used against her mother. Her mouth puckered, and she squirmed uneasily in Meg's arms. Meg spoke softly to ease her fright before she turned back to Jack, "The name is Meg Gibbs, and I think you're the one who'll be sorry. With your cattle fenced out and off other people's land, you're going to have to reduce your herds. Get rid of some cows, Jack, a lot of them. You've trampled this country and my people long enough."

He took a step toward her and looked as if he wanted to choke her. "You're a blamed woman, you can't talk that way to me!" His face swelled and turned beet-red. He clamped his hat back on. "Damned thieves, that's what you nesters are. You've stolen my land. This land out here was meant for cattle—not damned nester crops, and chickens, cows, pigs," he spat the words, "whole flocks of honyocker offspring!"

Meg stepped back from his menacing. "You're scaring my little girl, and I'd thank you to stop." He looked surprised, as though noticing the child for the first time and if his expression was apologetic it quickly hardened. She shook her head, her chin high. "No one stole this range from you, Jack. We came by it lawfully, by homestead right, and sometimes cash. You still have all the range you've ever been legally entitled to, and you'll have to learn to make better use of it."

She cuddled Vesta, humming shakily to her and smiling reassurance down into her nervous little face. After a minute or two, Meg went back to directing the loading of the wire, although Jack's glaring eyes made the hair on the back of her neck stand up. After a minute, she stole a look over her shoulder and saw him stalking away, his friends moving with him in a flotilla toward the saloon. Shafer trailed behind like an adoring puppy, his booted feet making little dancing steps to hurry before she could stop him.

She thought about calling out to him and ordering him home where he belonged, but didn't. Although she worried for him, she didn't own him.

Meg ran an ad in the *Echo* that the mercantile now carried barbed wire and word of mouth did the rest. Barbed wire fences sprang up on several valley farms in those next months. Most of those settlers bought stone posts to fasten the wire to and that kept Meg and Admire and the older boys busy cutting and hauling stone. Sometimes Meg was paid in cash, but she also took goods in trade for the stone posts: a calf, a few chickens, hogs, and seed grain. She shared with the others what she was given in surplus.

Settlers with the new wire fences took a deep, satisfied breath. They kept an eye on their animals for a while, checking that they were becoming accustomed to the fencing and wouldn't be seriously hurt while they learned better.

Dinah visited one day, complaining mildly about the gates she'd had to open to get there. While Vesta napped in the other room, Meg and Dinah had coffee at Meg's table.

"The word I'm hearing is that stock animals are getting accustomed to the barbed wire, and it's keeping them in," Meg said. "That's the whole idea, and I'm sorry about the gates. We had to do something to control the loose cattle."

Tiny lines formed between Dinah's fair blue eyes. "Jack hates it, but I don't have to tell you that."

"Like I told him," Meg said quietly, "I'm not fond of barbed wire, either, but he made it necessary. Folks in the valley had reached the end of their rope, trying to protect their crops, their children. There was nothing left to do."

Dinah nodded. "I know, and I understand. Jack has had to sell off huge numbers of cattle because—as he puts it—his range has been 'stolen.' It doesn't really hurt him to cut back, but he thinks it does." She shook her head. "He's cross as a bear over it. I don't know how many fights he's been in lately, but that seems his way to take out his frustration. When that no longer works, I don't know what'll happen. I wish I knew how best to calm him and make him see reason, but nothin' I say seems to make any impression on him. He hates to be forced into doin' anything not of his choosin'. I hope you all here at Paragon Springs will be careful. He could explode, and I don't know if I can stop him from makin' serious trouble."

"We'll be careful," Meg told her. "And we appreciate what you're trying to do." She took a sip of coffee and was thoughtful for a moment. "Jack has a new young cohort from here at Paragon Springs," she commented tentatively. "If Jack made trouble for us, his young friend could get hurt, too."

A cautious look entered Dinah's eyes. "You're talking about Emmaline's boy, Shafer."

"Yes. I wonder if it's such a good idea that he spends so much time with Jack? Shafer's young and a bit foolish. I'd hate to see him run wild and get into serious trouble. He rides off without a word to anybody and is gone sometimes for days, worrying his mother nearly to death. The word we have is that he's usually with Jack and his men, in Dodge City or wherever they are, involved in whatever they're doing."

"Jack's taken a likin' to Shafer. He wouldn't let harm come to him."

"Jack's idea of harm and mine are worlds different, I suspect," Meg said drily, although she didn't want to argue with Dinah. "It's the time he spends with Jack and his men in Dodge that worries me, not his work with them at roundup, or helping break horses. Those are tasks he loves."

On one of Shafer's wanderings on the plains this past spring, he'd killed an attacking bobcat with a quirt. For that daring accomplishment he'd become something of a hero to boys and men all over that country, not just to Jack.

"I'm not sayin' I agree completely," Dinah offered slowly, "but Jack believes that keepin' the boy here and tryin' to make a farmer out of him is wrong, against the grain of who the boy really is." She warmed to what she was saying, her eyes bright, her manner earnest. "Jack has taken Shafer under his wing as he might a young brother, or his son. He thinks a lot of Shafer. And I think teachin' Shafer about horses and cattle is good for Jack. They aren't bein' ornery in Dodge City all the time. For instance, did you know that Jack plans to have Shafer help him break the latest bunch of wild horses some of our riders brought back from Colorado?"

Meg didn't answer directly, but asked, "Has Emmaline approved?"

"She knows, but she's been afraid for you to find out just how close Jack and Shafer have become. She knows how you feel about Jack, and she's not ignorant to the facts of how he's treated you all here in the past. But she's afraid too tight a rein on Shafer will force him away for good. She's already lost a husband to wanderlust and the gold fields years ago. She doesn't want to lose Shafer in the same way. She believes that a few wild excursions won't hurt him, and she can have him close some of the time."

Meg hardly knew what to reply. Shafer wasn't hers to order around, but that didn't mean she didn't worry about his welfare, as she would anyone's in their community. She said as much now. "All this might be good for Jack, and maybe his association with Shafer might in the end stop Jack from totally destroying us here at Paragon Springs. But it's hard for me to believe it's good for Shafer. In the name of making the boy a man, Jack could pass on some real bad habits."

Disagreement and a kind of fear flared in Dinah's eyes. "Please don't interfere in this, Meg. I know how much you like to run things yourself, and folks have a lot to thank you for, but this really isn't your affair. If Emmaline doesn't like what's happening with Jack and Shafer, let her call a halt. But it's good for Jack to have Shafer around. I don't know if you're aware that Jack's first wife died in childbirth; and it looks like I can't give him a son—" she broke off and tears sprang to her eyes.

"Dinah, I'm sorry." Meg clasped Dinah's hand. Her own tears were close, just thinking how lucky she was to have Vesta, who was beginning to make noises that she was awake in the other room. "You're right. This isn't my affair and I'll stay out of it." She sighed, realizing that she ought to have more trust in others. They knew best how to work out their problems, and it wasn't like she didn't have enough of her own.

Although she'd promised, Meg struggled mightily as time passed to mind her own affairs and ignore the growing friendship between her worst enemy and her good friend's son, a beloved young member of their community.

Led and encouraged by Jack, Shafer was clearly headed along the wrong path. He was too young to be spending so much time in activities designed to entertain Dodge City roughs and rowdies. He could get into serious trouble, landing in jail or being killed in a Dodge shootout. There were seventeen saloons in Dodge City and every other house was a brothel. Money thrown away in a week there would keep the poor of the valley for several months.

When he was home, Shafer was a swaggering young loafer who saw himself as above work, and certainly above common farm folk.

It galled Meg when, after several months, Jack began to ride openly to Paragon Springs to ask the boy to go with him whenever he wanted, as though God had anointed him the right.

One warm and windy spring day, she was hanging laundry on the line Hamilton had made for her of cottonwood saplings and rope. Vesta helped her. At two and a half, she enjoyed giving Meg the clothespins one at a time and hand up the wet garments. "Wait, angel," Meg told Vesta, when the sound of a growing argument filtered from out in front of the mercantile. She took Vesta's hand and they went to investigate.

In the store yard, Jack sat lazily in the saddle smoking, waiting and clearly amused as Shafer and Joshua stood nose to nose, shouting at one another. Shafer's horse, a fast little black mustang that Jack had given him months before for breaking horses, stood ground-reined nearby. The animal's ears flicked back and forth and he stomped nervously while the boys argued.

"You aren't leavin' here, today, Shafer Lee!" Joshua was yelling. "We've got plantin' to do and you know blamed well we can't get that and the cultivatin' done before we start hayin' if you aren't here to help." He was almost three years younger, but that didn't stop him from standing up to Shafer.

Shafer stood with one hip thrown forward, rolling the brim of his hat before he put it on. He'd started to smoke—rolling tobacco in a small paper in the fashion of many of Jack's riders—and a cigarette hung off his lip. A small bag of Bull Durham tobacco with its round paper tag showed from his vest pocket. "I'm goin' with Jack, farmer boy, an' you ain't stoppin' me. Huh, Jack?" He grinned up at him.

"What's going on here?" Meg left Vesta standing aside and moved between the two young men. She grabbed Shafer by the sleeve. "You know you're supposed to help the other boys. Does your mother know you're planning to leave?"

"She's got nothin' to say about it and neither do you, Aunt Meg." He shook free. "I'm a grown man, an' no woman's goin' to tell me what to do." He sounded so much like Jack, Meg itched to shake him.

In one graceful leap Shafer was in the saddle. Using his

reins to whip the horse, he pounded off without a backward glance.

Jack smirked at her and moved off in Shafer's dust.

"Wait, Jack!" She thought he'd ignore her and was surprised when he turned his horse and loped back to her.

"Somethin' on your mind?" he asked insolently while his mount danced, wanting to be off.

"You're going to ruin that young man, Jack. Leave him alone!"

"Leave him alone? I'm not forcin' him to come with me. You saw, he wants to come."

"Shafer belongs here. He's being very reckless and blind—he doesn't have a notion of the trouble he could get into with you and the company you keep."

He scoffed at her, "I'd killed my first Johnny Reb at his age and was earnin' a man's wages before that. He's man enough to make up his own mind how he wants to live. The boy is part Indian. For God's sake, let him be what he is. You women here at the Springs, tryin' to turn him into a farmer, would break his spirit. That's wrong, pure wrong, like I keep tellin' Dinah. I give him honest work with horses, that's what he's meant for."

"You give him some work, and that's fine. But everybody knows, Jack, that a lot of the time he's not working on your ranch. He's with you in Dodge City doing the same wild and stupid things you do: drinking, brawling, gambling."

Jack laughed. "You left out whorin'. He got introduced to that six months ago and I didn't hear any complaints from him."

"You're disgusting."

"And you're in the wrong country!" The humor left his face, and he spoke grimly, "Tryin' to make this territory over into somethin' it isn't, just like you and the rest of the women want to make a sissy out of Shafer. That boy's got some grit in him, an' I say it's you women ought to leave him alone—and this country, too." With that he whipped his horse around and rode hard after Shafer.

She'd almost forgotten Joshua until he spoke angrily a few feet from her, "Make him stay here, Aunt Meg, make Shafer stay an' do his part like the rest of us got to do!"

She walked over and put her arm around him. "I wish I could, Joshua." She smiled at him. He was a handsome, earnest young man, tall, gangly, with his mother's integrity and duty to work. "But it's not my place to handle him, it's his mother's. Emmaline doesn't want him running off any more than the rest of us do, but there seems no way to stop him, short of hog-tying him to the plow or throttling him with the seed bag. She doesn't want to do that." She sighed. "I'm sorry so much of the work falls on you and David John when Lad is off to school most of the year, and Shafer runs off with Jack. It isn't fair. But I want you to know how much everybody appreciates what you do."

"Thanks, Aunt Meg," he almost choked on the words as he stalked off to the fields, a bag of grain seed over his broad shoulder, anger and resentment marking the line of his rod-stiff body.

Meg sighed. Maybe Jack was right and Shafer wasn't meant to be a farmer, but ignoring his chores, running wild, and breaking the law was hardly the right course, either.

She considered discussing the matter with Emmaline, but they'd talked about it several times before and she was sure nothing would change. Plus, she'd told Dinah she'd stay out of Jack and Shafer's friendship. There was nothing easy about it, though, nothing.

On an evening in late June, Meg sat at the supper table with Hamilton and Vesta. Meg poured a small cup of milk for

Vesta and handed it carefully into her child's chubby hands. Because Meg was eating for two again, she poured herself a second large glass of milk and took a second helping of chicken and dumplings. "More?" she asked Hamilton, holding the serving dish in her hands.

"You bet!" He grinned at her and held out his plate for her to fill. "I miss your cooking when I'm on the road, Meg. I miss my wife, and I miss my daughter." He reached over and tweaked Vesta's round little cheek. "Don't I, love?"

Vesta nodded. She noisily chewed her food and said, "Yeth, Daddy." She threw back her head and laughed at her antics.

"Eat your dinner nicely, now," Meg said, resisting a smile. She loved these evenings at home together as a family.

In his time in western Kansas, Hamilton had built as fine a reputation as a lawyer as he'd ever had in St. Louis. There was never a shortage of cases, and though he traveled and was away a lot, his times at home were that much sweeter. It might have been easier if they moved to Dodge City, but that was something she couldn't even think about.

If she had any regret, it was that she hadn't been able to build the town she'd so long dreamed of, and yet she knew it would come. The surrounding region, 864 square miles with Paragon Springs in the center and other small communities springing to life in the far reaches, had officially become *Hodgeman County.* Seven miles west of Paragon Springs, a farmer who had taken over the old Hague homestead had decided to build a town on the farm. He barely got the streets of Flagg plowed off before a group of crooked profiteers bought him out, and he left the country. Flagg was little more than a rowdy saloon and hitching rail and it disheartened Meg greatly that it had been named temporary county seat. County commissioners had been named, but actual governing had yet to take place. The town she envisioned Paragon Springs becoming should rightfully be made the permanent county seat and she meant to see that happen. In the meantime, she had Hamilton, Vesta, and the new baby on the way, and for that she was truly grateful. Those were miracles she'd been blessed with that had never been in any exact plan.

"Would you like to go to Dodge City to celebrate Independence Day?" Hamilton asked. "I'd like to show off my family to friends and business associates who plan to be there. There's going to be a parade, band music, bull fights and races, and of course, fireworks."

"Yes, if that's what you'd like to do." She didn't care that much for the town, and normally she was just in and out on business, but she'd like to meet the friends Hamilton was making. It could be good for his business and she wanted to do all she could for him in that regard.

Later, when she mentioned to Emmaline, Aurelia, and Lucy Ann that she was going, they decided they would attend with their families, too. Aurelia and Owen would travel with Meg and Hamilton, Emmaline and Selinda would travel with the Walshes. Paragon Springs would forego any celebration there this year.

Dodge City was dusty and filled with people, wagons, and horses, when they arrived. Music echoed from a dozen saloons; shouting and drunken laughter bombarded from all directions.

As they made their way through the milling crowds, Meg did her best to remember the names of people Hamilton introduced to her—but there were so many. A few she already knew, like Tog Elsberry and some others, from conducting business of her own with them. Today was the first time she'd met Henry Beverley, a likable Texan who'd once been a cattle drover but had recently joined a partnership with Robert M. Wright at his very successful general merchandise store. Sam Samuels, another employee of the store, was also new to her. He was an asset to the store because of his fluent Spanish, as a large part of its business was done with Mexican customers.

There were other friends of Hamilton's, as well as many folks she knew, and Meg spent the morning nodding, smiling, and shaking hands.

They listened to the speeches, watched the rip-roaring parade of cowboys down Main Street, and stood clapping to patriotic music played by a cowboy band from atop a wagon parked in the center of main street. Meg begged off from watching the bullfight, and Hamilton said he didn't care to watch it either, although she thought he said it just to be kind to her.

When the sun was noon high, they returned to their overnight camping place on the edge of town, in the shade of soapweed and prickly pear, to have their picnic lunch. There was a nice breeze off the Arkansas river. Meg was glad for the quiet, away from the commotion in town. Others seemed also to like the peaceful atmosphere, spreading their quilts nearby, and getting out their food.

A local hotel owner, J. L. Cox, heavyset and bearded, came over to ask Meg and Hamilton, "Are you going to watch the horse race?" Cox rocked back on his heels, his hat held to his vest out of courtesy to Meg. "Jack Ambler has put some big money on that Indian boy he's taken on. Will you be placing a bet, Hamilton?"

Hamilton hesitated, as though considering what Meg might like. "I don't believe I'll bet, but I'd like to see the race. Meg?"

She didn't really care to watch a show put on by Jack, but neither did she want to be a spoilsport. "Yes," she said, "let's watch."

There were a hundred people or more gathered at the site where the race would be held. A great deal of money was passing hands as men made bets. Shafer was there, grinning and cocky, on the black pony Jack had given him. The other rider, on a blood bay, was a wiry, mustachioed cowboy in his mid-twenties named Johnny Brooks. From overheard conversation, Brooks was as good a rider as Shafer and their horses were a close match so either could win.

Meg saw the Hesslers and waved to them. Bethany and Will waved back and, herding their flock of blond children before them, soon joined Meg and Hamilton.

"What a pretty little girl you are!" Bethany said, bending down to speak to Vesta.

"Say thank you," Meg directed gently.

"T'ank you," Vesta obeyed with a big yawn before turning to bury her face in Meg's skirts.

"She's sleepy," Meg explained, "I'm not sure she'll be able to stay awake for the fireworks. I may take her to the wagon so she can have a nap."

At that announcement, Vesta shook her head, no. She turned and stood straight, her eyes wide open.

The women chuckled.

"How are you feeling, Meg?" Bethany asked.

"Very well, thank you. I didn't have morning queasiness with Vesta and I haven't had with this little one, either." She stroked her stomach affectionately.

"You're going to have a boy this time," Aurelia said as she walked up then with Zibby by the hand. "You're carrying the baby low."

"If it turns out you're right, that'll be just fine," Meg told her. She asked the others, then, "Has anyone seen Emmaline?"

"I saw her earlier talking to the editor of the Dodge City

paper," Aurelia answered. "I suppose she was getting details about today to write up in the *Echo.*"

"I talked to her," Bethany said. "Emmaline's nervous about Shafer riding in this race with so much money in bets. She's worried trouble will come from it and he'll be in the middle."

"He's a good rider and he'll likely win," Meg said, keeping to herself her belief that Jack could get him into bad trouble any day of the week, not just at today's race.

Lucy Ann, Admire, and Rachel came to watch with them. And then in a body, the young people, Selinda and Lad, Joshua and David John, joined the home group, all eating large slices of watermelon, laughing at each other, and enjoying a good time.

Meg watched the young people for a few moments, glad they had this day away from hard work, for enjoyment. She turned back when shouting indicated that the race was about to start.

Jack had arranged for the race, and now, a few feet from the riders on their mounts, he drew his gun and pointed it skyward. "Ready, riders? All right, then, go!" He pulled the trigger and the shot rang out.

Shafer yelled, "Hi-yah!" Bent low over the pony's neck, he urged it flat out, belly to the ground. Brooks on his blood bay pounded a yard or two behind. Cheers and yelling rose above the soft thunder of hooves on hard dusty ground. Within seconds Shafer's black pony was a full two lengths ahead of the bay.

"Ride 'im, boy!" someone shouted.

"Show them, Shafer!" It was young Joshua Thorne. They might fight a lot, but they were still like family.

Above all the other cheering, Jack roared, "You can do it, son! Stretch that little bangtail out!"

Meg looked at Jack, seeing the pride and joy in his face.

She looked back at Shafer, now a small cloud of dust in the distance. In that second, his horse seemed to bend and break and Shafer's form was catapulted into the air to land on the ground. The horse staggered and went down not far from Shafer, who was an unmoving lump. Brooks saw what happened, slowed his bay, and stopped. He dismounted and ran to where Shafer lay.

The crowd fell silent, as unmoving as if they'd turned to statues. Then the murmurings, the cries, the curses and groans began. "Oh, hell!" Admire said.

Hamilton turned to Meg. "Stay here." He took off at a run.

Meg told Aurelia, "Watch Vesta for me, please." She ran after Hamilton. When Meg arrived, panting and breathless and afraid, there was a group ahead of her around Shafer's crumpled, unmoving form. She picked up his hat from the dirt and held it to her breast, her eyes wide with shock and her heart beginning to break.

Chapter Twenty-One

Hamilton knelt with others in the circle around Shafer. Meg caught his eye across the crowd and asked in a stricken voice, "How is he?"

Hamilton's expression answered even before he spoke. "He's badly hurt, but he's breathing. Find Emmaline."

She whirled and crashed into Jack. She stumbled back, looked up at him. He was white under his tan; his eyes were glazed with shock. She wasn't aware of feeling accusatory—she felt only numb and disbelieving—but something in her face made him say, "It wasn't my fault! I love that boy like he's my own son—I wouldn't have him hurt!"

She brushed by him, still in shock herself. "Well, he's hurt bad and I have to tell his mother."

Behind her someone was saying that the black horse had stepped in a gopher burrow or other varmint hole, and that's why he'd thrown Shafer. The black's leg was splintered.

Meg had gone only a few paces more when a shot rang out. She looked over her shoulder as she hurried and saw that Jack held the gun that had killed Shafer's pony.

She found Emmaline and told her what had happened. The blood drained from Emmaline's face. They rushed back to the accident scene. The crowd, staring and sad-faced, parted and let Emmaline through. Meg was close behind.

"I'm sorry," Hamilton said, meeting Emmaline and taking her gently by the shoulders. "He's gone. The fall broke his neck, and then his heart quit on him. I'm so sorry."

Emmaline fell to the ground beside Shafer. She took his still form into her lap and rocked silently back and forth while tears flooded her cheeks and pooled around her grimacing mouth.

A Dodge City minister rode to Paragon Springs to conduct Shafer's funeral. A somber crowd watched as his pine casket was lowered into the grave dug beside his grandfather's, in the crude little graveyard above Paragon Springs.

Selinda wept openly as dirt was shoveled into the yawning hole that held her twin. Lad Voss spoke softly to her, touching her arm, and Selinda turned to be held by him, while sobs shook her. Emmaline was in shock, repeating over and over, not to anyone in particular, "Shafer was a good boy. He just loved doing exciting things. But he was a good boy. He just didn't know quite where he belonged, and I didn't know how to . . . help him find . . . his place."

Later, after most folks had left, Meg returned up the hill. She knelt and, with shaking hands, placed a bouquet of wildflowers at the head of Shafer's grave. She rose and walked over to Grandma Spicy's grave—that dear old soul—and then to Helen Grace's small white tombstone, and finally to the joint stone that marked the graves of Mary Hague and little Ollie.

Tears ran from her closed eyes as she asked God to watch over Shafer, and to please let Shafer's burial be the last in the little graveyard for a very long time.

Three days after the funeral, Meg and Hamilton had just finished breakfast and were drinking a last cup of coffee when Admire arrived with a rush of news.

"Bobwire fences been cut all to hell in the valley—they ain't hardly a fence left standin'. Everybody's critters are mixed up. It's goin' to take days to sort 'em out and move 'em to where they belong. Longer'n that to get fences patched and up again. Nobody saw who did it; it was like a ghost come and took them fences down."

"It was Jack," Meg said. A chill ran down her back and she set down her coffee cup before she spilled it. "Alone or with help, this is Jack Ambler's doings."

"That ain't all," Admire said, looking grim. "I was up to Will Hessler's to see if his wire was cut same as mine. He ain't there. Bethany said he got up in the night when he heard a noise, and he never come back. She don't know what's happened to 'im. It ain't like Will to say nothin' to her before goin' off, but his spotted gelding is missin', too."

Hamilton looked thoughtful, his mouth set tight. "I'll wager that there is a connection between the wire cutting and Will's disappearance, that he was taken by force and had no choice in the matter. God willing, he'll turn up all right and tell us what happened. In the meantime, we'll arrange a search party right away and start looking for him."

Will Hessler didn't turn up, that day or the next, nor did the search party locate him. His horse was found wandering, still with the saddle on, three miles south of Dodge City. There was no sign of Will, no sign that he'd been injured or killed although a speck on the saddle looked like blood.

While Hamilton and some of the others rode with the sheriff to question Jack, the mostly likely suspect in both the wire-cutting and Will Hessler's disappearance, Meg took little Vesta and drove to see Bethany.

Bethany was distraught, her face drawn. There were dark circles under her eyes and her blond hair streamed around her face. "I should've gotten up with Will when we heard something outside," she said. "At least I might know what happened and where to look for him." She broke into tears. "It's my fault."

Meg put her arms around her. "You can't blame yourself.

Jack's behind this, I'm positive. We'll find Will. The sheriff and some of the men are questioning Jack now. They'll get out of him what happened."

"What if they never find out, what if Will's been killed? What if I never see him again?" Bethany cried harder. Meg held her in her arms, rocking back and forth, her own throat too choked to reply.

Hamilton came to Bethany's from the Rocking A, after talking with Jack. He shook his head at Meg's questioning look.

"Jack claims he knows nothing about what happened that night. He'd been on an all-out drinking spree for days and denies that it was him that cut the wire, or that he was the cause of Will's disappearance. I'm not sure I believe him, but he was convincing."

"He can't get away with this! He knows what happened!" Meg cried, gripping the arms of her chair. "The sheriff arrested him in spite of his denial, didn't he? Nobody else would've done this. Jack knows he's the one who did it."

"Until evidence turns up, the sheriff can't hold Jack. The sheriff is investigating, questioning people, but it seems so far that there were no witnesses to what went on, or at least no one willing to speak out against Jack, if it was him and he was seen."

"He's going to get away with this, just like always!" Meg held her balled fists to her temples in frustration, then her hands dropped hopelessly to her lap while furious tears burned behind her nose.

"I don't think so, Meg, I really don't. Calm down, honey, and think of the baby. We'll find Will."

"But where?" she demanded, getting to her feet. "Where is Will? What's Jack done to him?"

The settlers' loose cattle were rounded up, sorted, and returned to rightful owners. Fences were mended. After days of searching, Will Hessler still had not been found and, without a single clue to answer his disappearance, hope began to fade. There was even a lengthy search of the plains for a hastily dug grave, but none was found. It was generally believed that Will's disappearance would remain a mystery, a part of the region's history.

Bethany was doing her best to care for their children and survive without him.

Then one day, Meg and Vesta made the trip to Dodge City with Hamilton because he felt Meg should be checked by a doctor these last months of her pregnancy. She was so healthy that the doctor acted as though he wondered why she'd come. She wondered, herself. She'd consented to the examination only to please Hamilton. She let him pay the doctor, then suggested that as long as they were there, they should let Vesta watch the train come in.

Vesta loved watching the train and she bounced on the wagon seat, shouting at the train as its shrill whistle blew and it chugged into town. Meg held her back, and they sat watching the passengers disembark a few minutes later. Suddenly, Meg drew a sharp breath. "Sweet heaven, isn't that Will?"

The man was ragged and gaunt and he looked confused. Meg began to cry. "It is Will! Go bring him here, Hamilton, hurry!"

Hamilton led Will to their wagon and helped him climb up to the seat beside Meg.

"Will," she said, clutching his arm, touching his face, "We're so glad to see you! What happened? Where have you been?" It had been weeks since his disappearance.

"Take me to my wife and children," he mumbled tiredly,

running his hand through his yellow hair that needed cutting. "I'll tell you on the way."

As they rolled and bumped along the trace toward Paragon Springs, Will talked.

"I caught Jack cutting wire at my place in the middle of the night," he explained. "He was crazy drunk, out of his mind. He didn't like it that I've helped Meg settle folks here in the valley to 'take his land,' as he put it. He forced me to go with him at gunpoint. I went, rather than have Bethany become a widow, or cause her or the children to be harmed."

"You went with him where?" Hamilton asked, shaking the reins for the team to move faster.

"We rode south, hard to see in the night, but when we came to a barbed wire fence, Jack cut it. When we got to Dodge City the next day, he made me go with him to the railroad yard where he wanted to show me something, he said. I don't think he had any real plan; things just come to him. Nobody was around; I doubt if anybody saw him hit me over the head and knock me senseless. I figure he threw me into one of the cattle cars heading for Kansas City. The car was empty except for a lot of stinkin' muck; if it had been a loaded car I would've been trampled to death. He was gettin' meanness out of his system, I'm certain of that, and he might have thought it was a loaded car."

"He says he was drinking heavily and doesn't remember what happened," Hamilton said.

"He was as drunk as I ever saw a man; kept mumbling about Shafer's death an' the women at Paragon Springs being as much to blame as anybody for what happened. I couldn't make out much of what he saying, he was so drunk and mad, but I do believe he knew what he was doin'."

Meg asked in disbelief, "You went all the way to Kansas City?"

"Went a long way in that direction. I was found, conscious but mixed up, hurting like hell and covered with filth, when the train stopped at a little town, I never did know the name of it. Some fellas took me to the doctor. He said I had a concussion and kept me at his place till I stopped blacking out. Some good folks there put together a purse to buy me a ticket to get back home. I owe those folks; can't tell you how glad I am to be back, and alive."

Meg was livid at what Jack had done to Will, furious at the anxiety the incident had put them all through. But at the same time she was glad that this time they had Jack for something he could not worm his way out of. "Jack has to be arrested right away. Hamilton, will you take Will's case?"

"If he wants me to, you bet I'll take it."

The courtroom was packed, every seat filled with homesteaders and their wives, cowboys, Dodge City businessmen, gamblers, and prostitutes. Other saloon riffraff, more cowpunchers, and ranchers, lined the walls.

Meg and Hamilton had journeyed to Dodge City the day before and put up at the Dodge House hotel so they'd be on hand early. Meg remembered what Hamilton had told her as they left the hotel. "Keep in mind, Meg, I can present the evidence that will surely find Jack guilty," he'd said, "but it's the judge who'll decide his sentence."

He'd told her that Judge Locke Gillette was usually a fair man, but he was also a friend of Jack's. In off hours, the two were drinking companions. The sentence might be softened in Jack's case, or it might not. They'd have to wait and see.

Dinah, seated in the front row wearing a soft lavender suit, looked pale but held her head erect. Her gloved hands were folded in her lap.

"Your Honor," Hamilton was addressing Judge Gillette, a

craggy-faced man with bushy gray hair who, even in his dignified black suit, might have been a rancher himself from the
looks of him, "the accused, Mr. Ambler, did take Mr. Hessler
at gunpoint from his home in the night. He forced him to ride
with him while he cut the fences of innocent farmers. When
they arrived at Dodge City, Mr. Ambler bludgeoned Mr.
Hessler over the head with his gun, knocking him out cold.
With malice aforethought, he dumped Mr. Hessler's unconscious body into a cattle car that he knew would be leaving
soon for Kansas City. I ask that you find him guilty of mass
destruction, kidnaping, and attempted murder."

Everyone in the room seemed to hold their breath.

Judge Gillette scowled at Jack and thundered at him, "You
have heard the statements from Attorney Gibbs. How do you
plead?"

"I was drunk."

"Did you do what he says you did?"

"If I did do what Hessler and his lawyer say I did, I sure as
hell ain't sorry."

"Did you do it? Do you plead guilty, Mr. Ambler?"

"You all know I did it, and you know why! I'd do it again!
I'd like to take every last nester in this valley and throw them
on cattle cars headed east. It would serve them right, that's
where they belong. If you want to call that guilty, then, hell
yes, I'm guilty."

The judge pounded his gavel to still the uproar. "Stand
up, Mr. Ambler, and accept your sentence."

Jack sat there for a long moment, then got to his feet. His
eyes went to Dinah, and then found Meg. His face was a tight
mask, showing no emotion.

"On the charges presented here, to which you have pled
guilty, I give you a punishment of two years, Jack Ambler.
You can spend it in jail, or you can leave this country for that

period. Out, gone, not here."

"He's giving him a *choice?*" Meg whispered in astonishment to Lucy Ann next to her. "That's not right. Jack admitted his guilt, he should have the maximum punishment allowed by the law."

Admire leaned across Lucy Ann to whisper to Meg, "Judge Gillette and Jack are thick as fleas from way back. I'd give money to know exactly what they've talked about, between them, before this trial."

"Shhh," Lucy Ann admonished.

The judge was saying, "You'll serve two years in the Dodge City jail, Mr. Ambler, or you'll leave this country. What is your decision?"

Jack looked angry, but he answered flatly, "I'll go. I'll leave this damned country. I'll be glad to move my herd and never see another nester."

There were a few gasps heard around the room, but several of the Dodge City residents smiled and winked at each other. Something underhanded was going on beyond the obvious, but Meg wasn't sure what it was.

Above the growing murmurs from every corner of the room, the judge's voice boomed. "I hereby order that all fences in the way of Mr. Ambler's leaving be taken down. Anyone failing to follow my order will answer to the law."

A huge uproar rose in the room from the homesteaders. The judge pounded his gavel. "Now do you folks want him out of this country, or not? Till he's got his cattle and other stock moved, you'll take your fences down and keep watch on your own stock so they don't get caught up accidently. Later, you can put your wire fences back up."

There was still a grumble, but Meg quieted those around her by whispering, "It's all right! We'll obey the judge. Think what it's worth to be rid of Jack!"

Admire came to see Meg and Hamilton a week after the trial. "I suspected somethin' fishy was afoot," he told them, "when Judge Gillette said Jack could clear out, or go to jail, one or the other. Word is out, now, that Jack was talkin' of movin' his operation down into the Indian lands anyhow, way before the wire-cuttin' and other trouble. Judge Gillette knew about it and was just invitin' Jack to leave earlier than mebbe he planned. That judge himself has already got a large herd fattenin' down in the Strip."

Meg knew about the Strip, millions of acres of lush pasture that ran between the Indian Territories and Kansas. Although referred to for years as the Strip by cattlemen who trailed their cattle through it to market, the true name for the area was the Cherokee Outlet. It had been awarded to the Cherokee by the government, to be used as an outlet to hunting grounds north. With the buffalo almost gone, and settlements springing up in Kansas, the Strip was seldom used. Recently, under a vague common-law practice called "cow custom," cattleman had been taking advantage of those luxurious grasses to fatten their cattle, with a small fee per head paid to the Cherokee. Many cattleman paid nothing, seeing the area as one last stand of free grass.

At first Meg was angry that Jack hadn't been handed real punishment but would be going through with what he'd planned all along. Then she was just glad that he was leaving. If not pushed by the trial to do so, he might have changed his mind. Now he had to move, and they'd have peace at last.

Dinah came to see the women at Paragon Springs. She confirmed that Jack had been planning to move a large part of his operation down into the Strip.

"Are you going with him?" Meg asked.

"No, I'm stayin' here. Jack can't ever totally give up the Rockin' A. His heart will always be here on the Pawnee. He's turning the Rocking A over to me to operate. I'll visit him down in the Strip from time to time, of course. Maybe someday he'll be able to come home, and, God willin', time will have changed him."

"I never meant to run him off the way he tried to get rid of us," Meg told her. "I always wanted for everybody to live here together in peace."

"I know that." Dinah smiled.

Meg took her hands. "I'm so glad you're staying."

"I wouldn't leave. There's no place for me in Texas in my father's house. I have no desire to start over in the Strip, and my friends are here. It'll be a strange, long-distance marriage, but Jack, by breaking so many laws, leaves us no choice."

The fences came down in a mile-wide trail from the Rocking A north and southward to beyond Dodge City. The day of the drive, Meg was brought from the house into the yard by a strange sound that was faint at first and then became a growing cacophony of men's shouts, thundering hoofs, bawling cattle, and horses whinnying. She looked north and saw the exodus from the Pawnee Valley: dust-churning wagons, a remuda, twenty or thirty riders, and hundreds of bellowing cows, rolling like the waves of an ocean.

Meg and her friends, eyes shaded against the September sun, gathered to watch them pass. Once, Meg went back inside to check on Vesta who was taking a nap on her parents' bed. The noise hadn't awakened her. Meg smoothed her little red checked dress, touched her cheek, and went back outside. It was a wonder the child slept, what with all the yipping and yelling from both Rocking A cowboys and Meg's friends as they worked to keep the bawling cattle away from the settlement.

Meg watched in dismay as about fifty cows split from the

main herd and swerved toward the settlement. Some splashed through the spring pond and trampled cornfields not quite ready to harvest. She stood close to the house as others worked to drive the straggling cattle back where they belonged. Still the cattle came, the moving herd making clouds of dust that was filling their houses. Clothes that hadn't been taken from the lines would have to be washed again—if they survived the horns of straggling cattle passing through. Meg didn't like the harm being done to their claims, but anything was worth it to see Jack depart the valley. After so very long, the homesteaders would not have to endure his harassment, his constant efforts to dislodge them from their farms. They could live in peace.

Meg spotted Dinah, who'd said she'd ride with the group as far as the border where she'd tell Jack good-bye, and then return.

Then Meg spotted Jack, on the other side of the river of cattle. He rode out front a while and then trotted back to halt his sorrel in front of Meg, in her yard.

He shoved back his hat and wiped his forehead with his bandanna. His gold eyes were cold. "You think you've won, Plow-lady," he told her flatly, "but the facts are that in the long run, you and your kind won't last out here. You'll find that out the hard way and you won't need me to make it happen." He spurred his horse and rode away.

She felt a chill from his prophesy; she was tired and didn't want to watch the migration any more, anyway. She started to turn to the house when a flash of red in the midst of a dust cloud caught her eye. At first her mind balked, refusing what her eyes could see, then cold horror washed over her. "Vesta! Vesta!" Meg's cry was lost in the sound of the thundering, bellowing cattle. She began to run with clumsy chopping steps, molasses-slow due to her advanced pregnancy. Her child moved innocently, she seemed to be singing, as she faded in and out of a dust cloud, toward the churning hooves of the main herd. Meg grew faint, tried to hurry faster, almost fell.

She wouldn't make it in time, her child would be killed. Meg screamed from the roots of her being. Jack, riding away, looked back. He couldn't have heard her cry over the hoof-rumble, yet he had turned.

He jack-knifed his horse, almost somersaulting the animal on its nose, then whipped back toward the wave of running cattle approaching the child. Jack rode swiftly, reached down and snatched Vesta into his arms. He whirled his horse and rode out of the herd's path.

With Vesta in front of him in the saddle, he cantered to where Meg stood frozen, her hand to her mouth, unable to make a sound, waves of nausea in her throat.

Jack frowned fiercely. "I never meant that boy to be hurt," he said curtly. He handed a squirming Vesta into Meg's arms, and started to ride away when Meg's lips moved, "Thank you, Jack, thank you!" She wasn't sure she'd spoken aloud. She tried again, through a dry throat, "Thank you."

He didn't look back, there was no sign at all that he'd heard. But Dinah had seen what happened and she rode fast toward Jack. When she reached him, she stretched from her saddle and threw her arms around him.

Meg stood trembling, holding her child tight against her, afraid she couldn't keep her feet any longer. She stumbled toward her soddy. They'd never see eye to eye, her and Jack, but forever she'd be grateful to him for saving her child's life—even if she couldn't forget the horrible things he'd done in his determination to be rid of her and her friends from the land he blindly, cruelly, saw as his alone.

She would, however, be grateful to him from right where

she was. This was her home, the home she wanted, too, for her growing family.

Vesta squirmed and tried to get down, but Meg held her tight and on watery legs, her other child kicking inside her, stumbled into the house.

Jack had tried to run her out, and he couldn't. Nobody could. Ever.